BLOOD, FIRE & MERCY

Da'Valia Trilogy, Volume 2

Christina Davis

Character art by: Frostbite Studios

Map illustration by: Jennifer Tedmon

Cover design by: Ruxandra Tudorica of Methyss Art

www.methyss-art.com

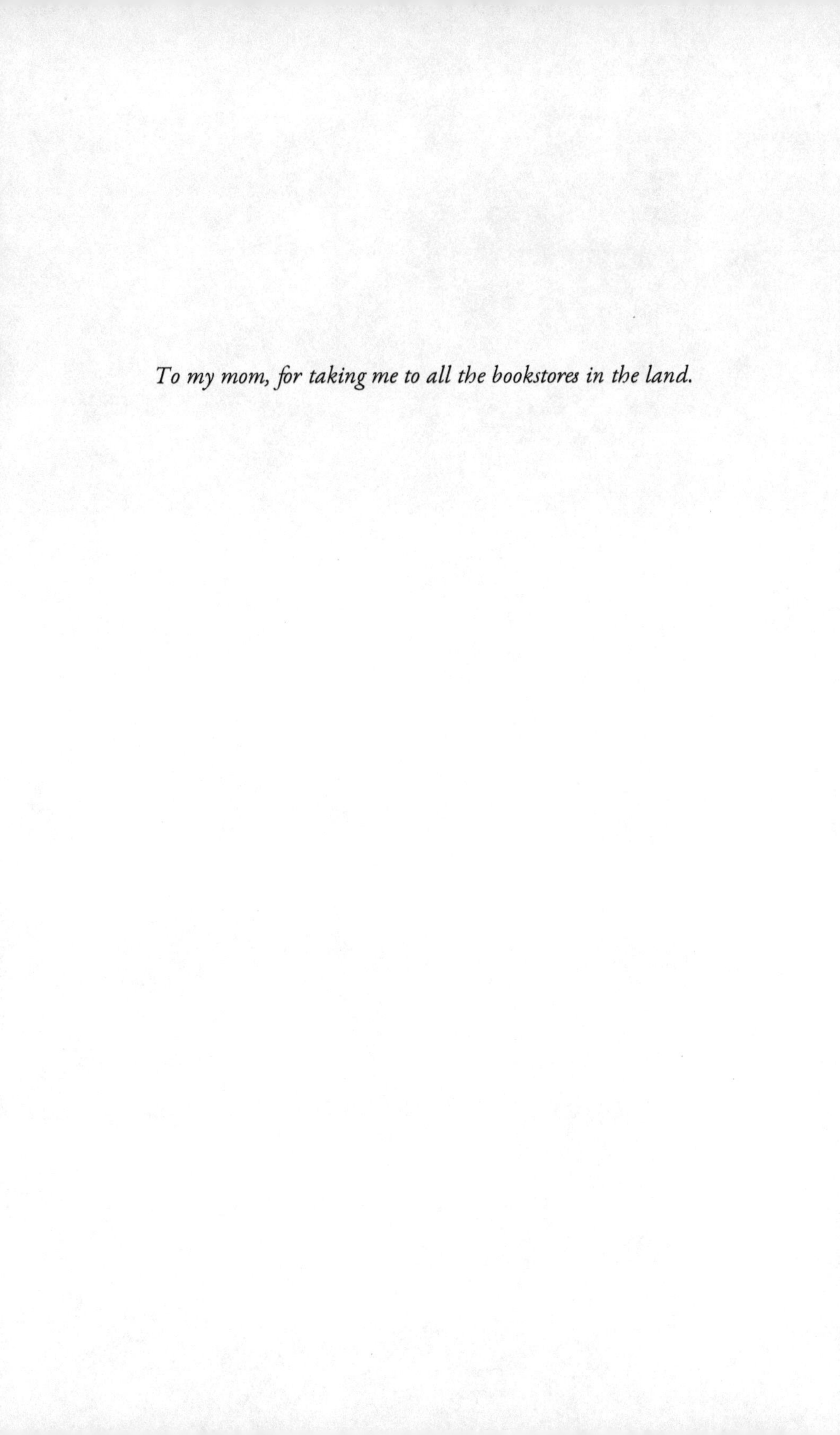

To my mom, for taking me to all the bookstores in the land.

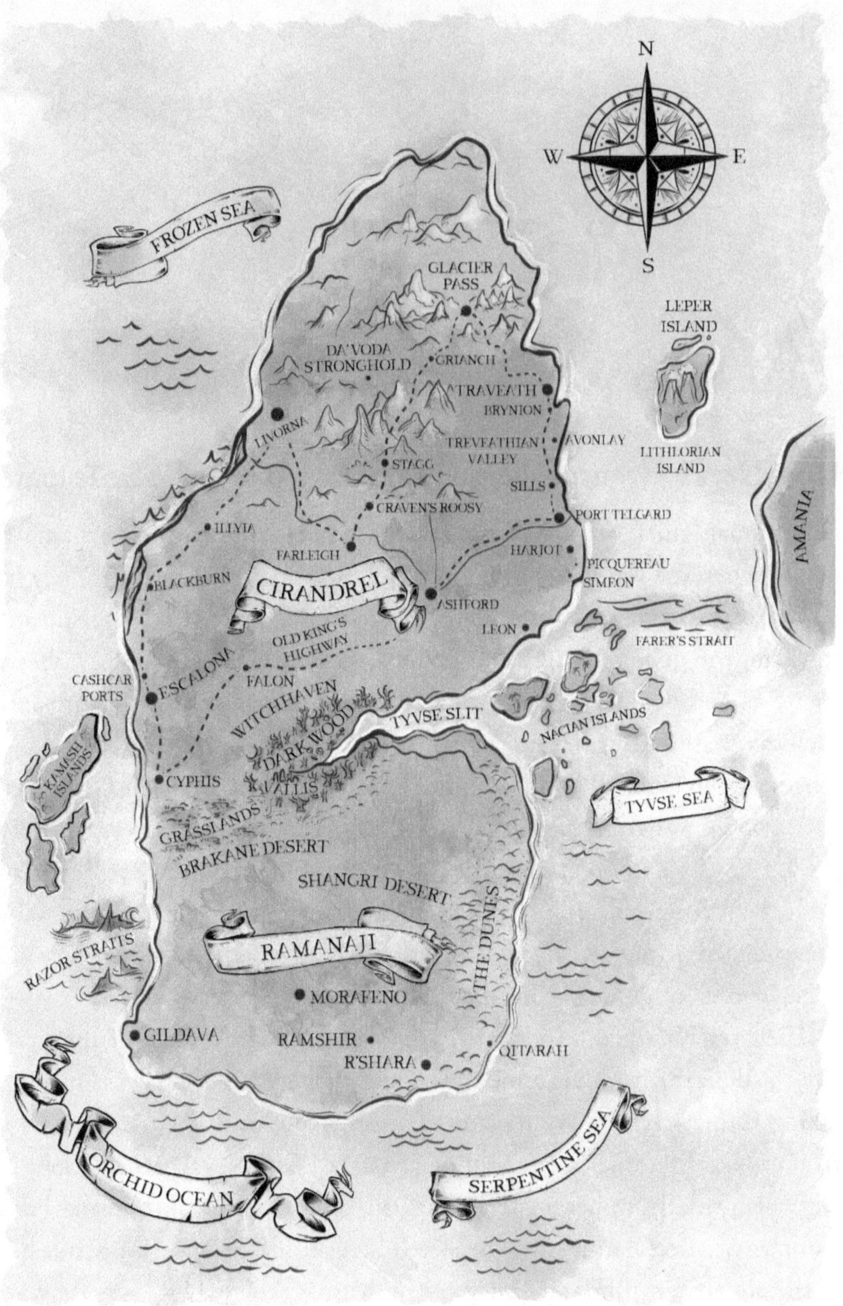

N
W
E
S
FROZEN SEA
GLACIER PASS
DA'VODA STRONGHOLD
GRIANCH
TRAVEATH
BRYNION
LIVORNA
TREVEATHIAN VALLEY
AVONLAY
STAGG
SILLS
CRAVEN'S ROOSY
PORT TELGARD
ILLYIA
HARJOT
FARLEIGH
PICQUEREAU
BLACKBURN
SIMEON
CIRANDREL
ASHFORD
OLD KING'S HIGHWAY
LEON
ESCALONA
FALON
CASHCAR PORTS
WITCHHAVEN
TYVSE SLIT
FARER'S STRAIT
DARK WOOD
NACIAN ISLANDS
KIAMSII ISLANDS
CYPHIS
VALLIS
TYVSE SEA
GRASSLANDS
BRAKANE DESERT
SHANGRI DESERT
RAZOR STRAITS
RAMANAJI
THE DUNES
MORAFENO
GILDAVA
RAMSHIR
R'SHARA
QITARAH
ORCHID OCEAN
SERPENTINE SEA
LEPER ISLAND
LITHLORIAN ISLAND
AMANIA

Recap of Born at Dawn

How Neva's adventure began in Book 1 of the Da'Valia Trilogy...

Half-human thief Neva Roberts was on the cusp of making a name for herself when she was interrupted mid-heist by Thatcher Sullivan. They had both been hired by rival Da'Valian clans to steal a goblet, but, unbeknownst to them, the goblet contained a godly power called the Eye. Neva bested Thatcher and made away with the goblet, but not before the Eye broke the spell that was binding her Da'Valian powers.

After receiving a warning from her mother's ghost, Neva left Glacier Pass with two Da'Valian soldiers, Astiand and Bryand, who were to escort her to the Da'Voda clan. Upon her arrival, she survived a fight to the death and underwent a firérite, a rite of passage, to gain control over her power. When she emerged with four horns instead of the normal two, many Da'Valia began speculating that she had been chosen by the gods.

Their ruler, Trinizhi, welcomed Neva into the clan as one of their own. But the donazhi's motives appeared to be two-faced, since she was known for taking ruthless action, even against her own people, and was once a bitter rival of Neva's mother. Living among the Da'Voda, Neva learned about her Da'Valian side from her austere guardian, Astiand, who encouraged her to embrace her true nature. She suspected he was hiding something, but even as she stole from him and snuck out to learn to fight, Neva was drawn to him. And she was drawn to another, too: Emiliand, the Da'Voda's best fighter. He and Vivizhi, the devout master at arms, taught Neva to fight in secret.

For the first time, Neva had a friend who knew what it was like to hide one's true nature since Emiliand was also a half-breed — one who could secretly read minds no less. They agreed to align their powers by forming an alliad once he finished a term of service with the nomadic Da'Roha army. Upon his departure, he gave her a magical tracking device so he could find her, and they kissed. Her relationship with Emiliand was a source of contention with Astiand, but it was unclear if he objected as her guardian or because he was developing feelings for her himself. They also ~~kissed~~ *really kissed* but were interrupted.

Neva learned a shocking secret shortly thereafter — that her mother had accidentally sacrificed Neva to the gods and put the Hand inside Neva while she was in the womb. The Hand, the Eye, and the Mouth were the three prongs of the Trishula, the greatest weapon ever created by the god of war. Their theft was the reason the god of war cursed the Da'Valia with the imbalance of power that often results in majilas, female Da'Valia, being driven mad or dying when they come into their power.

Meanwhile, the rival clan, the Da'Foha, threatened to harm her aunt if Neva didn't come to them. Her friend Adam tracked her to the Da'Voda enclave, where he was immediately imprisoned. With the help of Astiand's servant, Miland, whose confidence Neva had earned, she broke Adam out of the dungeon. She and Adam killed a soldier in the process.

In her return to Glacier Pass, she confronted the Da'Foha. She saved her aunt, but the Da'Foha's Vodou witch bound Neva's powers again. This forced Neva to admit who and what she really was to both her human friends and the Da'Voda to gain their assistance in saving her father, who had been taken hostage.

In an epic battle, Neva's powers were again released, and she lost control of the Hand, which decimated everything in its path. Only Trinizhi and the remaining members of her alliad, Astiand and Arroyand, were left alive. Privately, Astiand confessed to Neva that their mothers had been close friends and that he was honor-bound to protect her. He told her that the best way he could do so was to encourage her to flee to the desert, beyond Trinizhi's influence. Neva absconded with the goblet to live on the run with her family and Adam, who became her new thieving partner...

PROLOGUE

Fifth Fireside, 1651

Moonlight glinting off his ebony horns, Benjamand paced below a line of windows in a cavernous library. Violent rain pummeled the glass, running away in rivulets, and the ocean surged against the cliffs outside. The warlock's large, dark form was dwarfed by the towering shelves as he traveled along a row of polished tables and back again. Frown lines cut across his high forehead.

Neva watched him from under the arched entrance, where she was cloaked in shadows and a spider-black cape. She stood with one drenched boot on each side of the marble threshold, poised to flee. Da'Valia were unforgiving creatures, and as a member of the Da'Voda clan, her presence in the scholarly sanctum was not sanctioned. She had plotted several escape routes before daring to venture into the depths of the Da'Xana's fortress, and she was prepared to call on her trusty invisibility glamour and flee into the storm if the need arose.

"You never should have come here," Benjamand muttered. He thrust a hand through his silver-streaked black hair with a scowl.

"I didn't have a choice." Neva inched forward from her escape route. The shrouded goblet that hung from her belt knocked against her thigh.

"If my donazhi discovers you — the goblet — she'll —" Benjamand sputtered.

"I'll make sure that doesn't happen," Neva said.

"I hope that's true. For both our sakes."

"Just tell me, can you do it?" Neva asked.

"Whether I can or not is beside the point." He glowered down at her.

Neva tapped her fingers on her hip, thinking. Benjamand had spent decades studying magic craft among the Da'Xana. He wasn't a wordsmith, or even pleasant company, but he was the most learned warlock she'd ever met. She needed his help, but after all that had happened with her mother, she supposed that he was entitled to his reluctance. Nineteen years earlier, Monazhi and Benjamand had conducted a dangerous spell and accidentally sacrificed Neva to the gods not knowing that Monazhi was with child. A half-human child.

Against all reason, Neva had lived, and she would be forever burdened with the consequences of their actions.

The Hand, a powerful piece of the strongest weapon ever forged, dwelled within her. Centuries earlier, a Da'Valia had stolen the Trishula from their god, deconstructed the trident, and hidden the three powers it contained. Those powers — the Hand, the Mouth, and the Eye — had remained lost, until Benjamand and Monazhi used blood magic to unearth them.

For a long time, the Hand had been bound within Neva, but that had changed when she bonded with the power in her firérite, a supernatural rite of passage. She harbored the Hand and was, for all purposes, its master... except for the few times she'd lost her hold on it. Tears flooded her eyes as images of flame and blistering flesh flashed through her thoughts.

"You helped my mother before." Neva brushed the tears aside. "Help me now. Lock the Eye away inside me."

"What you ask is madness."

"If we don't, Trinizhi can still possess it," Neva pressed. "Is that what you want?"

"Of course, it isn't." A thundercloud passed over the moon, darkening his features.

Trinizhi was the selfish and cold-hearted ruler of the Da'Voda clan. Seeking to undermine Monazhi in their youth, the donazhi had conspired to have the dragon Lithlorian intercept the Mouth before Neva's parents could obtain it. In an ironic twist, the loss of the Mouth had been what prompted Monazhi to call the Hand into herself. With the Mouth going to Lithlorian's impenetrable island and the Hand being hidden once more, two prongs of the Trishula had drifted out of reach. Trinizhi had spent her ensuing reign focused on the remaining prong, the Eye.

In the time since Neva had stolen the goblet out from under Trinizhi, she had moved her family from city to city every season to stay ahead of the donazhi. It was a burdensome way of life. Not only was Neva getting low on coin to pay for new identities, disguises, and lodgings, but the Hand wasn't entirely within her control, endangering those around her.

When Neva first sought out Benjamand, her intention had been to ask him to lock the Hand inside her again. When he had explained that she'd bonded with the Hand in her firérite and that the spell wouldn't differentiate between her natural gift and the Hand, she'd shuddered at the thought. She wasn't about to become an easy target.

Neva's mother had written of Trinizhi's cruelty in her journal, and Neva had witnessed it when Trinizhi threw Adam in her dungeon and cut down Bryand. Trinizhi's aliado had betrayed her in the end, it was true, but he'd served her faithfully for many years. Bryand had been important to her, and she'd killed him anyway. Neva had only ever been a thorn in the donazhi's side. There was no question in Neva's mind that Trinizhi would do away with her if given the opportunity.

So Neva had come up with an alternative. She would transfer the Eye from the goblet, bind it inside herself, hide a spelled decoy for Trinizhi to find, and journey to the desert as Astiand had instructed her to do many moons before. Then, Neva wouldn't keep expecting danger around every corner. She wouldn't keep imagining what might have happened to her young cousins every time they were late for dinner. She wouldn't keep fearing the Hand breaking free, because she would be far away from everyone she loved.

What was more, she would be able to prevent Trinizhi from obtaining the Eye and exerting her influence over all Da'Valia. It wasn't as good as completing Monazhi's original mission of returning the Trishula to their creator, but it was a consolation equivalent to the one her mother had settled for, so it was good enough for her. At least this way, Trinizhi wouldn't win.

"I beg this of you, Benjamand," Neva said. "My mother trusted you, and I fear for all our futures if this is not done."

Lightning flashed through the windows and splashed across Neva's face. She pulled her cowl back. Removing the covering from her double set of horns was a calculated risk since her identity could be easily deduced if anyone saw her. But she'd done her research. The Da'Xana's sentries shouldn't have any cause to explore this level until their rounds, which weren't for an hour yet. And aside from blue eyes that matched her father's, Neva bore a strong resemblance to her mother. Benjamand had cared for her mother once. She prayed that Monazhi's memory would sway him.

Benjamand stared back at her. His mouth opened as if he was going to say something, but closed without uttering a word. Thunder rumbled over the stronghold. Would he agree? Or was he considering subduing her and turning her over to his donazhi? She might, if she were in his position. But keeping the prongs of the Trishula away from Trinizhi would honor Monazhi's memory. Neva trusted he would consider that paramount. He *had* to.

"You might not survive." His voice was strained.

"I will." She removed the goblet from her belt. "We have to do it, for the good of all Da'Valia."

"I'm not sure that I can complete the same spell your mother did," he said.

Neva swallowed hard. "We must try."

Chapter One

Sixth Cravell, 1651

If she slowed, they would catch her. Neva darted across the dry, cracked street and slid into a narrow alley between two sandstone buildings. The white material of her Da'Valian pants flowed behind her, and a traditional desert head wrap covered her horns. With so much of her hidden from view, she could pass as a native of R'shara as long as no one looked too closely, which they rarely did. It was safer to keep one's eyes averted.

Panting hard, she raced down the alley. She wished that the sun wasn't directly above and that some of R'shara's few shadows might shade her, if only for a brief reprieve. The air was so hot that sweat dried into salt on her arms almost as quickly as it appeared.

A group of children scampered after a ball made from leather scraps as Neva rounded a corner. Cringing, she skirted them and poured on more speed. She had left behind a spelled decoy for Trinizhi to chase in Cirandrel, but the relentless team on her tail could only mean one thing: Neva's plan had failed.

Neva's pursuers had already lured her into a trap in the Gem Quarter. The meeting she'd been waiting for since arriving in R'shara should have ended with the notorious Salaman, who operated a network of jewel thieves, agreeing to add her to his roster. Instead, a team of Da'Valia had sprung a trap, stopping her interview before it had begun.

When their illuminator had rendered her invisibility glamour useless, she'd found herself diving out a window to escape. The tang of blood still coated her mouth. She knew from past experience that she wouldn't be able to activate her invisibility glamour until the illuminator's residue dissipated.

Neva checked her surroundings frantically for landmarks. She was intimate with her little corner of R'shara, but this section of the city was less familiar. She just needed to keep ahead of her pursuers long enough to use her glamour.

She thanked the gods when she spied a familiar bathhouse. She was on the edge of the Textile Quarter. The path before her opened into a wide alleyway between rows of three-story factories. She jumped and manifested raw Da'Valian power. She shoved it down, scorching the cracked earth. Her physical prowess, along with the extra push, sent her two stories into the air. The tail ends of her silver-white power engulfed a laundry line of bed linens, which fluttered, burning, to the street below. She latched onto a window sill, and a splinter stabbed under her nail.

"Gods curse it." She sucked the splinter free and spit it out. She scaled the balcony above and jumped again, reaching for the hot tile of the roof's edge.

Fear ripped through her as an unknown assailant grabbed her by the wrist and yanked. She would have pulled away from her attacker and taken her chances of falling to the ground, but the grip was ironclad. *Da'Valia!*

Neva doubled her efforts, twisting to throw herself from the rooftop, not caring where or how she landed, as long as she was away from her pursuers. A broken bone or two was well worth her life.

"Nevazhi, don't." The deep male voice in her mind stopped her before she took reckless action.

"Emiliand?" Neva gasped, peering into the glaring sun. She stopped resisting and held onto his muscular forearm as he pulled her up.

Neva planted her feet on the terracotta rooftop and took inventory of her Da'Valian friend. Unlike majilas, whom Dhianz had summoned into creation at sunrise, ancient stories told of hilans, the males, being born of the darkest hour. Emiliand was only part Da'Valia, so a gray tint accented his dark flesh. Rugged stubble lined his firm jaw, and the ends of his hair dusted his shoulders. He wore a sword strapped across his back and a baldric of throwing stars across his chest. With his horns and his impressive height, everything about him demanded attention.

Concern gripped her as she noted the abrasions that riddled his horns. Da'Valian power was stored in their horns, and his appeared to have taken the brunt of an assault.

What happened? she wondered.

Emiliand swiped up a black quarterstaff, both ends barbed, and his silver gaze seemed earnest as he checked her over in return. He ended his inspection by catching her eyes with his. She couldn't believe she had forgotten how steady his gaze was. Her pounding heart skipped a beat.

Neva hadn't seen Emiliand since he'd left the Da'Voda clan for a term of service with the Da'Roha more than a year earlier. So much time had passed that she'd convinced herself more than once that she would never see him again. Her hand went to the silver pendant on her necklace. Emiliand had given her the spelled trinket so he would be able to find her. She rubbed the burning sun design as she had done many times since they'd parted ways.

"We have a lot of catching up to do," Emiliand said. His attention moved to the street, where four white, fluid forms sped below. "But I wasn't the only one searching for you. Let's keep moving."

They ran together, catapulting themselves over the breaks between buildings. They crossed back into the Gem Quarter, where stone cutters, refiners, and drillers processed the deposits that had been extracted from R'shara's mines. The farther into the quarter they went, the louder it got. Neva followed without question, but she peeked over at Emiliand more than once. She'd been on her own for so long that seeing him didn't feel real.

"They're not letting up." Emiliand's pace was steady as he used his unique brand of power to connect his thoughts to hers.

"I'm ready for a fight if you are," Neva responded. Emiliand was the most talented fighter she'd ever met. Her odds had just improved considerably.

Neva jumped off the roof and pulled the force of impact into a roll. She unfurled and drew her sword. Three majilas surrounded her. Judging by the length of their horns, they were toppels, some of the strongest of their kind — but so was she. They fired off shots of power, which she avoided without difficulty. What was their game?

The fourth majila never made it within striking distance. Emiliand plummeted from the rooftop and delivered a killing blow with his quarterstaff. Neva flung a series of rapid fireballs back at her pursuers. Undeterred, they advanced, knocking away the blasts as if they were mere nuisances.

The team's fifth dropped from the rooftops, landing behind Emiliand with a blade in her hand.

"Behind you," Neva warned Emiliand, but he was already pivoting to confront the majila, whose silver-white eyes looked like they might burn holes through him with their intensity. *Don't worry about Emiliand,* Neva told herself. He never lost a fight.

Neva threw up an unrefined power shield, deflecting the other majilas' strikes. She grunted as she blocked the downward stroke of a majila's sword with her own. A shot from another majila slammed into her shield, pushing her back.

They were trying to force her into a dead-end alley. Neva kicked the majila whose sword was locked with hers and flung her shield at the other. The third majila, with a patterned scarification across the bridge of her nose, went for Neva's head. Neva dropped to the ground and shot a blast at the scarred majila.

They were relentless, making it impossible for Neva to braid a stronger shield as she came to her feet. But she wasn't going down without a fight. Neva had honed her combat skills, practicing the sword with those in her caravan and joining in underground fights before that. She had planned to be ready if the donazhi ever caught up with her.

Neva launched a wave of power at her attackers. The majilas diverted the attack into the ground. Dust shot up between them. Neva swung her sword up and around in a sweeping arc. The scarred majila twisted out of its path, but another failed to recognize the threat until it was too late. Two down.

In Neva's peripheral vision, Emiliand flipped the fifth attacker over his head. That made three.

The scarred majila bolted forward while the other broke off to engage Emiliand. The scarred majila could have gutted Neva right then and there, but she snapped a smooth silver cuff over Neva's wrist instead. It locked, tight and unnaturally cold. The sensation brought back a flood of memories — of first knowing the Da'Voda, of a strong hilan named Astiand. Neva tensed, knowing what would come next.

The scarred majila invoked the painful anti-magic of the shacklay, sending an icy flow of black into Neva's veins and a bruise up her arm. Her shield extinguished in the dirt. The anti-magic intensified, wracking her arm so she dropped her sword. The scarred majila pounced, kicking the sword away and pushing Neva to the ground.

"You're coming with us, half-breed," the scarred majila said.

Neva could shatter the shacklay with the Hand, yet the thought of using it filled her with dread. It was the most powerful weapon she had at her disposal, but fear of losing control made her stop. She could not allow them to take her prisoner — the stakes were too high — but she also would never forgive herself if she released the Hand and it harmed Emiliand.

Still, she had to do *something*.

The coppery flavor on her tongue faded. Neva hissed the guttural incantation that would activate her invisibility glamour. The feeling of nettle stings riddled her from head to toe, and she disappeared from sight.

She flung her leg up, slamming her booted foot into the scarred majila's skull. The strike wasn't hard enough to knock out the majila, but combined with the element of surprise, it gave Neva the opening she needed. She yanked a dagger free from the small of her back and thrust up. Seconds later, the fight was over.

Neva untangled her legs from under the scarred majila in time to witness Emiliand finishing off the last of the squad. The threat had been neutralized. Neva dropped her invisibility and didn't move for a moment, catching her breath. Her throat was painfully dry.

"Are you all right?" she asked Emiliand, spotting a splotch of blood on his sleeve.

"I'm fine," he said. "The blood isn't mine."

You don't have to worry about him, Neva reminded herself again. Emiliand was as unique as she was. His father had been Colavalia. Legends told of how Dhianz, the god of war, created the Colavalia to guard the Underworld as a gift for the goddess of death. The Colavalia were concealed in mystery and mind-readers to boot — although that particular ability was not common knowledge.

Neva dragged her sword out of the dirt and wiped it on one of the fallen majilas, returning her blades home as Emiliand joined her.

"We should learn what we can and get them out of the way before the Upyri discover us," Neva said.

No one was traveling this way yet, but the storehouses and factories would let out in a few hours, and once that happened, potential witnesses would pepper the streets. The last thing they needed was attention from the Upyri or the mages who ruled Ramanaji Desert.

"You look well, Neva," Emiliand said as they moved the bodies to the flood ditch.

Neva paused in a crouch over the scarred majila's corpse. Appearances could be deceiving. She had been running long and far from everyone she cared about. That was how it needed to be. But she'd been so focused on putting distance between herself and Trinizhi, and between herself and those she loved, that she had become lonely without realizing it. Seeing

Emiliand in this foreign place reminded her of family, and that was something she hadn't allowed herself to think about in a long while.

"I'm better now that you're here," she said softly.

Emiliand placed a hand on her shoulder. She flinched, pulling away. She saw hurt flicker over his features, and regret tugged at her. She was pleased to see him, but she had ruined the moment. She'd had to. She couldn't bear to hurt him as she had so many others.

Emiliand sucked in a sharp breath.

"What is it?" she asked.

"Her scarification." Emiliand nodded at the majila's corpse. "I remember her."

Emiliand pulled the scarred majila's hair away from her neck to reveal an insignia at the base of her skull. The brand was familiar. Neva had a matching one. The donazhi of the Da'Voda had put it there when she had accepted Neva into their clan.

"She was sent by the Da'Voda," Neva said. She had assumed as much.

"Aye," Emiliand said bleakly. "She's a Ceasekin, one of Trinizhi's personal assassins."

Chapter Two

First Auton, 1640

Dear Little Elkizhi,

As promised, I pen this letter to you. We've been marching for weeks already, and we'll soon arrive at our position along Livorna's south bank. Bryand and I play dice with the other beasties in the evenings, and I've managed to win a few rounds. Bryand usually takes the pot, of course. Most days are boring with no action yet. I'm eager to prove myself, but I must be patient. You know patience is not my strong suit, so please keep me in your prayers.

Vivi was moved to another squadron, so we rarely see each other, but she said to tell you that you had better be practicing because you'll be big enough to spar with her when we return. Our mother is busy in wartime sessions, as is to be expected, but she sends her love.

With honor and pleasure,
— Astiand

"They weren't trying to kill me," Neva told Emiliand, shaking her head. "They could have if they'd wanted to."

Her cheeks warmed. It was embarrassing to admit such a thing to Emiliand, who had been one of her first teachers in the art of combat. But if the assassins hadn't been trying to kill her, it meant the donazhi wanted her alive. Had Trinizhi deduced that Neva harbored the Hand or the Eye, or both? Before today, Neva had convinced herself that the decoy she'd left for the donazhi had been successful. ...But what if she was wrong?

"You're sure they didn't want you dead?" Emiliand asked.

"I've never been more certain," Neva said. The scarred Ceasekin had slid a shacklay on Neva's wrist when she could have as easily cut her throat. "Let's get the rest of them out of sight, and then we can talk about it."

They finished dragging the bodies into the ditch, leaving behind bloody trails that instantly dried dark brown. The desert heat meant that the majilas' corpses would fester and the mages would discover them before long, but the Ceasekin were relatively well-hidden for the time being. The spelled trenches provided the people of R'shara with a modicum of protection during Fireside floods, now they were buying Neva and Emiliand time.

Out of compulsion, she murmured the prayer for a peaceful passing over the Ceasekin. Neva frowned as she pulled off the shacklay, useless with its master dead, and tossed it into the dirt beside them.

Several streets over, she nabbed a stretch of beige cotton and a white linen robe from a laundry line. They stopped in a pocket of shade, and Neva held the robe out to Emiliand.

"You need to blend in with the locals or the Upyri will give us trouble," Neva told him.

He hesitated.

"It's the kind of trouble we don't want," Neva insisted. "The kind of trouble that drove our people from the desert."

"Mages?" he asked, removing his shirt to reveal a plethora of small scars riddling his neck and shoulders. A surge of protectiveness flared in her at the sight.

"And Djinn," Neva confirmed, failing to avert her gaze. She hated whoever had done this to him. "Emiliand, what happened to you?"

Emiliand stilled with an unnatural immobility.

"Your horns, the scars..." Neva flushed.

"I messed up," Emiliand said with a grimace. "When it mattered most, I failed my squadron, and by extension, I failed my donazhi. I failed you."

"You could never fail me," Neva refuted. He was *here*. No matter what he'd lived through, he had followed through on his promise to her. That was all that mattered.

"I wish that were true." Emiliand gave a half-hearted smile.

"I mean it," Neva said more firmly. "I'm sure you did what you could."

"It wasn't enough," he said. The muscle in his jaw flexed, telling her the topic was not one he cared to discuss.

She fell silent as he finished changing. She tied the beige cloth around her waist to cover the blood splatter on her pants, and they made their way to a nearby marketplace. Neva led him through the crowd, ignoring the shuffling bodies, fragrant foods, and vendors' calls.

Hints of Da'Valian culture were everywhere — intricately woven rugs, beaded drums, and inlaid weapons. The scene appeared to captivate Emiliand. Neva swore she saw his nose twitch as they passed a cinnamon cart with a tower of sticky rolls, and she laughed when she saw him frowning at the dye booths. Dyes in Ramanaji Desert were pale in comparison to Illyia's famous royal colors back home, but the buxom women who called out their advantages claimed otherwise.

Neva also noticed the hitch in Emiliand's stride when he spotted the Upyr in charge of keeping order in the square. Several Upyri prowled around on a canopied platform in the center of the square. The head Upyr lounged above them on a stilted seat. With dark, gold-dusted skin that shone in the sunlight, no one could mistake him for anything but a Djinn, a possession demon. His yellow eyes roved the crowd as servants cooled him with enormous palm-leaf fans.

"Keep walking to the cantina at the south of the square," Neva warned Emiliand.

He did as she ordered. Neva held her breath as they passed beneath the Upyri's platform, far too close for comfort — and the Djinn, certainly, could sense their unease.

In their white uniforms, Djinn enforcers were stationed on street corners, near temples, healers' dens, and wherever else they wished. While the mages were reclusive, they employed the Upyri, an elite caste of Djinn, to keep order among the people. The Upyri had long oppressed the people of the seven cities, frightening them into obedience. Djinn could feed on emotions from close proximity, or from inside a host.

Neva had once seen a grandmother forced to dance under the hot sun for hours. The woman's family had been unable to do anything but watch until she collapsed in the dirt and the Upyr released her. Her crime? Not addressing the Upyr with his official title.

With a relieved sigh, Neva entered a cantina she'd been to several times before, usually when she was feeling lonely. Inside the smoky, dimly lit room, a trio of men played goat-hide drums for a sparse crowd. She held two fingers at the barkeep whose name she hadn't bothered to learn. In short order, he sent two tankards of junipero sliding their way. She paid with coins that she'd filched off a man at the door, and she and Emiliand found vacant seats in the back of the room. The cantina was cooler than the sun-drenched square, but Neva was still sweltering. She pressed her tankard against her face as they settled in at their table.

The cantina was where Neva had first met Porsha, the thief who'd agreed to introduce her to Salaman. Neva glanced over the tables, keeping an eye out for her. Thanks to Porsha's betrayal, Neva's plan for reviving her thieving identity, the Lynx, was blown. Her plan for a better future — one that didn't involve sleeping in the slums and stealing or scrounging to eat — was finished.

"Junipero?" Emiliand sniffed his tankard. "Thank the gods."

Junipero was one of the rare alcohols that could influence a Da'Valia. Emiliand downed the liquid in three long pulls, reminding her of several regulars who had frequented her father's tavern back home. Neva cleared her throat and gave him a quizzical look as she lowered her own tankard.

"Thirsty?" she asked.

"Always thirsty these days." He smiled ruefully, the friendly glimmer that had first drawn her to him surfacing. As quickly as it had appeared, his eyes darkened. "And it helps dim the voices."

Neva nodded. It wasn't easy for him to block out thoughts in a crowd. She reached out to touch his arm, to make sure he was real, but a second from making contact, she changed direction. She lifted her minty beverage to her lips with an ache in her chest. It was safer this way.

"I still can't believe you found me," Neva told him. "I wasn't sure the charm would work so far away."

"I paid good coin for it, but I never imagined you'd test it so far from home," Emiliand said, propping his elbows on the table. "Why did you leave Cirandrel?"

If he hadn't heard what had transpired while he'd been enlisted with the Da'Roha army, then he didn't know what she could do. That meant that Trinizhi's alliad, the only souls Neva had left alive on the battlefield outside Glacier Pass, must not have spread word of what happened.

As soon as she remembered the ash-blanketed battlefield, a low growl fought its way from Emiliand's throat. He must be reading her thoughts. A woman at a nearby table urged her companion away. The smoky air swirled in their wake.

"Show me," Emiliand said.

"I —" Neva shook her head, trying to think of anything else. If she could take it all back, she would.

"Neva, show me," he implored.

She squirmed and took a sip of junipero. She imagined his dismay, his condemnation. She couldn't stand it if Emiliand came to hate her for what she'd done. His friend Hanazhi had been one of those engaged in battle with the Da'Foha when Neva had released the Hand. Would he still want to become Neva's aliado after he learned what she'd done? Would he blame Neva as much as she blamed herself?

Still, even if he did, he had the right to know what had transpired. He'd come this far to find her, and he'd helped her fend off the donazhi's assassins.

"I just..." Neva cracked her knuckles under the table. *Know I didn't mean to do it, all right, Emiliand? I didn't mean for any of it to happen.*

She thought back to that time in the snowy mountains near Glacier Pass, just outside the city's wall. The Da'Voda and the Da'Foha had been engaged in battle when the Hand broke free from her control. To Neva's horror, the fiery power had obliterated everything in its path, save Trinizhi and her alliad. They'd only lived because Trinizhi had exhausted her power by erecting shields to protect them. Neva had pulled back the Hand, but too late. Afterward, she had knocked out Astiand and absconded with Dhianz's Eye.

"Dhianz's —" Emiliand choked, apparently in shock. He sat back, then leaned forward again and grabbed her tankard. He downed the rest of her junipero and wiped his mouth on his sleeve. "You're the Hand? And you already have possession of the Eye?"

The awed expression on his face made her sink in her seat. Emiliand, her friend and intended aliado, was gaping at her as if he had never seen her before, as if she was something special. He had it wrong. She had been an accidental sacrifice, nothing more.

"Both," Neva said.

"Where is the Eye?" He asked the question as if he expected her to pull the goblet from behind her back.

"Locked away inside me. Bound with a powerful spell." Neva swallowed hard. Then, with a waiver, "Both prongs of the Trishula are inside me now."

They stared at each other. Many Da'Valia believed that if they returned all three of the stolen powers to their creator, the curse on their people would be lifted. That had been Neva's mother's aim.

Finally, Emiliand posed the one question Neva hadn't wanted to ask herself since her run-in with the Ceasekin.

"How did they find you?"

Neva's heart dropped to the floor. The Da'Valia had avoided this region for centuries. With the Djinn at their side, the Obsidian Brotherhood had forced out the Da'Valia nearly three-hundred years before. Neva was the first who dared return.

She could think of one reason the donazhi would send Ceasekin to Ramanaji Desert, and it had everything to do with the only soul alive who had any idea where Neva was hiding.

Astiand.

If Trinizhi had discovered where to find Neva after all this time, it was because the donazhi's austere aliado had betrayed Neva as surely as she had knocked him upside the head when they had last parted. She couldn't believe she had ever trusted him. Ever kissed him.

"Astiand," Neva whispered, barely able to say his name aloud.

"He deserves Trinizhi," Emiliand said bitterly.

Why would Astiand betray her? When he had revealed that he was sworn to protect her, she had believed him. So what made him renege on that oath — an oath he'd claimed to have made to his dying mother?

But, really, his motivations didn't matter. Whatever Astiand's reasons were, he had betrayed her to her worst enemy. She couldn't forgive him for that. The donazhi's assassins hadn't killed her, but they could have, and she'd had no warning.

"We should leave," Emiliand told her. *"There aren't many places we can keep you from her, but we can go to the Da'Bruna and beg for asylum. No clan hates her more."*

Neva played with the leather bracelet on her wrist. The Da'Bruna were the most ruthless of the Da'Valian clans. They had excommunicated Emiliand's mother, and rumors said they ate their dead. She believed those rumors.

"What's to say their donazhi is any better than Trinizhi?" Neva asked.

"Any other donazhi is better," Emiliand said. "Shaundrazhi can be persuaded. We'll offer her something she can't refuse. We'll offer her information in exchange for asylum."

"What would she want to know?" Neva asked. She had a lot of secrets she intended to keep.

"I passed through Picquereau with the Da'Roha," Emiliand said with a half-shrug. "I picked up a lot of information while I was there, and I'm willing to leverage that if it will keep you safe."

That gave her pause. It was true, he could see the darkest thoughts of anyone he came in contact with. Maybe information would be enough to sway the Da'Bruna's donazhi in their favor. But even if word of what Neva did outside Glacier Pass had been contained, and even if no one had guessed that she harbored the Hand, the Da'Bruna would recognize her uniqueness as soon as they saw her horns. They might seek to use her for their own gain. From any angle, begging asylum from them was a gamble.

"We must act deliberately," Emiliand said. "Trinizhi monitors her Ceasekin carefully through enchantments. She will have known exactly when we dispatched them. She's probably already planning to retaliate. The only question we need to consider is, how long before she takes action?"

Given what was at stake?

"Not long," Neva said. "Not long at all."

She sighed. She had been fending for herself for a long time, moving covertly across the most brutal desert in existence, and she had become unaccustomed to others taking care of her. She'd had the help of a caravan and a disgraced Upyr as their guide, but that was different. She had bargained and paid for that. She didn't *deserve* help from anyone.

Unfortunately, whether she deserved it or not, she needed the Da'Bruna's help.

"I know someone who can get us back to Cirandrel." Neva calculated the amount of coin she had hidden. She had been saving it to finance her first big job under Salaman, and it was the last of what she had. It would have to be enough.

"I'll get us into the Da'Bruna from there," Emiliand said. "Who's your friend?"

Chapter Three

Sixth Auton, 1640

Dear Little Elkizhi,

Be proud of your brother — I've been elevated to sergeant. We've only been through one battle thus far, but everyone was impressed with my skill. The countless hours you watched me training with power and sword... they were all for this. Bryand taunts me, saying I'll become self-important, but I am confident I honor our god with every stroke of the blade. Our mother didn't say much, as usual, but I could see in her eyes that she is proud of me. I hope you are, too.

With honor and pleasure,
— Astiand

"I thought I might find you here," Neva said, approaching the Djinn who leaned against a mosaic temple wall.

Mari watched passersby with a predatory look, her yellow catlike eyes darting from person to person. No longer a member of the Upyri, Mari was left to scrounge for sustenance. Neva had seen her at this particular temple, a tribute to Riska, the goddess of death, more than once since their caravan had arrived in R'shara.

Crystals in the mosaic wall sparkled, reflecting an array of colors across the dry earth. Even now, when many city folk were working, or heading to and from the crocuta fights on the outskirts of R'shara, plenty still came to commune with their loved ones. A father ushered his daughters past on their way to the vaulted temple doors. They nearly trampled a blind beggar girl on the steps in their haste to move beyond the Djinn's sphere.

Mari shook her head after them. The waif scrambled to recapture her cup. Neva flicked a coin, which was her last from the cantina, into the receptacle. It wasn't enough for a meal, but it was the best she could do — and the least she ought to do on a day when she'd ended two lives.

Much of Mari's glossy black hair was pulled high on her head so the straight strands fell down her back like a tail, but a handful of wayward locks forced her to tilt her head to see as she turned her gaze on Neva. Mari wore long cream-colored skirts and a wrap that showed off her abdomen similar to Neva's own outfit.

"Neva," Mari purred in her smoky voice. "I didn't expect to see you again so soon."

Mari peeled away from the mosaic, her every move seeming intentional. Lethal.

Neva had made the right call by leaving Emiliand around the corner. His haunted eyes and newfound inclination to drink without reservation told her he was hurting. And Mari looked hungry.

"I need your help," Neva said. "An enemy has learned of my location, and I need to cross the deserts again, to return to Cirandrel."

"That's what I like about you, Neva." Mari cracked a smile. "You're always up to something. It's very Djinn of you."

Neva returned the smile.

"Will you guide us?" Neva asked. "I know you don't want to go back to Maither for employment. This way, you wouldn't have to."

Mari's brow furrowed at the mention of her brother, who was a high-ranking Upyr. The way Mari told it, their discord went well beyond sibling rivalry, and maybe even beyond this lifetime.

"You might persuade me," Mari said, cocking her head to the other side as if catching the scent of something that piqued her interest. "But that depends. Did you bring me a present?"

Neva didn't acknowledge the question and leaned against the mosaic, trying to pull Mari's attention back to her.

"You said you wanted to get out of here," Neva pressed. "Is that still true?"

Mari hummed, preoccupied with the corner of the temple. Specifically, the corner Emiliand waited behind.

"Da'Valian assassins may track us," Neva continued. "And then there are the usual threats. Time is of the essence. I can pay you, just not well."

Mari's attention shifted to Neva.

"You did bring me a present," Mari said with confidence.

Neva sighed.

"Emiliand, you might as well join us," Neva called.

Emiliand stepped out from behind the temple. In a blur, he leaped in front of Neva and held his quarterstaff at the ready.

Mari circled Emiliand slowly, inspecting him with an intensity that unnerved Neva.

"Where did you come from?" Mari sounded breathless.

"Your friend is a Djinn?" Emiliand's voice strained. "One of our mortal enemies?"

"Djinn don't have friends," Mari retorted, pausing in her inspection, her face even with Emiliand's shoulder. Her pink snakelike tongue darted out, tasting the air around him.

Neva rolled her eyes. Mari was playing with them.

"Mm. Distress and remorse." Mari slid a slender hand up to touch one of Emiliand's horns over the fabric that shrouded them.

Lightning fast, Emiliand caught her hand.

"You don't want to do that," he growled.

Mari took her time before stepping back. Neva frowned and crossed her arms, perturbed. Mari could feed off Emiliand's emotions from a distance without harming him, but if the Djinn was tempted to transform and possess him, his very soul could be at stake.

"I'm leaving, Mari, and I need a guide against the winds," Neva said. "Will you come?"

"That depends. This one's yours?" Mari asked again, still observing Emiliand like she wanted to eat him.

Neva licked her lips. They were promised in a sense, but dare she claim him? They hadn't discussed their agreement to align since they'd reunited.

"Does it matter?" Neva asked instead.

"Not if you have enough coin," Mari replied.

She didn't. Not really.

"He's mine." Neva's face warmed. "And he's coming with me."

Emiliand met Neva's eyes. The memory of their goodbye among the Da'Voda flashed through her mind. Impulsively, she had pressed her lips to his.

Oh gods, Neva thought. *Did he see that?*

Emiliand grinned.

"When do we leave?" Mari rubbed her hands together.

"At dawn."

"I'm attending a funeral tonight," Mari mused. "And I'll have to select something to wear for the journey, but I'll find you before the sun rises."

Mari slinked behind Emiliand and drew in a long breath as if memorizing his scent. She shot him a lingering look and wandered off down the street.

Groggy and parched, Neva awoke on the rough hay mat in her small hut. She was accustomed to the straw poking her in the back and the sounds of the slums. Somewhere, a baby cried, a couple fought, and dogs barked. Yet none of those were what woke her.

Her head was pounding. The Hand pulsated within the vault in the back of her mind, sparks of fiery power struggling free at the edges. She pushed against the destructive sparks and forced them back. Once she was satisfied that the Hand would not break free, she let out a quiet breath of relief. Soon, she would have to isolate herself outside the cities to release the power, as she did when the pressure became unbearable, but she estimated that she had at least a week before she needed to tend that need. Little by little, she was constraining it longer between releases.

She stiffened as she registered the warmth against her back and the scent of sandalwood. Emiliand. They had agreed to share opposite sides of the mat that occupied most of the floor space, but he had rolled closer sometime during the night. They both had.

She rubbed the sleep from her eyes before reaching for the water jug that she kept at her bedside. Carefully, Neva shimmied out from under Emiliand's arm and scooted to the edge of the mat. She took a long pull of water. Her hands trembled as she replaced the cork. She'd never intended to get so close to him.

Emiliand was attractive to her on a number of levels. He was trustworthy, protective, and loyal — and he understood her mixed parentage in a way few others could — but she hadn't allowed herself to be intimate with anyone since exiling herself to the desert. Her final moments in Ashford filled her nightmares, and she couldn't allow that to happen again. She *couldn't*.

A series of raps on the outside of Neva's hut startled her from the trap of her memories. An unfamiliar woman stepped through the low doorway. Emiliand lurched upright, yanking his sword free from its scabbard.

"Don't." Neva dropped the jug and lunged for Emiliand. She stalled his attack, but not before the tip of the sword was leveled at the woman's nose.

"Reporting for duty," Mari quipped with a mock salute.

Mari's face belonged to a stranger. Doe eyes were wide-set, and curly auburn hair fell about her shoulders. Though her deep red dress was long and flowing, the neckline was more revealing than anything Neva had seen anyone wear in public. Ever.

"Did I fail to mention we're attempting to be inconspicuous?" Neva asked.

"Haven't you heard of hiding in plain sight? This is as inconspicuous as it gets." Mari licked her plump lips. "No one is going to stop us, not if they want to avoid retribution by the Scarlet Mage."

"Scarlet Mage?" Emiliand murmured. Then, sharply, "our guide is an evokamor practitioner?"

"Do you want my assistance or not?" Mari's eyes flashed yellow-gold.

He glowered at her in response.

"Yes, we want your help," Neva reassured. They would never make it across the desert without Mari. "Emiliand, lower your sword. She has a point. No one will give us trouble if we're conducting business on the behalf of the Scarlet Mage."

"Not even the Scarlet Mage?" Emiliand asked doubtfully, but he lowered his blade.

"Then we had best get moving before he finds out," Mari said with a conspiratorial wink.

They headed to the stables in the blue-dawn morning. Neva said a silent good riddance to her cramped hut and the stench of the surrounding slums. The only thing she regretted about leaving was that she'd paid the slum lord rent through the end of Vestive. *Easy come, easy go,* she thought. She never had much luck at keeping coin in reserve. At least they had their transportation covered.

The evening before, Emiliand had ferreted out the Ceasekins' steeds and boarded them with instructions to have them saddled and packed. Most of the horses spooked and backed away from Neva and her companions as they entered the stables, but the Da'Valian steeds pawed the ground expectantly. Before mounting, she and her companions filled extra waterskins in the trough that ran along the front of the stables. The threats that could kill a person in Ramanaji Desert were numerous, but lack of water claimed as many lives as the winds, and their horses would need plenty.

Yellow light seeped over the horizon as they rode out, Neva and Emiliand in front of Mari, who had donned a long covering that left only her face visible. The rare red material was a statement of importance. Little about them called attention since it was perfectly usual for one of the Scarlet Mage's practitioners to travel with protection.

An Upyr took a few steps from her post but didn't stop them as they moved beyond R'shara's boundary, a low stone wall that kept out destructive herds of sand boars and hyenas.

They sped up once they moved beyond sight of the city, going as quickly as the horses could in the deep, glittering sands. Oases provided sporadic resting places, but they were infrequent and undependable. They came to one just before daylight faded and took advantage of their luck, setting up camp and watering the horses at the murky well.

That night, beneath the gray corkay trees with their powdery bark and dangling teardrop leaves, Emiliand collected fallen fronds and ignited them with his midnight flame. The temperature had dropped rapidly when the sun set, so they huddled together for warmth as Neva prepared a modest meal. She placed herself strategically between Mari and Emiliand, since they hadn't gotten off to an agreeable start, and filled a bowl for Mari.

"I'll pass," Mari said, shaking her head. "I have plenty to sustain me."

Neva could have sworn to Dhianz that she saw a flicker of despair on the evokamor practitioner's face at that statement, but then Mari was back. Neva tried to not let Mari's cavalier use of a human body bother her. After all, Neva had eaten all manner of animals throughout her life, and, if the stories were true, ancient Da'Valian tribes — her ancestors — had all been cannibals. Who was she to say what Mari could or couldn't consume to sustain herself?

After their meal, Neva slipped a dagger from her ankle sheath. She used the blade to notch two slivers out of the thick leather of her belt.

"The Ceasekin?" Emiliand asked, watching her work.

"Aye," Neva answered. It was a tradition among the Da'Valia to keep a record of one's kills. She had over twenty marks on her belt, and she remembered every single one. She made sure of it.

"And you think what I do is morbid," Mari said dryly. "At least I don't keep track."

"We do it to remember," Neva tried to explain. She had lost her own mother when she was young, so she had learned firsthand that more than one person suffered for every life she took. She owed it to those left behind to honor their dead.

"Looks more like you're punishing yourself," Mari said with a shrug.

Neva frowned. Her death count was growing, and that bothered her. Most of the lives she had taken were the result of failing to control the Hand. She was responsible for it, yet it had escaped her hold not once, but twice. She could blame no one else but herself.

For many Da'Valia, the victories that the marks represented were also a source of pride. Were her marks a form of punishment? Maybe. But otherwise, praying over her victims was the best she could do.

When she was done with the leather, Neva offered to mark Emiliand's belt for him. He paused briefly before unbuckling it. Neva accepted the waistband, the abrasive texture turning her hands clammy. Knowing what she would find, she turned it over and stared. Notches lined the entire inside, save for a few inches toward the buckle.

Neva raised her eyes to find defiance in his. Defiance, but also something more. It was as if he was daring her to hate him for killing so many people, as if he was bracing himself for the sting of rejection. Neva bit her lip.

Emiliand had always accepted her. She could hardly rebuke him now. Had he not been half-Colavalia and had he not been able to read minds, she suspected his belt would have a fraction of the marks. Other fighters didn't have the luxury of gleaning their opponents' intentions from their thoughts. She could be hard on herself for failing to keep the Hand reined in, but she couldn't judge him for being who he was.

Neva didn't say anything. She wasn't sure if he was listening to her thoughts or not, so she tried to keep her mind blank to avoid wounding him. She etched the lines into his belt.

"I'll not deny my purpose. I'll give a fight to anyone who wants one," Emiliand said as she handed it back. "But I have an idea of why we die so young. It's tiring to live with so much blood on our hands."

Looking at him, Neva was struck by the sense of peering into a mirror. She blinked away fledgling tears. Emiliand had always been accepting of who she was, now she understood him better, too. He had revealed a side that she hadn't wanted to admit was there. She had wanted to think him indomitable, but he carried invisible scars as clearly as he carried the physical ones. They were both killers, and they both bore the weight of it like stacking stones upon their chests.

Chapter Four

Second Fireside, 1640

Dear Little Elkizhi,

It pains me to write you with news of our mother's passing. She perished in battle, and hers was an honorable death. I was with her at the end. She spoke cryptically and made me swear to protect a majila I will likely never encounter. I cannot imagine what made her demand such a thing, but you know me. I take my oaths seriously. Perhaps even too seriously at times. Pardon my writing. I am in a fog of despair.

We were lucky to have our mother as long as we did, to not end up in the Orphague. I know that, but it's hard to keep sight of just now. I miss you, dear sister. I wish we could properly grieve together during this time, but the horn calls me back to the battlefield even now. May you hold a vigil in our mother's honor with your father. Send him my condolences as well.

With honor and little pleasure,

— Astiand

Heat rose in waves from the white dunes, permeating Neva's clothing and drawing sweat down her spine. Atop her horse, her backside had grown sorer, and the blisters on the insides of her thighs had chaffed until they popped. Earlier that day, she and her friends had embarked on the most treacherous part of their journey, setting out from Morafeno after they had broken their fast. Caravans that ventured north of Morafeno were few and far between, so they hadn't seen anyone since departing the metropolis. The silence this far from anything was oppressive.

Neva gnawed on a tough, peppery piece of dried sand boar and went to take a swig from the waterskin slung across her torso. She tilted her head back, shaking the last drops out onto her tongue.

"We've got renegades on the horizon." Mari pointed into the distance at a dust cloud, which was fast approaching from the east.

Neva dropped the waterskin and raised her hand against the sun. A party of renegades were headed their way, and not all of them were human.

"What would they want with us?" Emiliand asked, drawing his horse to a stop. "We have a mere five horses."

Not many, considering Neva and Mari's caravan had traveled with many more than that, plus wagons and donkeys. Five horses would fetch a significant amount of coin, but the renegades were endangering their lives coming this far north. It didn't add up.

"Hm." The sound of understanding came from Mari, and Neva cursed, catching on.

"They want the Scarlet Mage's practitioner," Neva said. Evokamor practitioners were highly skilled, and their mere presence could elevate the status of those around them. Sultans, mages, and Djinn alike would gladly exchange coin and information for their company.

"I knew your costume would cause trouble." Emiliand scowled at Mari.

"It got us out of R'shara and Morafeno without question, didn't it?" Mari shot back.

Neva ignored them as they bickered. If they ran and missed the next watering hole, it could mean their deaths. They didn't have enough water for themselves and the horses to last the day. On the other hand, they were outnumbered and renegades specialized in raiding — a blunt, unattractive method of thievery that left fields of corpses for the vultures. Renegades in these parts were known for their propensity for slaughter. It was as if Dhianz was testing her reluctance to use the Hand by putting them in her path, but perhaps there was another way.

"Are you two done?" Neva interrupted her companions. "They won't have seen Da'Valia in centuries. We might scare them off."

"Don't fool yourself," Mari scoffed. "They're renegades. It'll be us or them in the grave."

Neva pressed her lips together, annoyed. But Mari was right. She was being naive.

"I won't run from a fight," Emiliand said. "Let's show them that Da'Valia aren't easy prey."

"Just give me a blade," Mari said. "They won't like facing a Djinn either."

Emiliand tossed Mari a dagger. She caught it and kicked her horse into a canter to meet the renegades head-on.

"I see why you like her," Emiliand said. He took off after Mari and belted out a war cry. The renegades responded with wild whoops and hollers.

Neva untied the line for the pack horses, trusting they wouldn't stray too far, and kicked her own horse into motion. Racing across the desert, she squinted into the wind. Her stomach churned as the Hand pounded against its cage. *Us or them,* Mari had said.

"With honor and with pleasure," Emiliand told her. *"We fight for Dhianz."*
"For Dhianz," Neva echoed.

She gave herself over to her Da'Valian side. She manifested streams of power and deftly braided a shield, her blood awakening. She drew her sword.

Their groups clashed in a blur. Knocking away flying arrows with her shield, Neva slipped from the stirrups and balanced atop her saddle. A Jingali warrior, a hulking creature with a wild mane and a hairy chest, leaped at her. They collided in the air. They hit the ground hard and broke apart. The Jingali warrior's prehensile tail lashed out at her. She knocked away the blade it held and swiped aside his black claws with her shield.

The warrior advanced, chuffing through his lion-like snout. He was quick. She'd heard tell of Jingali relying on silker root to sustain them for days of fighting. She hadn't heard that it made them faster.

Out of the corner of her eye, she saw Emiliand bullying his way through the renegades. He charged as if this was the last battle he might ever take part in, sword-fighting against the mounted renegades and bashing his burning braided shield into anyone who came at him. Meanwhile, Mari was using her horse to kick and stomp renegades on the ground. They circled her but didn't harm her. Her body was the valuable prize.

Neva knocked away several of the Jingali warrior's hacks, unable to find an opening, and lunged away from a rider that came at her from the side. A flicker in the Jingali warrior's eyes gave her a second's warning that someone was rushing her from behind.

She crouched and pushed off the ground. She flipped over her attacker's head in a move she had practiced endlessly with a friend in her caravan. Neva thrust her sword forward with both hands, driving it through the renegade who had been behind her and into the Jingali warrior, piercing his heart.

The warrior snarled as he crumpled. A dozen renegades took his place, assembling around Neva with raised scimitars, several of them atop horseback. She yanked her blade free with a grunt and pivoted, striking out at those on the ground and shooting at those on horseback.

"Use me." The Hand swelled. Neva pushed it back.

Emiliand was making short work of his opponents while Mari cowered. The renegades had uprooted Mari from her saddle, but she'd somehow held onto Emiliand's dagger. Two men grabbed her arms, and the others tried to get ahold of her clothing.

"Mari," Neva yelled, spinning her burning shield around in a wide circle. "Stop playing with your food."

Mari gave an exaggerated groan.

"Fine." Mari ripped free. She slashed out, cutting one of the men on the arm.

"Dirty harlot," a renegade shouted. "You'll pay for that where you belong — on your back."

"Not on your life," Mari said, eyes flashing yellow. She threw herself on his weapon, impaling the body she wore. The evokamor practitioner's mouth opened wide. Golden dust shot out — Mari — and swarmed the man, sliding between his lips to take him over. The practitioner collapsed.

"Go with the gods, if they'll have you," Mari spoke through the renegade. She turned his sword on him. The next man who had been terrorizing her made it three steps before the cloud of Djinn dust shot toward him. Mari exploded against an invisible barrier — some kind of magical protection? Slower than before, her scattered dust re-formed and targeted another renegade.

Neva launched spheres at the mounted renegades, managing to oust two of them from their saddles. One was knocked unconscious, and the other screamed and rolled, trying to extinguish the flames enveloping his robes. Neva grabbed a dagger that one of the renegades had lost and threw it at the screaming man to end his misery. He went silent. A third rider jerked to a stop and pulled the reins to the side, whipping his horse to flee. A fourth followed suit.

She grinned. Others were running, too. They could see Emiliand snapping arms with his bare hands as he flung their comrades through the air. They could see Djinn dust overtaking their friends and forcing them to commit involuntary suicide. Not to mention Neva, who dispatched their Jingali warrior after he had tested her with only a few strokes. With the practitioner dead, they had little to gain and everything to lose.

It didn't take long for the remaining renegades to set off back toward Morafeno.

"And here I was expecting a challenge," Neva said wryly.

"They aren't running from us," called Mari, who had re-formed in flesh and bone, her hair in its holder atop her head. Her gaze was locked on something behind them. "The winds have come."

Already, faint screams reached Neva's ears. She spun around to see a tempest of sand and tormented souls. The sandstorm stretched across the desert in a manifestation so wide that there was no end in sight. Wind whipped her hair around her face. A bolt of terror shot through her, and her knees weakened. Despite facing several sandstorms on her journey south, and despite hearing stories about the winds burying caravans, she was unprepared for the breadth of the sandstorm bearing down on them.

"I've never seen anything like this," Emiliand said. "How do we fight it?"

"*We* don't," Neva answered, turning to Mari. Outrunning the winds was an impossibility. Only Djinn could fight the desert plague. "You got this?"

"Braid your shields, Da'Valia," Mari told them, raising her hands to the sky. "I'll do what I can."

The wind roared as it closed in on them, each squall a soul that had been pushed from its body by a Djinn. Centuries of lost souls cried in anguish, ready to pull apart any living creature they encountered. Legends said that when Goj, the evil trickster god, scattered the ashes of Dhianz's son on the wind, this was what became of the boy.

Emiliand coerced their now-skittish war horses into a cluster and urged them to lay against the ground, talking in calming tones. Being stranded without their mounts would be just as deadly as the other threats they faced, so Neva followed suit, ignoring the glazed gazes of the dead renegades. She lunged for a horse that they had left behind. She caught hold of the reins just before it skittered beyond her reach, but the animal reared. She had no choice but to let go, and it galloped away.

The storm bore down on them, blocking out the sun. The screams were so awful, so rife with torment, that they rattled her bones. Her enhanced senses were usually a blessing, but not now. The cries punctured her ears as she and Emiliand coaxed the horses together. They covered the steeds with blankets before throwing themselves between the animals and weaving their shields.

Emiliand put an arm around Neva and held her tightly.

"Don't let go," he shouted to her. Or maybe he had said he wouldn't let go. It was impossible to tell. Neva could barely hear anything above the wailing.

Neva ducked her head into his chest but peeked out to see Mari, who called Djinn power around them in a golden vortex. As the winds reached Neva and Emiliand, their shields held back the sand, melting it into a perfect circle of glass. But the souls cut through, pummeling them and forcing Neva to duck again. She had no weapon or shield fit to defend against vengeful energies.

For a moment, a melodic chanting rose amid the wind and pushed back the screams. The next, it was gone, and the howling took over.

The core of the sandstorm hit, and Mari began to glow. Yellow sand exploded against a current of souls, fighting back the onslaught, pushing, falling, and flying. Chaotic.

Emiliand yanked a blanket tighter over their heads, and the horses' terrified neighs joined the ear-splitting cries as Mari's power clashed with the sandstorm. The winds, which had been nearly deafening a moment before, amplified. Neva clapped her hands over her ears.

Sand piled around them. Their shields buckled briefly but held.

They were going to die. Panic climbed Neva's throat. All of those who suggested that Neva was chosen by the gods had been wrong. She hadn't been gifted with the Hand for a reason. She was merely a holding cell for the power before it moved on. As soon as she perished, where would it go?

Souls penetrated Mari's protective shroud and streamed through Neva's flickering shield. A gust hit Neva in the chest like a battering ram. She screamed at the onslaught, instinctively going for the Hand before she caught herself. If she released the Hand, Emiliand and Mari could end up at its mercy.

Neva jerked, crying out again. An icy pain stabbed her through the heart. The cold was excruciating. Crippling.

Emiliand went rigid next to her. In front of them, Mari spun in circles, still chanting. The Djinn wasn't fighting the sandstorm. That was a losing battle. She was fighting the current of souls that directed its path toward them. Bright golden sand turned brown as Mari worked to disrupt the ruthless gusts. Eventually, she morphed into dust and flew at the wind, holding it back until — suddenly — it was gone.

The sun reappeared. Neva gasped, sucking in the hot desert air. The souls assaulting her had left with the sandstorm, but an unbearable cold still gripped her heart.

"Emiliand?" Neva asked. He hadn't moved in too long.

"I'm alive," he said. A moment passed before he raised his head.

Neva surveyed the area. The winds had erased all evidence of their skirmish. Two of their horses had survived. The blankets that protected Neva and Emiliand appeared threadbare, with holes emerging from the folds. Mountains of sand as tall as Neva stood around them just beyond the perfect ring of glass. If the sandstorm had kept going, they would have been buried along with everything else.

Mari shuddered and faded before reappearing in her petite Djinn form. She walked toward them, but her knees buckled. She transformed into canary dust and closed the short distance.

"We should get moving," Mari said, her voice rising and falling as she faded and solidified with irregularity. "If I don't get another host soon, I might —"

She stumbled into Emiliand.

"Quick, put her down," Neva ordered Emiliand, who had caught the Djinn in an awkward embrace.

Moments passed, and Mari's eyelids fluttered.

"Hey there, Lover Boy." Mari grabbed Emiliand's arm, dragging her split tongue along the side of it, oblivious of the grime. "Glad you're here."

Neva winced, but Emiliand held still. Neither of them wanted Mari to perish, not when the vast expanse of desert before them could see more sandstorms in their path.

"Can you ride with her?" Neva asked Emiliand. She was breathless, as if she had been running for hours.

"Of course," Emiliand said, lifting Mari. "Keep your tongue to yourself, Djinn."

"If you say so," Mari murmured, half turning to dust for a moment so that gold specks littered his robes. She flashed Neva a mischievous grin over Emiliand's shoulder as they mounted.

Neva reached for her waterskin with trembling hands before remembering it was empty. She was parched. Her muscles kept locking in spasms. She prayed the next watering hole hadn't been covered up like their skirmish.

Licking dry lips, she re-cinched her saddle and climbed up. Her muscles cooperated, but barely. She was cold, a sure sign of illness for any Da'Valia, especially in such a hot climate. She fought to remain upright as they set out again, slumping lower in her saddle the farther they traveled. Even as she caught sight of the next oasis, desperation joined the chill in her chest. Her breath emerged in puffs of wintry fog.

"Emiliand —" Neva slipped in an attempt to dismount. She slammed into the sand. She tried to focus on Emiliand and Mari, who were standing over her. She rubbed the cold spot on her chest and gasped at the pain.

"Drink." Emiliand was by her side in an instant, holding his waterskin to her lips.

"You don't look so good." Mari dismounted and shuddered. "But you taste delicious."

"I'm so cold." Neva placed her hand on her chest. It was impossible to get frostbite in the desert, wasn't it? Clumsily, she pulled her wrap aside where it crossed in the center of her chest. The material parted to reveal an icy blue patch. Purple veins crept out, and steam rose from where the cold met the desert air. A fist-sized portion of her flesh had transformed into a flat, aquamarine crystal.

"What is that?" Emiliand's brow furrowed.

"It hurts." Talking took strength Neva did not have.

"Great Goj," Mari covered her mouth.

Emiliand cursed, apparently not liking what he saw in the Djinn's mind.

"Soul scourge," Mari whispered.

Chapter Five

Eleventh Vestive, 1531

Brother Osirus,

I have not received a message in response to my missive to Brother Cyrus. I understand the Serculus considers it of the utmost importance that I suffer, and I can assure you I have, indeed, suffered through a rain-drenched, dragon-plagued five seasons. The wardens are relentless, and the amenities scarce. I pray, Brother, that you will tell the Serculus as much. I continue to conduct my experiments, and I expect they will be very interested to hear the results.

Humbly yours,
Brother Alewiscious
Prisoner 173, Lithlorian Island

"It can't be." Emiliand's face turned ashen.

Neva's thoughts dragged, but soul scourge was a familiar term. The winds might not have taken her yet, but a soul scourge meant one thing: death was coming for her.

"I failed you," Mari said tearfully. "The scourge will work its way through you until it severs your soul."

"You haven't failed her yet." Emiliand took hold of Neva's hand. "The Da'Bruna could help if — Neva, will you align with me? Here and now?"

Neva shivered. According to the Da'Valian protocols she had read once, a majila almost always aligned with a hilan, and usually more than one. Stronger majilas, such as donazhis, would often align with three or even four. Forming an alliad allowed majilas and their aliados to exchange power.

But it also did something else.

Neva wracked her brain for an elusive memory, and it hit her. She had once seen a hilan so depleted that he had been on the edge of death. Bryand. Trinizhi had worked with a healer and an otima, a religious servant of Dhianz. Together, they had managed to save him.

Could the same be done for her, if she aligned with Emiliand now? Would the Da'Bruna even allow one of their otimas to help a majila from another clan? And a fugitive no less?

"We can't know for sure," Emiliand said. *"But there's no question of what happens if we don't."*

"What about the Hand?" Neva asked. When Melanzhi's aliados had touched the Eye, they had been incapacitated. Permanently.

"It's a risk, I won't deny that," he admitted. *"But this will align our powers, not pit yours against me. I'm willing to be your aliado, if you'll have me."*

"If?" Neva asked.

"I want you to know..." Emiliand's gaze strayed to the horizon. "I'm not worthy of you."

Neva frowned. She wasn't like other majilas, and he wasn't like other hilans. She couldn't imagine a hilan who would be a better match, but this was the second time he had alluded to being inadequate.

"How are you not worthy?" Neva asked.

"With the Da'Roha, we were hired by the Order to establish a line of defense south of the Farer's Strait," Emiliand started.

"The merchant sea road?" Neva asked.

"Aye. The Order suspected that the Amanians were using a woodsy area to conduct illegal trade. Tensions have been causing unrest in Port Telgard, and the Order needs proof to declare war. What we didn't know was that the Amanians had employed Vodou witches."

A shiver rushed down her spine.

"And, well, I'll show you."

Dizziness swept over her as Emiliand projected his memory to her. Instantaneously, she felt as if she'd lived the moment from his past and could recollect the tragedy as if it were her own.

Tree branches stung Emiliand's face in the dark, drawing blood as his legs tightened around a chestnut horse. Cool, salty air whipped against his face, and slim arms marred by rope burns wrapped around his middle. A void had replaced the pool of power he normally could pull from on a whim, as if he'd exhausted it in battle and it needed time to regenerate.

"Faster," a majila shouted behind him.

Emiliand leaned into the horse's mane as they leaped over a fallen tree. They crested a wooded hill to reveal the Da'Roha's central encampment below, where most of the soldiers were asleep.

Emiliand charged forward to warn his brothers-at-arms with his donazhi, Xandrazhi, mounted behind him. She was young, yet fierce. Her long hair flew out behind her, and her white-silver eyes were piercing.

"Who goes there?" A hilan emerged from the trees when they reached the outer perimeter. He held his sword at the ready atop his mount.

Yorand and three more of Emiliand's squadron were close behind.

"It's us, Gregand," Xandrazhi called back, her voice hoarse and rife with urgency. "Sound the alarm. Clear out the camp. Now."

The donazhi's order had the unit spinning and sprinting ahead. Air tainted by the electric edge of Vodou witch magic caught and lifted Gregand's cape so it carried out behind him, crackling blue in muffled flashes of light. He lifted a carved ox's horn. A low bellow roused the Da'Roha troops.

The relief that filled Emiliand was squelched as a strange glow appeared in the trees. Their horse stumbled, and he and Xandrazhi went flying. Emiliand tucked into a roll and catapulted himself forward in a full-out sprint.

Xandrazhi did the same. The perimeter guards disappeared into the trees. He forced himself to keep going. His brothers' lives depended upon it.

"Witches are attacking. Clear the camp." Emiliand called into the minds of his soldiers. He'd never attempted reaching out to so many minds. He hoped that they could hear him, and that they would heed him.

Ahead, the trees thinned and opened to an expanse of shoreline — shoreline that was dotted with fiery globes. Moonlight reflected off the black swells and incoming waves. Emiliand reached out with his mind, searching for the agents he knew must be nearby.

He saw the triad of Vodou witches with his mind's eye. At the farthest edge of his range, the women were aboard a dinghy on the bay, shrouded by an unnatural fog. He had never stretched his ability so far, but he could read their mal-intent. They raised their arms to the sky in unison, and the globes along the shore lowered and dimmed. The lead Vodou witch and her cohorts crouched to touch the water. Electricity crackled out in jagged lines, racing across the surface toward the glowing orbs.

"Down," Emiliand shouted to Xandrazhi.

She glanced back, but he was already barreling toward her with the last of his strength pounding through his legs. He caught her around the waist as the world illuminated around them. They went airborne and slammed into the earth behind a fallen tree. Lightning exploded, blasts rocking the shoreline.

"No," Xandrazhi screamed, struggling free of Emiliand's hold as a lightning bolt struck the base of a tree next to them.

She tore away from him and shot to her feet. Splinters and rock shards battered them as he lurched after her. Emiliand kicked Xandrazhi's ankle and grabbed the back of her wrap. He yanked her behind the fallen tree. His head slammed down on a rock, and his vision was wracked by bursting stars.

A wave of heat flooded over them. He held Xandrazhi down. The Vodou witches had drained both of their powers before leaving them for dead, and it was Da'Valian power that they had twisted into the perverse weapon that they wielded against the encampment. If Xandrazhi attempted to defend against the witches, it would mean her death.

Blood ran down the side of Emiliand's neck. He registered little of their surroundings. The light illuminating the shoreline had changed from a bright blueish white to an orange glow thick with smoke as fire climbed the trees. Emiliand could just make out the bodies littering the ground.

Emiliand's ears buzzed, obscuring all sound, but he heard Xandrazhi cry out in his mind. He wrapped an arm around her shoulders and held her.

"We must remain quiet. They are not far." *Emiliand warned her, stroking a hand through her hair.*

"I will not cower." *Xandrazhi lifted her head, oblivious to the gash on her cheek.* "Where are they? They will not survive the night."

Xandrazhi scrambled to her feet. She stumbled over branches and rocks as she made her way to the beach. Still, she seemed to hold her head higher with each fallen Da'Roha she passed. Emiliand followed, but he was disoriented, and he struggled to keep his balance. The scent of singed flesh mixed with sulfur and smoke was nauseating.

"Xandrazhi, stop," Emiliand shouted into her mind.

"Stop?" She spun and screamed at him. "Did you just order me to stop? I'm your donazhi. I should order you to come with me."

Emiliand doubled over and dropped his head into his hands. Xandrazhi was a good donazhi, the best he had ever known. They had fought alongside each other, and they had suffered through a few nights of peace, too, with Gregand's wretched singing to keep them entertained beside the campfire. Xandrazhi was courageous, fair, and humble. She had earned her position a hundred times over by seeking out prestigious work that kept her clan flush with coin and helped them find majilas to align with. Yet neither of them knew how long it would take for their power to renew, which meant that if she picked a fight now, she would not win.

"You'll lose," Emiliand shouted after her. "If you go after them tonight, you'll lose more than we've lost already."

The Vodou witches were leaving. They were almost beyond his reach. He needed to stall Xandrazhi just a moment longer. She kept marching to the waterline.

"Don't do this — not this night," Emiliand called. Enough Da'Roha had died. They should not lose their donazhi, too. "I will help you destroy them. No matter how long it takes, but not this night."

Xandrazhi turned to face him.

"You mean that?" she asked softly. Then, more forcefully. "You mean that, don't you? You think I need your help? You may be a toppel, but I'm a donazhi."

"Precisely. Who else will rebuild this clan if not for you?" He gestured around them.

Xandrazhi shifted, the incoming tide lapping at the hem of her pants. But she wasn't heading toward the water any longer. She was listening.

"On my honor, I will not leave this task to you." He knelt in the sand beside a body he recognized as Ictand, one of his squad leaders. "I beg of you to regroup first. Wait for your power to restore, collect your aliados from the other camps, and then hunt them down. Ictand deserves your vengeance. They all do."

Xandrazhi called to life a flickering flame in her palm. It quickly sputtered and died. The young donazhi swiped at the approaching waves with clawed hands, wailing in her grief. She collapsed in the shallow water.

"There is no making this right," Xandrazhi cried. A wave crashed into her, soaking her from the waist down. "I failed them."

"We both failed them," Emiliand told her. "But maybe, one day, we can avenge them."

Neva blinked rapidly, her eyesight adjusting to the harsh light of the desert as the harrowing memory faded. She hadn't realized it, but in the brief moment it'd taken Emiliand to transfer the recollection to her, tears had trailed down her face.

Mari cleared her throat loudly, observing them.

"Oh, good, you're still with the living," Mari said.

"You did all that you could for them," Neva told Emiliand, trying to rub some warmth back into her arms. "You can't see it yet, but this black mark isn't so dark."

"What is going on?" Mari crossed her arms.

"Emiliand and I are going to align," Neva said. Her lips were numb.

"I see. Lover Boy is getting his big moment." Mari glanced back and forth between them. "So what in all the realms are we waiting for?"

"We're not. We do this now." Emiliand shot Mari a warning glare. "And don't call me boy."

Chapter Six

First Cravell, 1547

Brother Cyrus,

Perhaps you did not receive my many letters, as I continue to eagerly await your response. As stated previously, I believe my punishment has been satisfactorily administered. My contributions to the Brotherhood are undeniable, and I insist the Serculus re-examine my case. As the Grand Magi, would you broach the subject at your next commune? Though my actions were admittedly brash, my research has benefited us, and will continue to benefit us for many years to come. However, as I am sure you have begun to notice, the physical side effects of aging are persistent. I have continued conducting my experiments, and I am optimistic that I will enhance my legacy.

Sincerely,
Brother Alewiscious
Prisoner 173, Lithlorian Island

As Emiliand dragged his boot through the sand to form a circle, Neva looked out at the barren landscape helplessly. She hadn't allowed herself to think about aligning with Emiliand in many moons, but she had imagined it on occasion, and she hadn't pictured it like this. The fantasy that had taken place in her mind was in a temple with their closest Da'Voda friends present and an otima presiding — and, of course, he saw it.

"These circumstances are less than ideal, but you do me a great honor, Nevazhi." Emiliand took her hands in his and led her to the center of the circle. *"Never did I dare to desire a majila as fierce and powerful as you. In time, I hope to redeem myself and to prove to you I can be a worthy aliado."*

It might have been the soul scourge, but Neva's heart skipped. She swallowed hard. She was supposed to be strong.

"I hope to be a majila worthy of you, too," Neva said. She meant it. The way he looked at her made her think they could do it. That everything would work out. The Da'Bruna would save her from the soul scourge, their alliance would be one that rivaled any other, and not even Trinizhi could touch them.

In theory, Neva understood how alliads were formed. An otima would ask for a blessing from Dhianz and oversee the exchange to form the connection between hilan and majila. But how could they accomplish such a thing so far from anyone?

"It'll be easy," Emiliand said aloud, presumably for Mari's benefit. "A formal ritual with a presiding otima is a luxury, but our people have aligned on battlefields for centuries."

"Mari, take a walk, will you?" Neva asked.

"Is that necessary?" Mari asked skeptically.

"Do it, Mari." Neva's teeth chattered. "It's not safe."

"All right, all right." Mari backed away.

"Are you ready?" Emiliand asked Neva.

"I don't want to hurt you," Neva told him. The image of flame biting into Adam's flesh came unbidden into her mind. How quickly that brief moment of passion had transformed into one of terror. Her exile here, her distancing herself from everyone she cared about... She didn't want to die, but if she harmed Emiliand, it would have all been for naught.

"You can do this," Emiliand said.

"How do we start?" she asked, mustering her courage.

"Take hold of my horns."

Touching one's horns could be considered a sacred act among Da'Valia. It implied complete trust. Neva placed her hands on his pitted horns.

Emiliand's pupils dilated. He slid his hands around her horns, and a torrent of heat scorched its way through her. An intense rush that was part agony and part bliss flared to life as their powers connected for the first time. She stepped into him, and the chill of the soul scourge thawed.

Emiliand appealed to Dhianz, asking for the creator's blessing. Gradually, Emiliand relinquished his power to Neva, so it flowed steadily through their connection. The combination of his power and the importance of what they were doing made her light-headed.

Neva was already full of her own power, the Hand, and the Eye, and the sensation of her mind stretching brought her to her knees. She dragged Emiliand down with her. She heard a whimper and was only distantly aware that it came from her.

"Inhale slowly," Emiliand's calming voice drifted through her mind.

Her lower lip trembled, and she sucked in a gulp of air. Slowly, she let it siphon out.

"This will work," she thought to herself. Da'Valia had been forming alliads for centuries. *"Let his power find a space."*

She seldom shied away from risk-taking, but this was different from spying or thieving. This was sacred and personal. On an exhale, she gave herself over to a new awareness. His essence, a midnight flame, joined the burning dawn coursing through her. Dhianz had created them to complement each other. She'd never truly known what that meant until this moment.

"Now, share your power with me," Emiliand told her.

Neva pushed her power through their connection at the slowest possible speed. He jerked as if he had been run through with a sword, but she couldn't pull it back. Their exchange quickened, and their energies catapulted back and forth.

Their power manifested around them, streaks of black and white flame against a blue sky. Emiliand pulled away, severing their physical connection. Neva lowered her hands to her sides, amazed that the current continued to flow.

"I'll be quick." Emiliand took a knife from his belt. The ritual could not be completed without a blood exchange.

Emiliand slid the edge of the knife along her arm for the barest moment. The cut was so shallow that it barely hurt. Blood dripped down her arm. In a ceremony with an otima, they would drink from cups. Here, alone in the desert, that wasn't an option.

The smell of fresh blood tickled her nose, and the sensation of his tongue on her skin made her squirm, but he held her gaze captive. There was something sensual about how he licked the wound. She forgot to breathe.

"Here." Emiliand held his arm out.

He made a cut, and she took his arm in her hands. Some Da'Valia clans drank blood to celebrate special occasions, such as the birth of a child, but she'd never done it. She gagged as the sticky liquid flowed down her throat.

"What do you feel?" Emiliand asked.

The coppery taste lingered on her tongue. Aside from that distraction, Neva was strangely aware of Emiliand. His smell and the feel in the air when he was around, those were familiar. But a newness had surfaced. An invisible string of power like a lure that a majila would cast to express interest in a hilan connected them.

"I feel ... you," she said.

Neva climbed to her feet and took several steps. The pressure of the lure changed. She closed her eyes and moved in the other direction. She spun around. Everything outside of them seemed to disappear. Even without the benefit of sight, she reached out and found him. They were perfectly aligned.

Emiliand added more power to the current. She followed suit, and the energy built. Their exchange heightened, and power shot through her from the tips of her toes to her horns. The Hand stirred, wanting to be used. Neva shook with the effort to contain it, but the persistent chill in her chest disrupted her control, and she found she couldn't deny the Hand completely.

She allowed no more than a teardrop of the power to escape. Fear clogged her throat. She felt it in her chest when Emiliand's heart stopped. His eyes grew wide. A beat passed, then two. Blood rushed to her head.

What have I done? Neva thought.

Emiliand's heart resumed beating. The current erupted, tossing Neva and Emiliand in opposite directions. Her head hit the ground, and a moment passed before she rolled over to see Emiliand wiping away a bloody nose. *What have I done?* she thought again. Her throat tightened. In allowing Emiliand to help try to save her, she had put his life at risk. His heart had stopped. Blood poured down his face. She felt sick to her stomach, and it wasn't from the soul scourge.

Neva drew her knees to her chest and hugged herself. His heart had stopped, and that was something she never wanted to experience again.

Unable to bear the guilt, she focused on the circle of sand that was scorched black between them. Like the patterns on a butterfly's wings or the veins in a leaf, the flowing marks had a complex symmetry, as if the formation of their alliad had been designed by the gods themselves.

Dimly, she registered that an invisible line, strong and steady, still linked them. The tension of the line diminished with each step he took toward her.

"I'm going to test our connection," Emiliand said.

He sent Neva some of his power. It flowed, intangible, to her. It tickled. She might have laughed if she wasn't so horrified at what she'd almost done.

"Now you try," Emiliand encouraged her.

Neva bit her lip and double-checked to make sure the Hand was stowed. Tentatively, she pushed a tiny amount of her natural power to Emiliand. He gave her an easy nod, a new light — was it pride? — shining in his eyes.

"That was quite the show." Mari walked over, apparently having concluded that the danger had passed. "But Djinn magic is better."

"Spoken like someone who doesn't have horns," Emiliand told her with the hint of a grin. He cleaned and sealed the cut on Neva's arm with his power before tending to himself. "C'mon. Let's keep moving."

Mari made a face at him before regarding Neva as if she were a succulent morsel of roasted meat.

"Stop looking at me like that," Neva said.

"You asked me to get you across the desert," Mari said. "Well, that's exactly what I'm going to do."

Mari morphed into golden dust and flew at Neva. The Djinn slid in her mouth and nostrils, choking her for a moment before taking full possession.

Neva's consciousness was pushed aside, and she could only watch while her hands rose in front of her face, turning from front to back. Mari stretched her arms as if getting comfortable in her new skin.

"Get out," Neva ordered Mari, trying to suppress the claustrophobia gripping her.

"Mari?" Emiliand asked in a voice Neva had never heard from him. "You had best explain yourself. *Now.*"

"Trust me," Mari said, her accent sounding odd coming from Neva's lips. "The scourge will shut her body down and tear away her soul, but I can keep her going."

"I said get out, Mari."

"You want me out, you're going to have to make me," Mari said. "I'm from the Upyri caste. I can do this. You're only hurting her if you fight me."

"Won't your possession sever her soul?" Emiliand said.

"Most likely, no," Mari answered.

"Most likely?" Emiliand echoed. His tone was rife with displeasure.

Neva tried to think. It was difficult with the Djinn occupying space in her mind. There really wasn't room for so much inside her, but Mari might have a point, especially if the Djinn could stave off the scourge.

"Neva, are you all right with this?" Emiliand asked.

"How did you get in here?" Mari asked.

"You're not the only one with gods-given talents," Emiliand said. *"Neva?"*

Neva would have been breathing hard with the effort it took for her to keep her thoughts straight, but as it was, Mari controlled even that ability now. The only thing the Djinn couldn't possibly control was the Hand. As for the Eye, well, that was locked deep within Neva, beyond either of their reaches.

"Are you certain?" Mari challenged Neva's assumption. Her tone said she was teasing.

"Can you?" Neva asked.

"Can't I?"

Neva wasn't, in fact, certain, but she had to admit that Mari's skill was exceptional. Even now, Neva's heart beat at a slower pace, stymying the scourge's progress.

"Let's not waste any more time." Neva conceded.

Once their water supply was replenished at the next oasis, which had been mercifully spared by the sandstorm, they set out at a furious pace, and they did not stop. Regular horses galloped, but the Da'Valian steeds practically flew. The thick white sands of the Ramanaji gave way to the cracked brown earth of Brakane Desert, and then the quagmire of the Grasslands.

Neva watched the terrain transform from a small corner of her mind over a day, or was it two or three? She couldn't be sure. This, being at the mercy of a Djinn, was the destiny that her people had fled Ramanaji Desert to avoid. She hoped she wasn't making a mistake.

The Grasslands, which were home to the Da'Bruna, were named for their tall reeds, which hid deep bogs beneath. The quagmire, fed by underground tendrils of the Tyvse Slit, presented another form of treacherous ground. They were nearing their destination.

Abruptly, Emiliand's steed tumbled head-first into a rocky pit with a shallow pool of stagnant water at the bottom. The horse's leg made a loud crack when it snapped.

Emiliand abandoned his saddle to avoid being crushed and put an end to the horse's agony. Neva's limbs were heavy. Despite Mari talking up her skill as a Djinn, Neva suspected that her physical form had grown so weak that Mari couldn't have come to Emiliand's aid if she needed to.

"We'll ride double from here." Emiliand reappeared at ground level, the corners of his mouth turned down.

"And slower methinks," Mari said.

Chills wracked Neva's body, and a kaleidoscope of colors overtook her vision.

"Emiliand, if I don't make it through this, I want you to know —" Neva started.

"Have a little faith," Mari admonished. *"This isn't my first life, you know."*

"You're going to make it through this," Emiliand agreed, staring straight ahead as he nudged the horse into motion. *"You have my thanks, Mari."*

"Do you see that?" Mari mumbled. "It's so bright."

The Djinn slurred the last of her words before slumping sideways.

Mari did not resurface after the world fell dark. Neva listened for anything that would indicate Mari was with her, but she was met with an all-consuming emptiness, an endless silence more grating than the isolation of the desert. Neva couldn't feel her limbs. Emiliand did not respond to her calls. She no longer had any sense of her surroundings. If Mari would wake up, Neva could at least see what was going on around her. If Mari would animate her again, Neva would trust that this wasn't going to last forever. But the sensation of losing all connection to her body was stifling.

One thought kept her hope alive: She could depend on Emiliand to get her to the Da'Bruna.

Neva lost track of time, the urge to scream building without release. She needed to focus on something, anything to avoid her soul going adrift like those trapped in the sandstorms. Lost. Tortured for eternity.

Were the circumstances different, she would have worked her worries away. She would have hidden behind the rush that came with thieving.

Yet she couldn't remain without something to anchor her. Her thoughts wandered, reliving her escape from the Da'Voda, how things had gone wrong while she was hiding in Ashford, and the Ceasekin ruining her interview with Salaman. She struggled to find anything that would ground her. *I am strong, powerful, and dangerous.* The words her mother's spirit had once delivered as a warning came to her. She imagined anchoring her soul to her body with steel hooks. She repeated the thought over and over until, eventually, Mari roused.

When Mari's eyes fluttered open, she thrashed about, frantically swatting at scorpions that appeared to be scurrying up her limbs.

"Get them off," Mari shrieked and bucked, trying to throw herself off the horse. Emiliand's grip tightened to keep her from losing her seat.

"They're not real," Emiliand said. *"We're almost there."*

Mari flailed in a bout of hysteria. The Hand railed against its cage, calling on Mari to release it.

"Don't do it, Mari," Neva begged. *"You can't let it out."*

Mari stretched her control into the deepest recesses of Neva's consciousness and tugged on the spindle wheel.

"This will work," Mari told her. *"You'll see."*

"No," Neva screamed.

Neva's soul surged, and she tried to shove Mari from her mind. Mari batted her away and went for the vault again. Neva gathered every last shred of willpower she had and heaved her consciousness at Mari. This time, the Djinn burst from her. Neva coughed on the dust and sputtered.

The scorpions sank their telsons into the center of Neva's chest. The soul scourge gushed forth, rushing to her extremities. Violent chills shook her. Neva whimpered, willing the creatures away and closing her eyes.

When she opened them, everything was white, so vivid it reminded her of the Fireside snowfalls. She was flat against a hard slab. Silhouettes leaned over her. Candlelight flickered over their features. Emiliand and an otima, who was neither hilan nor majila but who harnessed both sides of Da'Valian power. Astiand and Arroyand, who was Trinizhi's alliad and consort, were beside them.

This cannot be real. That was the last thought Neva had before a burning heat seared her insides, boiling her blood and obliterating the corpse-like coolness of the soul scourge.

"Keep fighting, Nevazhi," her mother's voice reached her from a far-off place. *"You are strong, powerful..."*

Lost in a moonless midnight sky, weightless and numbingly cold, Neva glimpsed movement in flashes against stars. Stars that were almost close enough to touch. A blur of black fur wove in and out of the fabric of her surroundings, and the sense that a creature was stalking her sent a shiver through her.

A giant black lioness with intelligent golden eyes leaped from between the stars and landed in front of her. Ripples like those in a pond fanned out from its paws.

"What are you?" Neva asked.

The lioness rose on its haunches, towering over her, and placed a paw in the center of her chest, emitting a molten heat.

Neva cried out and tumbled backward, free-falling in the darkness.

Neva jolted awake with a gasp, yanking at the neck of the modest nightgown that covered her. She tore the material in her effort to reveal the bizarre crystalline blue scourge. The wound was not molten, but it was far warmer than it had been in the desert. Four black dots along the top matched the claw marks from her dream. Had the marks arrived when she suffered the scourge or had they just appeared? She couldn't be sure. It had only been a dream... She badly wanted it to have just been a dream.

Emiliand stirred on a cot across from her, and several other beds in the room were empty. The pristine white sheets, spotless floorboards, and a combination of instruments and dried herbs hanging on the wall told Neva that they were in an infirmary. The cloying stench of patchouli incense had infused the space, making her nose wrinkle. Healing magic.

"You're awake," Emiliand said sleepily.

Neva gathered her shredded nightgown in a fist and sat up.

"How are you?" Emiliand asked.

"I'll live, I think," Neva said. "We made it to the Da'Bruna?"

"Aye," Emiliand said. "You know, if it hadn't been for Mari, we wouldn't have made it in time. I... I was wrong about her."

"Where is she? Is she mad?" Neva had a few choice things she wanted to say to Mari after the Djinn had almost unleashed the Hand, but Mari wasn't likely to be happy with having been exorcised either.

"She was at first, but I paid her, so that helped. Strangely enough, she hasn't left and seems to be enjoying herself. I think she'll forgive you."

"I had to do it. The Hand was calling to her, and she was losing control."

"I know."

Of course, he did. They fell quiet. Emiliand's eyes were heavy-lidded, and his lips were dry and cracked. Muffled footsteps sounded as someone passed by the exterior of the door.

"Will they grant us asylum?" Neva asked, almost afraid to hope. It had to be a good sign that they'd lent their otima and infirmary, didn't it?

"I'm not sure," Emiliand replied. "We'll meet with their donazhi at dawn."

Another moment of silence. Emiliand shifted, rolling onto his side. He folded down the top of the blanket and cleared his throat.

"You're not going to ask about him?" Emiliand asked.

"About who?" Neva's entire body went taut.

"Astiand."

"I thought I dreamed him," Neva replied. She'd thought she dreamed both Trinizhi's aliados. "He's really here? Arroyand, too?"

"Aye."

She shook her head to organize her thoughts. If she hadn't imagined Astiand and Arroyand amid the hallucinations, then Trinizhi had caught up with her despite Neva and Emiliand's efforts to evade the ruler.

"What are they doing with the Da'Bruna?" Neva asked.

"Another unknown," Emiliand admitted. "We were preoccupied with the healing, but I intend to find out."

"Trinizhi?"

"She's not here."

Neva slumped in relief.

"How did she find us?" Neva wondered. It seemed impossible that Trinizhi would anticipate them defecting to the Da'Bruna.

"I underestimated her."

"How?"

"I'm not sure." His tone was clipped. He gave a heavy sigh before saying, "There must be something I'm not seeing."

Neva shivered and pulled her blanket around her. What did that mean for their meeting with the Da'Bruna's donazhi?

Chapter Seven

Seventh Fireside, 1550

Brother Noridemus,

I have now been tethered to Lithlorian by my conviction marks for twenty years, which I must stress to you has been twenty years too many. You have always been fair and understanding. What I did, I did for the greater good. The Serculus should seriously reconsider my imprisonment, and I hope they will do so with the utmost haste. Please pass along my sincerest apologies. I trust you know I was a victim of Finneas's tutelage as much as anyone. If I do not hear from you soon, I will take matters into my own hands.

Brother Alewiscious
Prisoner 173, Lithlorian Island

Emiliand navigated a maze of extensive plank walkways as if he had been to the Da'Bruna stronghold before. As their footfalls joined the steady clatter of everyone moving about the compound, Neva wondered if he'd come here with the Da'Roha army. An enormous timber fence and watch towers to the north and south separated the enclave from the flat expanse of the Grasslands. A milky fog hovered over the bogs, concealing the bubbling mud pits, and reeds grew plentifully between the walkways. Neva reached out to brush the tips of her fingers against the bulbous, velveteen cattails.

Da'Bruna stared blatantly at Neva as she passed. Belatedly, she pulled the hood of her cloak forward to cover her horns, but she could still sense their attention.

The otima running the infirmary had insisted that Neva bathe and don fresh clothing before leaving. They had gifted Neva with a soft cream-colored cloak and a Da'Valian outfit that had both the color and sheen of a pearl. Instinct told her that the otima was one of those who subscribed to the notion that Neva was chosen by the gods because of the unique nature of her horns. While Neva did not share the opinion — her mother's diary had revealed her to be an accidental sacrifice and an unintended holding cell for the Hand — she wasn't about to turn down the chance to improve upon her travel-worn wrap and pants. Especially when it cost her no coin to do so.

She and Emiliand passed a group of Da'Roha recruiting for their clan. Their orange sashes marked them as members of the nomadic mercenary army. Emiliand's lips pursed as he nodded to them. They didn't nod back, and Neva heard one of them talking to a Da'Bruna about enlisting. A lowel Da'Bruna, Neva couldn't help noticing. That was unexpected. Usually, only toppels signed on with the Da'Roha.

"Do you wish you were still with them?" Neva asked.

"You mean over aligning with you? Never." Emiliand said. *"But as long as the deaths of those in my squadron go unavenged, my honor is tarnished."*

"You're honorable to me," Neva said.

"But what am I to them?" Emiliand asked. *"Nothing but a disgraced hilan who failed them."*

The tension in Neva's shoulders lessened when they entered a large dome-topped building at the center of the stronghold, shielding her from her audience. Emiliand led her through a series of hallways with long cerulean rugs running down the length of them. Neva slowed when she spied Arroyand, Trinizhi's youngest aliado. Neva's gorge rose at the sight of him.

He was leaning against the wall chatting with a hilan on guard outside a tall, iron-gilded door.

The last time Neva had seen Arroyand, he'd very likely saved her life — and she had very nearly ended his. It was a shame she hadn't. He had harmed her friend Miland for no other reason than because it was within his power, and she could never forgive that, especially not after Miland had helped her defy Trinizhi and escape from the Da'Voda enclave.

Arroyand's back was to them, but there was no mistaking his lean profile and curly hair, not to mention the dark green sash that declared him a Da'Voda. A shift in his stance indicated he sensed their approach. Arroyand whispered to the sentry as Neva and Emiliand arrived, and a majila standing guard on the other side of the door eyed them.

"The power from Glacier Pass graces us with her presence," Arroyand drawled as he turned to face them.

"Arroyand," Neva greeted him tersely.

"Where's your other friend?" Arroyand asked, looking down the hallway. "The Djinn?"

"Stay away from her," Neva said defensively.

"I'm not about to consort with a Djinn," Arroyand said. "*She's* the one that followed me to bed last night."

Neva frowned at Arroyand. Mari could do what she wanted, but messing around with Arroyand could be troublesome.

"I suppose that says something about what you do in the bedroom," Neva said. "Didn't happen to have an unwilling lover, did you?"

Mari liked to feed on terror, torture, and destruction, not lust.

"They're never unwilling," Arroyand refuted.

"Right," Neva said.

"You doubt me?" he asked, a hand over his heart. The sentry behind him smirked.

Neva didn't respond. She wanted out of this conversation.

"You're so wrong. Thurland could tell you." Arroyand caressed the back of the hilan's neck.

The majila on guard cleared her throat sharply. "Not if he's on privy duty."

"Step aside," Emiliand said to Arroyand. "We have business with Shaundrazhi."

"And I shall accompany you on Trinizhi's behalf." Arroyand adjusted his sash. "After all, you are Da'Voda."

Neva cursed her luck. With Arroyand there, how could her plea be heard objectively?

"What does Trinizhi want?" she asked.

Arroyand didn't answer, and his grin made Neva want to punch the smug expression off his face.

"She wants to hire you." Emiliand plucked the answer from Arroyand's thoughts.

"Shaundrazhi has been waiting for you." A toppel majila with silver charms dangling in her long white hair stepped aside to allow Neva, Emiliand, and Arroyand into a grand hall. The scent of fresh mushrooms wafted in her wake.

"That's Yolandrazhi, the Da'Bruna's top warlock," Emiliand told Neva as they passed the young majila.

"Really?" Neva wondered fleetingly what magic the warlock might have woven into the charms she wore in her hair, but the hall stole Neva's attention.

In contrast to the broken, steaming earth outside, the hall was elegant and refined. Inlaid stained glass decorated the dome ceiling, a creek babbled in the back of the room, and the air was cooler than outside. Candelabras and palms adorned the central dais, and four other elevated stone-carved seats were accentuated by all manner of plants. Neva recognized ferns, blooming lilies, and jasmine.

The svelte majila who lounged on the throne in the center of the dais played with a lock of her hair, which fell in lush waves past her waist. A bejeweled headpiece of diamonds and at least a hundred jet stones declared her station.

Shaundrazhi's upper lip curled upon their entrance, transforming her serene face into an ugly expression. Without warning, her white eyes locked on Neva's, drawing her consciousness into another plane of existence, a donazhi's landscape.

The walls and palms faded away, and the stone floor shimmered to reveal a wide pool with a waterfall feeding it from the dais. Water gurgled up from the center of the pool. Thick gray clouds circled above them, and raindrops speckled Neva's face and clothing.

"Tell me why you've come." Shaundrazhi's voice was husky and demanding.

The donazhi glided through the pool at the base of the thunderous waterfall.

Neva swallowed hard. She could hardly be in the presence of such a powerful creature and not fear that her very life was at stake. But this was what she had come here to do. Trinizhi's lackeys wouldn't be allowed to take Neva from Da'Bruna lands without permission. Getting Shaundrazhi on her side was the only way to stay beyond Trinizhi's reach.

"Donazhi, with humble respect, my aliado and I came here seeking asylum," Neva began. "Trinizhi has sent Ceasekin after me because of a transgression long past, and I wish to avoid further conflict with her and my clan."

"And you dare assume I would help you?" Shaundrazhi sashayed closer. "Your horns have given you a big head."

Neva licked her lips, nerves stealing the moisture from her throat.

"I merely hoped that you would be merciful," Neva said. "That you might consider granting me refuge."

"My mercy is not freely bestowed." Shaundrazhi yanked Neva by the hair, forcing her to bow at an awkward angle

"And I would never expect charity." Neva fought to maintain her composure, staying as still as possible.

"Pray tell, however will you endear yourself to me?" Shaundrazhi released Neva.

"An incentive," Neva said. "Information you might find valuable."

Neva straightened slowly and watched the donazhi. Neva needed Shaundrazhi's help, but she would be a fool to trust her.

"Tell me why she wants you," Shaundrazhi suggested. "I've known Trinizhi a long time, and if your claim that she sent her Ceasekin after you is true, you should have died twice over by now."

"Don't tell her anything," Emiliand interrupted. *"Shaundrazhi can't help us."*

Neva nearly jumped at the intrusion. She quickly schooled her features and hoped Shaundrazhi hadn't noticed. What if Shaundrazhi realized what Emiliand could do? His secret would be out.

"Why not?" Neva asked.

"She already made a deal to hand us over," Emiliand revealed. *"I'm only getting bits and pieces from her and Arroyand, but Trinizhi exchanged the Da'Voda's place along the coast for you. Shaundrazhi wants that glory, and Trinizhi has convinced her you're out to defeat all the donazhis for personal gain. It seems Shaundrazhi is under the impression that you killed the Da'Foha's donazhi."*

"You must have some notion, surely," Shaundrazhi insisted, presumably taking Neva's silence to mean that she needed more encouragement to talk.

Eddies swirled around Neva's ankles.

"Get out of there," Emiliand said.

Shaundrazhi grabbed Neva's wrap. The water reached their calves.

"Answer me." The donazhi's irises churned with power.

This donazhi was strong. This donazhi would be ruthless should the situation call for it. This donazhi likely excelled in her position, but Neva suspected that Shaundrazhi was no match for Trinizhi. If she were, she never would have agreed to a trade with the heartless ruler. Trinizhi was obsessed with dominion, and that made her infinitely dangerous.

Neva pried Shaundrazhi's hand off, calling her power to the surface to strengthen her control and block Shaundrazhi's probing.

"What are you doing? Stop this," Shaundrazhi demanded.

"Whatever Trinizhi told you about me was a lie," Neva said. "I can't say what she's planning, but you've underestimated her."

Shaundrazhi glared at Neva, and an ivory glow spread from her. Neva redoubled her efforts, blocking the donazhi. The world washed away in a rush of white rapids, telling Neva she had won the duel. In the grand hall again, Neva drew herself to her full height.

"You will soon rue the day you gave me to her," Neva told Shaundrazhi.

"I'm sure," Shaundrazhi said with a disbelieving tone. "Arroyand, as promised, you and Astiand may deliver the half-breed to Trinizhi."

"Do we fight our way out?" Emiliand asked.

"We can't." Neva had seen the compound. There was no way they could escape without bloodshed, and she wasn't willing to sacrifice any more lives. Plus, if Trinizhi really did want to hire her, perhaps the decoy had worked after all. Perhaps she actually had an advantage. *"We'll go with them. If Trinizhi wants to hire me, mayhap I can negotiate for my freedom."*

Her freedom. It had a nice ring to it. Neva could ask for absolution for herself and Adam in exchange for taking on a commission for the donazhi. Not to mention that reviving her career as the Lynx still held some appeal. Neva warmed to the idea as she mulled it over.

"The Da'Voda thank you for your cooperation in this matter, Shaundrazhi." Arroyand slid a collection of shacklays from within his cape and stepped toward Neva.

"Keep your hands to yourself if you want to keep them at all," Emiliand warned.

"Shaundrazhi, perhaps you could give Emiliand Da'Voda-Riga a tour of your dungeon?" Arroyand asked. 'We only have need of Nevazhi."

Arroyand and Emiliand stared each other down.

"It's fine," Neva said. She held her hand out, adding privately to Emiliand, *"I can just as easily take them off when he's distracted. Let him think he's won."*

Emiliand stood down. Arroyand grinned, oblivious to their silent discussion, and slid five shacklays up her wrist. Another five went on the other arm.

"Ten shacklays?" Shaundrazhi's voice went up an octave. "You're using ten shacklays to constrain her?"

"As soon as your troops arrive on the coast, ours will fall back to Picquereau," Arroyand said.

Shaundrazhi no longer looked as if she had won some long-raging battle. She looked as though she just realized she had been cheated.

"At the height of the next full moon," Shaundrazhi said. "Our troops will replace yours along the Tyvse Sea then."

"The Da'Voda are more than pleased to oblige." Arroyand slung an arm around Neva's shoulders. She responded by shoving her elbow into his ribs, forcing an audible grunt.

"I have no qualms about severing your limbs either," Emiliand elaborated upon his earlier threat.

"Well, you two are no fun." Arroyand dropped his arm, formally begged leave of Shaundrazhi, and headed for the door. "Come along, Nevazhi."

Arroyand sent a spear of anti-magic through one of the bracelets. Pain danced up her arms as if she'd plunged her bare hands into a snowbank.

"Where are we going?" Neva asked, ignoring the message that he was in charge.

"Trinizhi is at Picquereau."

Neva tried not to let her fear show, but her mouth went dry. Traveling from the Grasslands to Picquereau meant they would go through Ashford, where her family was hiding.

Chapter Eight

Twelfth Fireside, 1640

Dear Little Elkizhi,
We suffered heavy casualties again today, and by nightfall, our
enemies moved us into a disadvantageous position. They've cut
off our supply lines, and we'll be out of food in no time if we
don't act soon. It's so cold out that not even our power can
warm us. Fireside is a second enemy. Remember that when you
are called to fight during the cold season. Your enemy is not
one. It presses in on all sides... I do not mean to put fear into
you. I am certain we will prevail. I mean only to prepare you
for what you will encounter after your firérite.

With honor and pleasure,
— Astiand

The sight of Astiand had more of an effect on Neva than she had anticipated. Although he was just as handsome as she remembered — deep black eyes, wide shoulders, and an angular jaw designed to have majilas swooning in his wake — it wasn't desire that took her breath away. It was pure anger. How dare he give away her location to Trinizhi? How dare he lie to her and tell her he was sworn to protect her? How dare he betray her trust?

Neva tried to ignore the hot rush of blood that pounded through her veins when the tall, dark hilan stepped into the room. The Da'Bruna had furnished Trinizhi's emissaries with spacious quarters, and Astiand's presence filled the common room, demanding attention. Demanding retribution.

Unfortunately, Neva would be at a disadvantage if she lost her calm now, with the Hand stowed and shacklays lining her arms.

Neva's heart slowed as her eyes met Astiand's. A lifetime passed before his gaze swung to Arroyand. Neva shook herself.

"The carriage is ready," Astiand said. "Has she said anything of note?"

"Just that —" Arroyand started.

"That you can take your leash and shove it where the su —" Neva interrupted.

"So no?" Astiand brushed past Neva, coming so close that she could feel the heat rolling off him. In her mind, she played out going for one of the daggers strapped to her ankles and stabbing it into his kidney. Instead, she yanked free of Arroyand and the ridiculous leash he was trying to attach to a shacklay. Pointedly, she moved against the wall and crossed her arms.

"You still haven't disarmed her?" Astiand asked Arroyand.

"I was just about to."

"Must I do everything?" Astiand grumbled. He turned back to Neva and held out his hand. "Your blades."

"I'm not your prisoner," Neva said, her chin jutting up.

"That's exactly what you are." Astiand loomed over her.

The pressure of his presence was so intense that she tried to back away, but she was already against the wall. She bit her lip. His eyes dropped to her mouth. She caved and pulled the daggers from her ankle holsters before unbuckling her sword. She made a sound of disgust as she handed them over, directing her best glare at him.

"All of them," Astiand demanded once she was done.

Begrudgingly, Neva handed over the dagger she kept hidden in the small of her back.

"At least you've used enough shacklays," Astiand told Arroyand. "Still, keep an eye on her. I don't want to have to send a squad to track her down again."

Neva almost laughed. The only reason that the Ceasekin had been able to track her down in the first place was because she had been foolish enough to trust Astiand. She wouldn't share her secrets with him again. If she was forced to escape this time, they would *never* find her.

"I trust you're ready to set out?" Astiand continued, dumping Neva's weapons into his leather traveling bag.

"We only just finished with Shaundrazhi." Arroyand sounded indignant.

"So?"

The hilans entered a staring contest. Arroyand broke first.

"We'll be ready momentarily." The corner of Arroyand's mouth twitched. "We're just waiting on Riga."

Astiand dropped his bag, blades clanking.

"Would you mind repeating that?" His voice had a bite to it.

"I said we're waiting on Riga." Arroyand's eyes twinkled. "Emiliand Da'Voda-Riga. You remember him, I'm sure. Lethal hilan who left us for the Da'Roha — your ward casted for him in the Tiger's Eye, if I recall correctly. He should be back soon."

"That doesn't tell me why we're waiting on him," Astiand said. His jaw ticked. He was on the verge of losing his temper.

"Emiliand — my aliado — is fetching my things," Neva said.

Astiand remained perfectly still for a moment. Swiftly, he grabbed his bag and headed for the door, growling an order to meet him at the stables.

"Remember, it's your turn to drive," Arroyand called after him.

Neva glared at Astiand's back. Oh, how she longed to see him brought to his knees before her. With her blade pressed against his neck, would he apologize for reneging on the oath he'd made to his mother to protect Neva? Would he admit to betraying her, as well as dishonoring his family's memory? She looked forward to finding out. She was still daydreaming about it when Mari slid through the room's sole window, canary dust flying in on an invisible breeze.

"Where to?" Mari dropped onto Arroyand's bed, flexing her body in ways that shouldn't be possible as she morphed in and out of her dust form.

"Picquereau," Neva said.

"Djinn aren't invited." Arroyand clicked his leash onto a shacklay.

"She's a Djinn," Neva said. "That means you can't stop her."

Emiliand arrived in the doorway with the remainder of their meager belongings slung over his shoulder.

"We're going now, and we don't need an entourage," Arroyand said, yanking on the leash.

"Do you want me to come with you peacefully?" Neva asked him, yanking right back. "Because I can make things difficult for you."

"I can always make him do what we want," Mari said as if Arroyand wasn't in the room. "His aroma *is* quite delicious."

"If you possess me, I will end you." Arroyand shifted his stance and pulled the hilt of his sword to reveal the glinting blade.

"If I want to possess you, then you won't be able to stop me with a sword." Mari lunged at Arroyand.

His legs tangled in his effort to get to the door. Mari giggled.

"Move," Arroyand shouted at Emiliand.

Emiliand crossed his arms and turned so Arroyand had to squeeze past.

"Mari, have I ever told you that I knew I liked you from the first moment we met?" Emiliand asked as Neva passed.

Neva grinned at him over her shoulder.

"Glad you two are getting along now," she teased.

Shaundrazhi must have been determined to show the Da'Voda she was committed to their agreement, because a squad escorted Neva and Arroyand to the stables. Mari and Emiliand brought up the rear.

When they arrived at the carriage, Arroyand held the door open for Neva. She climbed into the sleek black contraption, and the Da'Bruna soldiers marched off. Da'Valian carriages were extremely well-built. The expert craftsmanship combined with warm weather meant their trip to Picquereau would be a fast one. Neva grimaced and settled into the cushioned corner.

Movement and enclosed spaces were not her favorite combination. And Astiand was a terrible driver.

Arroyand's arm shot out to block Mari from following Neva.

"I don't like this," Arroyand said. "You're kind aren't welcome here."

Mari's tongue tasted the air between them, her appraisal of him suggesting that she would be happy to feed off him if he didn't move out of her way.

"You don't have to like it," she said. She morphed into dust, flew into the carriage, and returned to her corporeal form beside Neva. The Djinn pulled aside the sheer curtain and flashed Arroyand a taunting grin.

Emiliand stepped up.

"You can remove your arm, or I'll remove it for you," Emiliand said.

"By all means." Arroyand dropped his arm.

Emiliand poked his head inside the carriage, and Arroyand admired him from behind.

"I'll follow on the horse," Emiliand said, depositing Neva's bag with her meager belongings beside her on the floor of the carriage.

"Keep an eye on things," he added.

Neva nodded, lamenting for a moment that she couldn't do the same. Arroyand's hold on the leash was firm. She doubted he would allow her out of his sight. He was probably anticipating the favor Trinizhi would bestow upon him for delivering her.

Emiliand mounted their remaining Da'Valian steed while Arroyand took a seat across from Neva and Mari.

"Look at that. It'll be just us." Arroyand stretched out his legs across from them as if he was entitled to more space than they were.

Astiand slammed the carriage door shut. His gaze landed on Mari behind the curtain and then shot to Arroyand. *Really?* Astiand's expression seemed to say.

"This has the makings of a traveling bazaar," Astiand mused. He made his way to the driver's bench. "We're moving out, and we're moving fast. Hold on, and keep your heads straight."

At least Astiand would be up top. Neva had no intention of spending more time with him than necessary. She had always had difficulty controlling her emotions around him, and right now, hatred rushed through her at the mere thought of him.

The carriage rocked into motion. When Neva had first left Glacier Pass, Astiand had sat inside his carriage with her and taught her about her innate ability to channel pain into greater focus — a vital skill for Da'Valia to master on the battlefield. The encounter seemed such a long time ago. Since then, Astiand had gone from begrudgingly helping her to aiding her escape to betraying her completely. She had thought she understood his motives once, but maybe she had never known him to begin with.

As soon as the timing was right, she would make sure they got to know each other a whole lot better. She would introduce him to her sword first.

The carriage rolled out of the Da'Bruna compound and onto the bumpy road that cut through the bog-ridden landscape. Neva dug her nails into her palms and focused on the pain to push aside her nausea. It was going to be a long ride.

Musings of what her family must be up to occupied Neva's mind as the carriage moseyed along unmarked roads, leaving dust in its wake. The inside of the carriage had filled with body heat and sweat. Faintly, she recalled a snowball striking her at the base of her skull and sliding down her back. Her cousins James and Kendall had always been fond of reenacting battles in the snow with her growing up in Glacier Pass. She missed that sometimes — when she let herself.

Craving fresh air, she peeked out the window to see if she could spot Emiliand, but the Dark Wood's low-creeping fog and twisted trees along the side of the road made her uneasy, so she drew the curtains closed.

They arrived in Witchaven along the north-eastern boundary of the Dark Wood by evening, and the forest absorbed the last rays of sunshine.

"Thank the gods," Arroyand said. "I could finish off a side of boar myself. Let's find something to eat."

"Yes, let's." Mari cocked her head at him. "I'm famished."

Arroyand shifted in his seat. Neva hid a smile. She was rather enjoying Mari toying with Arroyand.

When they came to a stop, Arroyand hopped out beside the stable, yanking on Neva's tether. She'd anticipated the action, so her first step onto Witchaven ground was a smooth one. She wrapped her hand around the other end of the leash and yanked right back.

"I need to relieve myself," she said.

"Allow me to offer my assistance," Arroyand said with a mischievous grin. "I specialize in lifting skirts."

Neva narrowed her eyes and considered kneeing him between the legs. Emiliand, who had arrived right behind them, swung down from the saddle and was on Arroyand before he could take another step. Quarterstaff shoved against Arroyand's throat, Emiliand backed him against the carriage.

"Care to repeat that?" Emiliand asked.

Astiand let out a long sigh as he rounded the carriage and spotted the spectacle. Neva loathed to be of the same mind as Astiand about anything, but she was annoyed at Emiliand jumping to her rescue. First with the Ceasekin, then with Shaundrazhi, now here. She could take care of herself.

"Jealous?" Arroyand's expression said he was entertained.

Emiliand pressed the quarterstaff harder against Arroyand's throat.

"Emiliand." Neva called him off. *"He's not worth it."*

"Go to the nearest inn, Arroyand." Astiand pushed the hilans apart. He jerked the leash from Arroyand's grasp and tossed him a pouch full of coin. "Procure rooms for us. Then meet us at that pub we passed."

Arroyand straightened his sash and held out his hand for the leash.

"She stays with me," Astiand said firmly.

"It was a mere jest," Arroyand said.

When Astiand didn't budge, Arroyand stalked off toward an inn up the street. Emiliand and Mari waved to Neva and backtracked to the pub while Astiand squared things away with a stable hand. Astiand took a pipe from his cape and packed it as he started in the direction of the outhouse. This part of Witchaven was quiet, but a bell sounded as a man entered a chandler's shop across the street, and a woman swept the boardwalk in front of the grocer next door.

Neva hurried after Astiand to avoid being dragged along.

"Bastard," Neva muttered.

"I'm no bastard." Astiand lit his pipe with a spark of power and puffed on it. "And a thank you might be in order."

She should be thanking him? What was in his pipe, exactly? Neva came to a standstill, pulling the leash taut. He stopped walking.

"Why, exactly, do I owe you my thanks?" Neva asked.

"I dare say there's a long list at this point," Astiand said.

"Pray tell, where shall I begin then?" Neva kept her voice low, but she was unable to keep it free from emotion.

"You could start with my helping you outside Glacier Pass," he said.

"You can have my thanks over my dead body," she said. The fingers on her left hand twitched, itching to go for a knife that wasn't there. The Hand surged, and sweat popped out on her forehead with the effort it took to subdue the power. It settled, but it left a headache in its wake.

"You look like you want to put a dagger in my chest," Astiand observed.

"Would you not deserve it?" Neva asked.

"I probably do deserve a knife to the heart for the things I've done." Astiand exhaled a ring of smoke, seeming to consider things invisible to her. Was it night falling, or her imagination that made his eyes appear darker?

Neva tore her gaze away.

"So you admit it," she said, her voice flat.

A pain that rivaled the soul scourge hit her square in the chest. Deep down, she had wanted to be wrong. She had wanted another explanation as to how the Ceasekin had discovered her in the desert. But this was Astiand's opportunity to confess or deny the allegation, and he wasn't saying anything.

"Is there anyone you won't betray?" She hated the tears that prickled behind her eyes. At least he didn't seem to notice.

"Time will tell," he replied.

The casual way he shrugged made her want to scream. She stepped into the outhouse before she could launch herself at him. She would not give him the satisfaction of having such an effect on her.

Chapter Nine

Ninth Cravell, 1641

Dear Little Elkizhi,
A break in the fighting has allowed me a moment to pen you
this letter. How I miss home and your company across the chess
board. I will challenge you to a game upon my return. Bryand
has become fast friends with a Da'Foha majila. I wonder if he
might join up with the Da'Roha after the war and make his
way to her. Corazhi is toppel, so she would be a good match. It
would be a shame to lose him, but he carries a fire for her. Vivi
even likes her, and you know how high her standards are. But
we first must make it through this alive.

With honor and pleasure,
— Astiand

Candlelight streamed out of the windows of the pub. The stone structure was adorned with the same thick gray moss that draped the skeletal trees of the Dark Wood like tangled yarn. Out front, a man wearing a stained apron turned a boar over an open flame. The man's audience, a semi-circle of townspeople, watched Neva and Astiand with leery expressions under the full moon.

Inside, a tavern wench delivered biscuits and gravy to customers. Emiliand was at the bar, a polished black counter lined with patrons and a barmaid tending it. The only vacant seats were beside him, so Neva took one. Mari nodded at Neva from her post in the far corner of the room, where she leaned against the plank-board wall next to a booth with one occupant, a hunchback drunk with greasy hair and a grizzly beard.

"Two more pints, my good woman." Emiliand slammed an empty tankard down on the counter and slid his coin to the woman behind the bar.

"You Da'Valia sure like to drink, don't you?" she asked, going about filling his order.

Neva refused to acknowledge Astiand as he came to stand beside her. Instead, she watched the barmaid, surprised by how at ease the woman seemed to be around them.

"You're not afraid of us?" Neva asked. Humans tended to shy away from Da'Valia. Neva had heard her kind referred to as 'beasts' or 'harbingers of death' more than once in her life.

"Lass, creatures in the Dark Wood scare me." The barmaid placed a hand on her hip. "Da'Valia who are supposedly helping the Order keep peace in Port Telgard with an eye on Amania? You do little to send a shiver down my spine."

"Well, I'm glad to hear it," Neva grinned at the woman. The barmaid clearly didn't have much experience with Da'Valia.

"As am I." Emiliand set down another empty tankard.

Emiliand slung an arm around Neva's shoulders, causing her to tense and check her hold on the Hand. She shrugged off the touch with a lump in her throat. She could feel Astiand's gaze boring into her.

"What say you we find a spot to sit down in this mess?" Emiliand asked, seemingly undaunted.

"You're going to follow us all the way to Picquereau, aren't you?" Astiand asked as if he already knew the answer.

"Wouldn't you?" Emiliand replied.

Neva crossed her arms as Astiand made an 'I'll allow it' gesture with his pipe. A table opened up, and they made their way across the room.

Neva was still annoyed with Astiand, but once they were settled, she dared to ask after a friend. "What happened to Miland after I left the enclave?"

"What do you think happened to him?" Astiand's jaw ticked.

Neva traced the lines in the rough tabletop thoughtfully. Miland had risked everything to help her break Adam out of the dungeon and escape from the Da'Voda. Astiand's response meant Miland had been punished for betraying the clan.

"He's gone?" Neva asked.

Astiand gave a sharp nod.

Their table grew uncomfortably quiet as Astiand stewed and Neva mourned. She hoped Miland was at peace in the next realm.

Even though she was deep in thought, Neva couldn't help noticing that Emiliand kept checking out the window. The way he squinted into the fog that wound through the black skeletal trees made her wonder if he could see things there that the rest of them couldn't. His father's people, the Colavalia, had been created to protect the gates to the Underworld. They did so at what was rumored to be the sole opening from this realm to the next, the mysterious city of Valis deep within the Dark Wood.

"*Are you thinking of your father?*" Neva asked.

"*Aye,*" Emiliand admitted. "*I listened for him my entire childhood, hoping I might meet him. A fool's endeavor, but I thought I heard something a moment ago.*"

"*You think he's out there?*" Neva asked. The swaying, inky branches gave her a bout of vertigo.

"*If he's alive, he's too far within the Dark Wood for me to hear him.*"

"*Is the Dark Wood so deep?*"

"*They say the Dark Wood is infinite.*"

Neva eyed Emiliand skeptically.

"*It has to end somewhere,*" she pointed out. "*I bet they've even put the boundary on a map.*"

Emiliand tossed a walnut halve from a wooden bowl at her. She caught it in her mouth but stopped chewing when she noticed the expression on Astiand's face. It almost resembled jealousy. She washed the snack down with a swig from her tankard. Astiand excelled at avoiding giving anything away, but the smolder that had flickered across his face made her question all sorts of things better left unearthed.

He betrayed your whereabouts to Trinizhi, Neva reminded herself.

She went back to ignoring him and tried to enjoy the familiar surroundings, which reminded her of her father's tavern back in Glacier Pass. Conversation increased around them as more patrons became accustomed to the Da'Valia in their midst and more townsfolk arrived to partake in the roast.

Under the table, Neva explored the shacklays around her wrists. The impenetrable metal bands had no clasps or hidden latches for release. If she was going to check in on her family when they reached Ashford, which she had every intention of doing, she wanted to be free of their anti-magic beforehand. She couldn't know for sure, but she pictured Arroyand adding a tracking spell to one of the bangles before he'd put them on her.

Her father had undoubtedly remained close to Adam, who had been a longtime family friend even before he'd courted Neva. If Trinizhi's aliados had discovered where either of them were, then her whole family could be in danger. Not only could her loved ones be used as leverage, as proven by the Da'Foha, but Adam had helped Neva kill a Da'Voda guard in their escape, making him an enemy of the clan.

A group of hunters burst through the front door, singing, "For he's a jolly good shot." They pushed ahead of them a large bloke with light blond hair and a quiver of arrows slung across his back.

"What's that about?" Neva wondered.

"The archer bagged an Onyx Wolf in the Dark Wood today," Emiliand tilted his head toward the blond man. "I heard someone mention it."

Many of the men were red in the face, as if they'd been enjoying spirits before their arrival. The pub would have been crowded even without them there. Neva had experienced first-hand how revelers often became unpredictable around a full moon. What she wanted was to be out of sight and with enough space between her and everyone else so that she didn't have to worry for their safety when she called on the Hand to break the shacklays.

"Well, we should congratulate him, shouldn't we?" Neva asked as Arroyand appeared at the table.

"Congratulate who?" Arroyand asked, taking a seat next to Emiliand.

"The man of the hour, the esteemed archer at the far side of the bar," Emiliand answered.

"What are you doing?" Emiliand asked Neva privately.

"Can you deliver a message to Mari for me?" Neva asked.

"I may be able to do better than that. What did you want to tell her?"

"To play along," Neva said. *"I'm going to stir things up."*

"I hear you," Mari said. *"I'm guessing I have Lover Boy to thank for that?"*

"You learned to link minds?" Neva asked. Emiliand had told her once that he thought he could link more than one mind together, but he had never dared create such a web among the Da'Voda in order to keep his secret.

"Just now," Emiliand said. *"I considered how I might do it for most of the day, but I wasn't sure it would work."*

"Well, you came to the right Djinn," Mari said, backing into the shadows under a set of narrow stairs that led to a loft. *"I love causing a ruckus."*

Neva suppressed a grin, liking that her friends were developing a bond. She marveled at the usefulness of Emiliand's mind-link. The applications for battle were impressive, and right now, it suited her need for private communication.

"I'm impressed," she told Emiliand.

"So shall we?" Neva said aloud.

"I'm fine where I am." Astiand set his pipe down and got comfortable. "I've no desire to mingle with the locals."

"I'll go," Arroyand offered, holding his hand out for the leash.

"Sure you can keep her on it?" Astiand asked.

"I am not incompetent." Arroyand scowled.

"That was a comment on my ward's deviousness, not your ineptitude," Astiand said.

Neva glared at him. He was joking, surely. She hadn't considered herself his ward since escaping from the Da'Voda enclave, and certainly not after he'd told the Ceasekin where to find her.

"I think I can handle it." Arroyand came to his feet.

Neva stood at the same time, bumping into him as she avoided the path of a tipsy couple. Neva's hands darted out, one relieving him of his purse and the other 'steadying' herself against his chest.

Astiand passed the leash to Arroyand.

"I'll be watching the door," Astiand said.

She rolled her eyes, and they maneuvered through the crowded pub to the merrymakers. She surveyed the hunters ahead and pinpointed the sweatiest, ruddiest man. Her target.

"Good evening, gents," Neva greeted everyone. "We heard you took down an Onyx Wolf today? An impressive feat."

The archer's eyes darted between them as if uncertain why a group of Da'Valia would approach him, but he lifted his chin proudly. "Indeed, I did. The biggest I've ever seen."

"He's lucky to be alive," one of his friends chimed in.

"Well done, my good man," Emiliand said.

"Might we buy you all a round of mead?" Neva offered. Almost as soon as she said the words, the barmaid had fresh tankards at the ready. Neva slipped the woman Arroyand's purse. By its weight, it would more than pay for the drinks — and it would need to because there was about to be a costly mess.

Neva reached past the sweaty man and took a tankard off the bar. She feigned losing her balance again and spilled the beverage on him.

"Oh my!" Neva imbued her cry with a ring of surprise.

"Oi," the man shouted at her. "Watch what you're doing."

She stumbled forward, and the man caught her, trying to right her.

"You don't have to push me." Neva pretended to try to pull away, grasping the man's forearm so it appeared as if he was holding onto her.

"Get off her, you lout." Emiliand joined the scheme. He moved as if to break the sweaty man's hold on her, and Neva went with the motion, stumbling into another townsman, knocking him over. The leash went taut.

Emiliand pulled back to punch the sweaty man and missed, hitting his neighbor instead.

While everyone was distracted, Mari morphed into her dust form and bolted inside a man who had his arm around a friend.

"How dare you touch my woman," Mari faked outrage. She slammed her forehead into the friend's.

Mayhem erupted at the Djinn's table and quickly spread. Neva wrapped the leash around her hand several times and darted under the bar flap. This time when the leash went taut, Emiliand crashed into Arroyand, forcing him to let go.

Neva moved fast. Arroyand and Astiand would notice her missing in mere moments. She murmured the incantation to bring her invisibility spell to life and launched herself out the side door. She hurried around back to the trash heap.

Scratching her neck for some relief, she dropped her invisibility and called forth a drop of the Hand. She shoved the power into the shacklays. They shattered, and the shards tumbled into the dirt. The metal glowed faintly before dimming to blend with the night.

Neva rubbed her wrists, pleased to be rid of the devices.

Astiand came around the corner, clapping. "Thought I might find you out here."

How had he caught up to her so quickly? The question must have been written on her face, because his next words were, "You forget, I know your tricks. I see you obliterated Arroyand's shacklays."

"What of it?" she asked. "The shacklays were pointless. Costume jewelry."

"Were they?" Astiand asked. "Is that why you started a brawl inside this fine establishment? To discard 'pointless' shacklays?"

"Why else?"

"Why else indeed?" Astiand stalked closer. "You wouldn't be trying to escape, would you?"

Neva didn't say anything and took a step back. The commotion inside the pub sounded like it was subsiding.

"Nothing to say?" Astiand's brow furrowed.

Neva gave him a death stare.

"There it is again," he said. "That look that tells me you want to stab me in the heart. I wish you would tell me what it is that I've done."

"You know what?" Neva blew out a breath. "Forget about it."

"No," he insisted calmly. "I want to know what you're talking about."

"Too bad. I'm done talking."

He closed the distance between them incredibly fast. Her cheeks warmed. Darn her traitorous body for revealing desires that she tried to keep dampened, and darn his traitorous actions for changing everything between them. She bit her cheek, using the pain to rein in her emotions.

"Can we call a ceasefire?" he asked. "I — I've missed you."

She nearly choked. He missed her? Surely his audacity was the only thing more infuriating than his betrayal.

"My house is quiet without you there," he continued.

… Because they weren't fighting? Because they weren't coming dangerously close to burning the walls down when words were no longer enough and only their power could speak for them?

She found it impossible to retort. In fact, not a single action came to mind, short of murder.

"I should have forgotten you," he spoke almost to himself. "I should have moved past you by now."

His words shook her resolve because as much as she wanted to hate him, she didn't. Rather, she understood exactly what he meant. How many times had she tried to forget him? How many times had she raced down a street, certain she'd seen his face on a stranger in the shadows? It shouldn't have been that way — because he was one of Trinizhi's sworn aliados. He was the worst possible hilan to get involved with.

"How —" Neva stopped, anger stealing her words. How could he claim to miss her? He had turned her whereabouts over to Trinizhi. "How dare you."

Astiand's arms dropped to his sides.

"I trusted you," Neva said. "Only to find out that you're nothing but a dishonorable liar."

She couldn't hold back her emotions any longer. She rushed him, slamming into him, her hands backed by power.

He stumbled and fell to a knee as her power roared against the midnight shield he raised as if it were second nature.

Neva backed away, her fingers trembling as she covered her mouth. She couldn't afford to lose control. Not like this, and not with the Hand.

"I put my life on the line for you," Astiand said quietly. "Trinizhi would have my horns in an instant if she discovered I let you go outside Glacier Pass. I'm here because I'm protecting you when I should be tending to other matters. So from where does your anger stem?"

"Oh, I don't know," Neva said bitterly. "Maybe the fact that there was only one person alive who had any idea of where I was when the Ceasekin found me, and that person was you?"

Astiand rose and stared down at her. She looked away. She didn't want to see the hurt in his eyes, didn't want to think she held that kind of power over him. He had hurt her, not the other way around.

"So that's how it happened, is it?" he asked.

"Are you going to try to tell me it didn't?"

"I shouldn't have to," Astiand growled, his sharp teeth distinct in the dark. "I made a promise —"

Arroyand sauntered around the side of the pub, his hair unruly.

"There you are," Arroyand said. "We've worn out our welcome." Trinizhi's consort had his cape off one shoulder and a speck of blood on the corner of his mouth. Emiliand and Mari followed him, Emiliand with a rip in his shirt and Mari with lazy yellow eyes.

"I'm done here anyway," Astiand said.

Anger clogged her throat as she watched him walk away.

They were not done. Not by a long shot.

"Someone's in a bad mood," Mari whispered to Neva as they rode in the carriage the next day.

The contraption swayed gently, and the Djinn had been staring off at nothing for some time. They were on the smoothest stretch of road they had traveled since R'shara. Ashford's waterways were important for trade, so the

Order of Cirandrel, the ruling government, kept the highway to and from the metropolis in good condition. Neva counted it as a blessing since the smooth ride lessened her motion sickness.

"Who — Emiliand?" Neva asked. Her aliado had downed enough alcohol the night before that she expected him to have a headache that rivaled her own, but she hadn't spied him since setting out. He was following more covertly today.

"Astiand." Mari stretched her arms up and phased her hands to dust as if she would reach through the carriage and feed off him.

Neva pressed her teeth against her bottom lip. If Mari had been talking about Emiliand, Neva would have cared, but her grudges against Astiand were multiplying.

"He's moody. Always has been," Arroyand butted into their conversation. "A fault if you ask me."

"No one did," Neva snapped. If she was being honest, she wasn't in the best mood since her interaction with Astiand either.

"All right." Arroyand held up his hands in mock surrender. "No need to get your drawers in a twist."

"And that's another thing." Neva glared at him. "Leave my drawers out of the conversation."

"Whatever the majila demands." Arroyand flashed her an infuriating grin. He seemed to have recovered from his displeasure at having found his shacklays in the dirt and his purse gone the evening before, but she preferred him unnerved.

Neva leaned on her elbow. With a yawn, she called a flame to life in her palm, twirling her fingers. Arroyand's glee faded.

There. Satisfied that she had shown him up sufficiently, Neva extinguished her power and made herself comfortable again.

Mari flashed her a conspiratorial grin, which Neva returned tersely.

Several hours into their travels, she nodded off, and she didn't awake until they arrived at the outskirts of Ashford, a city she hadn't returned to in many moons. Her dreams had been disturbing. She shuddered as old guilt resurfaced. Returning to Ashford stirred up memories she had suppressed for a long time.

"Sleep well?" Arroyand asked.

"No," Neva replied sourly.

"Well, you're practically home now, aren't you?" Arroyand asked. "Mayhap you'll sleep better tonight."

Neva froze mid-stretch.

"What did you say?" Neva asked.

"Just that you've come a long way from the desert." Arroyand's voice was too smooth. "Nice to be back in Cirandrel, I'd assume."

"Sure," Neva said.

She forced her eyes to the brick buildings outside the window. She didn't want to give away that Ashford had been her home for any length of time, but Arroyand bringing up the subject made her suspicious. How much did he know?

Chapter Ten

Tenth Fireside, 1642

Dear Elkizhi,

I've been promoted to Commander, making me the youngest of my generation to be granted the honor of such a rank. I didn't mention it before, but I rallied the troops at Craven's Roosy. Had I not, our losses would have been catastrophic. I suppose that was a deciding factor when they chose me. I wish I could say I am honored to accept the position, but so many Da'Voda died to make way for my ascension that not even Bryand jests about my promotions anymore.

This is a bloody, beautiful war, and I have no doubt that we will emerge victorious. Our donazhi seems determined in that. Her expression as she informed me of my promotion was unsettling. I suppose I should be pleased to catch her attention, but she lost an aliado a fortnight ago and, well, you know how she is. Vivi is displeased.

With honor and pleasure,
— Astiand

An orange hue cast over Ashford as the setting sun reflected off the web of waterways, shopkeepers closed their shutters for the night, and mothers called for their children to come inside for supper. Neva shoveled down the last few bites of her own meal at a wide window on the uppermost floor of one of the finer inns in the city.

She had spent enough time fretting over Arroyand's comment earlier. She had to be certain, now more than ever, that Trinizhi hadn't sussed out where her family was hiding.

She was counting on Astiand and Arroyand watching the exits downstairs, even with their contingencies in place. Arroyand had warded the windows and doors so they couldn't be opened from the inside, and they'd paid a human to keep an eye on her door from the hallway. But Arroyand had neglected to apply one of the barrier spells to the awning window in the washroom.

She'd already used a candle dampener to loosen the bolts and pop out the pane. If anyone came to check on her, Mari had promised that whoever reported back would say they'd seen Neva in bed, asleep.

Balancing on the armrests of the chair that Neva'd placed in the washroom, she pulled herself up and wiggled through the window, the sides of her hips scraping against the frame. She called on her favorite glamour, scratching her arms vigorously as she disappeared. She still remembered dropping four gold pieces — the most she had ever held in her life at the time — on the old mage's table to purchase the invisibility glamour. He had sold her the occasional spell up until then. But that day, following her release from the jailhouse, had been different.

"You're sure you want to do this?" the mage asked. His long gray hair was smooth and braided to the sides of his leathery face. His small apartment smelled of opium and rotten eggs, and Neva hardly wanted to touch his table.

"Of course." Her throat was parched with nervousness. She held her shift so that the material didn't cling to her. She wished the room was warmer.

"You're aware it can never be removed?"

The mage leaned into the candlelight as he threaded a long, curved needle with practiced fingers.

"Aye. That's rather the point." She would never be caught by the authorities again.

"You're aware this will hurt?"

She lay face-down on his table, determination stilling her. The ink from her first conviction mark was still setting, the skin of her wrist red and irritated. One mark was one mark too many, and three would be a life sentence at the mercy of the dragon wardens on Lithlorian Island. She wanted this done, and she wanted it done quickly.

"I'm aware. I'm ready."

The tortuous process had gone well into the night, but she never regretted it for a moment, for it had helped her move about whenever she wanted to go unseen. Just as it did now. No one on the street so much as looked her way as she climbed down the exterior of the inn with an exalted grin. Even the relentless headache she'd had since morning couldn't spoil her mood.

Ashford was a big city — that was why she and her family had chosen to hide there — so Neva saved time by boarding a gondola with a well-off merchant and his much younger wife. The flat-bottom boat swayed as Neva lightly hopped on behind the woman. The gondolier frowned, glancing around, but, seeing nothing, he got underway without delay.

Calabray's pub sat along a cobbled street in The Roses near the border of The Sorrows. The Roses was named for long rows of houses with red rose bushes between the canals. The plants had been seeded in honor of those who had perished during the War of the Canals. The Sorrows was a poorer district with tall tenement buildings that housed laborers and field workers, some who slept in shifts for lack of beds. Disease spread there every Fireside, usually taking children and the elderly with it.

Calabray's had a kitchen in the back, an apartment above, modest stores in the basement, and an array of rainbow bottles of alcohol in the main room. Neva climbed the stone stairs to the wrap-around porch and stepped into the shadows. She let her invisibility fade and tugged the cowl of her cape over her horns before she pushed through the swinging doors. One or two faces turned to see who walked in, but most conversations continued without interruption.

The big man behind the bar had peppered red hair and a smile that flashed in her direction as he passed two tankards of ale to a serving wench. The once-infamous thief, Sean Roberts, tucked his corkscrew into his apron pocket, and his eyes darted around the room nervously as Neva approached.

"What'll it be?" he asked her.

"Just an ale, sir," Neva said, sliding a coin to him across the sticky cured wood of the bar.

Shaun's hand rested over hers for a moment and squeezed before pulling away with the payment.

"I'll have that right up," he said.

Neva watched her father pour her drink.

"How's business?" she asked.

"Busier and busier," Shaun said with a shrug. "Trying times with the trade war brewing. A lot of folk have more reason to drink these days."

"And your family? They're all well, I hope?" Neva asked.

"All fine. All getting along well. The youngsters are growing fast." He passed her the ale.

Neva let out a slow breath. Trinizhi's people hadn't been around. The confirmation was a relief — for if anyone was watching them, her father would know.

"I'm glad to hear it," Neva said. "I can't stay long. I'm traveling through with some *friends.*"

Shaun's grin faded.

"Don't worry, though." Neva sat straighter. "It's for the best. I'm going to take care of some old business."

"Are you sure that's wise?" Shaun's voice wobbled with emotion. "I'd rather see you once a year for a moment than to never see you again."

"I have to. I can't keep living like this."

Shaun inspected her face as if he sought the truth. "Well, all right then," he said.

"Tell me about the boys," Neva redirected their conversation. She couldn't remain long.

"Oh, they've grown so much." Shaun wiped down the counter as he spoke. "They're almost Margret's height now."

No one was nearby to overhear them, so he told her how James and Kendall had picked up purse-cutting with ease. The twins showed a knack for small swindles, often inventing creative storylines to separate city folk from their coin.

Neva was attentive as he filled her in, so she was acutely aware when the pleasure disappeared from his face. The room quieted behind her, and the tell-tale squeak of a hinge told her that someone had just walked through the door.

"Don't anybody stop on my account," said a raspy voice with just a hint of the smoothness it used to carry.

Neva's shoulders tightened as uneven footsteps neared.

"What's that you were saying about taking care of old business?" Shaun raised a bushy eyebrow at Neva. He patted her hand before addressing Adam. "What'll it be, Son?"

"Just a pint, Shaun." Adam raised his good hand in salutation.

He took a seat on the stool next to Neva.

Shaun nodded, and Adam, with his wavy brown hair draped over the scarred half of his face and his damaged arm limp at his side, stared straight ahead.

"It's been a while," Adam said.

"Adam, I —" Neva searched for the right words, but what could she say when she had fled the side of his sickbed as soon as she'd had confidence that he was going to pull through? "How have you been?"

"They stop and stare like that all the time," Adam said, indicating the customers whose chatter had resumed. "Everywhere I go."

"I'm so sorry, Adam." Old habit made Neva want to touch his shoulder, but she didn't dare. They had become close, living in hiding and thieving together, but their relationship had been doomed from the beginning. She could see that now.

"Sorry for what?" He faced her, so she had no choice but to take in the scars that blemished his skin. "Sorry for lying to me? Burning me to a crisp? Or abandoning me when things got tough?"

"I — No, it's not like that." She shook her head in denial.

"Everything all right here?" Shaun placed a tankard in front of Adam with a stern yet concerned expression.

"I should go." Neva slid off her stool.

"Maybe you both ought to," Shaun suggested. "Seems to me you two have had a talk a long time coming."

Adam started to move but paused as if unsure.

"I'll keep your drink ready for you, Son," Shaun encouraged him.

Neva headed for the door. Her heart had squeezed at Shaun's use of the word 'son' again. There'd been a time that she thought maybe one day that title would be a legitimate one for Adam. An eon had passed since then. So much time, in fact, that she hadn't expected to be confronted with the damage she had caused. The damage he obviously hated her for.

Outside, Neva sucked in the cool night air greedily and raised her face to the sky, searching for the stars as though they might hold some age-old wisdom to impart when they never had before. She walked over to a honeysuckle bush that grew along the edge of the porch and picked a bud. She pinched off the bottom and pulled out the pistils as Adam's footsteps approached.

"I'm sorry," Neva said again. What else could she say? "I'm sorry for all of it. If I could take it back, I would."

"I guess that's where we differ, then, isn't it?" Adam rested his elbows atop the railing. "If you had stayed, I would have suffered through it all again if it meant you would never leave me."

"You can't mean that." Her voice cracked. She stared at the wooden planks of the porch unseeingly.

"Can't I?" Adam asked. "It's true. I never wanted you to go."

"Don't say that."

"Why? Because it makes you feel something?" His expression turned angry. "Neva, you ripped out my heart. If it hurts a little now, you deserve it."

"I didn't mean to."

"I'm sure you didn't mean any of it! Is that supposed to make it all right?"

"No — no, of course not." Guilt rose in her throat, choking her. "Just tell me what you want. What can I do?"

"What I want?" Adam lowered his voice. "What I want? What I want is my life back. You back."

He raised his damaged hand, all pink and white scars, and caressed the side of her face as he had so many times before. She shuddered and almost released the tears she was holding, but she forced herself to be strong. Breaking things off with Adam had been what was best for both of them, even if he didn't see it yet. She stepped back from him.

"Adam, you know I'll always care for you, but it can never be like it was." It was very nearly a miracle that he was still alive, and as it was, he had to live every day wondering if the Da'Voda would finally catch up to him. That was her fault, too. He might think he still wanted her, but she would only bring him more pain.

"Do I know that?" he asked, shaking his head. "It's not as if you've ever said as much. You just left. But it's your heart to give and take as you please, I suppose." He studied her for a moment. "Have you moved on?"

Her thoughts jumped to Emiliand. They weren't romantically involved, not really. But Emiliand understood her, he had aligned with her, and he made her feel safe. Was her heart taken? She wasn't sure, but her life had moved on to a place Adam couldn't follow. And he — Gods! — he was going to make her say it. Everything she hadn't had the courage to say before, when she had left the night the healer told her Adam would pull through. Everything she didn't want to say because it would wound him to the core.

How could she? She looked into his eyes. Beautiful, dark brown. She had fallen for him, those eyes, with every bit of herself that was human, and he had done the same. But in the end, they were different.

Infinitely different.

"We're not meant for each other, Adam." It was the simplest way to say it, but it wasn't enough, because it only scratched the surface of the truth, and they had too much history to leave it at that. "I loved you. I still do. I love everything we had together. I could always count on you, but when we were together, I lost control. I can't be involved with someone if I'm afraid at every moment that I will hurt them. I couldn't live if I... can you imagine?"

"And that's the truth of it, isn't it? That's how you feel?" he asked.

"Aye."

"Gods damn it. Gods damn you, Neva." He pushed away from the railing and moved as if he was going to take a swing at the side of the pub, but he dropped his arm at the last second. "You don't know how many hours I've spent wishing for your return. How many nights alone I've thought of you next to me. If you loved me, you would have been here."

"That's not —" She had been about to say that wasn't fair, but he cut her off before she could continue.

"Well, I'm done, Neva," he said. "I'm done with you. With waiting for you to see what's right in front of you. And with putting my life on the line for you and your family. If we were never going to work, you should have said so before you made me fall in love with you."

"I —" she struggled to respond.

"What, Neva?" The pain in his expression was too much. "What?"

She couldn't do this.

She ran.

Chapter Eleven

Ninth Auton, 1605

Brother Osirus,

I trust this missive finds you well. As the years have slowly progressed, I have come to the realization that the Brotherhood will only welcome me back if I bring something of worth to the table. If your bones have begun to ache as mine have, I trust you will agree that immortality in and of itself is not a gift. Finneas was right about the tethers, but he — and I — failed to recognize the importance of tending to our physical forms. Ebenezer will assist with my next experiment, and I will report back with the findings. I suspect they will be monumental in nature.

Brother Alewiscious
Prisoner 173, Lithlorian Island

Neva threw herself into the first alleyway she came to and flattened herself against the grime-covered wall. Her presence startled a litter of feral kittens, and they scrambled away from a pile of food scraps and down the alley. Neva let out a single sob and covered her mouth. She wanted to stop the tears, but her guilt was overwhelming. She let them fall.

Adam was angry and bitter, and she was to blame. He had become what he was because of her. She wanted to believe that he was still the same person who she had grown up with, but the truth of it was that she had injured him in more ways than one. His body, and his feelings toward her, would never be the same. And what was worse was that she'd come so close to dooming Emiliand to a similar fate during the ritual in the desert. To let the Hand out, even for a moment, was to flirt with disaster.

As if it sensed her attention, the Hand stirred. The faint headache she'd suffered for much of the day increased.

The whisper of a boot scraping on the cobblestones behind a large trash bin was the only warning she had before a muscular arm grabbed her around her middle and jerked her deeper into the alley.

"Quiet," Emiliand warned.

"What are you doing here?" she asked.

"I followed them. They don't know you're gone from your room," Emiliand told her. *"They're searching for an establishment that may sell junipero."*

Neva spied them. Astiand and Arroyand strode down the street with an air of entitlement. More than one person hurried out of their path.

Astiand's head swung in their direction, and he stared into the shadows. They were out of reach of the street lamp, but Neva was quick to awaken her invisibility glamour again. She scratched her neck, yet it did little to relieve the itch.

"What is it?" Arroyand glanced around.

"Nothing," Astiand replied. "Let's continue on."

"Did he see us?" Neva thought to Emiliand.

"He saw us all right. The question is, why didn't he do anything about it?"

Neva frowned. Astiand's motivations were a mystery to her, but he always had his own game pieces in play. Given that they continued past Calabray's, Neva guessed that whatever Astiand was up to tonight didn't have anything to do with her. She wasn't sure if she should be relieved or worried about what other intrigue was afoot.

Perhaps Emiliand could follow them and listen in on Astiand's thoughts — but while Emiliand blended in with the shadows well when he made an effort, he was not likely to go unnoticed. There was simply too much of him.

"We should get back to the inn," Neva said. She checked the street to make sure Astiand and Arroyand hadn't doubled back before she released her glamour.

Emiliand's eyes met hers. It was probably obvious that she'd been crying, yet he didn't comment on it. He just pulled her close and pressed his lips to her forehead, implying a million different things all at once. Most importantly, that he was there for her.

She swallowed around the rock in her throat. Gently but firmly, she took a step back. She had been crying over Adam moments ago, she had been obsessed with making Astiand suffer yesterday, and she didn't want Emiliand to end up a casualty of the mess that was her love life tomorrow.

Emiliand smiled faintly and headed out of the alleyway.

"Come with me," he said. "I want to show you something."

Curious, she followed him to one of the tallest structures within sight, a tenement building in The Sorrows. The few residents who crossed paths with them went wide-eyed before ducking their heads and scurrying past.

"Where are you taking me?" Neva asked.

"You'll see," Emiliand said.

He led her to the top floor, pushed open the window of an antechamber, and hoisted himself out. On the slanted rooftop Emiliand reclined against a dormer and interlocked his fingers behind his head. She joined him with a quizzical look.

"There's a lot of time to burn on patrols, did you know that?" Emiliand asked.

Neva shrugged next to him. She'd never given it much thought, but she supposed watching a border was similar to casing a place or waiting for a mark to set out on the town. Tedious.

"Well, this was always one of my favorite pastimes." Emiliand raised a hand overhead, and a black flame sparked to life from the tip of his pointer finger.

As she watched, he painted the gods in fire. Streaks of his midnight power connected the constellations of Dhianz and Ceris. Then faster — Riska and Maven. And faster still — Odonus and Goj. Emiliand moved so fast that Dhianz was only beginning to fade when he finished the fire sketch of Goj. Neva watched the shapes of the gods disappear above them, entranced.

"Again," she whispered. For reasons unknown, this felt intimate. Him sharing this with her.

She checked to make sure the Hand was contained and called her power to the surface.

"Use mine," she said when he raised his finger to the sky.

The white light of dawn flowed from Neva to Emiliand, and from Emiliand to the sky, as he traced the path from one twinkling star to the next. This time, he gave Dhianz his centaur form and the Trishula, gave Ceris her bow and arrow, and gave Riska her scale.

Neva turned her head and admired Emiliand by moonlight.

"How did you know this was what I needed right now?" she asked.

Silence.

"I wasn't reading your mind," Emiliand said. "I honor your privacy as much as I can. But I know what it looks like when someone needs a friend."

His words filled her heart. Before becoming her aliado, Emiliand had been her friend first. He was painfully good at it. But just because he was being her friend right now didn't mean they couldn't one day be more, and she feared he might want more than she was willing to give.

"What do you want out of this?" Neva asked. "What do you want out of being my aliado?"

The fire in his gaze made her stomach flip-flop.

"My feelings toward you haven't changed," he said. "You're still the fiercest majila I've ever met. I won't deny that I hope I will mean more to you one day, but no matter what happens, I will never regret becoming your aliado."

"And you're not judging me for getting close to Adam?" Neva asked in disbelief.

"Neither of us is solely Da'Valia," Emiliand said. "You can no more shut yourself off from your human side than you can deny your Da'Valian heritage."

Gods, he was so *good*. She wasn't sure she deserved anyone who was such a good person. She yearned to link her fingers with his, but she clasped her hands together. After seeing how she'd hurt Adam and feeling Emiliand's heart stop when they aligned, her mind was made up. Touching Emiliand was too big a risk.

"What if I need space?" she asked.

"I will always want more of you," Emiliand confided. *"But I will wait until you're ready."*

The tightness in her lungs dissipated. How was it that he could make everything seem all right when her life was anything but?

Waves crashed against the rocks in a steady rhythm, and moisture infused the air, even inside the carriage. Outside, sunlight played on the small peaks of water that stretched as far as the eye could see. The Tyvse Sea. Neva pulled aside the curtain as they rolled toward the grand gates of Picquereau, where the Da'Xana had resided since conquering the ancient fortress many generations before.

The white marble fortress appeared to have crawled from cliffs along the ocean like a creature from the stories of old, with columns fashioned after tentacles reaching out from the depths. The building had four wings, numerous gardens, and the barracks, where most of the Da'Xana resided. The core structure sported three levels above the palisades, with parapets and ramparts along the top.

Neva would wager that the gods themselves had some hand in Picquereau's creation. The first time she had infiltrated the alabaster city, she had stood, invisible and stunned, outside for a full minute. She had almost missed her chance to slide inside before the gates closed. On second impression, the sea-inspired stronghold was just as captivating and awesome enough for her to forget the pounding in her head, if only for a moment.

The Da'Xana took pride in preserving and studying ancient scripts. Many of the librarians specialized in oral histories as well and were trained to safeguard knowledge. Together, they dwelled with the books and scrolls in Picquereau's library, an extensive collection that was largely managed by one Da'Valian warlock: Benjamand.

Until Neva's mother defected from the clans, Benjamand had been one of Monazhi's closest confidants. When Neva had come to him for help, she'd shared her secrets with him. Together, they had cast a complex spell to call the Eye from its chalice and bury the power deep within Neva, binding it there for safekeeping.

But she could not appear to recognize him if they saw one another. To do so would raise suspicions among Trinizhi's alliad and the Da'Xana.

"What is this place?" Mari asked, leaning over Neva's shoulder.

Mari hadn't left her side since Neva returned with Emiliand the night before. Neva was pretending it was because Mari felt left out after everyone had abandoned her at the inn, but it took a lot of effort to convince herself that Mari wasn't feeding off her agitated state.

"That," Neva said, "is Picquereau. Home of the Da'Xana."

"Astonishing. Do the Da'Xana have horns like you, or tentacles?"

"Haha," Neva replied dryly.

"Too bad you won't be allowed inside," Arroyand drawled.

Mari's head whipped around, her eyes flashing.

"A Djinn might be tolerated among the Da'Bruna," Arroyand said. "But not here. The Da'Xana are the safe keepers of Da'Valian knowledge. They will not allow you to step foot on the grounds."

Neva frowned. She didn't want to leave her friend outside the gates. Mari had been instrumental in her making it this far alive.

Mari shot Neva a cocky grin, phased to dust, and flew at Arroyand. He jerked halfway off the seat and choked as the last bits of gold dust flew up his nose. He stilled.

"Ah, Mari?" Neva asked, uncertain if she was the only Da'Valia who could force a Djinn out.

"It's me," Mari said, stretching her new lips over her teeth a few times. Her accent was different from Arroyand's usual drawl. "I'm in control."

For a moment, a disgusted expression flickered over Arroyand's face. Then, it was gone.

"*Now* I'm in control," Mari corrected herself.

"Try not to talk much," Neva suggested. "It'll give you away — and don't expect him to be happy with you later."

"Happy? I'd expect homicidal," Mari said with a delicate snort. She attempted Arroyand's drawl: "But never fear. No one will ever know I'm here."

Mari peeked out the window as they stopped at the gate. Da'Xana guards, their eggshell sashes strung from shoulder to hip, inspected the carriage before they were allowed to continue past.

"What a shining example of Da'Valian defenses," Mari said sarcastically as they rolled through. "Are they always so thorough?"

"They must be expecting us," Neva surmised.

"Think it's safe if I come out now?" Mari asked.

"Not unless you want to get tossed right back out." Neva shook her head.

Neva's fingers tapped against her bouncing knee. Her moment of reckoning had finally arrived. She found it difficult to shake the desire to go invisible and stalk Trinizhi until she learned more about the donazhi's objectives. Neva tried to tell herself that this would be the same as any other commission, but Trinizhi had barely been willing to work with Neva before — when she offered up incriminating information on one of Trinizhi's aliados in exchange for the donazhi's cooperation.

Something significant must have changed for Trinizhi to want to hire her. A big something, too, since the donazhi had been willing to use valuable resources to bring her in and trade the Da'Voda's claim to a position along the coast for her. It was not Trinizhi, however, who awaited them at the entrance to the fortress.

"Who are they?" Mari asked, pointing out the window.

"Vivizhi, the Da'Voda's master at arms, is on the left," Neva said.

Vivizhi stood rigidly, one hand resting on the coiled metal-tipped whip on her hip. Her sleek horns declared her a toppel, and her long hair was in its signature pragmatic braid down her back. Unlike many majilas, she dressed in black.

Neva jumped out of the carriage before it stopped and smiled at her friend and former mentor. Vivizhi's lips stayed in a straight line, and her shrewd gaze swept from Arroyand to Emiliand, who was just coming up the drive, and back to Neva.

It was not lost on Neva that the master at arms was ignoring Astiand, which was interesting since he was glowering at her. Astiand and Vivizhi had a history, but it was an old one from what Neva could recall. Had something changed between them? Neva resented the flare of jealousy that heated her blood.

He betrayed you, she reminded herself for the umpteenth time.

Beside the master at arms stood another toppel, albeit a much smaller one. The petite majila stood with her hands clasped behind her back. Despite the taupe velvet cloak she wore with the hood pulled low, Neva could make out a smattering of jagged scars down the side of her face. There was something familiar about her.

The majilas descended the steps, Astiand swung down from atop the carriage, and Emiliand dismounted and came to stand beside Neva.

"Where's Mari?" Emiliand asked as Astiand rounded the side of the carriage.

"She went in search of something to eat before we came through the gate," Neva answered for all to hear, most notably Astiand. "Arroyand claimed she wouldn't be welcome here."

"She wouldn't," Mari drawled, acting the part.

Privately, Neva told Emiliand the truth, then checked to see if Astiand was buying the story. She discovered she need not have worried. Astiand was watching Vivizhi.

"I'm glad to see you've managed to stay alive." Vivizhi marched up to them.

"No thanks to some," Neva said, shooting another glance at Astiand. "Luckily, I had a wise teacher once, and her very first lesson was survival."

"Have you spoken with her?" Vivizhi asked Astiand.

Astiand scowled.

"You're welcome to tell her," he said. "She won't listen to me."

Emiliand cursed in Neva's mind.

"What is it?" Neva asked.

"It's the Mouth," Emiliand said, his tone disbelieving. *"Trinizhi wants to hire you to retrieve the Mouth."*

Neva's fingertips tingled. But that would mean... Her mind raced. Dhianz's Trishula only had three prongs, and she already had two of them. *Holy gods.*

"Are either of them thinking of the Eye? Did the decoy work?" Neva asked.

"Not at this moment," Emiliand said. *"I'll keep listening."*

"Well, time is short," Vivizhi said. "Trinizhi is expecting her within the hour. Neva, you can freshen up in my room."

The short, cloaked figure stepped from behind Vivizhi and pulled her cowl back. Most donazhis wore headdresses woven with black beads. This donazhi wore the jet in an intricate necklace that extended from just below her jaw to her bosom.

Neva's stomach clenched. She'd seen this majila before — in Emiliand's memories.

"Xandrazhi?" Emiliand's voice rang with surprise.

Chapter Twelve

First Auton, 1625

Brother Alewiscious,
Please stop sending me correspondence. Though you do not know it, you embarrass yourself by doing so. You obviously inherited Finneas's disregard for the Brotherhood's rules. You must be made an example of, and the Serculus stands by its decision.

Brother Cyrus

"Xandrazhi?" Neva echoed.

Belatedly, she realized she was staring, distracted by the scars. Xandrazhi's face was damaged, but upon closer study, the donazhi was still bewitching. It was as if the scars added another layer of depth to her beauty.

"Nevazhi," the donazhi inclined her head slightly to Neva, a significant show of respect. "A pleasure to meet one whose reputation precedes her so. Emiliand speaks highly of you."

"It's an honor to meet you as well," Neva managed.

Xandrazhi gave a small smile and turned her attention to Emiliand.

"It's time," Xandrazhi said.

"I'll catch up with you," Emiliand told Neva. *"I must speak with her."*

Neva glanced between them. What could she say? She'd seen for herself the atrocity that Emiliand and Xandrazhi had survived, and if Xandrazhi was waiting for him here, there had to be a good reason.

"All right, but hurry. The Mouth." She wasn't sure why she said it.

Emiliand excused himself from the group to accompany Xandrazhi. His horse trailed them as they strolled down the drive for a private conversation.

"How old is she?" Neva wondered, watching them go. She was immediately embarrassed. She hadn't meant to voice the thought.

"Old enough to know better," Mari said.

"She's sixteen now." Vivizhi ignored Arroyand. "The youngest donazhi the Da'Roha have ever had, and also their biggest failure. It's an atrocity how many prime warriors have perished under her rule."

Neva's stomach sank as she continued to watch her aliado walk away with the young donazhi.

"Come," Vivizhi ordered. "Time is short, and I'd like a word."

Vivizhi took the stairs two at a time and moved through the smooth marble hallways with ease. It was a fashion quite the opposite of how Neva had lurked in the shadows the last time she had roamed Picquereau. Astiand matched pace with the master at arms. Together, they reminded Neva of co-conspirators on a mission, their single-minded intent uniting them.

Neva and Mari brought up the rear, and as they walked through the halls, a number of Da'Xana lowered their eyes to Neva. The action was a step shy of bowing one's head, but the show of respect still spoke volumes. First the Da'Bruna and Xandrazhi, now the Da'Xana were acknowledging her. Neva bit her lip. The clans would loathe her if they uncovered the truth — that she was merely a sacrifice, that she had both the Hand and the Eye in her possession, and that she was keeping them to herself.

She wished the Da'Valia wouldn't put their faith in her. They were bound to be let down.

"Don't they hate Da'Voda here?" Neva asked.

"Things have changed somewhat in your absence," Astiand responded.

"And your horns give you away," Vivizhi told her. "It's no small thing to be the most powerful majila we've seen in generations. Those wisest among us understand the importance of it, and the Da'Xana are the most knowledgeable of all the clans."

Eventually, they arrived at Vivizhi's sparsely outfitted room in one of the lower levels of the fortress. The space was furnished with a small cot, an even smaller desk and chair, and a padded kneeler for prayer.

"They really went out of their way to make you feel comfortable, didn't they?" Neva asked.

"I requested this room," Vivizhi said. "I prefer solitude in my free time."

"Will we all fit?" Neva asked, looking pointedly at Astiand.

"Arroyand is going to make himself useful and confirm Trinizhi is aware of our arrival," Astiand said.

"Ah..." Mari stalled in the doorway.

Neva nodded covertly, brushing back a long lock of hair to hide the motion.

"That was my intention, of course." Mari hurried off.

"Well, that was easy," Vivizhi said.

"Too easy," Astiand agreed as he took the room's only chair for himself. "If he's possessed by a Djinn, I'll claim I never noticed a difference."

"What?" Vivizhi asked.

"Nothing," Neva said quickly, closing the door behind her.

As soon as they were alone, Vivizhi placed her hands on Neva's shoulders.

"You must agree to whatever it is Trinizhi asks of you." Vivizhi's eyes were alight with a heady energy. "The job she wants to hire you for. You must agree to it."

"So now everyone knows I'm a thief?" Neva stepped away from the master at arms, startled.

She glared at Astiand as another of his betrayals was unveiled, but, truth be told, she was more befuddled by Vivizhi's fervent support of the donazhi's crusade. When they'd first met, the master at arms had agreed to help Neva learn to fight in secret. Vivizhi had done so knowing it would not be something the donazhi would appreciate.

"I'm hardly 'everyone,' but that's not what's important," Vivizhi countered. "We're on the verge of something bigger than all of us."

So that was it. Vivizhi was devout. She always had been. It was a big part of why the master at arms had chosen to help Neva in the first place. It made sense that Vivizhi would want the Da'Valia to reclaim the Mouth.

Neva had to admit that discovering the job was for the Mouth changed things — but how much it changed things depended on what the others knew. Did they know that she had the Eye and that the chalice she'd hidden for Trinizhi to find was just a decoy? Did they know Neva was the Hand? She had so many questions, but she couldn't ask them without hinting at her own secrets.

"I'm open to a conversation, but not with *him* here." Neva pointed at Astiand.

He propped his legs on the bed, leaned back, and crossed his arms.

"Astiand is not important," Vivizhi said with a careless wave in his direction. He frowned.

"Then tell me what is," Neva suggested.

"Trinizhi wants to hire you to steal the Mouth," Vivizhi said excitedly. "This is what you're meant to do. It must be."

"Let's spend a little less time on conjecture, shall we?" Astiand interrupted, apparently unmoved by Vivizhi's intensity.

"Let's," Neva said.

"Fine, fine, fine," Vivizhi hurried forward with her case. "We'll say for argument's sake that it's not your destiny to return part of the Trishula to the Da'Valia, despite your peculiar firérite and horns. But you are a talented thief, and it remains that the item Trinizhi wishes to hire you to steal is the Mouth. Do you understand how momentous this is?"

Neva's lips parted. If only Vivizhi knew... Neva had the Hand and the Eye. With the third prong of the Trishula, Dhianz's greatest weapon could be restored and returned to its rightful owner. Many believed that Dhianz's forgiveness would follow. After centuries, redemption for the Da'Valia was a real possibility.

That had been her mother's mission, her life's work: Redeem the Da'Valia to their creator. Monazhi had fallen horribly short of that goal by becoming pregnant with Neva, which had resulted in Monazhi fleeing from the clans before proof of committing a taboo act became irrefutable. But before she'd left, Monazhi had called the Hand into herself in a move of desperation. The action had put the Hand in Neva, protecting it from Trinizhi, who sought to abuse the influence it would bring her. But it also meant that the imbalance of power among the Da'Valia persisted.

A millennia ago, S'donzhi, Dhianz's jilted lover, had stolen the Trishula. Dhianz had been furious and cursed all majilas born from then on as retribution. As a result, every majila faced the possibility of death or insanity when going through the firérite.

Neva recalled Ellazhi, the young majila who had gone through her firérite at the same time as Neva. Neva had come out with greater control over her power while Ellazhi had emerged with a broken mind. The pain, suffering, and overabundance of power the young majila had encountered during the firérite had been too much for her to bear. And she had been little more than a child at the time.

Neva might not put the wellbeing of others ahead of her own desires often, but she could not honor her mother's memory by allowing the imbalance to continue. Not when she was so close to being able to complete Monazhi's life's mission. Not when majilas were still forced to suffer such fates.

Neva sat down on the bed. Realizing how close she'd placed herself to Astiand, she jumped up again and listened to Vivizhi.

"If you bring back the Mouth, so much good might come of it. With trouble brewing between the Order and Amania, the clans are cooperating with each other for the first time in many years. The timing is fortuitous. I believe — we all believe — that this is what you're meant to do, Neva." Vivizhi motioned to Astiand, around the room, then at the ceiling above as if pointing at the entire Da'Xana stronghold. "Dhianz wouldn't bless you with so much power without a purpose in mind."

So Trinizhi had the decoy, and from the sounds of it, she thought she had the real thing. Neva smiled, piecing together a new scheme.

"You can stop trying to persuade me," Neva said. "I'll do it."

"What I'm saying is, for the greater — wait, you will?" Vivizhi had been so wrapped up in her speech that Neva's spontaneous agreement seemed to have surprised her.

"Yes, I'll take the job."

Astiand pulled a flask from a hidden pocket and took a long swig before offering it to Vivizhi and Neva. They both declined.

"She'll be expecting us," Astiand said. Neither of them had to ask who.

Neva squared her shoulders.

"Our faith is in you," Vivizhi said. She opened the door. "I knew we made the right decision to bring you back for this."

"The right decision?" Neva asked.

"We'll talk more later," Vivizhi said. "Trinizhi is waiting for you now. Go."

Neva let Astiand usher her through the door. Her gut tugged at her, telling her that things were not as they had first appeared.

"What did she mean, Astiand?" Neva asked more insistently.

Astiand glowered at her and walked away as if expecting her to follow.

"What do you think she meant?" Astiand threw back at her. "I told you, I pledged once to keep you safe. I am your guardian twice over. What kind of hilan would I be if I sent Trinizhi after you?"

Neva hurried blindly after him.

It had been Vivizhi all this time? Vivizhi had told Trinizhi where to find her? Vivizhi had all but sent the Ceasekin to R'shara? Neva gave a mental groan. Her friend and former mentor had obviously done what she thought was right, but that meant Neva was in the wrong. Her mind had already been made up by the time she saw him at the Da'Bruna stronghold. She had held Astiand responsible without ever truly hearing him out. With every fiber of her being, she'd blamed him. She stopped mid-stride.

"I faulted you," Neva said. She had fantasized, quite seriously, about impaling him more than once.

Astiand checked to make sure the coast was clear before he yanked her into an alcove under the stairs. Their eyes locked, and her breath caught. It was just his hand on her arm, but his touch stole every bit of her attention. She ripped free and backed away a step.

"Vivizhi was persistent," Astiand said, seeming not to take notice of her retreat. "She started spending a lot of time in the same places as me, always curious if you had said anything that might indicate where you'd gone. Maybe I should have tread more carefully around her. She's always talking about what Dhianz has planned for you.

"Maybe you should blame me. I knew better, but eventually, it slipped, and I couldn't keep her from going to Trinizhi with the news. I count myself lucky that she left my part in your escape out of it."

Neva was quiet. Confused.

"I can't trust anyone," she whispered. Where was Emiliand? She wished he was here and not off with Xandrazhi.

"That is not true." Astiand took a hesitant step toward her. He reached out, and the pad of his thumb stroked her neck. It was such a small touch, but it undid her. Their surroundings disappeared. Her knees locked. Her throat constricted. She wet her lips as a delicious warmth spread through her.

"Do you hear me, Nevazhi?" Astiand asked. "That is simply not true."

The air between them grew palpable, and he leaned down.

"I would never betray you. I am yours to command."

She didn't move. Didn't speak.

I will never betray you. I am yours to command. His words swam in circles. *I will never betray you. I am yours to command.* How had she ever doubted him? *I will never betray you. I am yours to command.* Yet he was not. He couldn't be, because he was Trinizhi's aliado.

But they were alone, and no one need ever know what transpired between them in this dark corner of an endless fortress. Her resolve buckled.

"Use me," the Hand whispered.

Neva jerked away from Astiand and stumbled into the hallway. The Hand railed against its cage, and her headache intensified. Black spots danced over her vision. She gritted her teeth, turning the spindle wheel tighter on the vault in her mind.

"Neva." Emiliand stopped at the bottom of the stairs. "Is everything all right?"

The spell broken, Neva dragged her awareness away from Astiand and focused on her aliado. She brought Emiliand up to speed quickly and telepathically.

"Is that so?" Emiliand inspected Astiand. *"It would take me days to dig through his secrets. You're sure you trust him? You're sure you want to do this?"*

"Everything is fine." Neva stepped toward the stairs and gathered her wits about her. "Let's go meet with Trinizhi. In honor of my mother, this is something I have to do."

She could count on both Emiliand and Astiand to understand her reasoning. Astiand gave her an undecipherable look and ascended the stairs. She rubbed her temples. The Hand was becoming more insistent. She would need to release it soon.

"Where's Xandrazhi?" Neva asked Emiliand.

"In the stables," Emiliand said. "She's overseeing preparation of the horses."

The way he said it, as if it were an apology, made unease unfurl in Neva's belly.

"You're leaving." Her words were hollow.

She'd felt so alive only moments ago, thinking of taking on a job that would enable her to complete Monazhi's mission. But Neva's spirits were dampened at the prospect of going after the Mouth without Emiliand by her side. She had been alone and on the run for so long that she'd learned how not to rely on anyone. But Emiliand was her aliado, and she wasn't sure if their bond was strong enough to survive more time apart.

"Yes, I must go with Xandrazhi," Emiliand said. *"You will still have Mari."*

"Xandrazhi found them — the Vodou witches?" Neva asked.

"Aye," he confirmed. *"And she's been recruiting. The time has come to seek revenge."*

"Go," Neva said. She didn't want him to leave, but she was afraid that if he didn't depart now, she would ask him to stay. And if she did that, she'd never forgive herself. "You don't owe me an explanation."

She wanted retribution for Emiliand and Xandrazhi both, for all Da'Roha. Could Neva put off Trinizhi to fight alongside Emiliand? Could she aid in the Da'Roha's recruitment efforts? Could she go with Emiliand and lend the Hand to the cause? But no. Vengeance would benefit the Da'Roha. Redemption would benefit all Da'Valia. That was why her mother had pursued it. Neva's mission was the Mouth now, and Emiliand's was to amass an army strong enough to fell their Vodou witch enemies.

"I don't have to leave yet," Emiliand said. "I promised you that we would face Trinizhi together."

"And that's not a promise I'm about to ask you to keep," Neva said. She would have preferred the edge Emiliand could have provided during negotiations, but he'd already gleaned enough information for her to enter her meeting with Trinizhi with confidence. "I can handle her alone. She needs me more than I need her."

"Once this is done, I will again be worthy of you," Emiliand said.

"You've always been worthy," Neva told him.

"I'll find you as soon as I am able." Emiliand pledged, his eyes dropping to the pendant that rested in the hollow of her throat.

"Not if I find you first." Neva used a flirtatious tone that she'd perfected while waiting tables, but her delivery was subdued by apprehension.

"Take care of her," Emiliand told Astiand.

Astiand raised an eyebrow. "Have you not noticed? She can take care of herself."

The corner of Emiliand's mouth twitched. He lowered his head to Neva and strode off toward the main entrance. She watched him quietly.

May this quest for vengeance heal their wounds, Neva prayed to Dhianz.

Chapter Thirteen

First Cravell, 1642

Dear Elkizhi,

It has been too long since I've written. Your big brother has an awful lot of responsibility now, and our donazhi is very demanding. Vivi and I have only managed to steal away a few moments together. Now, our donazhi has decided to send Vivi's squadron to another location. With Bryand spending so much time with Corazhi, I fear I am lonesome in the rare times that I am not sending out new orders and reviewing our strategy. On that, a scout has just returned, requiring my attention, and I cannot say when I will be able to write again. Know that I think of you often.

With honor and pleasure,
— Astiand

The wing of Picquereau where Neva was to meet with Trinizhi was bright and airy. Colorful wool rugs cushioned the marble floors, and a sweeping staircase with an alabaster banister led to the second above-ground level. Da'Xana of all stations were busily moving about, tending to house-keeping tasks, delivering goods and messages, and carting repaired weapons toward the practice yards.

Neva's headache subsided as they neared their destination. Absent-mindedly, she fiddled with the pendant that rested in the hollow of her throat. Emiliand was leaving with Xandrazhi to take on deadly Vodou witches, and she worried for him. But fretting wasn't going to help anyone. She dropped her hand and turned her attention to Astiand. She was surprised to find him silently regarding her. She averted her eyes. Looking at Astiand put her better judgment in jeopardy, and that was a luxury she could not afford around Trinizhi.

They turned down a hallway decorated with paintings. Neva recognized a few famous battles and a piece depicting Dhianz and Goj with S'donzhi between them. They each grasped one of the majila's shoulders, and she seemed to peer out of the painting with tears in her lifelike eyes. In the songs, bards told of the brothers striking a wager to win S'donzhi's affection. That their cruel game centuries ago had started the chain of events that had led Neva to this very place and time was nearly unbelievable.

Neva's attention was diverted when Mari, still possessing Arroyand, entered the grandiose hallway from the other end. Neva groaned inwardly. The Djinn's groin-led swagger was exaggerated to the extreme, almost comical. Neva was grateful to have Mari at her side, but she wasn't sure how long they would be able to keep up the charade.

"Trinizhi is ready for us?" Astiand asked.

"Hard to say for certain," Mari drawled. "I got turned around and just made it here myself."

"Unbelievable," Astiand said, raising an eyebrow at Neva.

"Let's just do this," Neva said, pretending not to notice.

Astiand pushed open the double doors that led to Trinizhi's suite. A salty sea breeze fluttered in from the open balcony. Water sparkled under clear blue skies beyond. Trinizhi stood against the railing, staring off into the distance with a gleam of what Neva suspected was triumph in her eyes. A majila Neva had never seen before was seated at a large corner desk. She had an arched nose, dark eyebrows, and silver charms dangling in her long hair.

Their arrival startled Trinizhi out of her reverie.

"Nevazhi." Trinizhi stepped back into the room, a smile overtaking her face. The breeze caught the ends of her hair where it fell below her black beaded headdress. "I'm so glad you have arrived. You and I have much to discuss."

As custom called for, Neva lowered her head.

"Sit." Trinizhi held out her arm to the settee much like Neva imagined a practiced hostess in any of the Order's Houses would. Only they weren't trained killers. "This is Nikolazhi, one of our top warlocks."

Nikolazhi watched them from her perch, fiddling with one of her charms. Neva acknowledged the warlock and sat next to a white bearskin blanket, its head stuffed and its jaw locked in an eternal roar.

"Let's skip the niceties, shall we?" Neva asked. "The Da'Bruna patched me up. I'll live."

Astiand closed the doors, sealing them off from the rest of the fortress. Mari perched next to Neva on the edge of the couch.

Trinizhi studied Mari. The donazhi's lips curled back, revealing sharp teeth. In a blur, Trinizhi embraced Mari and murmured something. Power flared in the donazhi's eyes, and the aroma of burnt hair filled the room.

"Be gone," Trinizhi hissed.

In a burst, gold dust spewed from Arroyand's nose and mouth. Mari's dust form undulated around the room, catching on their clothing and hair as if she was disoriented. She slammed into a glass window, shattering it and flying free of the fortress. Nikolazhi rushed to the window, raising her hands.

"Halt! Let it go." Trinizhi clenched her fists and turned to Neva. "You dare bring that creature here?"

"I could hardly stop her," Neva said calmly. Mari was her own person.

The Trinizhi that Neva remembered would have called for some punishment, but the donazhi in front of her merely fumed. Rare color came to the donazhi's cheeks, and her hands clenched into fists.

Arroyand went to Trinizhi. His eyes were bloodshot, and a new depth had appeared under his cheekbones. He wrapped an arm around the donazhi's waist. That was where Mari had slipped up. Arroyand wouldn't have sat next to Neva. He would have gone directly to his donazhi.

"And you," Trinizhi targeted Astiand. "You're supposed to be the responsible one. Why isn't she bound with shacklays?"

"Funny story, that," Astiand said. "She took them off."

"Don't worry, my donazhi." Arroyand nuzzled the crook of Trinizhi's neck, drawing her attention away from Neva. "We got her here in one piece, just as you asked, and none of us are worse for wear."

"Do you know what Perzhi would do to us if she found you brought that *thing* here?" Trinizhi's words dripped venom. "All my efforts rebuilding our relationship would have been for naught."

"Shh." Arroyand traced Trinizhi's lip, lingering until her posture softened. "The Djinn is gone now, and I'll kill it if I ever see it again. Perzhi will never know what we don't want her to know."

"I suppose." Trinizhi seemed mollified. She turned her attention back to Neva. "We have a history, you and I."

Neva narrowed her eyes. That was putting it lightly.

"Really," Trinizhi continued, "you've made things quite difficult and frustrated me to no end."

That was more accurate.

"But you also showed your true allegiance when you informed me of Bryand's betrayal and left my goblet for me, so I'd like to put the past behind us." Trinizhi shifted as if the words were painful to say. "I'm not sure if you've heard, but things have changed since your departure. If Bryand's betrayal taught me anything, it was that the Da'Valia need unity among the clans. I've been taking steps to make that happen. You'll notice we're welcome on Da'Xana land. No one has threatened us. No one has asked us to leave."

Neva ran her tongue over her teeth. It was true that both the Da'Bruna and the Da'Xana had been unexpectedly welcoming. It was ironic, though, how Arroyand had consoled Trinizhi just moments earlier by saying that they could keep their secrets from Perzhi. Weren't good relationships built on trust and honesty? Neva would give Trinizhi credit for being diplomatic enough to rebuild relationships to this point, but time would tell whether she could maintain them.

"Just as I have taken steps to better the Da'Voda's relationship with the other clans, I would like to mend ours as well," Trinizhi said.

"Is that why you sent a team of highly trained assassins after me?" Neva asked coolly.

"Not highly trained enough, it seems," Trinizhi said sternly. "Moving forward, it is my hope that you will be open to compromise."

"And is this compromise something you devised before your Ceasekin failed to kill me, or after?" Neva asked.

A warning glint surfaced in the donazhi's eyes. Neva pressed her lips together. Playing hard to get had seemed like a good strategy to stay above suspicion, but perhaps she'd gone too far.

"Look, I wouldn't be here if I wasn't willing to negotiate," Neva said. "But I want my human friend Adam and I left alone for the rest of our lives. I don't want you, your Ceasekin, or anyone else coming after us again."

Her romance with Adam may have died the night she'd burned him, but he was like family. It was her responsibility to protect him. To make things right if she could.

"That's not out of the question, of course," Trinizhi allowed. "I understand the promise of your friend's safety would mean a great deal to you, just as it would mean a great deal to me if the Lynx agreed to acquire a certain item for me."

"Very well," Neva said. "Shall we establish an accord?"

"Indeed," Trinizhi said. "The clans have agreed to a summit at the end of Cravell. We haven't held one attended by all the clans since the Great War, so this is momentous. There is an item of great power akin to the goblet you stole for me in Glacier Pass. This item may play a pivotal role in the summit, but it won't be easy to obtain. Nearly impossible, in fact. If you bring it to me, I will absolve you and your friend, and I will pay you handsomely for your effort."

"Nearly impossible?" Neva questioned.

"I could send my own troops after it," Trinizhi hedged. "But they have not spent years honing the unique skill set you have at your disposal."

Neva crossed her arms, waiting for a real answer.

"You will find the Sword of Elon in the lair of the Lithlorian wardens," Trinizhi finally said.

Neva let out a bark of laughter. When no one else joined her, she took in their serious expressions. Her grin faded. Waves broke against the cliffs outside, and a gull squawked in the distance.

There were several very good reasons no one had ever stolen from the dragons on Lithlorian Island. Most importantly, they could eat you alive. Secondly, there was no possible escape. Plus, the island wasn't claimed by any of Cirandrel's crime lords, so anyone running a job would be doing so without support.

By Neva's count, there were three ways onto the island: in the grasp of one of the wardens, in the custody of the Order, or aboard a pirate ship. In the first scenario, she would be as good as dead, but she reasoned that privateering was a viable option. With her background and Da'Valian talents, she would be able to contribute aboard a ship if she could overcome her motion sickness and her inability to swim. But with Trinizhi's deadline, time would be a major factor. The same would be true if she infiltrated the island from aboard the Order's prison ship.

Neva couldn't believe Vivizhi had encouraged her to take on such a risky assignment, but she doubted that the master at arms had known the location of the Mouth. In a sword on Lithlorian Island? How could anyone know? By the tick in Astiand's jaw and Arroyand's raised brows, neither had been privy to these details until now.

"How, precisely, do you intend for me to accomplish such a feat?" Neva asked.

"I will help you get to the island," Trinizhi said. "And I will leave the rest up to you. After all, you're the expert."

Neva's spine straightened with pride as she considered how best to approach such a job. She would need to gather supplies, a crew, and insider knowledge of the island. She would also need to secure passage back to Cirandrel, but if she had all that, she might be able to pull it off.

But did she dare? Because if she acquired the Mouth, she certainly wouldn't be handing it over to Trinizhi when she returned. That meant all bets would be off for her safety and Adam's. The summit would be the perfect stage for completing her mother's mission. As long as Neva prevented Trinizhi from being the one to promise the Da'Valia redemption, the donazhi would gain no power over the other clans. It seemed worth the risk, given what was at stake.

"How handsomely are you willing to pay?" Neva asked. Just how much was Trinizhi good for? Five-hundred silver, perhaps? That would be difficult to carry, but she would never need to work again.

"Name your price," Trinizhi said.

"The cost of an operation like this is high... A hundred gold pieces should suffice." Neva heard Astiand choke on air.

"Done," Trinizhi said a little too easily. "And I'll need you to sign a contract."

"Of course," Neva managed to say. She could scarcely believe Trinizhi was going to give her a hundred gold pieces. "So we're in agreement?"

"It seems so," Trinizhi said. "You will fetch the Sword of Elon from Lithlorian Island and return it to me here before the summit commences."

Nikolazhi removed a thick sheet of parchment from an ornate box atop the desk and lifted a feathered quill. She dabbed it in an inkwell and added a notation to the document.

"It is a blood contract," Nikolazhi said. "You must sign in blood."

"A blood contract?" Neva asked, trying to recall what she'd heard about the expensive magic. She'd never imagined she would encounter it herself. "I'm not signing a blood contract."

"That doesn't seem necessary," Astiand agreed.

"It's merely procedural." Trinizhi adopted the expression of a patient parent, as if she had anticipated this response.

"Well, you're the donazhi," Neva pointed out. "Can't you change procedure?"

"I can change a lot of things." Trinizhi's tone was cruel. "For instance, the Da'Voda haven't had a need to spend much time in Ashford as of late, but perhaps they ought to."

Neva's throat constricted. Trinizhi's implication was clear, and Neva would not allow her family to become victims of Da'Valian affairs again.

But dare she sign a blood contract? Wasn't there a cost if she failed? Where had she heard that? Neva didn't doubt that Trinizhi wanted her to steal the Sword of Elon, yet she couldn't trust the donazhi to be on the up and up. Not for a moment.

Nikolazhi stepped aside to allow Neva to scrutinize the verbose scrawl and the wax seal of a professional scribe. Neva could read cursive in the common tongue and Da'Valian, but her limited schooling had not been legal by any means. She went slowly, spending more time on unfamiliar words to deduce their meaning. She was thankful when Astiand leaned in to review the document as well.

Near the end of the contract, Neva saw it:

In the case of failure to deliver the Sword of Elon, a consolation will be furnished in the form of indentured servitude over the period of twenty years, or until Nevazhi Da'Voda-Roberts' death, whichever comes first...

Rage turned Neva's vision red. Vivizhi had once told her that Trinizhi would use Neva to benefit herself if given the opportunity, but this sly attempt to turn Neva into the Trinizhi's vassal was unconscionable. And given that Neva had every intention of double-crossing the donazhi, agreeing to then do her bidding for decades to come was a serious thing — especially because Neva had the Hand under her control. What would be the point of keeping the first power from Trinizhi if it meant Neva must hand over the second?

But there would undoubtedly be a sliver of time when Neva had all three prongs, when she could do whatever she wanted with them. Would working for Trinizhi for a finite period of time be worth it? Yes — her mother would have condoned it, in fact. It was a small price to pay for something much bigger. *"Bigger than all of us,"* Vivizhi had said.

"What happens to my horns if I become indentured?" Neva asked. When Trinizhi had turned Miland into an indentured servant, she'd sheared off his horns, preventing him from using his power ever again.

"Not a thing," Trinizhi said. "I think you'll agree that you're of more use with your power intact."

"I don't like this," Astiand said darkly, a crevice forming between his eyebrows.

"Do I need to remind you of your allegiance?" Trinizhi asked. "Or have you forgotten whose aliado you are?"

"I forget nothing." Astiand's steely eyes clashed with the donazhi's.

"Then you will remember that I prefer insurance for my investments." Trinizhi's smile turned icy.

"It's all right," Neva murmured to Astiand.

"The magic of the contract will force you to comply," Astiand said.

"I won't fail," Neva said.

"But if you do?" Astiand asked.

"I think it's safe to say we all hope that doesn't happen," Trinizhi said. "Wouldn't you agree?"

Neva nudged Astiand's ankle under the desk. He was treading dangerous waters with little to gain. Neva wasn't going to back down now, not with the chance to make Monazhi proud on the horizon and Trinizhi's threat against Neva's family still hanging in the air. If Trinizhi thought Neva was working for her, she had no need to go poking around Ashford — but what would happen to her family when Neva's betrayal came to light? She needed an assurance.

"I want guaranteed safety for my family and Adam, no matter the outcome," Neva said. "Forever."

Trinizhi nodded to Nikolazhi. The warlock added a second notation.

"'Further, this contract ensures that no harm directed by the Da'Voda, their agents, or their sister clans shall come to the Roberts' family or Adam Tate for sempiternity,'" Nikolazhi read the notation aloud.

"Sempiternity means forever?" Neva asked.

"Indeed," Astiand said, his tone still displeased.

"Will that suffice?" Trinizhi asked.

Astiand made a barely perceptible gesture, implying he wasn't going to stop Neva from signing.

"Aye," Neva said.

Trinizhi passed the quill to Neva. With a subtle twist, the donazhi drew blood along Neva's thumb with the razor-sharp center of a calla ring.

"Ow." Neva yanked away with a scowl. "I could have done that myself."

"Now you don't have to," Trinizhi said magnanimously. She turned the flower on her ring. It glistened red and retracted.

Neva milked the wound and dabbed at it with the tip of the quill, letting the blood slide up into the hollow shaft. Holding her breath, she signed her name. She didn't like the pinpricks of magic that stung her fingers or the uneasiness in her belly.

"There. You have it." Neva dropped the quill and stepped back. Her nostrils burned with the scent of sewage that wafted off the paper.

"Very good," Trinizhi said, nicking the side of her own thumb to add her signature.

Nikolazhi recited a spell and summoned her power, using an infinitesimal flame to burn a sigil into the parchment.

"It is done," Nikolazhi stepped back.

Trinizhi lifted the contract against the light from the shattered window and blew on the signatures.

"Wait — what is that?" Neva reached for the contract. Had she seen writing on the back of the parchment?

"Have a look." Trinizhi placed the contract back on the desk.

Neva flipped the parchment over a moment before something slammed down on her skull. She slumped to the floor.

CHAPTER FOURTEEN

Seventh Fireside, 1631

Dear Osirus,

Surely, now that a century has passed, the Serculus will welcome me back into the fold. I understand their hesitancy, but I sincerely believe the time for making an example of me has come to an end. Especially since I've discovered how to mitigate the effects of time. I eagerly await your response.

Brother Alewiscious
Prisoner 173, Lithlorian Island

When Neva came to, she discovered that a new throbbing sensation had joined the Hand's siege on her head. In the dark, she reached back and touched her bare scalp. Her fingers came away sticky with half-dried blood from an open wound. When it healed, she would have an impressive scar. She checked again, confused by the absence of her hair. Someone had shaved her head.

She struggled to sit up. Her brain sloshed inside her skull, and her vision swam. Some of the moldy straw that was strewn across the uneven stone floor stuck to her cheek.

Neva tried to take in her surroundings, but her senses were condensed into a sort of tunnel vision. Nothing was very clear. Nothing was focused. Tendrils of the Hand slipped through the seals of its prison, and she battled it back. Where was she? What had happened? She wasn't sure how much longer she could constrain the Hand, but this was not the time to allow it to manifest — she wasn't alone.

Sounds echoed around her. Someone cried out, another person coughed, and more moaned as if trapped in nightmares. A particularly loud woman shouted obscenities before wood rapping on metal forced her silence. The stench of body odor and excrement was near enough to push Neva over again. She waited for a bout of nausea to pass before leaning against the metal bars behind her.

Bars?

"No," Neva whispered. *She wouldn't have.*

She forgot to breathe as she discovered her head wasn't her only source of discomfort. She turned her hand over and stared at the blurry marks tattooed on her wrist. Three black Xs ringed by perfect circles.

Neva's vision darkened around the edges, and she wasn't sure if it was because of her head wound or anger — no, pure fury — at having been duped.

She had earned one of the marks on her wrist outright in Glacier Pass, when a scuffle with the Watch had concluded with one of their men's ankles being wrenched under her and his comrades capturing her. She had stashed the goods, but not well enough, and that had led to her first conviction tattoo. Combined with the two new marks... she had been sentenced to life on Lithlorian Island.

Her stomach clenched and bile burned the back of her throat. She didn't doubt that Trinizhi was sending her to Lithlorian because she wanted the Mouth, but the conviction marks would last forever. For all intents and purposes, Trinizhi had condemned her. Three marks among the thieving community? Neva would be blacklisted. Not to mention that even if she survived this job and somehow voided her contract, few respectable employers would neglect to check for conviction marks. While she could hide one or two with a glamour, three was cause for any hedge witch or mage to alert the authorities, because it would be more lucrative to turn her in.

Neva grabbed the bars and attempted to pull herself up. Could she find an escape? She swayed on her feet before collapsing, but she'd seen enough to confirm her fear. Her cell was one in a long line of barred enclosures under an extensive arched stone tunnel. The cells, the conviction marks, the sheer size of the lockup... She was in the docking bay of the Port Telgard jail.

Trinizhi had likely paid a hefty bribe to get her here. Neva doubted that her head injury could have kept her out for more than a day, and Order legal procedure would have taken much longer than that for a conviction from the House of Madrona, Port Telgard's ruling house. While most of the houses were known for expeditious court proceedings, the House of Madrona was not one of them.

Had Astiand gone along with it? Neva couldn't imagine how Trinizhi and Arroyand could have deposited her here without her guardian's cooperation, but her mind was working slower than usual, and she was having difficulty collecting her thoughts. Neva dropped her head into her hands and clenched her teeth so hard that her jaw twinged. She was mad at Astiand. Or maybe she should give him the benefit of the doubt this time? No, she was pretty sure she was furious with him. She swore and slammed her hand against the bars.

A woman with a rat's nest for hair and mere rags covering her rotund form grumbled near Neva's ankle. The woman rolled over in a deep sleep, and Neva moved her foot before it was trapped.

She wanted to challenge Trinizhi to a kilstroke. She felt like an ice pick was being hammered into her head. Emiliand was off with the Da'Roha none the wiser. Mari obviously hadn't tracked her here. Her father thought she was putting old disputes to bed. She was in what her Uncle Archibald would call a shite situation, and she could barely think, let alone formulate a way out of it.

With a start, Neva discovered an old woman staring at her from the next cell. The woman's beady eyes were pinned on Neva.

"When will we be shipped off?" Neva asked, half expecting the woman wouldn't answer.

"Not long now. They'll come for us as soon as the sun is up." The old woman held a shawl around her slumped shoulders. Her skin was wrinkled like dried mushrooms, and the frayed ends of the shawl dusted the ground, picking up bits of dirt and cobwebs.

"To Lithlorian?" Neva asked in a hushed tone.

"Where else?" The old woman's gaze was fixed on Neva's horns.

"Where else indeed?" Neva muttered, lamenting her imprisonment and her stupidity. Oh, her stupidity... She groaned. The warning signs had been there. A hundred gold. A magically binding contract. But the safety of her family and the potential to complete her mother's mission of redeeming the Da'Valia had seemed worth it. Still, she couldn't help but wonder if she could have found another way.

"You're not supposed to be here, are you?" the old woman asked.

"No," Neva said, although she supposed that was a matter of opinion. "Not really."

"I thought as much. I saw them bring you in, you know." The woman coughed up a wad of phlegm and spit it into the straw. Neva heard a rattle from deep within the woman's chest. "I would suppose a wretched uncle needed to be rid of you, but I've never seen horns like yours before."

"Nothing so tragic," Neva said. After all, she had agreed when Trinizhi said she would get Neva to the island. For good and bad, Neva had signed on for this.

The contract... She'd seen writing on the back of the contract before Trinizhi knocked her out. What had it said? What else had she agreed to — in blood?

"I'm Willi," the old woman said after a moment of silence.

"Neva."

"How old are you?"

"I've seen eighteen firesides," Neva said.

"Eighteen firesides. So young." Willi rubbed at her throat, which sounded raw. "It's not fair that they put you in here. You haven't even lived yet."

"They'll get what's coming," Neva promised.

"Isn't that the truth of it?" Willi asked. "The gods like keeping a balance. I killed my husband, and we pledged our hearts 'til death. Now I'm going to die, too, so it seems fitting, doesn't it?"

Neva was quiet. She'd heard the rattle in the woman's chest. Willi spoke the truth. If the voyage to Lithlorian Island didn't kill her, infection would.

"How did it happen? Why?" Neva asked. She had lived with the guilt of accidentally being responsible for many deaths for a long time now. But someone she loved? That was one of her greatest fears. She couldn't imagine what this woman must be going through.

"Why?" Willi asked, her voice peaking. "Decades upon decades of his confoundedness, and I couldn't take another moment of it. I considered pushing him out the window more times than I can count, but we only lived on the second story so I never could do it. I didn't want to end up taking care of an invalid for the rest of my days. But in the end, it was more of an accident. He came home, late for dinner as usual, and ornery as ever after I'd slaved over that meal for him, so I bashed the bastard's brains in with my good cast iron skillet."

"An accident?" Neva echoed weakly.

"Aye," Willi said. "I didn't mean to kill him, but when I tried to explain that to the magistrate, all he heard was a confession. Seems I've reached the end. And don't tell me I haven't. I know how it is. Someone my age will never survive Lithlorian. I'd be easy pickings. Doesn't seem fair, does it?"

"Not fair at all," Neva allowed. Agreeing with a disturbed person seemed better than angering one.

"You're a good listener," Willi told her. "Take my shawl. I won't need it where I'm going."

Willi passed her shawl to Neva through the bars and placed her gnarled hands in her lap as the distant sound of metal gates opening reached them. Morning light peeked through the series of small windows along the stone ceiling, casting a purple glow about the space. Prisoners shuffled down the row of cells with guards herding them. They would all be dragon fodder before long.

"This is it," Willi said, moving to the door of her cell with her head held high.

"Already?" Neva wrapped the shawl around her shoulders and struggled to her feet again.

"Everybody up," a guard shouted. The guards raked their clubs along the bars to underscore their orders. "Line up at your door. No pushing. No shoving. Yer all going to the same place."

Willi's door opened, and the old woman stepped into the throng.

"Lovely to know you," Willi croaked back at her.

Willi's farewell registered as a bout of dizziness washed over Neva, and the door to her cell rolled open. Neva tugged the shawl over her horns and prayed to Dhianz that she would make it through this. She feared she was concussed. She was walking like she was already aboard the ship, slipping too easily on the slick stone and relying on the bars to hold herself upright.

From the holding cells, Neva and the rest of the women — hundreds of them from every corner of Cirandrel — were driven like cattle down the long tunnel to the loading bay. The stench of mildew and festering body odor was replaced with that of seaweed and fish guts as they approached the massive timber doors blocking their way.

Ahead, guards worked screeching cogwheels to slide the doors open. A startling morning glare forced more than one prisoner to cover her eyes.

When Neva's vision cleared, she discovered the wide opening that let out at the docks was well above the sea. Narrow planks jutted out from the jail to a cargo bay of a giant ship. None of the planks was wide enough for more than single-file loading.

"Keep moving. Mind your step. You won't survive the fall." The guards called out warnings and jabbed their clubs at prisoners.

Neva swallowed, failing to moisten her throat. She was unsure if she would even make it aboard the ship, let alone across the Tyvse Sea and to Lithlorian Island.

As she approached the planks, Neva saw Willi step out onto one. The old woman turned to the guard nearest to her.

"You'll never take me alive." She threw her arms out and fell backward.

A shout lodged in Neva's throat as a faint splash sounded. Neva pulled the shawl around her hands tighter, cutting off the circulation to her fingers. Every several feet, there was another muted splash as a prisoner fell into the watery depths. Neva flinched away from a woman who bumped into her.

"Mercy, pray. I beg your mercy." Another woman screamed as she was pushed toward the entrance by the mass of bodies behind her. "I can't go. I can't leave my little ones."

A step from the edge, the woman flung herself at one of the guards. His club made a sickening cracking noise as it hit her head. She fell to the ground unconscious, blood oozing from her brow line.

"Anyone else can't go, come see me," he shouted, waving his club.

Neva and the prisoners next to her moved around the woman's unconscious form and to the ledge. Neva couldn't help looking down as she stepped onto the plank. It would be easy to get across, really — if it didn't sway quite so much and if she wasn't still seeing double. The water below was tinted pink where the waves crashed against the rocks. For a moment, Neva saw the fin of an ocean predator break the surface.

"Move," a guard yelled at her.

Neva willed her vision to correct and inched across the wooden plank. She could feel the guard itching to use his club on her if she didn't start making progress. By the time she reached the other side, she was shaking with the effort it took to avoid falling.

"Keep walking." Another guard yanked her into the cargo bay. "Head on to the back. We have scores more to fit in here."

Neva scrambled with the rest of the prisoners, careful to keep the shawl covering her horns. She imagined the crowd succumbing to hysteria should her true nature be revealed. She didn't want to become a target among those who had nothing left to lose.

She almost giggled at the morbid thought that murder carried no additional punishment in their present situation. Then, she thought of how she came to be in this predicament, and she sobered. She hunkered down, packed between a woman mumbling prayers and another who was bawling.

One by one, the prisoners packed into the ship's hull until, finally, the guards closed the opening, sucking out the last drop of light. It took a moment for Neva to adjust to the pitch darkness, but when she did, all she could see was the bald heads of hundreds of deviants.

Her mouth parted. How had every person here committed crimes that the Order deemed so horrible that they should be exiled to Lithlorian Island and relegated to dragon fodder? But then the Order did only ship its prisoners a few times a year.

Many of those around her either sat in shock, mourned the people they had left behind, or otherwise wallowed in their unfortunate luck. Seeing them, determination rose within her. Her situation might be shite, but at least she could still double-cross Trinizhi. She imagined the expression that Trinizhi would wear when she realized that Neva held all the prongs of the Trishula. Neva would succeed if it was the last thing she ever did.

The mass of bodies had pushed Neva to the center of the hull, so she worked her way to the watering trough to tend to her head wound. She dipped the edge of her shawl in the water while pretending to take a sip. No one would take kindly to someone washing with the drinking water. Neva made space for herself against the side of the ship and cleaned the wound as well as she was able. Working by touch, she pushed her scalp back together and used the smallest bit of power she could manage to seal it shut.

"What was that?" someone whispered next to her. "Did you see that?"

Neva let a low growl unfurl in her throat.

The whisperer scrambled to find another spot.

Neva fought nausea, which intensified as the ship disembarked. Even with all the bodies surrounding her, she was very much alone. This was the first time she had been without Emiliand and Mari in weeks, and she missed them. Even their bickering.

Neva quickly became acquainted with the cargo bay. There were two troughs in addition to the one holding their drinking water, one on either side of the ship. They were fed in one trough once a day, so the other became the de facto toilet, which let out to the sea on either end. When it was time to eat, guards dumped buckets of slop into the food trough. Women turned animalistic, shoving each other aside. Some formed groups to get to the food. Three or four would fight off others while the rest shoved the gruel down their throats, and then they would switch positions. Two women were killed at their second feeding.

Neva's dizziness was improving, but she had no appetite. Her motion sickness grew as the ship pitched this way and that, and she was soon forced to visit the waste trough to vacate her stomach.

Several days into their journey, the guards identified about a dozen dead and carted them out of the cargo bay to dump them overboard. The deceased had been in the groups that hogged slop at feeding time. They had neglected to appoint lookouts throughout the night.

Neva dozed occasionally, but she did so lightly. When feeding time came around the fifth day, a guard with cauliflower ears emptied his slop bucket in the food trough and stomped over to Neva. She averted her gaze, hoping he would pass by her.

"Hey, you, still alive?" The guard nudged her with the toe of his boot.

Neva didn't respond and was startled when something dropped in her lap. Her gaze shot to the guard's face. The hairy man's eyes flashed a brief, bright yellow.

"Mari." Neva relaxed. She draped the edge of her shawl over the ginger root Mari had dropped in her lap.

"Are you all right?" Mari asked in a hushed tone. Her caution was unnecessary. Everyone was preoccupied with mealtime.

"I'll be fine," Neva assured her. "I can't believe you found me."

"I told you, I may have let you down once, but I won't do it again."

"You're a good friend."

"Djinn don't have friends."

"Uh-huh," Neva said, skeptical of Mari's motto.

"The captain says the winds are turning favorable," Mari told her. "We'll arrive at Lithlorian in a few days' time. I'll find you when we do."

Mari departed, smacking her club against a beefy palm, calling for any bodies that needed to be removed. Neva ate the ginger root and was relieved when it calmed her nausea. When the next feeding came, she pushed her way to the food trough and shoveled down a couple of handfuls. It would have to be enough to sustain her for the rest of the voyage.

You're not alone, Neva told herself as she rested. The modest meal brought heavy fatigue over her. *Everything will be all right.*

But the Hand had other plans.

CHAPTER FIFTEEN

Eighth Fireside, 1631

Dear Alewiscious,
Brother Osirus tells me you have unlocked the secret to tethering
not only our spirits but our physical forms for life everlasting.
Can this preservation be done for all the Brotherhood? We will
reconsider your imprisonment if you can provide detailed
instructions.

Brother Noridemus

Neva lurched awake in the middle of the night. Mild vertigo made her vision spin as she jolted away from the side of the ship, but the rest of the maladies from her head wound had dwindled since disembarking. The Hand pounded like a war drum. Beams of light broke through the vault's seals, pulsating in time. The Hand wanted to be used, and it wanted to be used *now*.

She counted how many days had passed since she last released the power. More than an entire moon's cycle.

Too long.

Far too long.

How the godly power had not yet broken free of her hold on it, she didn't know. She hadn't slept since boarding, not really, and with little food, she was wearing down. She had to prevent the Hand from rising. Her belt had too many marks already, not to mention that the Hand would consume the ship, leaving her at the mercy of the Tyvse Sea.

Neva closed her eyes. She would do what she could to keep everyone alive. She had to.

"Dhianz, give me strength," she prayed. Then, because she wasn't sure he would hear her: "Maeve, strengthen my resolve."

She braced herself and snapped her pinkie finger backward, breaking the bone between the lower joints. The pain was sharp and immediate, and her Da'Valian ability to channel pain into greater focus made all of her senses sharpen. Every creak of the ship's hull sounded louder. The stale air carried a deeper chill. The reek of the toilet trough made her gag. The Hand leaped, demanding her attention with renewed vigor.

Gritting her teeth, Neva constructed the largest vault she could conceive around the one that held the Hand. She slapped her palm against the hull each time the sting faded, renewing her focus. When the time came to put the lock in place, the spindle wheel was as large as the helm of the ship. She spun it until the door to the new vault was firmly locked in place. Still, the Hand continued to rail.

Neva imagined a wide expanse of nighttime desert and dropped the vault in the middle. The dry earth cracked underneath it. In the distance, gray snow-capped mountains surrounded her in every direction. Stars twinkled in a moonless sky, and though there were no clouds, snowflakes drifted down from above. If there was ever a place the Hand would not escape from, she was counting on this barren landscape to do the job.

She didn't know how long she stayed there, standing motionless in the middle of the hull. A day? Two? Each time the vault heated, she called on snow in the imaginary place, using her force of will to cool the Hand. She was sweating and starving and fatigued, yet she couldn't relinquish her hold on it.

Finally, the carrier slowed and the sound of wood scraping against one side of the ship alerted her that they had reached their destination. Neva lined up with the rest of the women, keeping her breathing even and her concentration steadfast. The Hand would turn prisoners into ash and the dock into embers. She needed to make away from everyone to release it safely before it broke free.

As soon as the hull opened, convicts streamed out. Neva squinted against the blinding white haze of daylight, tears clouding her eyes. Men and women from different levels of the ship sprinted down the dock to the beach, while others jumped into the shimmery blue water. At least, at first. The screams from those that were yanked under were warning enough to prevent anyone else from going in the water.

Neva stepped off the boat, and the marks on her wrist flared to life as if they'd been freshly made with a branding iron. She walked through the crowd wholly focused on the Hand. She was barely aware of her boots touching the sand or of the warmth when it seeped through. Distantly, she recognized that prisoners were being led by others already on the island up the beach, past the tree line, and into the jungle. Crudely made knives flashed as a group of women from the island descended upon a man in the crowd. Briefly, Neva spied the tattoos marking him as a rapist.

Don't get distracted, Neva told herself.

Somehow, she kept moving down the beach toward a rocky outcropping. She curved around the budding cliff edge and away from the inmates. A ganger, one of the convicts who had obviously been on the island for some time, shouted after her, but no one followed. She entered a cove well beyond sight of those on the beach and turned toward the water. She mustered her courage and walked into the oncoming tide.

The water weighed down her long Da'Valian pants, each receding wave beckoning her deeper. Neva allowed the sea to bring her into its embrace until the water crested her navel. Her feet were still touching the ground with each swell, but barely. This was far enough. Paranoia that she would get swept under nearly shattered her concentration. A creature brushed against her leg, and she flung her arms out.

The Hand surged free. It poured into the water, intense and steady. It canceled out waves that would have broken, melted the sand beneath into a smooth glass slide, and wiped out all the creatures in its path. Never had the Hand emerged from her with so much desire to consume behind it. The sheer force of it pushed back the ocean, and steam rose as far as she could see. Warm blood gushed from her nose.

Frantic screams warning of a sea monster sounded from the beach, but the convicts who'd arrived with her would live. With stories of a new creature to fear in the deep, perhaps, but they would be around to tell those tales. The sea was already returning to its natural rhythm.

"Thank you, Dhianz," Neva said. "Thank you, Riska."

Calm and with a clear head at last, Neva washed away the trails of blood from her nose. She dried her face on her wrap, her gaze shooting to the sky when a shadow flickered over her.

Her neck craned, and she caught the scream that welled in her throat. Above her flew a dragon with cerulean scales that flexed and glinted in the sunlight, horns that curved in the direction opposite of her own, and black talons, each as long as her arm. Its wingspan was twice the length of its body, making it the largest creature she had ever seen, and when it flapped its scaled wings — once, twice — it sounded like steel blades scraping against whetting stones.

Neva raced back to the beach and witnessed pandemonium break out. Prisoners streaming from the ship bolted for the tree line, bald heads bobbing. She hit the ground, trying to decide her next move.

"This way if you want to live," a grime-covered ganger with long dreadlocks shouted.

The dragon dove and snatched two convicts from the ground. In its wake, another dragon, this one the color of honeycomb with sunflower streaks, plummeted and plucked up another convict. People screamed, running for their lives.

The tree line was spotted with sunburnt convicts draped in weathered clothing, all with blue strips of cloth tied around well-defined biceps. Each held a spear, and they funneled the new arrivals into the jungle, a tangled web of giant trees and exotic plants. Neva had never known there were so many shades of green, but she would allow herself to marvel at them another time. She couldn't stay out in the open.

Three more shadows brushed over her. She rushed to join the flood of convicts embracing the protection of the trees. Fleetingly, she spied twin volcanic peaks, the storied ashmounts, spewing black smoke in the distance before the jungle's canopy hid them from view.

The change from the sandy terrain of the beach, where her feet sank several inches with each step, was gradual until her boots barely made impressions on the mossy ground. Flies swarmed the crowd, biting at will. Shade grew thicker as the trail narrowed.

After climbing a short incline, Neva emerged with the others in a charred clearing. Blackened remains indicated that the area had been leveled by fire, but it had a smattering of shrubs and saplings, so the fire hadn't been a recent one.

Enormous trees surrounded the clearing, and Neva tracked the flashes of movement in the jungle canopy. People were in the trees. Too many to count. All of them studying the newcomers. They were well-camouflaged, but Neva guessed their numbers were in the thousands.

So many people. How would she find Mari? And more immediately, what did they want?

Neva was so busy watching them that she bumped into the man in front of her, unable to continue on. The new arrivals stood, effectively penned in a circle of the wide tree trunks and spear-toting convicts. The man she had bumped into jabbed his elbow back at her. Neva growled and punched him in the kidney.

"What will they do to us?" a woman whimpered.

More weathered convicts emerged from the heavy foliage, and Neva discerned distinct groups among them. Several dozen men and women with children behind them carried crudely fashioned spears and daggers. The adults wore black mud smeared beneath their eyes while the younger ones didn't, but they moved united. Next to them, she spied the women who had taken out the rapist on the beach. Beyond them, another group of ... Neva frowned. Nobles? They were armed, and some of them comfortable in stances that hinted at formal combat training. Definitely nobles. She could spot that posture and haughty air as easily as a fat purse in a coat pocket.

The gangers comprised all stations, all genders, all ages. Save for the children, the only common attribute among them was their conviction marks. Pirates, swindlers, traitors, thieves, and murderers were all represented. Neva rubbed her wrist, unable to shake the sense that she belonged among them. Had she not earned a spot on this island many times over?

Guilt constricted her windpipe, and her eyes drifted to the next group as she searched for a distraction. A handful of men were dressed neck to toe in shining amber armor. They wore swords at their hips. One of them carried the largest crossbow she'd ever seen. The apparent leader stood ahead of the rest, his arms crossed as he examined the new arrivals shrewdly. His head was shaved, and his scalp was tan as if he'd spent a lot of time in the sun.

"Hear ye, hear ye," a ganger bellowed through coned hands. "Allow me to present your new king."

Chapter Sixteen

Ninth Fireside, 1631

Dear Noridemus,

Let me first express my joy at receiving your message. I have waited many years for the Brotherhood to accept me back into the fold. Tell me, how is Osirus? I send missives to him regularly, but I have not received a response. Of course this form of tethering can be done for all the Brotherhood, but it does require substantial power. A relic of the gods would suffice. Please send a ship to fetch me, and I will complete my research among the Brotherhood.

Brother Alewiscious
Prisoner 173, Lithlorian Island

Neva's eyes doubled in size. Of all the rogues she might have run into on Lithlorian, this was the last she would have expected.

"Greetings, gangers," the king welcomed the crowd. His light blond hair was pulled back in a holder, his once clean-shaven face was sporting a robust beard, and his skin had tanned several shades darker. But that bent nose, that too-comfortable swagger — those were familiar. Neva had last seen the thief when she'd bested him and broken his arm as they'd both attempted to steal a goblet from the House of Trescony.

Thatcher Sullivan. Under the moniker the Chameleon, he was notorious for taking unsanctioned jobs across Cirandrel. A thief among thieves.

After he'd disappeared that night in Glacier Pass, she had speculated about his fate once or twice. He'd been hired by Vodou witches and Da'Foha, neither of whom were very forgiving, to steal the Eye. She'd wondered if he had managed to stay alive and out of the hands of the Order. Apparently not.

"If you've made it this far, you've proved your worth." Thatcher motioned to the jungle theatrically. The blue strip of cloth on his upper arm flashed, matching those of the men on the beach.

He nimbly leaped atop a charred log and scanned the blow-ins.

"But just because you're still alive doesn't mean you'll survive this island. We've got dragons, all manner of poisonous fruit, ashmounts, snakes that will try to share your bed, strangling vines, lepers, and sea creatures galore. The dangers are endless.

"Us gangers? We know this island intimately. The Crown does especially so." He gestured to the gathering of gangers that stood behind him. "And since we run things here, we'll be selecting a few of you to join us."

Thatcher motioned his gangers forward. They picked through the crowd. Each ganger eventually singled out one newcomer to join their ranks.

"Weed out the lepers," Thatcher commanded.

The gangers prodded at their selections with the blunt ends of their spears, moving clothing aside to check underneath.

"Clean."

"All good here."

The gangers brought their selections into the fold behind Thatcher, doubling their size. Only two of the Crown had shown any interest in Neva, but apparently some combination of her horns and head wound were not up to their standards.

"The Crown thanks you for your generous contributions to our ranks," Thatcher said. He stuck his fingers in his mouth and gave an ear-splitting whistle. His gang merged into the jungle, many of them climbing the footholds etched in the trees to secure higher vantage points.

"The rest of you may choose the gang you join." Thatcher nodded to the gang to his left. "But choose wisely. No gang likes castoffs."

"We're the Anchorweights." A barrel-chested man with a long, parted beard squinted at the crowd. Nearly a hundred gangers clustered around him, a mix of men, women, and their youngsters. "Former pirates, mostly. With all the connections you could want on the high seas and all the fish you could want for dinner. We've no patience and a terrible thirst."

Joining their gang would have value. Neva didn't imagine other gangs would start conflicts with the Anchorweights, given their strength in numbers, and access to a network of pirates would make getting off the island easier. But they weren't her only option.

"We're the Ashmount gang," said the man with charcoal slashes under his eyes. "If anyone wants clean water, they have to go through us."

Neva considered the man. How many convicts would attempt to join his gang merely for the promise of drinking water?

"The Revenants." A woman at least twice Neva's age stepped forward with brown braids wound about her head and several children clinging to her ratty skirts. "I'm Mandana. We've no time for cheats or thieves. This is your new life now. We raise our children here, we live here, and we mean to live here well."

Several more gangs introduced themselves — the Undertakers, mostly murderers; the Aristocracy, loyalists to the Old King; the Harpies, women who were committed to ridding the island of rapists. The list went on, but none of the remaining gangs had more to offer, Neva judged. That is, until the final gang leader stepped forward.

"And we're the Dragonslayers." Tattoos covered what she could see of the leader's arms. He'd kept his head shaved but had a robust mustache. A bright yellow songbird was perched on his shoulder. "We mean to take back the island from the dragons one day and liberate ourselves with their riches. We welcome any who would join us."

"A suicide mission," someone shouted from within the Anchorweights. "Just ask where the rest of them went."

"We've kept you alive more times than I can count, Spyke," the leader yelled back. "Don't make us regret it."

Four men stood behind the leader of the Dragonslayers. Neva frowned and counted again, taking care to see if she had missed anyone. The Dragonslayers had remarkably low numbers. Five men against even one dragon did, indeed, sound like a suicide mission. But they didn't have a Da'Valia yet.

"Let's get on with it," the leader of the Ashmounts called out. "Blow-ins, pick your gangs."

As the new arrivals milled about, Neva studied the Anchorweights, then the Dragonslayers. On one hand, the Anchorweights would keep her fed, and they had contacts she could take advantage of to get off the island. But on the other hand, the Dragonslayers presumably had knowledge that would be invaluable to her. She needed a viable plan to steal the Mouth before she could plot her escape. With any luck, the Dragonslayers might already have a plan she could adopt.

Neva took a tentative step in their direction and shot a final glance over her shoulder at the Anchorweights. They had much better numbers and plenty more muscle. She hoped she was making the right decision.

"What are you?" A Dragonslayer with a mop of brown hair and startling blue-green eyes studied her. He carried a quiver of oversized arrows across his back, and an extra-large crossbow leaned against the tree next to him.

"Da'Valia." Neva lifted her chin.

"I've never heard of a Da'Valia with four horns before," another Dragonslayer commented as he cut into a piece of fruit with spiky green skin. With his sharp cheekbones, Neva imagined her Aunt Margret would say he was easy on the eye.

"You'll have to take my word for it," Neva said.

"No ganger's word goes very far," the leader said. "We're happy to have you on, but you haven't proved yourself to us yet. Until you do, your word isn't worth dirt."

"Sounds fair." Neva supposed she shouldn't have expected anything more. "So, you'll have me?"

The men exchanged glances.

"Aye," their leader confirmed. "I'm Ballard. This is Warbler," — he stroked the black spots on the songbird's head — "That's Durant," — he pointed to the ganger eating the fruit — "Tavo," — he pointed to a fellow about Neva's age with black hair, a neatly trimmed goatee, and a wide stance — "Valentine," — the tall man's skin was leathery, his beard braided, and his eyes beady like a rat's — "and that's Rinaldo."

Ballard's introductions finished with the ganger who had asked Neva what she was.

"But first, we have to inspect you." Valentine grinned at her in a way that made her skin crawl. He took a step toward her.

She moved in tandem, keeping distance between them. She could knock him out cold, but it didn't seem the best way to start things off with her gang.

"Anyone touches me, and I'll break their fingers," she said evenly, conjuring a glacial look. "One. At. A. Time."

"That would be your prerogative," Ballard said. "But we do need to check you over for the safety of everyone here. We all get checked."

Neva noticed the other newcomers were stripping down to their undergarments.

"Rot's a real problem," Durant explained.

"Leprosy?" Her gorge rose. She prayed she hadn't unknowingly contracted the flesh-eating disease. "Check me if you have to."

"I'll do it," Ballard said before Valentine could take another step. Ballard didn't seem to want his gang distracted by its new member. "You're welcome to some privacy. Call me over when you're ready."

Neva ducked behind a tree. She was stripped down when she heard a commotion start up from the clearing.

"Leper! We've got a leper here."

"I've got one, too."

"To the beach, you. Move."

Neva peeked from behind the tree to see several Anchorweights and Ashmounts prodding two male convicts back toward the beach with their spears. She called to Ballard, and he checked her over in quick order.

"Nothing to worry about," Ballard said finally, eyeing her horns. "Get dressed."

"What will happen to them?" Neva yanked on her wrap as more lepers were rounded up.

"They'll be given a dinghy, oars, and the chance to make it to the Outpost on Leper Island," Ballard answered matter-of-factly. "The colony there will take them in. If they try to sneak back, the Crown or the Anchorweights will stop them."

"I don't envy them," Neva said.

"Nor should you. I'd expect that with all the magic workers in this world, someone would have stumbled upon a cure, but it eludes them." Ballard held out a waterskin and piece of fruit. "Here. Figured you'd be hungry."

Warbler tweeted a brisk staccato, sounding perturbed.

"You've eaten today," Ballard told the bird sternly. "She hasn't."

Neva accepted the offerings with thanks. She bit into the tart fruit and juice dripped down her chin as she rejoined the Dragonslayers. She took stock of the two other newcomers who stood with them.

"I'm called Crowe." New growth on the younger convict's scalp suggested that he would have a dark widow's peak when his hairline filled back in. His skin was clammy, his lips were dry, and he reeked of vomit. "I've some experience fishing, and I'm all right with a bow."

"And you?" Ballard asked the other man.

"Name's Debo," the short red-head flexed his giant biceps. "I'm a bruiser, and I'm strong. I can carry as much as my own weight and then some. My uncle was a blacksmith, and I apprenticed some, so I can work metal, too. I'm damned loyal."

He might have been exceptionally short, but judging by his muscles, Neva didn't doubt Debo's claim to strength.

"And dragons don't scare you?" Ballard questioned the newcomers.

"Dragons scare the piss out of me," Debo said. "But I'll not run from the monsters. I'm a fighter first."

"I just want to go home," Crowe said.

"What do we think, 'Slayers?" Ballard asked the gang.

Neva voiced her approval with the others. There was safety in numbers. They could use all the help they could get.

"All right." Ballard leaned back on his heels. "You're in if you pass inspection. Strip."

Neva averted her eyes. Several of the gangs had taken off, but the rest milled about. She noticed a man in long, faded robes, standing apart. He was pale compared with most of the gangers. His beard was scraggly, and his peppered hair reached well down his back, proving he'd been on the island for a long time. The tattoo on his forearm was an upside-down triangle that overlapped the bottom third of an upright triangle. She had seen that symbol before in the desert, at a temple of Yokam's.

"Who's that?" Neva asked.

"Apothecary," Durant responded. "Keeps to himself. Can get you any tonic you need. I heard someone say he was the first deviant chained to this rock — the only one to ever make it off the island, too."

Neva's head snapped around.

"He made it off the island?" she asked.

"Two things keep us here." Tavo held up his wrist, which was marked with an <u>M</u>. "Conviction marks, and the wardens. The rumor is that the wardens scooped the apothecary out of the sea and dropped him at the base of the ashmounts more than once."

"Our conviction marks can keep us here?" Crowe pulled his pants back up. He and Debo had passed their inspections.

"The Order has the ink spelled," Ballard explained. "Your marks were activated as soon as you got off the ship. I've seen more than one ganger perish from magical poisoning after trying to be rid of them. It's an ugly death. But if the apothecary managed to cut them off and survive, at least we know it's possible."

That answered one of her questions.

"Can a dragon be outrun?" Neva asked.

Tavo guffawed, and Durant chuckled.

"You have much to learn, Da'Valia," Ballard said, a grin peeking out from his mustache.

Chapter Seventeen

First Vestive, 1643

Dear Elkizhi,

The fighting is escalating, and I sense a precipice is on the horizon. If all goes well in the coming weeks, we will win this war and I'll be home by Seventh Vestive. Corazhi was wounded in a skirmish at Stagg and sent back to her village, making Bryand insufferable. If you think I'm grouchy after a restless night, you should see him. I pity our foes, for the next time he steps foot on a battlefield, no one will hold him back.

Vivi was furious that her squadron was relocated. She thinks our donazhi did it only to separate Vivi and me. And I... I am not sure. I can find strategy in the move, but not much. Most nights, Trinizhi calls me to her tent along with Bryand, Helband, and Damiand after our official work is done. We share hagave. It's strange to think, but she seems lonely.

With honor and pleasure,
— Astiand

Rain clouds developed over the island as Neva and the Dragonslayers traipsed along overgrown footpaths deeper into the jungle. From the uneven ground to the lush canopy, the jungle was a living thing unto itself. Melodious birds hopped among undulating tree limbs. Neva found herself climbing over rotting logs that were wider than she was tall, side-stepping enormous rodent holes, and slipping on moist patches of mossy ground. Not to mention swatting away the many spider webs that caressed her face.

Ballard called out warnings with each new threat they happened upon. Venantulas laid their eggs in rotting wood and would sting them if they got too close. The snakes that coiled in the rodent holes had venomous bites. If anyone broke their tailbone falling over the slick moss, medicinal aid would be pricey or unavailable. Which led him to his next warning — if any Dragonslayer deigned to offer their charity, the newcomers had better expect that it would come at a cost.

The flies thinned out the farther they went from the congregation, but several buzzed around Neva, Debo, and Crowe. Neva breathed through her mouth to avoid the pungent stench that wafted around them, but it wasn't as effective as she hoped. If it weren't for the deadly sea creatures and her inability to swim, she would jump back in the ocean and drag Debo and Crowe with her.

After a while, Ballard's warnings petered out, and Rinaldo advised them on what plants were edible. His mother was a Revenant, so he'd been born on the island. As a result, he had intimate knowledge about the maladies that came with eating shriveled wahlberries or the wrong spotted melons.

"I heard all the natives became pirates," Debo said, swatting at a fly. "Why aren't you on a ship somewhere?"

"I had reasons to stay," Rinaldo said. An emotion — was it sadness? — shone in his bright eyes.

"Our camp is just ahead," Ballard said. "We'll get you three cleaned up and suited up, and then we'll show you the lay of the island. There's no telling when the next hunt will be, but with this much fresh blood, it's bound to be soon. The dragons you saw on the beach were only after a snack."

Neva shivered. If that had been a snack, what would a true dragon attack look like?

"Never get caught unawares," Tavo added as they climbed a steep incline. "If you're a Dragonslayer, you have to be on your toes at every moment, or else you risk all our necks."

"And keep clean. Plenty of gangers have been carted off to Leper Island with mistaken rot. Here." Durant whacked at the base of a nearby plant with a wicked short sword and passed one stem each to the newcomers. "Chew on this. Ingo stalk will keep your teeth from cracking and help your breath to boot."

Neva chewed on the fibrous stalk as instructed, enjoying the earthy flavor. They arrived at a well-concealed camp, deep in the jungle, before long. The Dragonslayers removed a leafy bough from over a small fire pit and pulled back vines that were draped over the footholds carved in a tree trunk. Following the path of the footholds, Neva spied several platforms on the branches above. Likewise, a food store of melons and several barrels had been concealed with foliage.

Warbler took flight and disappeared in the branches overhead.

"This is it," Ballard said. "We move camp every season, just in case the other gangers get any ideas."

"They don't often target us — we're the only ones who fight the wardens when they strike," Durant said. "But you can't be too cautious."

So, this was her new home. Neva took it in. If she could keep the food down, she would consider it a vast improvement over the ship.

"Have a seat." Ballard directed them to the fire pit.

Neva followed Durant's lead, sitting on one of the thicker mossy patches of ground. Crowe did the same, and Debo perched on a boulder.

"First thing's first — do not go anywhere alone," Ballard said.

Neva inspected his tattoos as he talked. The dragon that looped around his wrist held obvious meaning, but a spider web of rope stemming from his elbow meant nothing to her, much like the symbols on his neck that were reminiscent of the pins the Order used to denote rank among its soldiers. The last one made her reconsider. Lots of men were paid to fight, and he had the bearing of someone who could issue orders.

"Gangers have been known to jump others the first few days on the island," Tavo added. "Initiations."

"That's right, so we partner up," Ballard continued. "If you need to go somewhere, you take another Dragonslayer with you. Got it?"

They nodded.

"I'll need to hear you say it."

"Got it." Neva responded with the others.

"What, uh, what are our initiations?" Crowe asked, wiping his palms on his tunic.

"We don't hold initiations," Ballard said. "When the wardens attack, that will be enough of a test."

"I'll partner with the she-devil," Valentine offered from behind Neva.

Neva fixed an icy glare in his direction and imagined setting his shoes on fire. She didn't want a confrontational start with the Dragonslayers, but she would not be opposed to making Valentine dance.

"Rein it in." Ballard advised Valentine. "She's one of us now."

"I'll partner with her," Tavo offered. "By the looks of her, she'd be an asset in a fight."

"I'm trained up." Neva assured Tavo.

"Second thing," Ballard resumed his speech. "We haven't got a beef going with anyone, and I want to keep it that way. The Crown runs things. Do your best to stay out of their way. And we're playing nice with the other gangers, too, at the moment. As soon as that changes, you tell me. Got it?"

"Got it," Neva and the others echoed.

"Right. Third thing, we don't care what you did to get here. We've all had our run-ins with the law. The moment you stepped on this rock, those things don't matter anymore. They don't define you."

Ballard stared at Neva as he spoke, and she squirmed under his scrutiny. The eerie sensation of being known too well made her want to switch gangs and go find the Anchorweights. Had she been letting what she'd done define who she was? Maybe.

"Starting now, you get to define you," Ballard continued. "The Order may have thought it was sentencing us to die on this rock, but what we've really got is a second chance."

"And a chance at riches any of us has only dreamed of," Tavo chimed in.

"Aye," Ballard said. "Now, are you with me?"

"Aye." Neva got to her feet with the others.

"Good." Ballard pounded Debo on the back. "Go through the pile for some suitable armor, and we'll head to the watering hole so you can clean up. You lot would send a skunk into hiding."

Valentine pulled a collection of vines away from yet another hiding spot, and Neva followed Debo and Crowe to the pile of shining amber-colored armor. They rummaged around, creating a racket that frightened nesting birds nearby into flight.

So much for hiding places, Neva thought. Anyone who was paying attention could determine their location. But, like Ballard said, the Dragonslayers were on good terms with the other gangs.

Neva picked up one of the pieces of armor. Light as a feather, the armor gleamed as if it had been shaped and polished that very morning. How was it so lightweight? She eyed the breastplate and set aside the piece, its plackart, and a backplate. She briefly considered a fauld, but she didn't have the codpiece to fill it out appropriately, so she passed on that, too.

The Dragonslayers' armor was not designed with the female figure in mind, nor was it designed to accommodate horns. Trying not to seem ungrateful, she collected armguards from under a helmet and grabbed several blades to replenish the ones Trinizhi had divested her of.

"What metal is this?" Debo asked.

"This here is dragon armor," Tavo bragged, puffing his chest out. "We had a 'Slayer a few years back who was an expert metalsmith. We managed to confiscate some dragon scales, and he reformed it so we could wear it into battle."

"Dragon armor?" Crowe questioned at the same time that Debo said, "You've a kiln?"

"The rarest metal in all the realms," Durant confirmed. "It won't dent. You'd be hard-pressed to find a stronger metal. And the island practically *is* a kiln closer to the ashmounts."

"Resources are limited," Ballard said. "You'll learn to get creative as we have."

"Doesn't wearing the armor antagonize the dragons?" Neva asked.

"So what if it does?" Rinaldo replied.

"Where does one take a piss around here?" Debo asked, glancing around.

"If that's all you need to do, any tree will do," Durant said. "Otherwise, make sure you take the shovel on your way to that shrub on yonder."

Neva took in the rusted shovel, then the shrub as the other newcomers nodded. Of course the Order hadn't invested in making the island comfortable for its prisoners — being sent here was as good as a death sentence. She was half expecting their watering hole to be a mud pit.

"Enough chatter," Ballard said. "Let's go. Rinaldo and I will take you to wash up. It's Durant's and Valentine's night on grub duty."

Warbler perched on Ballard's shoulder again, flapping his wings as if he was excited about the excursion. Rinaldo led the way to a clear blue watering hole at the base of a towering waterfall. Debo slid on the slick moss, nearly bowling Neva over as it came into view. She caught him by his collar and yanked, keeping him on his feet. He gave her an out-of-breath thanks and scrambled up the incline.

Below the raging falls, the water churned and spread out to form a shallow pool where more than a dozen naked gangers washed their clothing and themselves. Reeds ringed the watering hole, and a stack of volcanic rocks partitioned off a deeper second pool. A ganger filled a waterskin at a smaller third pool.

Several gangers were posted at the top of the waterfall and in the trees. The black smudges on their cheeks marked them as members of the Ashmounts. Ballard approached a group at the water's edge and passed something to them. Payment, Neva imagined.

"Go on and get cleaned up," Ballard called out to them. "Rinaldo and Tavo will watch your belongings."

Neva eyed Rinaldo. She wasn't so sure. He seemed to be having a hard time not ogling the gangers in the water.

"Rinaldo?" Ballard attempted to catch his attention.

At the second mention of his name, Rinaldo's ears turned strawberry red.

"On it," he said.

Neva took in the crowd around the watering hole. At least Valentine wasn't here.

She undressed, covering the remnant of the soul scourge with her palm, and followed Debo and Crowe into the shallowest section. The water was tepid and rather enjoyable, even without potions or scents. She scratched at her scalp, dislodging grime and dried blood. She missed her long hair deeply and resented Trinizhi for its loss, but she enjoyed the abrasive sensation against her fingertips. When she raised her head out of the water, she was refreshed.

She growled at a skinny pox-marked lad with a mess of short, matted blond hair who was giving her horns far too much attention.

"Whelp, that did it," Debo commented.

"Did what?" Neva asked distractedly.

"You've made him piss himself."

Neva chuckled and shook her head as Debo and Crowe waded off into deeper water. She remained content in the shallows, preferring to keep away from the other gangers and near the edge of the pool. She imagined the other new arrivals would be trying to establish their reputations. She didn't want to be targeted or provoked.

When she finished bathing, she moved on to scrubbing her wrap and pants. She was almost done when she noticed the pox-marked ganger who had been staring at her horns earlier had returned to blatantly watching her. Water sloshed against him as he started toward her.

Neva tossed her clothes aside as another man — this one taller and clothed — headed in her direction along the edge of the shore. He was dwarfed by the reeds, but he was at least Neva's height. A woman with chin-length, dirty blonde hair also turned her way.

In her peripheral vision, Neva saw Ballard on the far side of the pool deep in conversation with one of the Ashmount gangers. Debo and Crowe had gone to explore behind the waterfall, and Tavo and Rinaldo were nowhere to be seen, even though they had been tasked with protecting the gang's meager belongings.

The few other gangers in her vicinity scattered, leaving Neva in the shallows with her pursuers. She opened her hands, ready to unleash if necessary. Her natural shield warmed the water, and steam rose around her.

"What're you doin' here?" the woman asked. Her crooked teeth gave her a slight lisp, and her eyes were wild.

"The Da'Valian queen sent you here, didn't she?" The man on shore put his hands in his pockets. His voice was calm and steady. "To make sure we're doin' what we signed on to do?"

"I don't know what you mean," Neva said. "No one sent me."

"Our time isn't up," the pox-marked lad said.

Da'Valian queen... Their time wasn't up... Neva clenched her teeth. It was a miracle that she didn't crack a tooth. Clearly, these three were here for the same reason that she was. Trinizhi must have taken out two commissions for the Mouth.

"I'm sure you have plenty of time left," Neva agreed. "But, like I said, no one sent me."

"Liar," the woman screeched. She launched herself at Neva with her arms outstretched, dirty nails aimed at her throat.

"Hey," Neva shouted, swatting away the attack. Her feet slid on algae-covered rocks, and water crested her collarbone. Panic shot through her in the brief moment it took to regain her balance.

"Rein it in, Cass." The pox-marked lad restrained the woman, pinning her arms to her sides.

"Who does she think she is? We're the Crocuta Crew. We don't need anyone checking up on us." Cass sprayed spittle as she struggled to break his hold. "I want her gone, Ian. I want her gone right now!"

"Cool down." The pox-marked lad recaptured an arm that Cass had wrestled free. He dragged her, kicking and screeching, to another section of shore.

The Crocuta Crew? Neva hadn't heard of a thieving ring going by the name. Perhaps they were still establishing themselves. She hadn't been out of the game that long, had she?

"No one sent me," Neva said more firmly to the man on shore. She showed him her conviction marks.

He took in the marks, and he withdrew his hands from his pockets. Neva was relieved to see they emerged empty. Dodging flying weapons was one thing, but dodging them in water over algae-covered rocks was a touch more difficult.

"You're not here to check up on us?" he asked, cracking his beefy knuckles.

"No."

"But you are a thief."

Neva swore in her mind and didn't say anything.

His brow furrowed, and his eyes told her he knew the shape of things. "May the best thief win, then."

"If you say so," she replied.

"Neva," Ballard called out to her.

The man's gaze darted to Ballard. "If you know what's good for you, stay out of our way."

Neva tilted her head, acknowledging the threat. The man retreated. She watched him until he reached the opposite side of the pool. United with his crew, he headed up the hill and into the trees. She could respect that they were here to do a job, but so was she, and she couldn't afford to let them win.

"Curse it," she muttered. She dunked her head under the water.

Chapter Eighteen

Tenth Fireside, 1631

Brother Alewiscious,
I suggest you not send any further correspondence until you can
guarantee physical preservation for the Brothers. We are not
interested in hypothetical suppositions. I will, of course, come to
your aid, but you must help me first.

Noridemus

Rinaldo emerged from the reeds mere inches from where the Crocutas' ganger had stood moments before. "You sure make friends fast."
Surprised, Neva slipped on an algae-covered rock and cursed again.

"We watch each other's backs, remember?" Rinaldo grinned. He returned a curved knife to the holster on his belt.

"Hm." She frowned. She prided herself on being aware of her surroundings, but she was exhausted, and by attempting to keep her attention on the three threats in front of her, she'd failed to identify her own backup. "Are you always so stealthy?"

"This is my jungle," Rinaldo said. "I learned to blend in young. Wasn't safe not to."

"I'm beginning to see that." Neva grabbed her clothing and climbed out of the pool.

"They won't be coming back," Rinaldo said. He was watching the Crocutas scale the mountain. "Not today, anyway."

Neva dressed. She would have called her power to the surface again to dry her clothing, but the clouds opened above and released a warm downpour. Ballard and Tavo approached from the other side of the pool.

"My youth has been restored," Tavo said jovially as he lifted a jug to his lips. A white residue painted his goatee when he lowered the jug.

Neva studied him. Surely, he was close to her own age.

"You still look like an old man to me," Rinaldo goaded.

"I'd make you pay for that comment," Tavo said, "but I'm in too good of a mood."

"You see Olivia?" Rinaldo asked.

"Aye." Tavo puffed his chest out. "And she smiled at me."

"Doubtful," Rinaldo said. "My sister has better taste."

"You have a sister?" Debo asked, wiping raindrops from his freckled forehead as he climbed from the pool.

"First things first — my sister is off-limits, got it?" Rinaldo pushed Debo into Crowe, and they crashed back into the water.

"Unless she makes the first move, right?" Tavo asked, his levity dimming. "That's what you said before."

"Unless she makes the first move," Rinaldo said. "Which she won't. Can we stop talking about my sister now?"

Neva bit her lip, trying to ignore Ballard. His expression remained neutral, but he hadn't stopped staring at her since the Crocutas had left.

The Dragonslayers were doing a passable job of integrating her, offering armor and a dip in the watering hole, but she wasn't sure if she could trust them yet. Undoubtedly, her hesitation was tied to being burned by Shaundrazhi, Trinizhi, and Astiand. And even though she didn't want to add his name to the list, some part of her resented Emiliand for not being by her side, too. Sometimes, it was easier to not depend on anyone else — but if she couldn't depend on her aliado, who could she depend on? She buried the budding resentment.

The gang's journey back to their camp was a short one, but it was productive as they collected kindling along the way. The Dragonslayers spread out so they were all in sight of each other. The constant pattering of raindrops landing on giant leaves in the canopy offered a soothing background noise. The foliage higher up held much of the water from reaching the jungle floor, leaving the wood they collected dry.

Neva was expecting Ballard to seek her out, so she kept snapping the branches off a dead shrub as he squatted beside her.

"Have anything you want to tell me?" Ballard asked.

Like what, the truth? she wondered. The details of her deal with Trinizhi were laughable. She barely believed them herself.

Warbler's head twisted from side to side as if he was inspecting her.

"Nothing comes to mind," Neva told Ballard.

The other Dragonslayers seemed oblivious to their exchange. Ballard shook his head, looking down. Looking disappointed, Neva might have said, but he hadn't known her long enough to be disappointed. In his own words, she still had to prove herself.

"You're part of our gang now, Neva," he said. "If trouble finds you, it finds all of us, so I'll ask again. Do you have anything you want to tell me?"

"I can handle myself."

"That's not how things work here."

"Any trouble that finds me won't spread to the rest of you." Neva willed sincerity into her words.

"I truly don't know you, but here's how I see it," Ballard said. "Like all of us, you've done something so terrible that your punishment was banishment to this rock. To die."

Neva flinched.

"Your crimes — thievery, according to your conviction marks — have offended the gods so that they've turned their backs on you and left you at the mercy of the dragons."

She rubbed at the marks on her wrist. Had she offended the gods? Considering the way things had been going, it added up.

"And in less than a day, you're already stirring up trouble with the locals."

"I'm not stirring —"

"I'm not done." Ballard stood and crossed his arms. "I want you to think real hard about what kind of person you want to be. The kind no one would risk their own necks for — or the kind they would risk everything for?"

Neva pressed her lips into a thin line as she watched him stomp off toward their camp. She wanted to punch him, and she also wanted to cry, alone in the jungle somewhere. She'd been that person once, someone worthy, but that had been a long time ago. She wasn't sure she could be that person again.

Ballard was punishing her. Neva wanted nothing more than to sleep until morning, but he had delegated first watch to her, which meant she could get half a night's sleep at best. She mustered her resolve. She'd chosen the Dragonslayers, and this was what it meant to be a part of their gang.

"The wardens are unpredictable, so we never know when they will strike," Ballard had told her next to the campfire. "When they do, we must be alerted as soon as possible. We can't fight all the wardens together, so their hunts are the best chance we have at picking them off."

Neva sighed and leaned out of the path of the smoke that shifted in her direction. She was part of the gang now. She needed to pull her weight.

"What do I do if I see a dragon?" she asked.

"Scream," Valentine said.

"Valentine." Ballard said the ganger's name as if he were calling a dog to heel.

The gang fell silent. Valentine mumbled an apology.

"Crowe will be up after you," Ballard told Neva, reaching for the handholds in their tree. "Unless there's a hunt, nobody wakes me until dawn."

Neva followed him up. The Dragonslayers had constructed wide platforms to sleep upon between the limbs of the tree. Neva kept going past the first landing. She wanted a space to herself and a good vantage for watch duty. Farther up, near the top of the tree, she found a branch to settle down on.

Soon, the Dragonslayers' snores joined the frogs, crickets, and jackals that called out in the night. Both Durant and Valentine snored in fits and starts, Tavo might as well have been sawing through a tree, and Debo emitted a high-pitched whistle with each exhale. It was no worse than the sounds that had lulled her to sleep in the slums of R'shara.

Neva stared up at the sky, thinking of Emiliand painting the gods in the constellations. She would never be able to gaze at the stars again without remembering their private rooftop excursion in Ashford. She wondered where Emiliand was now. Was he looking at the stars and thinking of her at this very moment? Something gently tugged on the invisible thread connecting them. Or perhaps it was her imagination.

The wind kicked up, and gooseflesh sprouted along her neck, putting her on alert. Before her, a black snake swung onto her branch from a neighboring tree. Neva struck out at it with a blast of power so fast that Mari's golden sand form narrowly escaped. The snake writhed and hissed, flames enveloping it. The far end of Neva's branch drooped as Mari materialized atop it.

"Thank the gods," Neva whispered. "What took you so long?"

"What's your hurry?" Mari picked up the smoldering carcass.

"Uh, a blood oath due at the end of Cravell," Neva said.

"Come again?" Mari made a face and poked her pointer finger at the dead snake.

Neva hadn't told Mari what had transpired with Trinizhi, so she caught her friend up on the contract, the Dragonslayers, and the competition.

"Neva, you're the only person I know who would sign a blood contract without consulting a mage first," Mari said.

"An oversight." Neva said. She didn't want to dwell on her mistake. "Besides, I didn't exactly have a mage on hand. Where have you been?"

"Around. I love it here. I may never want to leave." Mari sighed contentedly, gazing across the island, which glowed orange wherever a campfire burned.

"Well, *you* have got to be the only person who feels that way," Neva replied.

"Mayhap," Mari said, tilting her head. "But I'm hungry all the time. I crave what they have here — and over there."

Neva followed Mari's line of sight to Leper Island.

"Mari," Neva said her friend's name more sharply than she intended. "They're sick."

Mari sighed again. This sigh was twice as long.

"I mean it," Neva pressed. "Those people aren't in good health. It would be wrong to feed off them."

"Arguable, but that's a topic for another time," Mari said. "I have something for you."

"What's that?"

"A gift from your guardian. Give me your knife."

"You're working with Astiand?" Neva left the blades the Dragonslayers had given her sheathed.

"Let's just say we came to an agreement," Mari said, holding out a hand. "He told me where to find you."

"Hm." Neva didn't like the idea of Mari working for Astiand, but Neva certainly didn't have any coin with which to pay her, so that left the question: would Mari be here otherwise? "I hope he's paying you well."

Mari shrugged. "Your blade?"

"Whatever he sent, I don't want it."

"That's what he said you would say," Mari informed her. "And he told me to tell you, 'whenever, wherever.'"

Neva's spine went rigid. *Does he know me that well?* Neva wondered. She raised a hand to run her fingers through her hair before remembering she no longer had any. She dropped her arm to her side.

"Those were his exact words?" Neva asked.

Mari nodded.

Neva handed over a dagger, resigned. She'd bargained for Astiand's help once, to save her father. In doing so, she'd promised Astiand a favor: whenever, wherever. Even though she was still upset with him for not preventing Trinizhi from tossing her in the Port Telgard jail, she still owed him.

Mari planted her foot on the snake's head and held the tail end to slice its middle open. She worked something free from its belly. The Djinn passed Neva an oval foxed mirror small enough to fit in her palm. Neva accepted it with two fingers and used a leaf to clean off the entrails.

"You brought me a looking glass?" Neva asked.

"An enchanted mirror that will allow you to speak with him," Mari said. "You're to check in once a day as long as you're here."

Neva's reflection in the looking glass mocked her, but her own moral code wouldn't allow her to renege on the bargain. Her father had taught her better.

"Let's get this over with," Neva muttered, cupping the mirror in her hands and following Mari's instructions to coat the surface in power. White flames flickered over the splotchy surface.

Nothing happened.

"Try thinking about him," Mari encouraged. "How does he make you feel?"

Neva shot a glare at Mari. As a Djinn, Mari would know exactly how Astiand made Neva feel. Bitter. Betrayed. He made her burn.

The mirror flashed, and his face appeared on its surface.

"Nevazhi." Astiand's eyes darted from side to side as if checking to make sure no one could overhear him. "Tell me you're all right."

"No thanks to you," Neva replied.

"What would you have had me do?" Astiand said levelly, as if he expected her rebuke. "It's irrefutable that Trinizhi has taken notice of my preferential treatment of you."

"Does your preferential treatment always bring her to bash majilas over the head and *convict them*?" Neva questioned. Their deal meant she had to contact him, not that she had to be pleasant.

"You have no idea," he said. "I would have prevented both if I'd had a choice."

"Prove it," Neva said. "Tell me what the other side of the contract said."

"I couldn't read it," Astiand admitted. "Trinizhi has been more secretive than usual, and she locked it away as soon as you were incapacitated."

"Then find out," Neva said. "I need to know what I've agreed to."

"It's not going well on the island I take it." Astiand's statement made her want to throttle him.

"No — it's not that." Neva took a deep breath and stopped herself before she rehashed how she'd come to be on the island in the first place. She tried again, more calmly. "I didn't say that."

"So you have things well in hand?" Astiand pressed.

Throttling him would be too kind. Astiand deserved a slow death.

"Did you know she hired another crew to go after the sword?" Neva asked through gritted teeth.

"She did what?" Astiand sounded surprised.

"A crew called the Crocutas," Neva confirmed. "They're not pleased with my presence."

"I didn't know," Astiand said. "She must have hired them a long time ago. Think you can take them?"

"Of course," Neva said. That wasn't the point.

"Very good," Astiand said. "I wanted you to know, I have your sword and your necklace in a safe place."

Neva's hand flew to her jugular, where Emiliand's necklace usually rested. The pendant had become her worry stone, and the sword was the only connection she had to her mother's bloodline. That Astiand had saved the items for her evoked a fluttering in her stomach, dampening her exasperation. She waffled over whether she still wanted to be vexed with him or not.

"I — that's ... you didn't need to do that." She struggled to form the words to thank him properly. Frustrated, she settled for falling back on old habits. "Is that all?"

His eyes softened, and she shifted under his gaze. He wasn't telepathic, so why did she feel like he could reach through the mirror and read her thoughts?

"That's all," Astiand said.

"I'll ... see you tomorrow," Neva said.

"Until then, may Dhianz watch over you," Astiand told her.

As his face faded away, she was reminded of Ballard's words earlier. Lithlorian Island was a blind spot from the heavens. No deities were looking out for her, not here.

But Astiand seemed to be, and she wasn't sure how she felt about that. A childish part of her said it was the least he could do after allowing Trinizhi to hit her over the head and convict her. Or perhaps he was doing it because he'd come to care for her?

Astiand projected a stern outward appearance, but he'd taught her about her people, he'd sat by her sickbed after her firérite, and he'd told her where to hide from Trinizhi. If things were different...

Who was she fooling? Trinizhi made the future Neva envisioned an impossible one. Neva pushed down the fantasy with a groan and covered her face with her hands.

"What do you need?" Mari asked.

"Can you find out where our competition is?" Neva asked. "And uncover their plan? I must get the Mouth before they do, but they've been here longer. They have a significant advantage. I can't have them fouling things up for us."

"I'll find them," Mari said with a salute. She leaped off the platform, transforming into dust. Neva watched her friend fly away. It was a big island, but if anyone could find the Crocutas and discover their plans, it was a Djinn.

Chapter Nineteen

Seventh Vestive, 1644

Dear Elkizhi,

It appears I am coming home a war hero. Bryand, too. We chose well when we agreed to side with the upstart Order. With Dhianz's blessing, this will be my final letter to you and I will see your face soon.

With honor and pleasure,
— Astiand

Bleary-eyed, Neva climbed down from her perch to discover that breakfast was a meal of gamey roasted seagull and raw sea slug. It had been a year since she'd enjoyed her aunt's cooking, but she almost cried from missing the comforts of home as she forced herself to swallow sea slug entrails. Durant had scooped its innards out in front of them, declaring he'd throw it back in the ocean when he was done and that once it healed, they could eat it again the following month.

"These are for you." Ballard handed out three heavy spears to the newcomers. One end sported a metal-tipped point and the other a steel ring.

"We have you properly outfitted now."

Neva wiped her hands on her pants and grabbed her spear. The wood was smooth from use, but the tips had recently been replaced. She spun it around in a figure-eight, picking up speed. Neva recalled Emiliand wielding his staff against the Ceasekin and the renegades. She would need to practice with the new weapon to really know how to use it, but she had some idea.

"When will the dragons make an appearance do you suppose?" Debo asked.

"Good question," Crowe commented. His eyes were red-rimmed.

"The birds will go quiet," Tavo said. "You'll get no more warning than that."

Warbler tweeted a sing-song melody and preened.

"I imagine the wardens will go on a hunt before too long," Ballard added. "They haven't attacked as often the past few seasons. Used to be every day. But we still see them take flight every week or so. When would you say, Tavo?"

"I said to rely on the birds," Tavo grumbled. "Counting on my calculations is a gamble."

"You weren't too far off the last time," Durant said.

"The last time?" Neva asked.

"Tavo's calculations were a few hours off," Ballard acknowledged. "But he gave us the most forewarning we've had in years."

"Needs to be better," Tavo deflected.

"Surely you had some method," Neva said, friendly but serious. If she could learn when the dragons would hunt, then she would know when their lair had the weakest defenses.

"I'm not keen on sharing much with a ganger who has mysterious nighttime visitors while she's on watch," Valentine interjected.

"Nighttime visitors?" Ballard asked.

"Are you saying you saw someone here last night?" Neva challenged Valentine, knowing that it would be impossible to prove. Mari hadn't left any tracks.

"Why didn't you alert the gang?" Ballard asked Valentine.

"I would have noticed a ganger climbing past me, even if I was asleep," Durant said.

With as loudly as he snored, Neva wasn't so sure, but she wasn't about to point it out since he was taking her side.

"Suppose I didn't see anything," Valentine said after a moment. "But I heard voices."

"Maybe it's time to move camp," Ballard said with a frown.

Neva continued to spin the spear, enjoying the weight and balance of it. It blurred in comet trails around her as she considered how she might use the looking glass again without her gang discovering that she was talking with Astiand. If she didn't contact Astiand as promised, he wouldn't be pleased.

"And in the meantime?" Tavo nodded to the newcomers.

"Right," Ballard said. "It's time you learn how to gut a dragon."

Neva shared an excited grin with the other newcomers, forgetting their cringe-worthy meal. Ballard led them to the beach, where driftwood formed the border of a large rectangle in the sand.

"The space you stand in would be incinerated in seconds should a dragon set its sights on you," Ballard told them. "We'll start with sprints, but keep in mind that dragons hunt in groups, so if you make it beyond the range of their dragonfire, you'll do well to keep moving. Watch out for the telsons on their tails, and if you look them in the eyes, you're done for. No creature is capable of escaping enthrall."

"Enthrall?" Crowe asked.

"Picture this: You're on the run. All the critters around you scatter." Ballard raised his hands to the clouds. "A dragon lights up the sky behind you. You steal a quick look. That's when it has you in the death lock. Then, it comes in for the kill, and you're done for."

"How can we fight that?" Neva asked.

"We focus on their horns. Near enough to their eyes that you'll be able to tell which direction they're looking, but you won't be trapped. It's not foolproof, but it's the best way we've learned to fight them."

Ballard launched into the rest of their training, describing the creatures' speed, stealth, and cunning. He sketched a caricature in wet sand and identified their weak points — of which there were few. The heart. The head.

No extremity would suffice if the Dragonslayers' intent was to kill. And a blade had to go under their scales before it could do any damage. Neva almost asked about their horns, but she stopped herself. She had no desire to call attention to her own weaknesses.

After sprinting from one side of the driftwood rectangle to the other no less than fifty times, Ballard declared that they were adequately warmed up. The time to learn to snare dragons had come. To start, Durant and Rinaldo demonstrated how to fashion long ropes into lassos and attach them to the newcomers' spears. Taking down a dragon required skill and coordination, and Ballard showed them a variety of ways they could capture a dragon as a team. Most depended on their surroundings, but Rinaldo's crossbow was their best tool for trapping a dragon's wings.

A dragon could only be held down so long before snapping their ropes, so they practiced tug-of-war in the sand. Tug-of-war against a dragon was no children's game, which Ballard pointed out numerous times. He showed them holds that would be less likely to result in severed hands or limbs. The information kept coming. Dragons were pack animals. They rarely allowed themselves to be cornered. If their gang managed to pin a dragon, it was imperative they went in for a fast kill.

During a brief break, Rinaldo took a turn lecturing the newcomers.

"Lithlorian was the original warden, but no one has seen him in years," Rinaldo said. "We don't even know if he's still alive, so don't concern yourself with him. What you do want to concern yourself with are his offspring. Enoch is the most deadly, and the oldest, but he only emerges for a few hunts each year. Malakai and Lennox, those two are the ones you want to keep an eye out for. They relish wreaking devastation, they're the youngest, still growing, so they're hungry. Then, there's Farakai, Zephyr, Erlach, Andreo, Chaard —"

"They're all male?" Neva asked.

"Aye," Ballard answered. "The island was almost overrun with females a few years back, but one day, they flew away."

"Where did they go?"

Her question was met with silence.

"Da'Valia are no dragons, but we have the same creator," Neva commented. "We harness fire, and our females are often fiercer than our males. Are dragons the same?"

"Not to our knowledge," Ballard said. "But one less dragon is one less dragon, and we can only fight what's in front of us."

Neva nodded slowly. Rinaldo had named seven dragons, and that sounded like plenty to her.

"As I was saying," Rinaldo continued. "They dwell in the spire of the Old Fort halfway to the ashmounts. When the fog rolls in and they swoop down from the lantern of the spire, it's one of the most fearsome things you'll ever see. Until they light fire to your home."

A hush fell over the newcomers. As Rinaldo continued with his lecture, Neva watched him with renewed respect. How many times had the wardens burned his home? Yet he still stood against them.

As each respite came to an end, Ballard would take up their training again, stressing the need for strength, speed, and agility. Upon learning that Neva possessed superior strength, Ballard doubled their workload. All of a sudden, dragging a half-dozen logs down the beach wasn't enough. They needed a full dozen. Their obstacle course, which was a series of trenches in the sand, soon had mounds between every pit.

Warbler flew alongside them as they trudged back and forth. Neva pretended his sing-song calls were those of encouragement, but deep down, she suspected he had a high opinion of himself and had appointed himself as their drill instructor.

She could sense animosity coming from Debo and Crowe as the difficulty of their drills increased. Still, they didn't say anything — possibly because none of them wanted to spur on Ballard's apparent sadistic streak, or possibly because they were all breathing too heavily to talk.

Once Ballard was satisfied they wouldn't 'so easily die' in the next hunt, Neva and the other newcomers were assigned responsibilities for the good of the gang. Weaving nets, collecting food, preparing food, gathering kindling and firewood, mending weapons, maintaining weapons... The list went on.

After a grueling day toting fallen trees up and down the beach, Neva and her companions collapsed in the sand. They hadn't eaten since they'd broken their fast — the island was a two-square-meals-a-day place — and she was dizzy from having burned through the meager provisions. Da'Valia were stronger and faster than humans, but they needed sustenance.

"Day's not done yet," Tavo told her.

Neva lowered the arm she'd thrown over her eyes and glared up at Tavo.

"You're jesting, surely?" Neva asked. Was it too much to hope that he would handle grub duty without her?

He started down the beach. Neva forced her head up to watch him go. He wasn't slowing down, but she couldn't bring herself to move.

"You want to eat tonight?" he shouted.

Her stomach grumbled. She dragged herself up with a groan. Sand showered down around her, eliciting complaints from both Debo and Crowe. She threw an apology over her shoulder as she trotted to catch up with Tavo. Every movement strained her fatigued muscles so they quivered. She cursed Ballard's work ethic. She felt as though she'd spent the entire day in the underground fights back home.

When she caught up to Tavo, she asked, "Is Ballard always like this?"

"You mean the drills?" Tavo asked.

"Yes," Neva winced. "The drills."

"He does like to run the new gangers." Tavo chuckled. "Ever hear of the Army of Onidas?"

"He was part of the Army of Onidas?" Neva asked, impressed. The Army of Onidas hadn't been around long, but they had waged a successful crusade deep in the Serpentine Sea, overcoming all manner of monstrous sea creatures. Or so she'd heard a bard tell once.

"Aye," Tavo said. "Rumor is he came from the Tavish Fleet, but he fought with the Army before they disbanded. The way he trains new gangers, I suspect there's some truth to it."

The beach ended at a series of rocky outcroppings that jutted into the water. They climbed the low cliffs and traversed the tide pools until they came to an inlet where the Dragonslayers had strung a net across in the water.

"Go on." Tavo encouraged her with a shooing motion. "Nothing you can't take care of yourself."

Tavo plopped down against the cliff and cleaned the dirt from under his nails with a pick. He clearly expected her to do the heavy lifting as a new member of the gang, so she begrudgingly got to work. Neva peered over the edge of the inlet. The net was made from thick rope, and it was soaked through. Despite her dislike of seafood and despite barely having the strength left to lift the net, a thrill rushed through her as she spotted bright green crustaceans caught in the webbing.

Tavo chuckled at her squeal of delight. She hoisted the net the rest of the way up before dropping it at her feet. She opened it wide and reached for one of the clawed critters.

"Look out for —" Tavo's warning didn't come soon enough.

"Ouch!" Blood welled between her thumb and pointer finger, and she dropped the crustacean. She cursed as it scurried off the rock and splashed into the water below. Tavo hurried over from his respite.

"Don't let the other —" Tavo gave up on his words of caution as the remaining crustaceans broke free from the net and disappeared over the edge.

Bleeding hand be damned, Neva yanked the netting up to salvage the two remaining crustaceans. She stared at Tavo bleakly through the ropes. He cursed a stream of colorful obscenities that left Neva wondering what a *shizit* and a *pussole* were, although she did have a couple of guesses. Embarrassment climbed her cheeks. She had just made a costly mistake.

"It was an accident," she said quickly.

"I'm sure the others will appreciate that when we're sharing these two for supper."

Her heart dropped. She wasn't used to having others rely on her, and irritation nagged at her for having failed her gangmates. They weren't Da'Valia, but they were just as hungry.

"I won't eat," Neva said, aware that the sacrifice wouldn't make up for her blunder.

Tavo shook his head as he shoved the crustaceans into a net sack, careful of their pincers.

"Just put the net back," Tavo told her.

Neva did as instructed and then followed Tavo to a boiling pit of clear sulfur not far from the trap. If grub duties were a test, she had failed. She tried unsuccessfully to not dwell on her blunder as Tavo demonstrated how to lower the sack into the pit to cook the crustaceans. Afterward, he put her to work bashing them open and removing the meat. There wasn't much.

Neva avoided the glares from the other Dragonslayers when she returned to camp with the fare. She excused herself and climbed to her branch. When she heard chatter begin below, she activated the enchanted mirror. Her expression must have given away her mood because Astiand asked what was wrong as soon as he saw her.

"It's nothing," Neva whispered. As much as she wished she could confide in someone, deepening her connection with Astiand would not be good for him. People who spent too much time around her tended to get hurt. Plus, they didn't have much time before the Dragonslayers finished their pathetic meal and climbed up for the night.

"You'd tell me if something was wrong?" Astiand asked.

She sucked in a breath. Would she?

"Of course," she said slowly. "What did you find out?"

"Nothing yet," Astiand said darkly. "Trinizhi is scheduled to be in extended wartime sessions with the Order in the coming days. I'll have to be with her for much of it, but I may be able to slip away long enough to put the contract under a candle."

"I have to go," Neva said abruptly. She could hear Crowe bidding the others good night already.

"Check in with me tomorrow," Astiand said. "With any luck, I'll know more then."

Neva extinguished the flame in her palm without saying goodbye. She spent her remaining moments awake regretting it.

After another day of Ballard's strenuous training, in which he'd made Neva climb no less than a dozen trees without footholds, she and Tavo had been tasked with trading for eggs in Town. The comforting scent of meat pies welcomed Neva as she trailed Tavo out of the jungle. A collection of lean-tos and outdoor communal areas formed the shantytown, where the majority of gangers regularly gathered to imbibe, trade, launder, and otherwise mimic civilized society as well as they could given their location.

"Steal anything here, and you'll be gutted before you can enjoy the spoils," Tavo cautioned Neva.

She acknowledged his warning with a nod. Members from every gang milled about, so Neva kept an eye out for the Crocutas and kept her hands to herself.

Across the island, gangers were awaiting Docking Day. Many descendants of Lithlorian prisoners became pirates, and they returned occasionally to make repairs, visit, and bring news. Most gangers were running low on supplies, since Docking Day, which kicked off a week of trade with the pirates, hadn't arrived yet.

Tavo explained that Docking Day always took place after the first big hunt following the arrival of a prison ship. The Order had brokered the temporary peace, which enabled Cirandrel's ships to transport goods without interference, the wardens to languish following their meal, and the prisoners to be self-sufficient.

But until the pirates arrived, Town was the primary place that goods exchanged hands. Valentine and Rinaldo were off fetching water, while Durant and Debo were after a bottle of rum. Crowe and Ballard had free time. Their leader was taking Warbler to compete in a songbird tournament, which was the principal form of entertainment on the island. Neva enjoyed a battle between two vibrant Revenant songbirds before moving deeper into Town.

Tavo acted as her guide, sharing details about many of the gangers they passed. Neva saw a blond man they all called the Baker, whose wives and children were baking pies in stone ovens; a group of Harpies, who offered washer services; a smaller group of women, who were operating a smokehouse out of a modified lean-to; Anchorweights, who were performing drunken tricks on a tightrope; and Thatcher, who was laughing at the story one of his gangers was telling him.

Neva tensed as her eyes locked with those of the self-proclaimed king. Thatcher's smile faltered, and he studied her closer. A puzzled frown flickered over his face.

She held her breath and quelled the tension in her limbs. Thatcher stopped staring to say something to one of his gangers. She relaxed. Apparently, Thatcher couldn't place her from their brief run-in so long ago. It was possible that the sight of her horns had been what caught his attention. After all, they had been an ocean away from here when they first met, and her appearance was quite different. Perhaps her luck was changing.

Durant and Tavo conducted a handful of transactions, trading a fishing hook for a bag of salt, rope for rum, and so forth. Durant was an expert negotiator and seemed to get more of everything he wanted. She said as much, and Tavo credited Durant's past as a swindler.

"A past that got me here, so I mustn't've been very good," Durant said wryly before he and Debo split off toward the Anchorweights' open-air pavilion.

A ganger with a blue swath tied around his arm approached Neva as she and Tavo arrived at the Baker's pens, where he had a flock of chickens to supply his meat pies and a side business selling eggs.

"You're to follow me," the ganger beckoned Neva. His teeth were crooked, and his beard was patchy.

"Spyke." Tavo stepped in front of her. "What's this about?"

"Thatcher wants an audience," Spyke said.

Neva dropped her shoulders. It looked like her luck wasn't changing after all. Thatcher must have remembered her.

Tavo grunted. "She goes, I go."

"Fine by me," Spyke said with a shrug. "This way."

He led them through Town to an orbo hut, which was constructed out of the same dark red wood as the trees towering over them and was large enough to fit a dozen people inside.

The gangers in the vicinity were all well-armed and had a darkly suspicious bearing about them that was common in Cul Corner, R'shara's slums, and some squalid parts of the Sorrows. No one smiled. At the entrance to the hut, a man sat on a stump, sharpening a long knife.

"Spyke's back," the man shouted.

"Send him in," Thatcher's voice carried through the opening.

"Leave those here." Spyke pointed at their spears. "Knives and sword, too."

Tavo propped his spear against the side of the hut, and Neva did the same. They staked their blades in the ground.

"They better be here when I get back," Tavo grumbled.

Neva hesitated, unsure of what she was walking into. Tavo cocked a groomed eyebrow at her. She rolled her shoulders back and pushed past the hide.

"Welcome," Thatcher greeted them.

She stared into his steely blue eyes, too cunning for her liking. Thatcher waved away the woman who was feeding him berries off a vine.

"Chameleon," Neva said.

"The one and only," the king replied. He smiled as if she had confirmed something by using the moniker. "The question is, who are you, dove?"

She judged that he was about twice her age. He had the same arrogant bearing she remembered from the last time they crossed paths, when he'd tried to steal her commission straight out from under her.

Thatcher was surrounded by the biggest, burliest men she had seen yet on the island, and the most well-groomed women. Women who, even in this remote location, had scrounged for combs, rouge, kohl, and revealing clothing.

"My name is Nevazhi." She widened her stance.

"So you *are* Da'Valian," Thatcher said, stroking his beard. "Or something close to it. I had wondered with so many horns. Well, regardless, it strikes me that the tables have turned since we last met."

"When we last met?" Neva feigned forgetfulness.

"Come now," Thatcher's tone said he didn't believe her for a second. "You remember me."

"I remember that you were poaching," Neva said, eyeing the men who moved to flank her.

"Ah, but my memory is sharper," Thatcher said. "As I recall, you broke my arm, and I demand repayment."

Her stomach turned to stone.

"That was a long time ago," Neva started, ready to state her case.

"Break her arm," Thatcher ordered.

Neva's blood thrummed, awakening for a fight. Thatcher's men grabbed her and restrained Tavo. She got a couple good kicks in, but the Hand stirred, and the distraction cost her. One of Thatcher's lackeys swung a heavy club down on her arm just below her elbow. The bone cracked. She fell to her knees with a yelp. Tavo cussed at the gangers holding him back.

Neva struggled to dampen her natural response to unleash her power and decimate Thatcher and his henchmen. The Hand wanted to be let loose — and she wanted to let it. But a broken arm was bad enough. If she released the Hand, Tavo would be lost in the blaze, and the dragons would learn that a new power had arrived on the island.

She might be able to take on a good number of the Crown and win, even with only one functioning arm, but not without causing significant damage to the surrounding area and townsfolk — and not without the risk of sustaining more injuries herself.

All of which was decidedly going against her current mission.

Neva whimpered. Gods, her arm *hurt.* She fervently wished she could go back in time and do more than toss Thatcher across the room when he interrupted her heist in Glacier Pass.

"Have you learned your lesson?" Thatcher asked.

"Make no mistake, I will remember this," Neva ground out.

"That's rather the point." Thatcher said. "I trust that you'll steer clear of what's mine from here on out."

Tavo struggled against the lackeys, using more colorful language to curse them, their mothers, and their bedmates. Thatcher motioned to the henchmen. They shoved Neva and Tavo out of the hut and into the dirt.

They had been dismissed.

Chapter Twenty

First Auton, 1644

Dear Elkizhi,

It pains me to pen this letter to a memory, for I do not know if you would be able to read my writing at all. You failed to recognize me when you emerged from your firérite, and that broke what was left of my heart. It seems only yesterday that I wrote to you from the field, so it feels natural to return to it. We miss the sound of your laughter, the sweet melody of your song. Our home is empty without you.

Forever your brother,
— Astiand

Tavo kicked the dirt and grumbled, snatching up his spear and returning his blades to their proper places. Neva collected her own weapons and followed him as he charged down the well-worn path that wove between the Crown's huts. He groused about the Crown's inferiority, loudly, until they were out of earshot of Thatcher's henchmen.

Neva's face was hot with anger and embarrassment, and her arm was throbbing. With her broken finger and her broken arm, she counted herself lucky that she was left-handed. Still, it would be impossible to keep up with Ballard's drills now.

How had she ended up in this mess? If only she'd dealt with Thatcher another way in Glacier Pass, if only she'd had the courage to use the Hand against him and his lackeys... If only.

"Are you all right?" Tavo glanced back at her.

"Da'Valia, remember?" Neva said, forcing false confidence. She was sweating, and her arm was the opposite of all right.

Tavo grunted and veered down a narrow path. "Right. Well, try to keep up, Da'Valia."

Tavo used his long blade to hack away the branches that encroached on the path. Neva kept on his heels to avoid the spider webs.

"Stay back." Tavo stopped abruptly.

"What is it?" She peered over his shoulder.

"See that blue vine there? See how it sways?"

The greenish-blue vine was as wide as her forearm and dangled from the canopy all the way to the jungle floor. As Tavo said, it was gently swaying, yet no wind disrupted the surrounding vegetation. She didn't hear any critters above, either.

"Strangling vine?" she asked.

"Aye." Tavo inched around it and motioned for her to do the same. "Worse than a snake, it'll snare you and feed off your decomposing corpse for months."

"That's disgusting." Neva grimaced.

"Welcome to Lithlorian Island."

In an effort to give the strangling vine a wide berth, Neva slipped on a mossy rock. Her arm jolted, and her vision sharpened. Sweat ran down the sides of her face. She didn't acknowledge the sympathetic expression Tavo directed at her. She was Da'Valian, and this was just a broken arm. She'd survived far worse.

"Ever killed a man, Neva?" Tavo asked.

"N-No." She cleared her throat. "None of them were men."

"More like you, then? Da'Valia?"

"Aye," Neva confirmed. A pale yellow snake slithered across the path behind her.

"Just as well, I suppose." Tavo's conviction mark flashed at her from beneath his cuff. "Fairer that way. I never fought fair. I moved about in the shadows. I didn't want to be well-off, understand. I wanted to be filthy rich. Jewel encrusted cutlery and the like. It made me blind to what I didn't want to see."

"And what was that?" she asked.

"That a deal that sounds too good to be true usually is." Tavo sounded more disgruntled than usual. "The Baroness Fysk — you've heard of the Fysks of the House of Balmoral? She promised me all the riches I desired and more if I got rid of her troublesome husband. She never intended to pay, mind you. Sold the Order on some story about another noble hiring me to do the deed. Later, waiting to ship out, I heard her husband had pissed away their entire fortune. She never had the coin to pay my fee in the first place."

Neva winced. She was intimately familiar with deals that sounded too good to be true. His story was salt on an open wound.

"You trying to distract me, Tavo?" Neva asked.

"Is it working?"

"Mayhap."

"Well, then, let's continue." Tavo stopped where the path split again, unhooked a ceramic jug from his belt, and took a swig. "What about you? What'd they ship you off for?"

"What would you say if I told you I was innocent?" Neva asked.

"I'd say to pull my other leg." Tavo snorted, passing her the jug. "They don't send innocents to Lithlorian. You pissed somebody off."

"I suppose that's accurate." Neva held up her conviction marks and took a sip.

"So what do the Crocutas want with you?" Tavo asked.

They resumed walking.

"I'm not sure." Neva tilted her head. She had the sneaking suspicion that she'd been lured into an interrogation. "Nothing, I hope."

"Well, I've got your back," Tavo said gruffly. "My man will set your arm and give you something to prevent infection. Maybe something to help you heal faster. My advice? Don't let the folly that got you here become anything more."

"Who's your man?" Neva asked.

"Al — Alewiscious — the apothecary," Tavo answered. "Baker's eldest son might've tried to set the bone, but I've seen his handiwork. You can thank me later."

She stalled mid-stride. The apothecary? The strange man with the triangle tattoo that she'd seen upon arriving on the island? Her gut told her that he warranted caution so she almost wanted to decline, but her broken arm was a serious setback. She resumed walking. The break needed tending.

They traversed up what Tavo called 'the ramparts,' which were black cliffs with the ocean battering them below, until the gentle breeze transformed into a bitter, salty wind that stung Neva's face. The orbo trees creaked as they swayed in the wind, and the stench from a rotting animal carcass permeated the area.

"Here we are," Tavo said.

They broke free from the jungle, and Neva took in the monstrosity in front of them. Cubed red laterite made up the walls of the sizable dwelling, and black spears of porous volcanic rock shot out from the ground at a steep slant to form the roof. Spikey black moss and vines with thorns as long as her fingers clung to the building like knotted fishing nets.

Calling upon her Da'Valian sight, she saw the white glow of magic like an aura around the dark glob. It pulsated at her, sending waves of rotting sweetness and an intangible alienness that raised gooseflesh along her arms. Not a rotting animal carcass. Magic. She wanted to run the other way, but an invisible hook pierced her gut and yanked at her, bringing her closer. Tavo banged on the door and pushed it open without waiting for an answer.

Neva stepped inside after him, her feet landing on a carpet of mold. She shuddered as dizziness passed over her.

Insects scattered away, and flickering candles illuminated the space. With all manner of potions, powders, and plants on display, the dwelling reminded her of the hovel of a hedge witch she'd visited once as a child. The witch had given her a tonic to temper her fever, but the woman had also taken three milk teeth as payment. It was not a pleasant memory.

"What's your poison?" a raspy voice greeted them from a shadowy corner.

Neva stared at the apothecary, taking in his long burgundy robes and sharp bone structure. His gray eyes didn't roil with power the way a Da'Valia's did sometimes, but the aura and reek of cast magic seeped from his pores.

Despite having been let out mere days before, the Hand struggled in its cage. The weapon always seemed ready for a fight at inopportune moments. She pushed it back.

"What are you?" Neva asked. He was no mere apothecary.

"I believe I asked the first question," he said.

"No tonic, Alewiscious, not today," Tavo said. "We just need you to set her arm."

"You're a fool, Tavo," the apothecary said, leaning on a cane as he emerged from behind a wooden counter. "Do you know this horned wench could snap you in half without a moment's hesitation?"

"We're working together," Tavo replied, seemingly unperturbed. "Mayhap she'll snap *you* in half for me. What do you say to that?"

Neva pretended that color didn't climb her cheeks, but she rather liked that she had won Tavo's acceptance. She turned her attention to the dried herbs hanging from the ceiling. The air smelled so foul that she half expected to find spoiled game in the rafters.

She spied Alewiscious's triangle tattoo again, and it hit her — the Obsidian Brotherhood. Neva took an involuntary step back as the apothecary moved about his lair.

"You're a mage," she said.

"She has a keen sense about her, Tavo." Alewiscious poured water from a blue glass bottle into a ceramic mug and placed them both on his counter. "One might wonder why she's saddled herself with the likes of you."

"How did a mage end up on Lithlorian?" Neva asked. The Obsidian Brotherhood would never allow one of their own to be taken prisoner — and the island was Order territory.

"How did a Da'Valia?" Alewiscious shot back, pinning his gaze on her horns. "If that is what you are."

"It is," she said.

"Humph." The sound was disparaging, but Alewiscious's irises turned inky. He steepled his fingers, giving her the impression that he was pleased with her answer.

She narrowed her eyes. She didn't like him one bit.

"May I?" The apothecary inspected her arm.

Neva steadied herself against the counter as another wave of dizziness washed over her. Stomach acid climbed her throat.

"What's your assessment?" Tavo asked.

"It's a clean break, just below the elbow," Alewiscious said. "You're lucky."

Neva winced. Lucky wasn't the term she would have picked.

"With some of my reparation elixir, it should heal in no time, though I can't say how long. I've never treated a Da'Valia before." Alewiscious gathered more items, moving with a grace that belied the supposed need for a cane. He added leaves to a mug before handing it to Neva, along with a stick.

"Heat it and drink," he said. "It'll speed up the healing. And the stick's for biting."

Neva called her power to the surface, warming the mug. At the eruption of flame, Tavo jumped away from her and cursed. She ignored the sensation of the mug tugging on her power, and extinguished the flame. *Strange*, she thought. But then, everything about this place was unusual.

"I'll be damned," Tavo said. "The stories are true."

"I often find a string of truth in every tale of lore," Alewiscious said. The corners of his lips turned down. "And I did warn you."

Neva had a niggling sense that the apothecary was disappointed. He had no reason to be as far as she knew, but she failed to shake off the hunch.

"As soon as Ballard finds out you can do that, your drills are going to get a lot more interesting," Tavo told her.

Neva downed the bitter tea and placed the mug on the counter, channeling the pain from her arm to avoid gagging.

"Tavo, hold your friend still," the apothecary instructed.

"My name is Neva," she told him.

"Bite on the stick, Neva," Alewiscious said, not missing a beat.

Neva did as instructed, and Alewiscious wrenched the bone into place. Neva jerked and bit down so hard that the stick snapped in half. Tavo fell backward.

Neva spit the splintered wood onto the moldy floor. "Great Dhianz, that hurt. Sorry, Tavo."

"I'm fine. I'm all right. A slip. That's all." Tavo scrambled to his feet and knocked on his breastplate.

"What do we owe you?" Neva asked the apothecary. Her tongue was heavy, and her stomach roiled.

"Depends. You're not a virgin, are you?" Alewiscious scrutinized her.

"Not that it's any of your business, but no." Neva conjured a fiery glare.

"A shame," the apothecary said. "Been awhile since I had virginal blood to cast with."

The image of Alewiscious pouring blood into a cauldron rose unbidden in her mind. She swallowed, her spit tasting sweet. She was going to throw up.

"Tavo, can you pay the man? I can't stand it in here." Neva clapped a hand over her mouth and darted for the exit.

Outside, Tavo caught up to her and pounded her on the back as if it was helpful.

"Apothecary's potions can knock you on your butt, but they can also do a world of good," Tavo commented.

"I hope that's true." Neva wiped her mouth on the back of her hand. So far, she wasn't impressed.

"You're less green already," Tavo remarked.

"What do I owe you?" she asked.

"I haven't decided yet," Tavo said, scratching his head. "The apothecary charges Dragonslayers less than other folk, since we're the only ones that'll take a stand against the wardens, but that cost me my last good fishing hook."

"What if I light all our fires?" Neva asked.

"Ballard will have you doing that anyway." Tavo barked with laughter. "C'mon. Let's get you back to camp before that tonic really kicks in."

Chapter Twenty-One

Third Auton, 1644

Dear Elkizhi,

Privacy is a luxury I no longer have, and I cannot condemn myself, so this message will burn before it ever reaches you. What I will write would have shocked you. I have aligned with Trinizhi. Our donazhi is powerful and persistent, and I cannot believe that I once felt sorry for her. I had thought her lonely, but who would want to be friends with one as manipulative as she? She threatened you, Little Elkizhi. Not in so many words, but the threat was there all the same.

There was a time when I thought that all I would need to do to honor Dhianz was my power and skill on the battlefield, but I have learned that I need to be more cunning. Bryand, too. I'm not certain what our donazhi used to persuade him. Corazhi was permanently maimed, and perhaps that was his tipping point. Regardless, we're both a part of Trinizhi's alliad now, and there's no way around it.

Vivi will no longer speak to me. She won't even look at me, and the truth is, I cannot blame her. Trinizhi made her watch when we aligned. ...Vivi has applied to lead an expedition to the Nacien Islands, and I'm afraid that as her commander, I have no reason to deny the request. And I'm afraid that as her friend, I endorse it.

With little pleasure,
— Astiand

At the base of the Dragonslayers' tree, Neva burned with fever under a threadbare blanket Durant had lent her. By the time she and Tavo rejoined their gang, her eyelids had drooped and her limbs had weakened until she could no longer stand. She was supposed to contact Astiand, but the effects of the apothecary's healing tonic meant she couldn't raise her head without the jungle spinning around her. She was vaguely aware of her gangmates guzzling rum around the fire next to her, but she didn't have the presence of mind to socialize.

When she'd stumbled back into camp, an arm draped over Tavo's shoulders to hold herself up, Ballard ordered her to sleep on the ground. Neva had collapsed next to their campfire, avoiding the stares of her gangmates. First, she'd caught the attention of the Crocutas, then she'd squandered their supper. Now, Thatcher had broken her arm and she couldn't even keep herself upright. If she were her gangmates, she wouldn't think very highly of herself either.

"It's time we cut the dead weight," Valentine whispered in the tree above later that night. "The Da'Valia is more trouble than she's worth."

Neva strained to hear more. It was obvious Valentine didn't like her, but she wanted to know what the others would say.

"Did you have such an easy time when you first arrived on the island?" Ballard asked.

"You've heard the stories," Valentine insisted. "We all have. Da'Valia are dangerous to have around. And now with Thatcher? She's a burden."

Neva willed tears of self-pity to stay put. It figured that Valentine was the first to suggest what they must all be thinking, but that didn't make it any easier to hear.

"I see what you're doing, Valentine, and I'll not stand for it," Tavo said. "I know exactly how you like to *cut* dead weight. She's indebted to me, so unless you're prepared to make good on what she owes, leave her alone."

"She carries a log all right," Debo said. "I don't mind having someone on the team with enhanced strength if we're fighting dragons."

"Durant?" Ballard asked.

"The nets can be tricky if you're not used to them." Durant spoke as if deep in thought. "But I am concerned about whatever past she has with the Chameleon, and whatever's stewing with the Crocutas. That's a lot of unknowns."

"Rinaldo?" Ballard called on the native.

"My mother always said Da'Valia were created for battle. Seems premature to dispose of her before seeing how effective she is against the wardens."

"Crowe?" Ballard asked.

"Can any of *you* carry a tree?" Crowe responded.

The gang fell quiet. Someone took a swig from a bottle.

"The wardens will attack any day," Ballard said. "I didn't spend all this time training Neva for nothing. I hear your concerns, Valentine, that she may be a liability. If that turns out to be true, I'll deal with it."

"We should deal with it now. While the creature is incapacitated." Valentine's voice rose.

"She can make fire," Tavo said. "That's a talent we should exploit, not turn our noses up at."

"We all can start a fire," Valentine said. "That's no reason to keep her."

"That's not what I said," Tavo corrected. "She can call fire into being on a whim. It answers to her."

Someone cursed and another — Rinaldo? — murmured a prayer for protection.

"This discussion is over," Ballard said firmly. "Everyone has shared their opinions on the matter, and I've decided. We'll give her a few more days as a Dragonslayer, see how things play out. Stand down, Valentine."

"You're too soft, Ballard," Valentine said bitterly.

"And you're a cold-hearted bastard who likes to use a blade on anything without a prick," Tavo shot back. "But you don't see us trying to be rid of you just because we don't like you."

"I said, that's enough," Ballard said. "I'll confirm that Thatcher is appeased. Go to bed. Sleep this off."

Neva waited until she heard the medley of snores coming from above before dragging herself, half-delirious, off into the jungle. She didn't go far. She would need her gang to think she was relieving her bladder if whoever was on watch saw she was gone. Plus, she had to fight to remain upright for the few steps she took.

She hunkered down behind a tree, her heart pounding. She wiped her sweaty brow and cupped her hands around the looking glass. It was very late, and if Astiand was asleep, he might not be thrilled that she was reaching out. She thought about the times she'd seen his ire rise before. His desire. His passion. Warmth spread low in her belly, and she chided herself. He was undeniably alluring, but he was Trinizhi's aliado. He was embroiled in Da'Valian politics. He was, to put it simply, a bad idea.

Why did the bad ideas always sound so good?

Neva sighed and rested her head against the tree behind her. Astiand did not appear in the mirror. She waited another few moments. Why did she feel so hollow inside? Did seeing Astiand really mean that much to her? She slid the mirror back into her wrap. Then, she stilled. Could the looking glass connect her to Emiliand? She didn't have anything to lose by trying.

Please work, she pleaded. She called on her power again, letting white flame heat her palms and flicker over the mirror. She recalled parting ways with Emiliand, huddling with him in the path of a sandstorm, seeing him for the first time in so long in R'shara, sharing her power with him on the rooftop in the Sorrows. Gray smoke swirled on the face of the looking glass, and her heart leaped. The smoke faded. The face of the mirror remained empty.

A hand wrapped around her neck and squeezed. Neva's eyes shot open, and she sluggishly went for a knife before she recognized that a steel dagger was pressed against her cheek. She froze and squinted at the beady brown eyes mere inches from her own.

"Quiet, little dragon," Valentine whispered, his breath reeking of spirits.

The Hand pounded on the walls of its vault. *Use me.*

With effort, Neva called snow into her landscape to cool the Hand and pushed it back.

"What do you want?" she asked Valentine.

"Now there are the words I've been waiting to hear you say," Valentine said, breathing faster. He squeezed her neck and kept the knife tip pressed below her eye. "Next, I want to hear you whimper."

"Get off me," Neva demanded.

He didn't seem to hear the threat in her voice.

"Or what?" Valentine asked, grabbing the place where her arm was fractured.

The pain was a hot poker. Her blurry vision sharpened, and her nausea receded.

"Use me," the Hand whispered again.

Neva's fingers twitched. She was committed to keeping the Hand contained, yet her own power could do plenty to incapacitate Valentine. The question of what would happen afterwards was the only thing that stilled her. Dealing with Valentine might prove his point about her causing trouble for the Dragonslayers.

A silhouette appeared in front of the fading embers in the fire pit.

"Don't make me gut you, Valentine." Ballard spoke dangerously low. He pressed a rusted, curved blade to Valentine's side.

Valentine released Neva's arm and twisted away from Ballard. The pressure of the blade on her face disappeared, but not before the tip nicked her cheek. Neva rolled away from Valentine, coming up into a crouch. Spots swam in her vision, and she struggled to keep herself from falling over.

"She's a menace," Valentine said, saliva flying. His attention jumped between Neva and Ballard.

"And you're a dead man." Neva manifested two burning orbs.

To his credit, Ballard didn't appear distracted by the appearance of her power. He held up a hand, suggesting she hold off on harming their gangmate. She started forward and tensed, lifting the orbs higher.

"You're no longer welcome here," Ballard said to Valentine.

"You won't kick me out," Valentine refuted. "I've been with you for years."

"Wouldn't I? You should know I could never stand for this," Ballard said. "Leave."

The Dragonslayers stared each other down. Finally, Valentine turned toward their tree.

"I said *leave*," Ballard reiterated.

"What about my things?" Valentine's eyes bulged.

"Count yourself lucky that you're leaving with your life." Ballard kept his blade pointed at Valentine.

"You'll change your mind when the next hunt happens," Valentine said.

"No, I won't."

Ballard didn't budge. Neva swayed. She couldn't remain standing much longer, so she flung a burning orb at Valentine's feet. He jumped and backed hastily into the jungle.

"We better not see you around here again," Ballard shouted after him.

Neva shot another orb at Valentine's heels as he retreated. As soon as he disappeared from sight, she dropped to her knees.

"What's going on down there?" Durant called from above.

"Nothing," Ballard answered. "Just settling a dispute."

"Valentine?"

"Aye."

"Taken care of?"

"Aye."

"G'night then."

Ballard's eyes found Neva's. She didn't imagine he was happy to lose a ganger with such low numbers to begin with, so she was surprised when he fetched the blanket and covered her with it.

"You look terrible," he commented.

"I've been better."

He took a seat on the boulder next to her.

"Rest up," he said. "I'm on watch the rest of the night. You and I are going to have a long talk in the morning."

When Neva awoke the next day, everyone except Ballard had gone. He reclined beside the fire pit, chewing on ingo stalk and staring into the trees. Warbler was serenading him with a lively, up-tempo tune. The air was hot and moist, smelling of damp earth, and gray clouds shrouded the island.

Neva wiped the dew off her face and pushed herself into a cross-legged position. She froze. Her arm throbbed with a dull ache instead of the sharp pain she had expected. She held her hand in front of her, flexing her fingers. She gently rolled her arm back and forth.

Her bones would undoubtedly ache for some time to come. Otherwise, she felt as good as — no, *better* — than she had since arriving on Lithlorian. Her scalp was no longer tender, and she had enough energy to run laps around the island. Uneasiness settled over her despite her appreciation for such a gift.

Ballard's eyebrows lifted as his attention shifted to her. "Apothecary must have trained in the dark arts."

"Or some such thing," Neva agreed with a frown. Alewiscious had said he'd never given the tonic to a Da'Valia before, so anything was possible. Still, the speed with which it had taken effect seemed too good to be true, a happenstance which made her nervous. Her stomach growled. She was so hungry she could eat a bucket of sea slug innards without a second thought.

"Where is everyone?" Neva asked.

"Training at the beach," Ballard said. "It's time for our chat."

Neva swallowed.

"The seed of doubt has been planted," Ballard continued. "Last night, Valentine made a case for why you shouldn't be a part of the gang. I insisted you get the same fair shot as the rest. I need you to prove me right."

She let out a slow exhale and nodded.

"You'll be on grub duty again with Tavo today," Ballard continued. "Try not to let any charubes escape."

"I won't," she agreed, annoyance arising at the reminder of her blunder.

"Your little demonstration last night impressed me. Starting now, you're going to use your power for the good of the gang. Daily, for our fires, and we're going to train you up to use it against the dragons."

"I can do that." Neva cringed, feeling like she was being chastised by a teacher.

"Any other special talents you care to let me in on?" Ballard asked.

She hesitated. She wasn't willing to use the Hand if it meant more people would die, so she couldn't tell him about it. "I can throw a knife and do this..."

She murmured the incantation to awaken her invisibility spell. Nettles stung the length of her neck and inside her throat. A genuine smile overtook his weathered face.

"You've been hiding more than I suspected," he said, petting his mustache.

"It didn't come up in conversation," Neva replied, dropping the disguise. "It rarely does."

"Right," he said wryly. "That brings me to my final stipulation. You have until this time tomorrow to come clean about whatever quarrel you have with the Crocutas. I don't want another situation like we had yesterday with Thatcher."

Neva nibbled on her bottom lip. She could trust Tavo, but the others?

"What if I don't?" she asked.

"Then you'll have proved me wrong." Ballard tossed his ingo stalk into the fire. "And I hope you won't do that."

Chapter Twenty-Two

Fifth Fireside, 1644

Dear Elkizhi,

I get a strange sense of comfort when I write to you, even though I now burn every letter I write. With mother dead, you locked up, Vivi turning away, and being bound in an alliad that neither Bryand nor I want, my life has turned from dream to nightmare. It pains me to have become this person, and I'm not proud of it. I will finish my term as a commander and then move firmly into the political realm. I am confident that I can act honorably by doing our donazhi's bidding as is expected, but I fear I will not like it.

With little pleasure,
— Astiand

Upon Ballard's insistence, Neva moved their camp while the other Dragonslayers trained. Valentine was the type to seek retribution, Ballard told her, and so their camp was no longer a safe haven. They scouted and selected a new location not far from the Revenants. Their new camp was high enough on the side of a hill that they would be able to defend the space properly.

"This'll do," Ballard said, kicking a lava rock back toward a deteriorated campfire ring.

The trees in this part of the jungle bore black scorch marks, although the foliage was vibrant and green.

"Dragons?" Neva asked, gesturing to the scorch marks.

"Undoubtedly, but that was before my time," Ballard said with a shrug. He reached for the handholds in the trunk of a nearby tree. A couple of the old platforms were still tied to the branches above. "I'm going to get some shuteye. You can finish moving camp."

"Alone?" Neva asked.

"I pulled a double shift on watch last night," Ballard replied. "And besides, I think you can take care of yourself, Firechild."

Neva made a face at him. In the old stories, Firechild had been a poor boy at whom other children would throw stones. During a long and deadly Fireside, his family on the brink of freezing, the boy prayed to the god of fire to help warm his family. Teonets gifted Firechild with the ability to start fires with his mind. Firechild saved his family and provided warmth to villagers across the countryside. His brothers and sisters had never gone hungry again. The parallel Ballard implied made Neva uncomfortable. Firechild had been a hero. She was just a thief.

With a sigh, Neva got to work. She'd had too few moments to herself on the island, so she wasn't about to pass up the opportunity to enjoy some solitude. She still wasn't sure what she was going to do about Ballard's ultimatum, and she had some thinking to do.

She dropped the belongings she had carried from their original camp and headed back to collect their hidden desirables. She was well past her deadline for checking in with Astiand, since he hadn't appeared in the mirror the night before. Halfway between camps, quite certain she was alone, she stopped next to a burned-out tree hollow and ducked inside.

She pulled Astiand's looking glass from her wrap and cupped it in her hands. She bit her lip. Neither Astiand nor Emiliand had answered last time, and what was worse, she didn't know who she'd wanted to answer more.

She shook her head to clear it. Her love life hardly mattered unless she made it off this island. She thought of what it was like to lose herself in kissing Astiand, to ride into battle with him. Her power flared to life, the mirror brightened, and his face rippled into focus.

"Nevazhi." The crease between his eyebrows smoothed.

"Astiand."

"I was worried when I didn't hear from you." Astiand cleared his throat. "Are you all right?"

"A minor complication, that's all."

"What happened?" His voice deepened.

"Old business," she said. "It's finished now."

She shifted under his scrutiny. She didn't want him to think less of her for finding herself at the mercy of humans. Any Da'Valia would count allowing Thatcher to throw his weight around to be an embarrassment. Not to mention Valentine getting the drop on her, even if she had been under the influence of Alewiscious's concoction.

"I hope that's true." Astiand's tone was rife with worry. "You must return with the sword by the end of Cravell."

"What is it?" Neva asked. He'd found something.

"I read the rest of the contract."

"And?"

"It's not good."

"Come out with it then." Neva couldn't help rolling her eyes.

"Your power will be forfeit."

The ground dropped from under her. The looking glass tumbled into the moss as she reached out to steady herself. Neva closed her eyes and counted to ten, ignoring Astiand calling her name in the background. When she could breathe again, she picked up the looking glass. First things first.

"Would this be instead of indentured servitude?" she asked.

"No."

"Is there any chance you're wrong?" she asked.

The look he gave her said he was insulted she asked, but all he said was, "No."

The string of curses that ran through her mind would have made Tavo proud. Her power couldn't be forfeit, not if she wanted to complete her mother's work. But that dream was drifting out of reach. If the Crocutas got the sword and returned it to Trinizhi, then the magic of the blood contract would ensure Trinizhi got the Hand and the Eye from Neva. Trinizhi would effectively command all three prongs of the Trishula.

"Figure out how to break it," Neva demanded.

"No one can break a blood oath," Astiand said.

Neva pinched the flesh on the inside of her arm. The pain helped, but only enough for her to think of one possible way out of her predicament.

"Seek out Benjamand Da'Xana-Escriva. Tell him what happened. He'll help. I know he will." Neva massaged her temples. If anyone could sever the binding magic of a blood contract, it would be Benjamand. As for whether or not he would help her... Neva couldn't be certain. "Tell him — tell him our mothers would want him to."

Astiand was quiet.

"Say you'll do it." Neva tried to mask the sound of fear in her voice.

"Your focus should be returning with the sword," Astiand said. "If there were a way to break a blood contract, no one would use them anymore."

"Astiand, so help me gods," Neva said through her teeth. "If you don't go to him first thing and get down on your knees to beg for his help, I will never speak to you again."

"Nevazhi —"

She threw the looking glass into the jungle with all of her might so that she wouldn't hear whatever else he was going to say. Fear and anger warred within her. Fear of what was to come, and anger at herself for having stumbled headfirst into Trinizhi's trap. Neva had been so certain she could trick Trinizhi... Neva felt like an amateur.

She had mere hours before Ballard would kick her out of the gang if she didn't tell them all why she was on the island. And she hadn't learned enough about the dragons to infiltrate the Old Fort on her own.

With a moan of frustration, Neva walked in the direction she'd thrown the looking glass. She was going to need the confounded thing so Astiand could tell her when he found a way out of the blood contract. Unfortunately, the jungle had tried to swallow it up. She spent over an hour searching for the mirror.

After she pocketed the device, Neva went about moving the rest of the Dragonslayers' goods — their food stores, armor, and bedding. Thankfully, her gangmates had taken their personal belongings and weapons to the beach. If she had to move their smelly socks, she would have revolted.

Once Ballard awoke, they joined the rest of the gang on the beach, and Neva ran sprints with Debo and Crowe to get out some energy. As the late-afternoon rains cleared up, Neva and Tavo separated from the main group to check their nets. They both cursed when they arrived at the inlet. The rope that awaited them on the rocks had been severed, and the netting was nowhere to be found.

"I'll kill Valentine when I see him again," Tavo declared, red in the face.

"You think he did this?" Neva asked.

"I know how that louse operates." Tavo yanked the remnant of rope free and chucked it into the sea. "Besides, who else would tamper with our nets?"

"Thatcher?" Neva ventured, but the self-proclaimed king's maliciousness seemed opportunistic, not scheming. Breaking her arm had been a quick strike against a newcomer who had bested him before, establishing his dominance in the hierarchy. He wouldn't keep coming for her. That left... *The Crocutas?* She didn't dare voice the thought aloud.

"Humph," came Tavo's response.

"What are we going to do?" Neva asked. She had moved the remainder of their food stores earlier that day. They had crumbs left.

"Dig for sand crabs, I suppose," Tavo said bitterly. "Let's head back to the beach."

The heavy fog creeping in from the sea blocked the sun, making the hair on the back of her neck stand up. The wind kicked up, carrying a taste of the ashmounts, and the island grew cold. As the other Dragonslayers came into view down the beach, the birds serenading the jungle fell silent.

Neva lowered her center of gravity and gripped her spear with both hands. Her eyes flew to meet Tavo's.

"Run," he whispered.

Chapter Twenty-Three

The dragon's roar pushed down on them, rattling Neva's teeth as she ran across the sand. She lost a fraction of ground with each step, but she didn't dare change her trajectory. A shadow flickered over her, and the Hand stirred.

Too close. The dragon was much too close.

Ahead, the Dragonslayers stopped mid-drill and spun in their direction. They abandoned much of their gear and ran for the tree line. Warbler shot after them.

"Use me," the Hand urged her.

She matched Tavo's pace. He huffed beside her, pumping his legs at a speed that was astonishing for a human. The fog rolled over them, so thick that she couldn't see the dragon, but she could hear its wings flapping.

The sole Dragonslayer still on the beach ahead, Ballard shouted and gestured frantically. The wind pulled away his words before they could reach her, but the expression of horror that took over his face next didn't need translation. Neva threw herself into Tavo, sending them both rolling into the sand.

Tavo's profane shriek died as the dragon finished its stoop in a spray of sand and razor-sharp talons in the exact spot they'd just been. The dragon pivoted and shot back into the fogbank. Red scales flashed amid the fog, then vanished.

"Malakai," Tavo uttered, his mouth hanging open.

"You can thank me later, Old Man." Neva yanked Tavo to his feet by the front of his gorget.

"I'm not your grandpa," Tavo huffed, apparently uninjured.

Tavo grabbed his spear out of the sand, and they darted for where the Dragonslayers had gathered at the edge of the jungle. Rinaldo had propped his large crossbow against a tree growing in a V. He had one of his impressive arrows notched with a length of rope hanging off the end. Rinaldo's gaze tracked the flashes in the clouds back and forth across the sky. Ballard arrived last.

"You called it," Ballard told Tavo. "The hunt is on."

Tavo grunted, but didn't let his focus stray from the heavy gray clouds — as if he could see through to the dragons if he wanted it badly enough.

Another roar sounded in the jungle, shaking the ground under Neva's feet. Her power hummed to the surface.

"They're behind us," Debo called, spinning to face a threat none of them could see.

"Malakai is young," Durant spoke up. "He may have acted prematurely. From the sounds of it, the hunt is just beginning."

A single scream pierced the air.

"To Town," Ballard shouted.

As if he had done it hundreds of times before, Rinaldo kicked his crossbow off the tree and swung it over his shoulder. He carried the arrow in a fist as he sprinted for Town, apparently not sparing it a second thought. His single-mindedness reminded Neva that he had family on the island. Tavo swept up one of their practice nets, and the rest of them followed Rinaldo in formation. On the edge of Town, they split into two groups.

As they'd practiced, Neva, Ballard, and Tavo moved toward the center of the village, and the others sought out higher ground. Gangers and their children fled the area en masse, abandoning their trees and their belongings, dashing from huts. Neva saw tears running down children's faces, but aside from a few sobs escaping, many of the gangers were eerily silent as they ran, mouths covered.

The sound of wings slicing through the air warned Neva before a spray of flame erupted over her head in a giant *whoosh*. She dropped to the ground with the other Dragonslayers, and the fiery attack enveloped one of the Crown's huts. The flickering fire reflected on the dragon's dark cerulean scales as the creature latched onto a tree and launched back into the air. It disappeared into the mist.

Neva regained her footing and peered into the cloud cover. *Where are you?* she wondered. The cerulean dragon reappeared in a nosedive. She raised her spear and ran forward. She failed to find a good angle before the dragon plucked a fleeing convict off the ground.

Blood poured from the punctures, and the ganger screamed.

"Use me!" The Hand railed against its prison.

Neva's grip tightened on her spear. The townsfolk continued to flee, trampling over anything in their way. There were too many people. It was too chaotic.

Lizard-fast, the cerulean dragon took off into the fog again. The Dragonslayers pushed against the crowd, scanning the sky.

"How many are there?" Neva asked, hoping her more experienced gangmates might know.

"There's no telling," Tavo said grimly.

"There," Ballard shouted.

Malakai's lethal form emerged from the fog. He circled them. Neva followed the arch of his back with the tip of her spear, but she didn't have a good shot. He was still too far away. Her gaze skipped to Rinaldo, whose crossbow had better reach, but his arrow was still nocked. Neva pulled her power to the surface. She didn't want the wardens to learn that a Da'Valia was in their domain if she could help it, but if her life was threatened, she wouldn't hesi —

"Break," Ballard shouted.

They lurched away from one another, abandoning formation. Neva threw up a rudimentary shield behind her as she ran at a hut, kicked off the side of it, and used her momentum to catapult herself atop the neighboring structure. She pulled herself up. Malakai screeched and shied away from her blazing shield, his attention shifting to easier prey: Ballard. The dragon pounced, snapping its impressive teeth as Ballard leaped head-first into the opening of a burning hut. Malakai crashed into the hut after him. Neva let loose her spear.

The weapon struck at a severe angle, sliding between the scales to pierce dragon flesh. It held, giving her hope for a moment, before falling free. The dragon roared at the assault. Neva flung herself off the hut and smacked into the ground. She narrowly escaped a catastrophic spray of fire that engulfed the hut she'd been standing atop.

"Oi, Neva," Rinaldo shouted. He took his shot.

The dragon's roar told her the arrow had found its mark. Ballard struggled free from the burning shelter with a guttural sound and rammed his own spear, net affixed, into Malakai's other side. The dragon bucked, flinging him away like a rag doll, and roared again.

Neva darted underneath the enraged creature and went for the arrow embedded in its upper thigh. She grasped the dangling rope from Rinaldo's arrow. She attempted the same maneuver she'd used to scale the hut, but Malakai thrashed about too violently.

Debo and Crowe taunted the dragon in the distance. They threw their spears, springing away as soon as Malakai turned in their direction. Assuming that was the best distraction she was going to get, Neva grabbed the arrow and swung herself up. She straddled the dragon without a firm hold.

Frantically, she pulled the end of Rinaldo's rope through Ballard's net. She dropped off the other side and yanked the rope around the nearest tree.

"Dragonslayers, to me," she called.

She planted her feet against the base of the tree and pulled until her muscles were at the point of tearing. Her gangmates soon crowded her and lent their strength. Everyone — save Ballard and Durant — was pulling the rope, forcing the dragon to remain grounded.

Malakai roared again and flared his free wing in an attempt to take off. Durant dove between the dragon's legs and shoved his spear under Malakai's scales, into his chest. The rope held.

"Pull," Ballard shouted.

The Dragonslayers redoubled their efforts, cinching the net and forcing the dragon lower onto the spear. Neva's heart jumped as she spied a fray in the line of rope. Malakai bucked. How much longer could they hold him down? If he escaped, the rest of the wardens would learn that a Da'Valia was on the island, which meant she would lose the element of surprise.

Malakai roared again. Neva wanted to believe the cry sounded feeble. The rope was cutting off the circulation to her hands, which reddened with blood. Crowe's eyes were wide. Debo smelled of urine. The rope slipped. Durant heaved the spear up again. Malakai keened. Black tar-like blood gushed from the wound. With the angle of his spear, there was a good chance Durant had nicked the heart.

"It's not going to hold," Ballard shouted. "Everyone, take cover."

Durant rolled clear. The Dragonslayers released the rope and hurled themselves into the seclusion of the jungle. Malakai shook off the netting like a dog shakes water from its fur. He launched off, his body heaving with every bat of his wings. His movements were sluggish, and blood continued to flow. Malakai crashed into the treetops in an attempt to fly out of the canopy.

"Look," Neva called out.

The Dragonslayers turned in time to see the great beast twist and falter. Branches cracked and snapped as Malakai tumbled to the jungle floor.

Shrill cries sounded from within the fog, distinct at first, then blended into one awful vibrato. Neva covered her ears. Shadows flashed among the clouds as the wardens sought the body of their fallen comrade. Their cries transformed into a haunting funeral song.

Neva and the Dragonslayers huddled in complete silence, waiting for the dirge to end. They stayed that way for so long that pins and needles prickled Neva's legs. She and her gang couldn't see Malakai from within the dense jungle, but they could hear the dragonfire erupting after the keening faded. An orange glow painted trees on the other side of Town.

"And nothing will remain of a dragon but ash," Durant murmured as if reciting from memory.

"Quiet," Ballard ordered in a stage whisper.

The Dragonslayers watched the wardens take flight and circle over Malakai's remains. The wardens glided off.

"It should be safe now," Ballard said.

Neva stood and shook out her legs. She couldn't recall when night had fallen. Slowly, the Dragonslayers headed back to Town, except for Neva and Tavo, who was watching her closely.

"Something wrong?" Tavo asked.

Neva bit her lip, the truth of her situation sinking in. She had no chance against the wardens. Not on her timeline. Besting Malakai — the youngest and least experienced warden — had taken all of the Dragonslayers working together, and they'd only narrowly accomplished it.

Stealing the Sword of Elon and returning it to Trinizhi before the summit by herself was out of the question. She needed help. She might even need a miracle. But at the very least, she needed the Dragonslayers on her side.

Tavo patted her shoulder awkwardly when she didn't answer.

"No one will judge you if you need a moment," Tavo told her.

"Tavo." Neva shrugged off his touch and pulled herself to her full height. "I have one question for you."

He raised an eyebrow at her.

"How would you like to be filthy rich?" Neva asked.

"I'm going to need a fresh pair of pants," Debo was saying as Neva and Tavo rejoined the gang at the site of their scuffle with the dragon.

"You smell the same to me." Tavo guffawed while Debo glowered at him.

Neva rolled her eyes. She hoped her cousins grew up to be more mature than her gangmates. Her gaze landed on the black puddle of dragon blood. Was it only virginal blood that mages coveted, or was other blood — say, the blood of a dragon — equally as appealing to them?

"Crowe, toss me your jug," Neva said.

With a dubious expression, Crowe removed the jug from his belt and handed it over. Neva poured out the water and used a leaf to scoop black dragon blood into the container.

"Uh, do you expect us to eat that?" Debo asked, glancing up from rewrapping a long scrap of material around a gash on his leg.

"I have a hunch." Neva was shaking with excitement. If she was right and the apothecary required blood for his magic, dragon blood had to rank above virginal blood, didn't it? They may have just gained an important negotiating tool.

"What are you up to?" Ballard asked.

"We're getting off Lithlorian," Neva replied, plugging the bottle. "I didn't want to say anything before, but I think I know how to do it."

"Say that again," Durant said.

"Tell us about it later," Ballard cut in. "When there aren't so many lugs to hear it."

Thatcher emerged from the jungle opposite them, approaching with a cadre of spear- and torch-toting gangers following in his wake. He held his arms wide and turned, taking in the scene and behaving as if he'd orchestrated the chaos at the same time. Despite the charred remains and smoldering structures, his attention ultimately landed on the Dragonslayers.

"Ah, and here are the men of the hour," Thatcher proclaimed.

Neva wiped her hands on the mossy ground and fastened Crowe's jug to her belt. Ballard and the others stepped in front of her, as if blocking her from Thatcher's view could prevent hostilities between them.

"How shall we thank our saviors?" Thatcher asked no one in particular. "Spyke, see if there is any rum left in the underground. That ought to do nicely."

Spyke scurried off.

"We're not going to have any trouble here are we, Thatcher?" Ballard asked.

"Trouble? Of course not." Thatcher's smile failed to reach his eyes. "I believe your thief and I understand each other. Besides, half our huts are still standing. We owe you our gratitude. Let's leave our bygones in the past."

"Glad to hear you say it," Ballard replied.

"Now, shall we go see our prize?" Thatcher strode off toward Malakai's remains. "It's not every day we take down a warden."

Neva frowned at his use of the word 'we.' Ballard turned his head and shook it slightly, telling her — or maybe all of them? — to let it go. Warbler reappeared and landed on Ballard's shoulder, trilling furiously as if recounting the action.

The warden's metal scales had been reduced to a molten puddle. Raindrops hissed when they landed, and steam rose to meet the fog around Malakai's sable ribcage. Ash drifted away on the wind, taking the scent of smoke and charred meat with it. The dragon's skeleton soon became a spectacle as more Town residents returned to salvage what they could.

Neva looked away from the tears on their faces. This island was a job for her, but this was their life. The huts that had burned were their homes. The people who had been eaten were their friends. The items they had lost were tools for their very survival. Yet as more of them gathered, she saw their fear give way to relief, which manifested in music, dance, and food. The gangers didn't wallow in what was lost. Rather, they reveled in what they still had.

Neva pondered that as the Crown, and other gangs alike, celebrated the Dragonslayers, showering them with gifts. Buttery roasted gulls. A loaf of bread. More bottles of rum than they could drink. Neva tore into the stale bread. A substantial meal wasn't something she'd enjoyed in a long time, so she made it count, savoring the salty flavors, varied textures, and the contentment that followed.

Before long, the black dragon bones cooled. Neva dared to touch a femur, amazed that dragon bones didn't burn to ash. Children pretending to be Dragonslayers scampered over the remains and scaled the ribcage with excited shouts. An Anchorweight chased them, growling and flapping his arms, holding the edges of his cloak to appear as though he had wings. Tavo, a bottle of rum in hand, shooed them away.

Declaring that the skull would fetch a high price on Docking Day, Tavo called over Ballard to help him secure it away from the children. Tavo made sure Rinaldo's sister was watching before he puffed his chest out, flexed his biceps, and squatted down with Ballard to lift the colossal specimen.

Throughout the revelry, Neva's gangmates' eyes returned to her. Ballard had been more than patient with her already, and they wanted answers. As soon as the Crown's presence dwindled and the gangers around them succumbed to the lull of rum, they hauled the skull to the beach, where they collected their belongings. Neva led the way, using her power in place of a torch.

The rain cleared, taking the fog with it. When they reached their camp, with its new vantage, she could see clear to the ashmounts.

"I'm here on a job." Neva came out with it. "A job that will make us all very rich."

Durant and Debo sat down, Debo still favoring his injured leg. Crowe and Rinaldo exchanged a look. Ballard waited expectantly. She took a deep breath. This was her chance to persuade them to join her quest.

"What kind of job?" Ballard asked.

"A dangerous one." Neva was honest. "But also the kind that could see you off this island with gold to boot."

Dragons were famous for hoarding treasure, and she only needed the sword. That meant there would be plenty of other riches to go around.

"You've been here less than a full season, yet you aim to do what countless others failed to?" Durant asked. "What makes you so special?"

"You saw my shield in Town," Neva pointed out. "But I can do more. Here, Debo, let me see your leg."

Neva knelt next to Debo and removed his makeshift bandage. A ganger had gifted him with an old pair of pants, but he still smelled faintly of urine. She rolled up a pant leg and washed the wound. She instructed him to press the flesh back together and summoned her healing flame, sealing the cut. Debo jerked but stayed in place. Crowe walked over to poke at the pink scar tissue. Neva's gangmates had been curious before, but they turned rapt.

She pressed on. "Have you heard of Dhianz's Trishula?"

"The weapon? Isn't that a myth?" Rinaldo asked.

"What about it?" Ballard asked Neva.

"I have the second prong," Neva said.

The Dragonslayers glanced around as if confused.

"Where?" Rinaldo asked skeptically.

"It's inside me," Neva said.

Rinaldo took a step back. He pressed his thumbs together and splayed his fingers out on one hand. The sign to call Ailish, the goddess of courage and protection.

"Prove it." Durant crossed his arms.

"This does seem far-fetched." Ballard stopped short of calling her a liar.

"All right, fine." Neva manifested power in front of her again. It wasn't the Hand, but she didn't think any of them would know the difference. "Pick a target."

"That tree," Ballard pointed at a massive orbo tree that grew not too far away.

"No," Durant pushed down Ballard's arm. "The rock face."

Moonlight shone on the light gray rock face that protruded from the hillside in the distance. There was a chance her power would burn up before reaching it — and that was if her aim stayed true over such a distance. *This is your* only *shot,* she reminded herself.

"No problem," Neva said. She bit her lip.

So far, the Dragonslayers had only seen a fraction of what she could do — healing fire, an unrefined shield, and small orbs. If she managed to hit the rock face, she would be immensely proud of herself, and she would impress the Dragonslayers enough to win their help. They could pull off the job, and she could return to Cirandrel victorious.

But if she missed and was cast out from the gang, she wasn't sure she would be able to feed herself let alone infiltrate the wardens' lair.

Neva grew the hovering sphere, feeding it more power but leaving the Hand locked away. Determined, she pulled her arm back and flung the sphere forward in a lofty arc, willing it to stay on its intended trajectory. Its tail streaked across the sky. The fireball slammed into the rock face and burned out. She would expect to see scorch marks in the morning.

Neva looked back to find Debo and Crowe with their mouths hanging open. Durant wore an undecipherable expression. Tavo clapped.

"Huzzah," Tavo exclaimed. "A myth my arse. You've been holding out on us."

"Great Dhianz," Durant murmured. "We might be getting off this gods-forsaken rock."

Neva would never say so, but she saw tears glisten in his eyes.

"If we're lucky and we work quickly," she said. "Yes, my aim is to return by the end of Cravell."

"That was quite the show," Ballard spoke up. "Anything else you'd care to share before we consider what you've told us tonight?"

Neva didn't have to ask if he was referring to the incident at the watering hole. She wouldn't get his vote unless she earned his trust.

"I want to be forthright before you agree to this," Neva said. "You all should know, I was hired to steal the Sword of Elon, but so were the Crocutas." She filled them in on what had transpired at the watering hole. "I have someone working on that."

"You've a partner?" Ballard asked.

"A friend," Neva said. "She'll ferret out their plan."

"She won't get far," Rinaldo scoffed. "Cass has a reputation for being overly suspicious."

"Mari will."

"How do you suppose?" Ballard asked.

"She's Djinn."

"Those are real, too?" Rinaldo went pale.

"As real as I am," Neva said.

"Is it true they can take over our bodies and make us do whatever they wish?" Debo asked.

"Aye," Neva said. "But she won't. I'll vouch for her."

Neva hoped Mari wouldn't make her regret the promise. The Djinn was a bit of a wild card, even if Astiand had employed her to assist Neva on Lithlorian.

"What about the blood?" Crowe asked, eyeing the jug.

"There's one person who made it off the island, right?" Neva asked.

"The apothecary," Tavo sat straighter on his log. "Al *is* a connoisseur of exotic substances."

"You all said he severed the magic in his marks? We can offer to exchange dragon blood for him doing the same for us."

The Dragonslayers' chatter died out.

"Men, let us consider this offer and all it implies." Ballard beckoned everyone over.

Neva tapped her foot as they huddled. Her gaze roamed, and she found herself staring at the eye hollows of the dragon skull across from her. She shivered, trying to ignore the sense that Malakai was peering out at her from the Underworld.

"I will not die here," Durant told the other Dragonslayers. "Nine years, I've been looking for a way back. In all that time, Neva is the best shot I've seen."

Crowe and Debo blanched when Durant had said 'nine years.' Hope sparked in Neva's chest.

"I like the sounds of this as much as the rest of you," Ballard said. "I have some unfinished business I've long waited to attend to on the mainland, but finding passage back to Cirandrel won't be easy."

Ballard cocked an eyebrow at Neva. She shrugged in response. She didn't have a solution for getting back to the mainland.

"Does that mean you're with me?" Neva asked.

Ballard glanced around at the Dragonslayers a final time.

"Aye, we're on board," Ballard said. "But we need the apothecary to agree as well. Otherwise, we're sunk before we've begun."

CHAPTER TWENTY-FOUR

Second Vestive, 1645

Dear Elkizhi,

Trinizhi's favorite method of persuasion is coercion, so letting anyone get too close only gives her more material to use against me. These are the lessons I am learning. How to oppress those who are weaker. How to evaluate allegiances and use people as leverage. With each new task I am burdened with, I find myself clutching at the remnants of my honor. This happens more often than I care to admit. I never know who is listening, so I have no one with whom to share this plight, save for these letters, which turn to ash almost as quickly as I write them.

Your brother,
— Astiand

In the hours between Neva's demonstration and the first rays of sunlight peeking between the ashmounts, she lit a fire and the Dragonslayers gathered around. They agreed on new safety measures — among them, moving about in teams of three and four. They wanted to meet Mari, and

Neva assured them that the Djinn would check in soon. Ballard announced a new training schedule, which included double sessions. If she could make a braided shield, he said, she could weave a net. He showed her the basics and had her practice with her power.

Tavo whistled between his teeth. "I see why this queen of yours hired you."

"She's a donazhi," Neva said bitterly. She knotted off the row of netting that she'd been working on and let her power fade.

"Right, let's go see the apothecary." Ballard set his empty rum bottle down.

The trek to the apothecary's hovel had seemed to take forever the first time, but it flew by the second. Despite the fact that they hadn't slept in more than a day, the Dragonslayers tittered with newfound excitement.

"First thing I'm going to do when I get back is find my wife and show her a good time," Debo fantasized.

"I'm going to check in on my mum," Crowe said. "She had gout when they dragged me in, and I haven't seen her since. I'm not sure the local healer would mix a tonic for her after what I did."

The Dragonslayers fell silent. They all had people back in Cirandrel.

"What about you, Rinaldo? First time on the mainland — you must have some idea of what you'd like to see." Tavo hacked down a branch blocking their path as he addressed the younger ganger.

"Not sure I care as long as we make the wardens suffer," Rinaldo said thoughtfully. "Suppose I'll find employment somewhere, try my hand at a regular job."

"You could always fall back on dragon slaying," Neva teased. "Plenty of need for that."

Rinaldo grabbed a handful of stickers off the bush next to him and threw them at her.

"Hey," she exclaimed. The stickers decorated the front of her wrap. He laughed as she picked them off and threw them back at him. Suddenly, she knew what it was like to have brothers.

With a sigh, Neva rubbed her nose. The scent of damp ash and sweat permeated her clothing. As they traipsed through the jungle, she wondered if taking down Malakai might have earned them all a complimentary dunk in the watering hole. But she didn't imagine the Dragonslayers would be inclined to make another trip to the watering hole anytime soon. They were consumed with the promise of escape.

Nausea swept through her as they approached Alewiscious's stone cabin. The Dragonslayers gathered around the door as Tavo banged against it.

"Out of bed," Tavo shouted. "You've got company, Al."

"Tavo?" A latch released with a *clunk* on the opposite side of the door, and Alewiscious's raspy voice carried to them from beyond. "What's happened?"

Alewiscious poked his head out.

"Excuse Tavo," Durant said politely. "We're in need of your services, good sir."

"Good sir?" His eyebrows rose to his hairline. "This must be serious."

The door swung open, and the Dragonslayers filed into the hovel, coming to stand across from Alewiscious. The old mage hunched over his cane and inspected them.

"What is it you want?"

"There's a story that's been going around," Ballard said, frowning at the bottle of preserved toads that sat upon the shelf next to his face. "We're wondering if it's true."

"Ah, I take it you mean my daring escape." The corners of the apothecary's mouth tugged up to reveal rotten teeth.

"Indeed," Ballard confirmed.

"So, is it true?" Tavo asked. "Can you break the magic in our marks?"

"Can I?" the apothecary asked. "I'm the only one who can. The question is what do you have to offer? This particular spell took me decades to develop. You've done nothing but disturb my morning."

"Dragon's blood," Neva said with a ring of pride.

"And?" Alewiscious asked.

"Loads of it," Neva clarified, removing the jug from her belt and placing it atop the counter. *Shouldn't that be enough?* she wondered. Alewiscious made no move toward it.

"We're willing to negotiate, of course. What's your price?" Durant stepped in front of the jug.

Neva tried to keep breathing evenly. He sounded too eager.

"You couldn't afford my services," Alewiscious declared. "But we might come to an agreement. Tell me, what's your plan for escape?"

"We'll have passage aboard a ship," Ballard said. "We intend to outrun the wardens."

"Is that so?" The apothecary scoffed.

"Aye," Durant said. "We're going to loot the wardens' keep, Neva is going to hold off the dragons, and we will sail far, far away from this rotten island."

"You think this horned wench is going to hold off the dragons?" the apothecary asked. "Tavo, you're even dumber than I thought. She's Da'Valia, she's dangerous, and she could incinerate the lot of you, but she does not stand a chance against the dragons."

"We've seen what she can do," Rinaldo refuted. He crossed his arms defensively. Debo and Crowe nodded in agreement, and a blush climbed Neva's cheeks.

"I'm sure whatever parlor tricks she showed you were awe-inspiring," the apothecary told them. "But her power is nothing against them."

"We took down a dragon just last night," Neva said.

"I said, *nothing.*" The apothecary came forward and leaned into her face. "Taking down one is nothing. You're prepared for death then, young one?"

His eyes, the whites aged yellow, held hers.

"I am," she bluffed.

"We'll make it out alive," Tavo butt in. "She's Dhianz's Hand."

Neva flinched.

"Tavo," she said his name sharply. She hadn't wanted to share her secret with anyone else, but perhaps the situation called for it.

Alewiscious staggered back, leaning against his cane and staring at her like he … wanted to own her? Greed was written across his face. It made her want to high-tail it off the island, conviction mark or no conviction mark.

"Well, that changes things, certainly," the apothecary murmured. Beads of sweat decorated his forehead despite their dank surroundings. "But perhaps you might clarify? Where is it, exactly?"

"I carry the Hand, and it answers to my will." Neva shot an annoyed look at Tavo.

"The dragons won't know what hit them," Tavo boasted, oblivious to her censure.

"I can begin working on the spell today," Alewiscious said. "But for me to remove your conviction marks, you'll need to fetch something first. Visit Leper Island. Find Ebenezer Tavish — Ballard will recognize him — and persuade him to give you six beads of obsidian salt. Then, bring them back to me. I'll accept your offering of dragon's blood." Alewiscious pulled the jug toward himself. "And you'll take me with you when you leave the island."

The Dragonslayers erupted, everyone sharing their opinions — loudly. Ballard didn't know an Ebenezer Tavish, Debo thought an old man would hinder their getaway, and no one wanted to go to an island they might not be allowed back from. Durant let out a shrill whistle. The commotion stopped. The former swindler spat on his palm and stuck out his hand.

"We have an accord," he told Alewiscious.

They shook on it.

Warbler serenaded the gang as they trudged back through the jungle. Even though Alewiscious's terms were different from what Neva had expected, her mood lightened. A day trip to Leper Island and an additional passenger for their escape was a fair enough trade for their freedom.

"It's time we talk about how we're getting back to the mainland," Ballard announced. "We promised the apothecary that we'd secure passage."

Warbler twittered as if he didn't appreciate being interrupted. Ballard acknowledged Warbler's masterful vocal control, then returned to the matter at hand, asking if anyone had any ideas.

"I'll check with my contacts and see if anyone has the space to take us on," Durant spoke up. "Docking Day will be our best chance to arrange passage. There will be no shortage of pirates to negotiate with, and they're all plenty used to evading the Order. We'll just need to convince them that Neva can fend off the dragons."

"I could get word to Myles," Rinaldo offered, swatting away a caterpillar that swung onto his cheek from a nearly invisible thread. "See if the Channel

Siren will take us on."

"The Channel Siren is too slow," Ballard countered, using a large curved blade to hack away at a strangling vine that reached for him. "No point in fleeing from the wardens if the Order will just catch us on the open ocean and bring us back."

"The Ezmerelda is fast," Tavo said. "We ought to see about getting aboard the Ezmerelda."

"Zeerust and his crew are just as likely to gut us and take the treasure for themselves," Ballard said. "We'd be better off with a captain who doesn't have a reputation for disappearing people. Not to mention that if we approach the wrong ship, we may give up valuable information to the Crocutas. We need to be cautious."

"Or mayhap a little reckless?" Neva proposed. At the dubious looks Ballard and Rinaldo gave her, she continued on. "I'm just saying, yes, we should think things through, but no one else has ever done what we are about to do. We can't expect to succeed without being daring."

"I'd wager no one is working with Merrick," Durant said thoughtfully.

"Mad Merrick?" Tavo scoffed. "Everyone knows the Sandpiper changes direction on a whim."

"He *has* never been caught," Ballard said.

"The Dancing Sandpiper is one of the fastest ships around," Durant said. "Mad Merrick didn't get his name by being cautious."

"He outran the Order in the Razor Straits a while back, didn't he?" Crowe asked. "It's a miracle they made it out alive. We should find a sane captain if you ask me."

"Well, no one did," Durant snapped. "You'd be hard-pressed to find a pirate who isn't peculiar in one way or another. Anyhow, I'd gladly trade my claim to sanity for my freedom, and you should do the same."

Crowe narrowed his eyes at the swindler, making Neva wonder if she was going to need to jump between them and break up a fight.

"You leap into battle with dragons, yet you think you still have a claim to sanity?" Crowe asked, deadpan.

A beat passed. The Dragonslayers laughed, dissolving the tension.

"Merrick has a skilled enough crew and a fast boat," Durant said. "I say we present an opportunity he can't turn down."

"What about the Fleet?" Debo asked as they arrived back at camp. "Would any of their ships have us?"

The veteran Dragonslayers regarded Ballard uneasily. Their leader's expression had turned grim.

"We, uh, we don't deal with the Tavish Fleet," Tavo said.

Interesting, Neva thought. She dusted the splinters off the top of a half-rotted log and took a seat. With Ballard's tattoos and his history with the Army of Onidas, she hadn't expected him to have strife with the most powerful pirate families in the Tyvse Sea. Perhaps his tattoos only told part of the story. Or perhaps a falling-out with the Tavish Fleet was why he was on Lithlorian in the first place.

"So the Dancing Sandpiper it is." Mari materialized next to the empty fire ring with a flourish of sparkling gold dust. She shook out her long black ponytail. Gold flecks fell, disappearing before they hit the ground.

Tavo spewed out the mouthful of water he'd just taken a sip of, and the rest of the gang lurched away. Without giving it a second thought, Neva quickly embraced the Djinn.

"We're hugging now?" Mari asked, blinking as if bemused.

"I was beginning to wonder when I was going to see you again." Neva was careful to avoid saying 'if.' She wanted the Dragonslayers to continue to operate under the impression that Mari could be a trusted member of the team.

"Mari, I presume?" Ballard asked.

"The one and only," Mari declared, flipping her ponytail over her shoulder.

Neva made quick introductions, and Mari waved her fingers in greeting. The Djinn sauntered around the fire pit, halting in front of Rinaldo.

"Hello, there," Mari purred, her tongue flicking out to taste the air around him. "Aren't you a sight to behold?"

Rinaldo stiffened, glaring at the Djinn. "Stay away from me."

"Must I?" Mari asked longingly.

"I told them you wouldn't possess them," Neva admitted.

"Neva." Mari pouted.

"We're working together now." Neva scooted over to make space. "Have a seat. We're glad you're here."

"Speak for yourself," Rinaldo said, backing away from their visitor.

"Isn't this one delightful?" Mari asked, giving Rinaldo an exaggerated wink. "And he has a delectable aura."

"What did you discover?" Neva asked Mari. She was hoping for some good news.

"The Crocutas are embedded with the Anchorweights," Mari announced, plopping down. "And they're worked up about you, that's for sure."

"Good." Neva smiled. The more distractions for her adversaries the better. Gods knew she had enough of her own problems.

"I'm not so sure it's good for you," Mari told her. "Cass has a mean streak, and she talks about you an awful lot. Have any trouble with your fishing nets lately?"

"That was the Crocutas?" Tavo asked.

"Aye," Mari said. "A ganger named Val gave them the tip a few days ago."

Valentine. Neva clenched her jaw.

"A few days ago you say?" Ballard asked.

"Did the right thing, kicking him out," Rinaldo said bitterly. "He was still in the gang a few days ago, which means he betrayed us to get rid of Neva."

"People do stupid things when they're afraid," Crowe commented. Neva got the sense he was speaking from experience.

"One might argue that the decisions we make when we are afraid are the decisions that count the most," Ballard said. "He'll get what's coming to him."

Warbler voiced his agreement.

"Likely, since they've teamed up," Mari agreed. "Cass is quick to temper, and Ian is hardly any better. If they weren't family, they'd have turned on each other by now."

"Have they arranged passage to Cirandrel?" Neva asked.

"In a way. They've spent much of the past year fixing up a boat that ran aground on the other side of the island," Mari informed them. "It's small, and it doesn't require any additional crew. Their conviction marks are fake, so their plan is to sail away and keep the wardens' treasure for themselves, with the exception of your relic, Neva."

"I bet the ship is the Fairline," Tavo told them. "It's been grounded for a couple of years, so it might not take much to get her sailing. And she's small enough for a three-man crew, if no one sleeps."

"Small, but not fast," Ballard said matter-of-factly. "And a three-person crew against the Tyvse Sea? The Fleet would pick them up in no time. Or the Order."

"Speed might not be very important," Mari added, twirling the ends of her hair through her fingers. "They have explosives stockpiled."

"Explosives?" Neva echoed.

The Dragonslayers all started talking, hypothesizing about the Crocutas' plan and quizzing Mari on how the explosives were guarded. Ballard shouted to get them to settle down.

"You have been busy," Ballard said, giving Mari an appreciative look. "Anything else we should know?"

"Rumor has it that pirates have already been spotted off the coast," Mari said. "They'll start arriving tonight. The Crocutas are conspiring to kill Neva on sight at Docking Day tomorrow."

"Is that so?" Neva asked dryly.

"I'd like to see them try." Debo cracked his knuckles.

Neva's lips twitched. She'd been thinking the same thing. She regretted not having done more than singe Valentine's heels the last time she'd seen him, but she could always make up for that.

"They won't have the chance, not if I have anything to say about it," Tavo chimed in.

"Now, now." Ballard made a shushing motion. "We can avoid them easily enough. This is not the time to pick a fight or get distracted. This —" he paused dramatically — "is time to train."

The Dragonslayers groaned on cue.

Chapter Twenty-Five

Second Vestive, 1650

Dear Elkizhi,

My head is spinning. I met someone this evening, and I think she is the one our mother made me swear to protect with her dying breath. She resembles Monazhi, making me think for a moment that I was seeing a ghost. Nevazhi is nearly full grown but only just coming into her power. It seems some cruel joke the gods have chosen to play on me at this moment in time, when my alliad is rife with discontent. I've failed to sleep at all this evening, and dawn is approaching. If the half-breed survives her firérite, I've no idea what I will do with her.

Your brother,
— Astiand

Neva found it disconcerting to walk about in the middle of the day without a shadow. Usually, she used her invisibility glamour in darkness or near-dark, but after Ballard had ordered her to stay behind with Mari in an effort to keep things peaceful at Docking Day, she decided to deviate from her modus operandi. He was being unimaginative. She could easily attend without anyone finding out. She followed on Debo's heels in her invisibility glamour, her attention pulled in all directions. Docking Day was a spectacle.

A mess of ships, ropes, and pulleys transformed the shoreline. Pirates scraped barnacles off their ships' hulls, bird masters battled their songbirds, and gangers traded for stolen goods, restocking their stores. Gangs and crews alike performed recitations, plays, and poems. The Baker's children ran toasty pies from their stone oven in Town to the beach. Rum bottles littered the sand. The island was 'toasted,' as her Pa would say, by noon, with fights breaking out, numerous Anchorweights dozing in their hammocks, and lovers pairing up.

Neva crept behind the Dragonslayers as they came to a stop at the pier, where the Dancing Sandpiper was moored along with the Ezmerelda, the Interceptor, and several others. Neva's lips parted when she saw Mad Merrick's crew forcing him to walk the plank.

Mad Merrick waved his arms in an animated fashion and adjusted his floppy leather hat. His crew jeered and cheered him on, one of them poking him with a long stick. Mad Merrick teetered. The wind caught his hat, tipping it off his head, and the cheers doubled.

The taunting was too friendly for an authentic plank-walking, Neva surmised. Nevertheless, the theatrics were dangerous. She had heard the screams from the convicts that jumped into the water upon their arrival. The creatures that dwelled in this part of the Tyvse Sea enjoyed human flesh.

Neva held back a gasp as Mad Merrick reached for his flyaway hat. He yelped and tumbled off the plank, free-falling and hitting the water with an impressive splash. A second figure followed Merrick off the ship. A woman dressed in trousers, a loose tunic, and a fringed vest arced into the water like a seabird, her dark dreadlocks flying out behind her.

The Dragonslayers hurried to where Mad Merrick stumbled out of the waves, his hat once again atop his head, dripping seawater along the brim. The woman who followed was more graceful. For a moment, her skin glistened like a fish's scales. Neva called on her Da'Valian vision but failed to see the glow of magic around the woman. Still, she hadn't imagined the scaly iridescence. The woman might look human, but she was something supernatural. She plucked an eel from the water and chucked it back into the sea.

Meanwhile, Mad Merrick spun in circles, punching the water like a — well, like a mad man.

"I told you — I'm unscathed." Mad Merrick laughed victoriously. He grabbed one of the large flesh-eating fish he'd punched and tossed it onto the beach as if he'd done so many times before.

"This guy is our way out of here?" Crowe asked.

No one answered. Neva wondered if they should have taken Mari up on her offer to possess the captain and orchestrate their escape. But Mari didn't have any sailing experience, and Durant had insisted that, while Mad Merrick had a reputation for being deranged, the captain wouldn't turn them down. If he did, Mari had free reign.

On the shore, Mad Merrick snagged a cloudy glass bottle from a crewmember and took a long swig before shoving the man away. Chatter from the crowd of pirates muddled the air, with bouts of laughter breaking through the baseline hum. The Dancing Sandpiper's crew moved up and to the far end of the beach.

The Dragonslayers stood by as the crew propped up an old wooden target on the edge of the jungle and dropped crates of goods in the sand. If Neva squinted at the target, she could make out a handful of splinters that were still red in the center, but the rest of the wood had been nicked and bleached by the sun so it had no color left.

She recognized those nicks. She and her friend Mikel had spent many hours throwing knives in her father's basement before they'd started competing in tournaments, and their targets, tree rounds from the Garen Warehouse, had looked much the same when they were done with them. Aunt Margret had called their activities time misspent, but Neva's knife-throwing skills had come in handy more times than she could count, so she begged to differ.

"Durant, you're up," Ballard said.

Durant mingled with the crowd of pirates, greeting those he seemed to know as he went, and a knife-throwing competition got underway. Neva watched as the crew took turns throwing against their captain. Their methods went from precise and tame to theatrical and dangerous as time wore on and the crowd's enthusiasm grew. A pile of empty rum bottles was accumulating, half-buried in the sand.

Each time Durant tried to approach Mad Merrick, someone would stop him — namely, the woman with the dark hair. Since emerging from the water, she had added a belt with an impressive sword affixed to her ensemble. She bounced on the balls of her bare feet while she tapped her fingers on the hilt as if she was itching for a swordfight.

"Genivra looks extra feisty today, doesn't she?" Rinaldo commented, passing a piece of melon to Ballard.

"Don't let her hear you say that," Ballard said, holding the fruit so Warbler could eat the seeds before he took a bite.

Neva nearly failed to hold back a sigh as Mad Merrick performed a trick she had seen him do twice already, where he stood on his head and threw a knife as he flipped to his feet. The crowd went wild, hooting and hollering.

She glanced at the Dragonslayers. Were none of them going to do anything? Mari was dancing in her dust form in the wind channels above them. Honestly, she'd been up there so long, it looked as if she'd given up on them and was playing with the seagulls.

Mad Merrick won his next throw, too. Neva wondered if the crew was afraid of besting their captain. It seemed unlikely that none of them would be any good. And that was unfortunate because it seemed that the crazy captain was inclined to keep throwing until his arm fell off. Confident he would fatigue soon, Neva locked her fingers and twiddled her thumbs to pass the time. She nearly fell over when Mad Merrick switched from his right hand to his left hand and *kept throwing.*

Neva checked for the Crocutas or Valentine. She didn't see them, and her gaze landed on Ballard instead. She respected him when he wasn't being unimaginative. She didn't want to draw his ire. But someone needed to do something. The way things were going, Mad Merrick would still be throwing come the end of Cravell.

Durant raised his arm in salutation and called out to Mad Merrick again. The action prompted Genivra to shove him backward, the rum in her bottle sloshing out. Neva clenched her teeth. The Dragonslayers tensed, and Durant's face turned a peculiar shade of crimson.

Neva'd had enough. Not interested in examining the flare of defensiveness that arose on Durant's behalf, she acted on instinct and darted into the jungle. She dropped her invisibility glamour and emerged next to Durant. She placed her hands on each of his arms, steadying him.

"Are you all right?" she asked quietly.

"What are you doing here?" Durant checked over his shoulder at Ballard, who was glowering at them.

"I want to throw," Neva said loudly.

"What's that? A new challenger," Mad Merrick exclaimed. He swaggered over from the throwing line and inspected her. "Hm... I'm not sure I like the looks of you."

"Looks haven't a thing to do with it," Neva said, squaring her shoulders. "I'm a good shot."

"How good?"

"Better than you," Neva replied.

He chortled and shot her an admonishing look. "Be gone with you."

He started back toward the throwing line.

"Oh, I see," Neva said. "It's all right. I understand... if you're afraid." She waited. She was taking a gamble. A big one. But she'd been watching the captain from afar for well over an hour, and he didn't seem the type to let a public slight go unanswered.

"What did you say?" He stopped walking.

"Well, now, Merrick," Durant rushed to console. "She didn't mean it. Everyone knows you have courage in spades. Ignore her. We just want to talk."

"Durant." Neva turned to her gangmate. "I did mean it, but it's all right. He's too nervous to go up against a Da'Valia, and, well, he should be."

"I'm not —" Mad Merrick spun to face her again. She had him. Neva flashed him a cocky smile.

His eyebrows drew together.

"You want to talk, Durant?" Mad Merrick tapped the flat side of a knife on his palm. "What shall the stakes be then? Methinks we should make it interesting. For instance... claim the victory and you can bend my ear, but fail and I keep yours."

He made a sawing motion with one of his knives, guffawing as if he'd told the joke of the century.

"Genivra could fashion me an earlobe necklace." He swiped tears of laughter from his cheeks.

"Certainly, Merrick." Genivra's voice grated on Neva's nerves.

Neva smirked at Genivra and flipped a knife. She caught it with a mastery that hinted at the years of throwing she had under her belt.

"Try not to make it too easy, Merrick." Neva adopted Genivra's lilt, earning a glare from the captain's second-in-command. "I like a challenge."

"Indeed," Mad Merrick said. "A game of Knight and Knave ought to decide the victor. What say you, Da'Valia?"

Neva had played Knight and Knave with Mikel and his friends plenty of times on the streets of Glacier Pass. The rules were simple. The lead player would throw twice to set the challenge, and the others would try to match the throws. If the lead player threw underhanded behind their back and hit the bull's-eye twice from ten paces, then any other player that failed to do the same got a mark against them. To make the competition fair, the lead player would switch for each round. Any player who suffered three marks fell out of the game (the Knave), and the player who lasted the longest won (the Knight). Any player who missed the target automatically earned a mark, ending their turn whether they were in the lead position or not. Neva had witnessed Mad Merrick's knife-throwing antics for enough time that she was confident she could match him.

"A game of Knight and Knave sounds perfect," Neva said.

"Let's see if you can keep up." Mad Merrick chuckled.

They tossed a coin to decide the lead thrower. Mad Merrick. He backed a dozen feet from the throwing line and took aim. *Thunk — thunk.* Two blades stuck in the faded center circle.

"Child's play," Neva said, taking care to copy the stance he'd used. She didn't want to gain a mark on a technicality. Her blades crowded his in the center circle a moment later.

Several more rounds passed before they each had a mark against them. Neva huffed out a breath and backed up another dozen steps, testing the distance where she could still hit the target. Her blades hit the faded paint, one in the center bull's-eye and one just inside the middle ring. Mad Merrick took another long pull of rum and matched her throw. Neva scowled. In her experience, throwers didn't get better the more they imbibed, but Mad Merrick seemed to be the exception. His crew cheered him on.

He tossed his hat into the crowd and scaled the footholds of a nearby orbo tree. He scooted out on the lowest limb and fell backward, his legs hooked on the branch. Upside down, he took aim. Both his blades hit the target just outside of the center circle. Neva was already climbing up for her turn when Mad Merrick flipped down. He stumbled and landed on his butt in the sand.

"You can tap out now," Mad Merrick heckled.

"I wouldn't dare," Neva called back, flipping upside down.

Neva let her blades fly. They stuck next to Mad Merrick's with a satisfying *thunk — thunk*. The Dragonslayers were the loudest of her supporters. Neva nodded to them and flipped down onto her feet, then onto her butt for good measure. It earned her a few laughs from the crowd.

"This one's outside the ring," a pirate called from the target. He was pointing at one of Neva's blades. "That's a mark against the Dragonslayer."

She frowned and scraped her teeth over her bottom lip. She needed to win a round to even the score. She chose to perform the trick she'd seen Mad Merrick do three times already — with one major difference. She balanced in a headstand and flipped to her feet before releasing. She used a straight throw instead of a rotation. Often, when a thrower practiced a certain move repeatedly, his muscles had difficulty adjusting to slight changes. She prayed that would be the case for Mad Merrick.

"Match that," she challenged.

"My specialty," Mad Merrick declared with a chortle. But he wasn't laughing a moment later when he bungled the release on his first throw. He didn't bother with the second. He'd already lost the round.

"What were you saying about your specialty, Captain?" Neva asked.

"It's of no matter." Mad Merrick brushed past her to collect his blade. He cursed as he struggled to pry it free. "We have a tie-game. Anything can happen."

"Mayhap," Neva allowed. "Or mayhap I have you right where I want you."

"Is that so?" He turned to Genivra. "Get me a blindfold, would you, Geni?"

Genivra raised her eyebrows and remained where she was, her arms crossed in front of her. "A blindfold? Do you think that's wise?"

Neva glanced between them. Whatever Mad Merrick had planned for the next round, Genivra seemed to know what it was.

"The blindfold," Mad Merrick snapped. "And Ruffo — carry that melon to the target."

The pirate named Ruffo lifted the large striped melon he was about to carve into. "This one?"

"Yes, that one. Go on."

"Where do you want it?" Ruffo asked as he arrived at the target.

"Atop your head, you fool." Mad Merrick dropped his hands to his sides in an exasperated motion.

Genivra passed a black strip of cloth to Merrick. Neva hid a smile, because while throwing knives blindfolded was extremely difficult, her senses were enhanced, and they gave her a distinct edge.

The protuberance at Ruffo's throat bobbed as he backed against the target. He lifted the melon to his head with shaking hands.

"I do not want to lose another crew member to your shenanigans, Merrick." Genivra was the sole voice of opposition.

"He's not afraid." Mad Merrick pointed to Ruffo, who, contrarily, looked like he was about to lose control of his bowels. "And if he needn't be afraid, you needn't be afraid."

"You're insufferable," Genivra bemoaned.

"Such vitriol. You wound me." Mad Merrick placed his hand over his heart.

"Oh, get on with it," Genivra said, but the creases in her forehead deepened.

Mad Merrick returned to the original throwing line and donned the blindfold.

"Say something so I know where you stand, Ruffo," Mad Merrick ordered.

"Uh — I — I'm here. Over here!" Ruffo choked out. "For the love of the gods, I'm right here."

Neva shook her head. The ways this stunt could go wrong were numerous.

"Very good, very good." Mad Merrick raised a knife and shuffled his feet comically in the sand. "And the melon is still on your head?"

"Y-yes." Ruffo's breaths were coming quicker now.

"Brilliant," Mad Merrick said cheerily. "Now, I want you to hold very, very still."

The crowd went silent, everyone seeming to hold their collective breath. Mad Merrick let his knives fly. *Thunk — thunk.* The blades protruded from the target on either side of the melon. Ruffo dropped to his knees, barely containing a sob. Neva took in the sight of the melon resting atop the blades. Slowly, the melon rolled forward and plopped down in front of Ruffo. It split open, and its sticky-sweet innards spilled out.

Mad Merrick ripped off his blindfold.

"Splendid." He threw his hands up, laughed, and did a high-knee dance, kicking up sand with his heels. "Match that, Da'Valia."

Neva flipped her daggers as she approached the throwing line. She had no shortage of confidence in her ability, but the outside chance of missing and ending someone's life gave her pause.

"Get down there, Durant," Mad Merrick shouted.

Wait, Durant?

"Me?" Durant's voice cracked.

"Was this not your idea?" Mad Merrick challenged.

"It certainly wasn't," Durant said.

"It's all right." Neva tried to sound encouraging. "I've got this."

Durant remained rooted in the sand. The pirates tittered, and Genivra kicked Durant's backside to get him moving. The Dragonslayers chanted his name as he approached the target.

Neva wiped sweaty palms on her pants. What should have been a simple game had escalated quickly. If she thought about everything that was at stake at this moment, she would unnerve herself, so she focused on the target. Once Durant was in position with a melon atop his head, one of the pirates tied the blindfold on her. She replayed how Durant had approached the line.

"Say something so I know where you stand," Neva called out to Durant.

"If you kill me, I will come back to haunt you," Durant declared, drawing chuckles from the crowd.

Some of the tension in her shoulders dissipated. She pictured him in her mind. She impersonated Mad Merrick's sand-kicking and planted her feet.

"Good, and the melon is still in place?" she asked.

"Aye. Just get on with it," Durant called back.

He didn't need to tell her twice.

Thunk — thunk. The sound was right. Neva's heart skipped. Or was it? She ripped off the blindfold and watched for the longest moment of her life as Durant collapsed on the beach. The melon wobbled in place atop the knives. A woman in the crowd gasped, and the melon pitched forward, falling into Durant's lap. The crowd went wild.

Neva grinned as Durant picked himself up and rejoined the Dragonslayers. His face was devoid of color. Mad Merrick swaggered over to Neva and tossed his empty rum bottle aside. He got close enough that the floral odor on his breath tickled her nose. A floral odor that most definitely was not rum. Her gaze shot to the bottle in the sand. He'd been faking his inebriation. She crossed her arms. That was fine with her. She wouldn't mention it — just as she wouldn't mention the almost imperceptible flicker of golden sand that had swooped down and kept her from gaining a third mark, nudging the melon off the knives.

Thank you, Mari. Neva would have to do something nice for her friend when they returned to civilization.

"Da'Valia, hm?" Mad Merrick sounded thoughtful. "Geni, remind me that Da'Valia are expert throwers next time we see one, will you?"

Geni shook her head at him.

Enough games. It was time to end this. Neva backed up another twenty paces from the farthest throw line. The crowd skittered to make way. She stopped at an unthinkable distance from the target.

It almost didn't matter where she hit the target as long as she hit it because there was no chance Mad Merrick could throw accurately from this far away. Neva filled her lungs, took aim, and threw, her leg kicking out behind her. She nailed the bull's-eye, then the outer ring. The Dragonslayers cheered.

Mad Merrick's levity fizzled as he took up a spot at the line, squinting at the target. He drew back and let his blade go. His knife bounced off the bottom of the target and into the sand.

"I'm the Knave?" Mad Merrick sounded stupefied.

"A little more practice and you'll be a decent shot before long," Neva said in a reassuring tone.

Mad Merrick's head jerked her way. "Before long —" He barked out a laugh. "It takes a real pair to show me up." He stuck his hand out. "Gods know I'm tired of these fools tripping over their own feet. Tell me your name, Da'Valia, and what you need of me."

"Trust us when I say you'll want to hear this in private," Durant interjected.

The Dragonslayers soon found themselves being led toward the Dancing Sandpiper. Neva and her gangmates were on high alert, scanning for the Crocutas as they made their way through the impromptu open-air market that spanned the beach. They were almost to the pier when Neva spotted them. Tavo elbowed Ballard. The Crocutas were marching straight for Neva and her gang, pushing anyone in their path out of the way. Cass was screeching like a wildcat, and Valentine wasn't even trying to hide the dagger in his hand.

"Friends of yours?" Genivra asked, noticing the impending threat.

"Debo, Crowe, Rinaldo," Ballard said their names like an order.

The Dragonslayers split from the group and went straight for the Crocutas to hold them off. Abruptly, an Anchorweight howled and bowled into the Crocutas from the side. Neva grinned. She was going to have to do something *extra* special for Mari. A ruckus ensued, with more Anchorweights hurrying into the fray, throwing punches and breaking bottles over heads. The Dragonslayers leaped into the fight. Debo especially seemed to relish the activity, cursing and name-calling at will.

The rest of them continued to the Dancing Sandpiper uninterrupted. On deck, Durant filled in the captain and first mate on the basics of the Dragonslayers' mission. He threw around words such as gold, gems, and endless riches. His spiel was so persuasive that it would have had Neva signing on again if she wasn't already bound by blood, but Mad Merrick was guarded.

"It's impossible," Genivra said dismissively. "You cannot do what you say and live."

"They said no one could sail the Razor Straights, too," Durant pointed out. "Yet here you stand."

"It's our busiest plundering season in years," Mad Merrick countered. "You may not have heard, but Amania is waging a trade war, and the spoils thus far have been splendiferous."

Durant flicked his eyes from Neva to Mad Merrick, tilting his head in a 'go on' motion.

"See, Durant?" Neva picked up on the cue quickly, slumping her shoulders in defeat. "They're not interested. After all that, we ought to have just hired a faster ship."

A dead silence fell over their confab. She'd set the trap, but had she overplayed her part? She hoped not. She couldn't backtrack now.

"Faster ship?" Mad Merrick was the first to speak. He sounded incredulous and highly offended. "There is no ship faster than the Dancing Sandpiper."

"She's swift on the high seas, Neva," Durant said softly.

"That's why we agreed to approach them in the first place," Tavo chimed in.

"But has the Dancing Sandpiper ever outrun a dragon before?" Neva asked as if someone needed to explain it to her.

"No ship has ever outrun a dragon." Mad Merrick threw up his hands. "It cannot be done."

"But what if we told you it could?" Durant sprung the trap. "I'd rather it be you, Mad Merrick. Your crew deserves the notoriety, the respect. Your ship deserves the reputation. We can deliver. We will escape the dragons, and it's only up to you to decide to be a part of it."

"Perhaps you should tell us just why you're so confident?" Genivra suggested. Her blue-gray eyes were alight with a curious glint as she studied Neva's horns.

Genivra, it turned out, carried even more clout with the captain than any of them had given her credit for. Neva paid closer attention as Durant ponied up all the details of their plan, even the ones Neva wasn't keen to share. When Genivra nodded, Mad Merrick nodded. When Genivra frowned, Mad Merrick frowned. Upon mention of the Hand, Genivra got quiet. So did Mad Merrick.

We should have been trying to convince her the whole time, Neva thought. But they were both listening now, and that was what mattered.

Genivra rested her hand on Mad Merrick's shoulder.

"What's the take?" Mad Merrick asked, indicating he was ready to negotiate terms.

"Depends on how much we can carry out," Durant said matter-of-factly. "If you lend us a few of your crew, it's bound to be more than we could make away with on our own."

"More to the point then — what's the split?" Genivra asked.

They would be taking home mountains of gold if they were successful. The question on all their minds was how the treasure would be divided.

"Sixty to us, forty to you," Durant opened. "It's a fair split since we've done all the groundwork."

"Eighty to us and twenty to you sounds a far sight fairer to me," Mad Merrick said after consulting Genivra. "You lot aren't just getting gold out of this deal, you'll be getting your freedom, too. The entire Order will be on the lookout for my ship."

"I see your point," Durant allowed. "But we'll also be starting with nothing once we're off this rock. If you can give us ten sets of hands to cart the goods to the ship and passage to any port north of the House of Halcyon within one month's time, a fifty-fifty split would be acceptable."

"And I get the Sword of Elon," Neva interjected.

Ballard cleared his throat loudly.

"And we'll need to borrow a skiff," Durant added.

"Anything else?" Genivra asked humorlessly.

"Gloves," Neva added quickly. "I'll need a pair of gloves."

Durant hesitated, looking at Neva before continuing.

"That's it," she mouthed at him.

"That's it," Durant said.

Mad Merrick blew air through pursed lips. "Eight hands — that's all I can spare if we're making a fast getaway. Passage to any port north of House of Halcyon in my own time, the cost of any repairs will come off the top, and we split sixty-forty in my favor. You may borrow a skiff and keep the sword. I'll throw the gloves in out of the goodness of my heart."

"Your own time cannot put us on the mainland past the conclusion of Eleventh Cravell, and we'll split fifty-fifty," Durant said. "Do we have a deal?"

"Returning to the mainland will take some time — a fortnight, maybe two if we get into a tight spot with the Order. We could pull that off, if we set sail no later than a week from today."

Genivra gave a subtle nod.

"We have an accord," Durant said.

Mad Merrick spit into his palm and held it out to Durant. They shook on it.

Tavo whooped, and Neva joined her gangmates in a group hug. Not even the stench of her smelly friends could stop the excitement rushing through her. What she had told Tavo was true: they would all be filthy rich before long. Mad Merrick wasn't the only one whose reputation would improve. Once word got out, her Lynx identity would be talked about as the most talented thief of her time. But best of all, she would be poised to trump Trinizhi.

Chapter Twenty-Six

Third Vestive, 1650

Dear Elkizhi,

How you would laugh if you could see me now. I've been alone for such a long time, now I spend every day in such frustration. Dhianz is surely trying me with Nevazhi. The half-breed majila is, indeed, the one our mother told me to protect. Monazhi's daughter emerged from her firérite with an unrivaled power level and four horns. Murmurings have begun that the gods have chosen her, and Dhianz help me, I have to agree. But she disregards my warnings, taunts me, tantalizes me, and I want nothing more than to meet her passion with my own. Although I am her guardian and Trinizhi's aliado, I know Nevazhi feels similarly about me.

I was resistant to aligning with Trinizhi once, even though I did it, but I've never felt so resentful over our bond before. It seems a cruel game to find someone who I know is the perfect match for me but to already be bound to another. The best way to protect Nevazhi is to stay far away from her, yet it takes all of my willpower not to give into temptation. Because if I did that, if Trinizhi even suspected that, I know she would drive a wedge between Nevazhi and me. I must contemplate the future and how I might play a part in Dhianz's scheme for this half-breed. Pray for me.

Your brother,
— Astiand

Neva didn't like having to check in with anyone, but as each day drew to a close, she'd be lying if she said that she didn't liven with anticipation of her nightly visit with Astiand. He was a reminder that she had allies on the mainland. That as troubled as certain parts of her future might seem, she had one of Trinizhi's own aliados on her side. Still, another part of her worried that the donazhi would find him out and Neva would be responsible for another catastrophe befalling someone she lo —

Looked up to, Neva amended.

The sense that she was condemning Astiand by continuing to meet with him niggled at her, but, surely, once more wouldn't see him under the wheel.

She settled against the base of an orbo tree and activated the enchanted looking glass. Astiand came into focus, and she took a moment to appreciate the fullness of his lips. He was in a bedroom, wearing a loose tunic and leaning against plush cream-colored pillows. He puffed on his pipe. Whenever she saw him smoking, she remembered the first time she'd seen him, dressed as a rich soldier on his way to the Trades at the House of Trescony.

"I wasn't sure you'd call on me this evening," Astiand told her.

"I'm not one to neglect a debt, if I can help it," Neva said, pretending she hadn't behaved like a brat the last time they'd talked.

"I hope that's not the only reason you check in with me," he said.

It wasn't.

"It is," she said instead.

He flinched. She had made a battle-tested, politics-proven Da'Valia flinch. It didn't feel as good as she might once have imagined. Neva told herself it was better this way. Easier. Plus, she needed to lay the foundation for parting ways before Trinizhi found him out. But she also needed him as her insider among Trinizhi's alliad and as a contact on the mainland a little while longer. At least, that's what she told herself.

"I approached Benjamand as you suggested," Astiand said after a beat.

"Can he do it?" Neva's mouth went dry. "Can he break the blood contract?"

"Perzhi, his donazhi, has devoted him to war preparations against Amania, but he says he will revisit some texts regarding blood magic in the archives."

"Did you tell him I don't have much time?"

"I told him everything."

Neva nibbled on her bottom lip. "Good."

"How are things on the island?" Astiand asked.

"As well as might be expected," Neva said, blocking the memory of his scent. Hagave, pipe smoke, and hilan. "We've — I've just arranged transportation back."

"That is a relief," Astiand said. "How are you?"

"Fine," Neva said. "And you?"

"Today was a bad day," Astiand admitted. "Preceded by a bad decade. Trinizhi wants to mobilize our younger beasties and majilas, even though they're not of age to enlist. Guess who got to deliver the bad news to Vivizhi."

Neva cringed. Vivizhi had high standards — not to mention a temper and a history with Astiand. Neva didn't imagine the news would have gone over well.

"Do you think she'll go through with it?" Neva asked.

"Trinizhi? I have no doubt," Astiand said.

"Do you wish you hadn't joined her alliad?" Neva got up the courage to ask. She reasoned that if he said yes, they might have a future together. But if he said no, she could infer he was only helping her because of the promise he'd made to his mother.

Astiand seemed to consider her question, swirling around the last few drops of hagave in his cup.

"You know, it strikes me that —" The door crashed open behind him, and he disappeared from the looking glass. It went dark.

Neva stared at her reflection a moment before lowering the looking glass. She stifled the desire to throw the mirror into the jungle again. She wasn't about to sign on for hours of hunting for the thing in the dark, but she really wanted to throw something. She settled for a rock.

She scraped her lower lip between her teeth, thinking. She hadn't had a clear view of Astiand's door, and she didn't doubt that Astiand could have provoked any number of people to barge in on him. But if it had been Trinizhi and if the donazhi had spied Neva's face in the mirror, the donazhi would have her aliado's horns.

A single shadowy figure awaited the Dragonslayers beside the Dancing Sandpiper on the far end of the pier, where a small skiff rose and fell with each incoming swell. Along the coastline, an otherworldly blue hue shone from within the breaking waves. The glow appeared this time each year, Rinaldo explained, signaling the mating season for water nymphs.

The gang picked their way through the minefield of snoozing gangers on the beach. While the island had celebrated the return of the pirates late into the night, the Dragonslayers had agreed to get an early start to Leper Island to fetch Alewiscious's obsidian salt. With any luck, no one would see them leave.

They marched down the wooden pier, and a cool ocean wind left a layer of salt on Neva's lips. The light of the moon revealed Genivra as the figure on the end of the pier as they neared. The first mate told them to abandon the skiff on the other side of the island near the ashmounts when they returned. She didn't need to explain that bringing the boat back to the Dancing Sandpiper straight away would be too public and that fear of rot would mean trouble if any gangers saw them returning.

"Exciting isn't it?" Mari asked, bouncing on her toes next to Neva.

No one else said anything. Mari was the only one treating this excursion like it was a special evening out in the city.

"You keep interesting company, Dragonslayers," Genivra said, eyeing the Djinn.

"She's one of us." Rinaldo cut off Neva, who had been about to say the same thing.

Mari preened at the declaration. Neva hid a small smile. There was nothing quite like brawling to cultivate team spirit.

The Dragonslayers piled into the boat, and Neva stifled a groan as it tossed this way and that. Crowe's greenish complexion matched her own. Rinaldo was the last to hop aboard after he untied the mooring line. It was a tight fit with so many of them, and the rowing was slow — far slower than any of them expected. The ocean lapped at the sides of the skiff as they crested swells and pushed on toward their destination.

Neva and Crowe were dry-heaving off the back of the boat when it came time for their turns to row, so the other Dragonslayers pitched in. Crowe's glassy eyes met hers in commiseration.

"What did we do to deserve this?" Crowe asked.

Neva was unable to answer. She had no doubt that she deserved every mode of punishment that the gods burdened her with. She had destroyed and ended so many lives: Adam, the Da'Valia outside Glacier Pass, a Da'Voda soldier, the Ceasekin, her cousin, Lindzhi. If Neva had to suffer now, it seemed only fair.

Neva let her head hang off the back of the boat as they approached Leper Island. She watched the wind carry the thick gray smoke from the ashmounts into the distance against the clear dawn. She could see the Old Fort with its grand spire glinting in the rising sun from here.

"Someone has caught sight of us," Mari announced.

"Are you sure?" Rinaldo asked.

"Aye, I'm sure."

The Dragonslayers looked onwards as the sky lightened, turning blue. The steep beach ahead remained vacant as they aimed for a dilapidated dock. The wood was gray with age, and more than a few boards were missing. Nearby, gulls pecked at a dead fish that had washed up, and flies hovered over globs of seaweed.

Rinaldo hopped out and tied them off. Neva and Crowe dragged themselves off the boat. She spat out the sweet, acidic residue of vomit and wiped her mouth on the back of her hand. She raised her eyes and skidded to a stop. She steadied Crowe, who bumped into her. A group from the leper colony stood on the elevated edge of the beach, weapons in hand.

"We get ourselves into some strange situations, don't we, Mari?" Neva asked, surveying their welcoming committee.

"We?" Mari asked. "I'm giving you all the credit should anyone ask."

"Hold on. Hold on." Ballard pushed to the front of the group. He unhooked his belt and directed the Dragonslayers to put down their weapons.

Spears, swords, knives, and Rinaldo's crossbow clattered onto the dock. Ballard tossed his scabbard into the sand. Neva looked at Mari, who shrugged. Together, they stepped aside so their companions could go first.

A tall man with black teeth and a caved-in nose stepped forward and seemed to take in their armor, weapons, and lack of obvious illness.

"You're not welcome here," he said.

"Forgive our trespass," Ballard called out. "We come bearing gifts."

Durant carried a small crate of pies and dried levasta root, a natural pain remedy, forward. They'd traded away a set of dragon scale armor at Docking Day to finance the trove. Neva hoped it would be enough to sway the colony.

"Are those the Baker's pies?" asked a shorter man, who stood next to the one in charge. This one was balding, and his lips were peeling.

"That you, Bertie?" Durant called out. "Glad to see you're still kicking. Aye, they're Baker's."

"Durant?" Bertie asked. "What are you doing over here?"

"We're looking for someone," Durant replied.

"Who would that be?" the tall man asked.

"Ebenezer Tavish," Ballard called back. "My grandfather."

Neva's gaze swung to their leader. Alewiscious had said Ballard would recognize Ebenezer, but Ballard had claimed not to know him. And Tavish... if Ballard was a Tavish, he was practically pirate royalty.

"My condolences then," the tall man said. "Because Ebenezer is dead."

No. Neva fought the feeling of losing her hold on things. It couldn't be.

Ballard dropped down onto one knee, Durant hung his head, and Tavo cursed. Neva struggled to maintain composure. All their planning had been for naught. They couldn't escape without the beads of obsidian salt.

Neva imagined writing her father of her fate and how he would become despondent when he learned that he would never see his only child again. She imagined telling Astiand that she had failed, even after he'd risked so much for her. She imagined the magic of Trinizhi's blood contract siphoning her power away. She didn't even know if that was how it worked, but the end result was what mattered. And what if Nikolazhi's magic conflicted with Neva's conviction marks? Would Neva be torn apart by magic?

Mari's eyes flashed yellow.

"Are you sure about that?" Mari asked.

"Buried him myself," the tall man confirmed. "Three years ago."

Bertie addressed the tall man in a tone too low for Neva to make out against the crashing waves and squawking gulls. Neva shot Mari a questioning look. For Mari to challenge the tall man's statement implied he was lying. Gods, how she hoped he was lying.

"It's very important that we speak with him," Durant persisted.

"Did you not hear me?" the tall man asked.

Bertie winced and held his hand out to Durant in a gesture of regret.

"Ebenezer is gone," the tall man reiterated.

Neva scanned the line of gangers, her gaze lingering on a blind girl with filmed-over eyes standing a few steps apart from the others. The waif's dreadlocked hair was so short that Neva nearly took her for a boy. The tall man was sticking to his story, but surely, someone here knew something. Surely, one of them would talk. But none of them moved forward.

Ballard came over to Neva.

"You like showing off," he told her. "Make it clear to them we're not leaving until we see Ebenezer."

Neva strode forward and threw her arms out, releasing dual bursts of power that streamed around her, looping through the air.

"We won't ask again," she called out.

"Neither will we." The tall man pushed up his ratted sleeves to reveal boils and discoloration that traveled from his elbows to his fingers, which were missing their tips.

The threat of leprosy wouldn't stand against Da'Valian flame, but the fact that he challenged her, unflinchingly, earned her respect.

"I've got this." Mari bent at the knees, a move Neva recognized.

"Wait," Neva stepped in front of Mari.

The waif was staring right at Neva. A shiver scurried down Neva's spine. Was the girl not blind as she'd first thought? The waif limped forward.

"I'll show them the way to Ebenezer," the girl said. Her childlike voice carried an undercurrent of something dark and powerful.

The tall man frowned, but her words were all it took to send them back into the jungle. Bertie scuttled over to collect the box of peace offerings and was the last to disappear with a friendly wave to Durant. The Dragonslayers collected their weapons, and the waif approached.

"I don't sense anything from her," Mari said with a frown. "And I don't like it."

"Is she looking at us?" Rinaldo asked, making the sign for Ailish.

"I don't see as you see," the girl said, stopping before them. "Try not to let it bother you."

"I know you," Neva said. She didn't know from where, but the waif was familiar.

"Do you?" the girl sounded amused.

"Who are you?" Neva asked, half certain she should've asked *what* the girl was instead. The wind pushed the girl's scent toward Neva. Dried rose petals like those that were buried with the dead, and smoke like that of a Da'Valian pyre. Neva's nose wrinkled, and she battled the instinct to put distance between herself and this creature, for the waif was no mere girl.

"Here, they call me Thana," the girl replied. "I'm a friend of Ebenezer's."

"What do they call you other places?" Tavo frowned.

"Many things, Tavo Ott." Thana smiled demurely.

Tavo's eyes widened. "I don't like this," he said out of the corner of his mouth. "She shouldn't know my name."

"I don't see anyone else lining up to take us to Ebenezer," Ballard said.

"Nor will they. I am your guide. Now, come." Thana beckoned them to follow her into the trees.

"I don't think we'll get a better offer," Neva said.

Ballard gave a nod and ordered Debo and Crowe to stay with the boat. Strangling vines parted to allow Thana into the jungle. The rest of them hustled after her. The path she led them down was bare where foot traffic had worn away the moss and undergrowth. Some of the foliage withered and turned brown as they passed. Unease coiled in Neva's stomach. She hoped she wouldn't regret this.

"You've come to see Ebenezer," Thana stated.

"We need but a moment of his time," Durant said.

"And he will need but a moment of hers," the girl said, pointing at Neva.

Neva swallowed, not liking being singled out. She couldn't imagine what Thana meant, but Neva could hardly turn back now.

Their hike to the colony was short. Moans filtered through the trees, reaching her before she saw the village. Compared with the colony, the shantytown on Lithlorian was a dump. Here, sturdy log cabins were situated in rows, streets — actual streets — were well-groomed, and gangers were lined up to fetch water from a stone well.

"The Outpost," Ballard murmured.

"How is it all still standing?" Neva asked.

"Dragons don't eat diseased flesh," Thana replied. "You won't have to worry about an attack as long as you're here."

"Yeah, dragons are such picky eaters," Tavo joked.

No one laughed.

"This way." Thana hobbled up the steps of one of the cabins. She pushed aside a beaded curtain. "Ebenezer, you have visitors."

The Dragonslayers filed into the room, shuffling awkwardly. A man lying on one of the cabin's four cots rolled over upon their entry. His face was bulbous with infection, and his long gray hair was gnarled, missing in patches. His arms were covered in faded tattoos of varying colors. One in particular caught her attention, the symbol of the Obsidian Brotherhood.

Her mouth went dry. Ebenezer was a mage.

Mari and Thana approached his sickbed, but when his eyes cracked open, they locked on Neva.

"I told you she would come for you," Thana told him softly, petting his hair away from his forehead.

"I don't want them here," Ebenezer said, glancing at the others. His voice was gravelly and strained.

Neva tried not to stare at the discolored nubs that protruded from the bottom of the thin blanket. Ebenezer's hands were missing all but a few digits. Thinking of the pain he must be in, she wanted to find Bertie and deliver all of the levasta root that they'd brought with them to Ebenezer. How was he still alive?

"You're Ebenezer," Ballard said, stepping closer. The other Dragonslayers hung back. "You've been missing for many, many years."

"Aye." Ebenezer took in Ballard. "I know you. Are you Misty's boy?"

"Her grandson," Ballard said. "And you... were her grandfather."

Neva exchanged a startled look with Durant. A quick calculation proved the unlikelihood of that. Under no circumstances should Ebenezer still be alive. Not five generations later.

"What's going on here?" Durant asked, and Neva guessed that he'd done the math, too.

"I'm not certain," Ballard said slowly.

"Alewiscious sent you?" Ebenezer presumed.

"Aye," Ballard answered. "For obsidian salt. How did you know?"

Ebenezer wheezed and groaned again.

"That's not why you're here," Ebenezer said. "Though I have no doubt that's what he told you."

Neva looked to Ballard in confusion.

"Then why?" Neva asked Ebenezer.

"You're here to kill me."

Chapter Twenty-Seven

Fourth Vestive, 1650

Dear Elkizhi,

Bryand is dead. He foolishly betrayed our donazhi, and this was the price for it. I'm bitter that he did not come to me, and at the same time, I know why he did not. I mourn in silence. Publicly, I condemn his actions, as is necessary.

I spent so many years dedicated to honing my strikes and the stroke of my sword. I spent even more time perfecting battle strategies and navigating political circles as one of Trinizhi's aliados. I have painstakingly put distance between myself and those I thought I could hurt. In short, I constructed such a wall around my heart, I thought nothing could ever penetrate it. But nothing could have prepared me for Nevazhi.

In the aftermath of Bryand's death, I encouraged her to run away. I acted out of fear. There are many ways that Trinizhi might mold Nevazhi in her image, kill her, or lock her away as she has you. I couldn't let that happen, so I had to let her go. Regret takes hold of me at night. Regret for having lost my best friend. Regret at having lost her. Regret at having let Trinizhi manipulate my life. It's time things start to change.

Your brother,
— Astiand

Neva stumbled out of the cabin and down the steps to the street, where she could inhale without being subjected to the stifling stench of illness. She gulped in air, but she couldn't catch her breath. Her vision darkened around the edges, and tingling ran from her fingers to her elbows as she struggled to control her breathing. She wrung her hands. This was wrong. All of it. What was Alewiscious up to, sending her on a kill mission?

Ballard followed in Neva's wake, and Warbler flew out after him.

"We shouldn't have come," Neva told Ballard. "I can't kill him. He's an innocent."

"But you can," Thana said simply. She pulled aside the beaded curtain and limped down the steps. "It is your destiny as Riska's chosen."

Both Neva and Ballard stared at her.

"I am not one of Riska's chosen," Neva argued, scrambling to collect her thoughts.

"Do you not bear her mark, the Crystal of Souls?" Thana asked.

"No," Neva said.

"Aye," Rinaldo said from the doorway, where the rest of the Dragonslayers were gathered. "She does. We've all seen it."

Neva jerked, and her hand went to the soul scourge crystal. It had been impossible to hide at the watering hole.

"That's just an old wound," Neva said.

"Hm." Thana approached and hovered her palm over the blue crystal in Neva's chest. Thana's hand glowed faintly with magic. "Mayhap you're not ready yet, but you will learn to accept your destiny eventually."

"That's..." Neva searched for the right word. "Absurd."

She backed away. She wasn't Riska's chosen any more than she was the queen of Cirandrel. True, Monazhi had accidentally sacrificed her to the gods when she was in the womb, and Neva did harness the Hand, and people frequently died around her, but that didn't mean — that *couldn't* mean...

"Is it absurd?" Ballard asked. "Maybe —"

"No," Neva said. The Hand was enough proximity to the gods for her. The Hand was *plenty* enough.

Thana lowered her arm. "The fact remains that you have an important decision to make here today. Talk with Ebenezer. If you still don't think you're meant to release him, then that is your decision to make."

"I can't," Neva whispered again.

"Leave us," Ballard commanded.

The Dragonslayers ducked back into the cabin, and Thana joined them. Ballard squeezed Neva's shoulder.

"I know that look," Ballard said. "What are you fighting against, Neva?"

She swallowed hard and willed herself not to cry. She had been suffocating under the burden of guilt for so long now, it was hard to see beyond it. When anything bad happened, it always happened around her. No matter what she did, people kept getting hurt.

How many more lives could she destroy before that guilt crippled her completely? Up until now, she'd killed accidentally or in kill-or-be-killed situations, and she would carry that burden forever. If she did this...

"What kind of person am I becoming?" she asked quietly.

"Haven't you been listening to me since you arrived?" Ballard asked. "This is your second chance. Every choice you make determines who you will be."

"But what about..."

"What about?" Ballard asked.

"What about what I've done?"

"There's no going back," Ballard said. "The only thing left to do is to forgive yourself."

"What if I can't?" she asked.

"You can," Ballard said. Warbler tweeted in agreement. "I've done it. Durant. Tavo. We all did things we're not proud of, but we've learned to trust ourselves to do the next right thing. It's all any of us can do. Dwelling on a past you cannot change will only lead to a wasted life."

"But what *is* the next right thing?" When every choice seemed to have an unintended consequence, how could she choose correctly?

"Go and talk to Ebenezer before you decide," Ballard said. "If you ask me, killing him would not only help the gang return home, but killing him would be a mercy."

Neva squeezed her eyes shut. She didn't want to waste her life. She wanted to complete her mother's mission, and there was only one way to do that. She opened her eyes and climbed the steps back to the cabin. She forced one foot in front of the other, pressure mounting until she stood by Ebenezer's bedside barely able to look at him.

"Tell me again why you think I'm here," Neva requested.

"Because I was a very foolish man once, and I made some mistakes — the kind that linger for generations," Ebenezer said.

Neva glanced at Mari, who shrugged. His answer didn't clarify anything.

"Why don't you start at the beginning?" Neva suggested.

"I have nothing but time," Ebenezer agreed weakly. "I was born in 1512. Every child born with power can be recognized by the blackness in his eyes. The Brotherhood can take the children by force, or their mothers can choose to relinquish them to the fold. Mine forsook me, abandoning me at one of Yokam's temples.

"I was raised in servitude to a mage who specialized in weather magic. His domain was the Serpentine Sea. Sailing with a weather mage was like cheating at times, but his moods would bring the rain as often as they would bring fair winds. When I came of age, he sent me back to the Brotherhood for a proper education in Qitarah.

"I rebelled against the structure that the Brotherhood provided, and the only other pupil who seemed to fall into as much trouble as I did was Al. He was brilliant and didn't deign to follow the rules. We enjoyed our fair share of fun and suffered more than our fair share of discipline.

"Al's mentor was Finneas, a mage who sought power and prestige above all else. Finneas's desire for immortality seemed unattainable to us at first, but he persuaded us to attempt an experiment that would give him life everlasting.

"The spell went awry and stole the life from him. When the Brotherhood found out that a brother's soul had been wasted, they were furious. They expelled us for ten years. Al and I fought over who was to blame, and since there was nothing left for me in Qitarah, I returned to the only other life I knew — one upon the high seas.

"I hadn't completed my education, but I'd come close enough to push a boat faster than it ought to be pushed. Mine ran aground on the coast of Amania in a storm, and that's where I met Jeaux, the most beautiful woman I'd ever seen.

"I lost my head over her, and our love lessened the sting of expulsion. She took my name and showed me what it was to have a family. We saved up to purchase a second boat, then a third. Magic helped. I was faster to intercept ships than the other pirates and quicker to make away. That's how the Fleet was born."

Ballard made a small sound in the back of his throat, as if Ebenezer's tale confirmed suspicions about his family dynasty. Mari gave a little sigh.

"I like to think things would have kept on like that," Ebenezer continued. "But Al had other ideas. He wanted prestige, and he had never forgotten how close Finneas came to attaining immortality. Were Al to finish Finneas's work, the Brotherhood would have no choice but to grant him a top position in the Serculus.

"After the Brotherhood conquered Ramanaji, it had grown complacent. The Serculus wasn't willing to risk brothers' lives for the advancement of magic. It was more worthwhile to sacrifice a brother's soul for tried and true spells. Finneas had figured out how to tether a soul, but he hadn't deciphered how to make a counterweight that would keep it in this realm. That was the missing piece."

"What's a tether?" Neva asked.

"Tethering is complex, but in the simplest terms, it's the means of anchoring magical rites." Thana held a mug to Ebenezer's lips. He took a sip before continuing. "Al absconded with one of the oldest, most valuable texts the Brotherhood possessed and came in search of me. I should have known not to trust him, but he was persuasive. We tested the limits of good sense and ultimately used the text to anchor our souls to this realm, to escape Riska's embrace. Unfortunately, the text was destroyed, but we were elated.

"Al convinced me to return with him to the Brotherhood to properly recount our completion of Finneas's work in front of the Serculus. They listened to what we had to say. They were more than happy to learn all they could from us and apply immortality tethers to themselves, but there was still the matter of the stolen text.

"Al failed to realize how furious they would be about its loss. A magical text isn't just a book, understand. It's imbued with power, often the life force of a brother who sacrificed himself. Anyway, the Brotherhood tethered us to each other and these islands. That's why, even though Al severed the magic of his conviction marks, he cannot leave.

"It was only through the passage of time that we came to realize the flaw in our magic. While our spirits remain in this realm, our bodies still wither with age, suspended on the brink of death.

"For me, our accomplishment has been more of a burden than anything else. Jeaux joined me on Lithlorian for many years, but she eventually passed. I watched our boys grew up to become fathers before they, too, died.

"I went to Al to see if we could devise a way to tether my family. But if I was a fool once, I was a fool twice. Al had been conducting more experiments, and when we went to cast immortality upon my remaining descendants, he changed the incantation and stole my power for himself. I presume he was trying to prevent the effects of aging, but I'll never know.

"After that, I showed the first signs of rot, as did several others on the island. We were sent to the Outpost to establish a colony. For some years, they sent supplies over from Lithlorian, but then they only sent more gangers who had been afflicted.

"This has been the long way of my telling you that we are bound together. Al and I are tied to these islands by invisible chains put in place by the Brotherhood. By the rules of the magic, one of us would have to die a true death to break the tether.

"If Al tries to escape, the magic will bring him back — be it by the tides, or the dragons, or a boat. Every time, he'll end where he began. And if I try to take my own life, my body will slowly, painfully heal, but only to the state you see me in now. He sent you here to kill me so that he may end his banishment."

Neva cleared her throat, trying to dislodge the shards of glass that she didn't remember swallowing. "I don't want to kill you, Ebenezer."

"And I want nothing else," Ebenezer told her. "Carry no guilt over this, Da'Valia. You will be doing me a favor. My flesh is rife with rot, but it goes deeper than that. Parts of me feel only pain, and worse still, parts of me feel nothing anymore. I am no longer a man nor mage. I am the shell of a man who has outstayed his welcome in this realm. Send me to Riska, and I will thank you. We both will."

Ballard had been quiet a long time, but he spoke up, "I'll do it."

Neva's knees nearly buckled in relief.

Ebenezer stared at his great-great-great-grandson with an emotion Neva pegged as pride. "You cannot. Only one with power bestowed by the gods may offer me a true death."

The Hand. Neva sank to the floor. If she didn't do this, the apothecary wouldn't remove the Dragonslayers' conviction marks, which meant that they would never escape Lithlorian. But what was more, an old man would continue to suffer for eternity. Not just a few days while he fought off a malady. Not just a few seasons wasting away before Riska claimed him. Years. She considered what would weigh heavier on her — action, or inaction.

What do I do? She stared at Warbler. The bird turned its head from side to side, meeting her gaze.

Ballard, meanwhile, was watching Neva intently, as if he was willing her to do the right thing. She didn't want to let him down. Slowly, she nodded shakily and rose.

"If I do this, what happens to Alewiscious? Does he die, too?" Neva asked.

"No, he'll live until his spirit tether is severed," Ebenezer said. "Our spirit tethers are independent of each other. It's our physical tethers that are intimately connected. If you grant me a true death, he will be able to leave Lithlorian."

Neva nodded slowly. "Any last words?"

"Only this," Ebenezer said. "Be leery of him. I have no doubt he has spent his imprisonment perfecting his dark arts. Don't be the fool I was."

"The beads?" Ballard asked.

"Thana will give them to you once it is done," Ebenezer replied.

Neva wrapped a blanket around Ebenezer and scooped him up and carried him to the nearest beach. Ballard and Thana followed her to the shore, but the others stayed on the edge of the jungle, presumably cautious of what was about to happen. Neva didn't blame them.

"You can leave," Neva told Ballard and Thana. "I'm not sure you'll want to see what happens next."

She wasn't even sure she would want to see it.

"I'll not leave him now," Thana said kindly. She squeezed Ebenezer's arm briefly and let go.

"Me neither," Ballard said.

"It may not be safe," Neva said. They didn't budge. "...Very well."

Neva lowered Ebenezer onto the sand and flexed her fingers over him. The Hand railed against its vault. She felt like a blacksmith was working a hammer and an anvil inside her skull. *I am in control,* she reminded herself, but the knot of unease in her belly persisted. Her fingers trembled. She twisted the spindle wheel in her mind and called the Hand to manifest. She channeled it like she did a healing flame. White fire appeared above her palms, and she stretched the power to the length of Ebenezer's body, perfectly controlled.

Ebenezer whispered a prayer to his god. After more than a century, Ebenezer's spirit would be at peace. Neva brought the flame down so quickly that he didn't even scream. A pile of ash was all that remained. The ash scattered across the sand and shallow water, dispersing into the air like snowflakes caught in a drift. Neva stood with Ebenezer until the last of it was gone.

Ballard and Thana still stood a mere ten paces away. Neva's relief that the Hand had done her bidding and nothing more, made her blood rush to her head. Though Dhianz and Riska may not be listening, she thanked them.

Thana hobbled over and peered up at Neva with her glazed-over eyes, offering a small leather pouch. Neva took it and counted the beads within. They were all there. She gave Ballard a reassuring nod, synched the drawstring, and tucked the pouch into the pocket of her wrap.

"Until we meet again," Thana said.

"Oh, we won't be back," Neva said.

A ghostly laugh danced around them as Thana turned and disappeared in a ripple, as if she were a mirage in the desert.

For once, Ballard was the one who called on Ailish for protection. He approached, avoiding the spot where Thana had disappeared. "You came through for us, Neva."

"Is it always this hard to do the right thing?" Neva asked.

"It gets easier," Ballard said. "But this was a heroic start. On the behalf of my family, I thank you. You granted Ebenezer a great mercy. Whatever past you're carrying, you should consider granting yourself clemency, too."

With that, the leader of the Dragonslayers returned to their gangmates. His suggestion lingered in her thoughts as they walked down the steep, winding beach to rejoin Debo and Crowe. Ballard probably meant well, but she couldn't bring herself to let go. She'd been holding onto guilt and fear for so long, she wasn't ready to relinquish it. She wasn't ready to forgive herself. If others still suffered because of her, she should suffer, too.

She was actually grateful when Ballard insisted they fill their time running drills. Things were easier when she didn't have to think about her past or her uncertain future. After the Dragonslayers were spent, they firmed up their plan for infiltrating the Old Fort. Rinaldo relayed details about the topography. The lava moat had once been a barrier formidable enough to keep predators and infiltrators at bay, but it had long since cooled, so it would provide an easy way in and out. If they were careful, the tall reeds that surrounded the Old Fort would hide their approach. Ballard questioned whether Mari could possess a dragon. The Djinn had never attempted such a thing, but she seemed eager to try.

They waited for nightfall to conceal their long journey back to Lithlorian. Mari gazed in the direction of the Outpost as they loaded into the skiff. For a moment, Neva wasn't sure the Djinn would accompany them back.

"Astiand isn't likely to pay up if you don't return with me," Neva joked, but the words sounded bitterer than she intended.

Mari looked at her sharply.

"I probably should have mentioned it before, but he isn't paying me at all," Mari said.

"What do you mean?" Neva let Debo board ahead of her. "Didn't he hire you to accompany me and deliver the looking glass?"

Mari was shaking her head. "He sent me in the right direction and asked me to pass along your trinket. That was all."

"But then, why do it?" Neva asked.

"My own brother turned me in," Mari said. "Accepting your offer has been the most fun I've had in this lifetime, but I also know you would never betray me like that. ...So mayhap I was wrong. Mayhap, Djinn can have friends."

They smiled at each other.

"In that case, do I get to say I told you so?" Neva asked.

Mari raised her eyes to the sky. "Fine, fine, go ahead."

They laughed and held hands as they climbed aboard.

Chapter Twenty-Eight

Fourth Vestive, 1632

Alewiscious,

I write only to tell you that this is the last response you will receive from me. Your behavior and words are unconscionable. Your actions put all of us at risk, and I suspect your promises of physical preservation are nothing more than chicanery. I offered to aid you in appealing to the Serculus, yet you refuse to reveal your supposed solution for physical preservation. Until you are willing to provide proof of physical preservation for the Brotherhood, don't bother contacting us again.

Brother Noridemus

"We've got trouble," Debo said gravely from the bow.

Neva stifled a groan as she lifted her head from where it hung over the back of the skiff. When she failed to identify any threats from above, her attention swung to Lithlorian Island. A group of Anchorweights and a dozen gangers from the Crown awaited them, toting spears and a few swords. Their torches cast a sinister glow, throwing angry shadows against the rocks.

As the skiff approached, Neva made out Cass ahead of the others, her torch raised high. Neva couldn't hear them yet, but Cass appeared to be shouting. Valentine stood next to her.

"The Crocutas." Mari said.

Now, Neva did let out a groan. Just what they needed. Their competition inciting an angry mob.

"We knew it might come to this," Ballard said. "No one wants rot spreading on Lithlorian."

"What do we do?" Rinaldo asked. He said a quick prayer for Ailish's aid.

Debo bit his nails, and Tavo rattled off a colorful string of obscenities. Crowe whimpered, his head still hanging over the stern.

"Getting the beads to Alewiscious is our first priority," Ballard said. "Getting Mad Merrick and his crew in motion is the second."

"Right, but we have to get through them first." Tavo jerked his thumb at the mob.

"I can take them," Neva croaked. She dry-heaved and wiped her mouth on her arm.

Ballard pretended she hadn't said anything. "You said Cass's boat was around here?" he asked Mari.

"The next cove over," Mari confirmed.

"That's Spyke next to Cass," Ballard commented. "Get us closer, and I'll try to talk some reason into him."

Durant and Tavo rowed faster.

"Oi." Ballard pushed to his feet, rocking the skiff. "What's the problem here?"

"What are you doing out there, Ballard?" Spyke asked.

"You're the problem, Ballard," Cass screamed over Spyke's question. "You and that Da'Valia, and your disease. Go back to Leper Island."

"Now, now." Ballard raised his hands, but his voice boomed out over the water with authority. Warbler flapped his wings and trilled. "We don't have rot. You're welcome to check us yourselves. Besides, if you don't allow us back, who will save your hides next time there's a dragon attack?"

A few gangers glanced around nervously, as if speaking of the wardens would call their attention. The gangers mumbled among themselves, and weapons lowered. Durant and Tavo stopped rowing, allowing the tide to lazily carry the skiff closer to the rocky shore.

"C'mon, Spyke," Ballard urged. "Let us back on the island so we can fend off the wardens on the next hunt. Tavo, when did you say there'd be another attack?"

"Oh, uh, any time now," Tavo shouted his reply. "Why, I wouldn't be surprised if they attacked again tonight."

"Liar," Cass screeched. "He's making it up."

"I ain't seen you out there protecting Town, Cass," said an Anchorweight.

"Think back to what I did for you on the ship that delivered us here, Spyke. It's better to be my friend than my enemy." Ballard lowered his hands, and Warbler ducked his head. "Now, we're coming ashore, and you can take my word for it — we're free of rot. You'll see. Tell your king to inspect the boat moored the next cove over. He can decide if we're the only ones who've ventured to the colony — or if the Crocutas are also at fault."

"You take your crew across, Cass?" Spyke asked suspiciously.

"Certainly not." Cass huffed. "I don't have a death wish."

"Anyone check you for rot since you've been back?" Spyke asked.

"We haven't gone anywhere," Cass shrieked.

"Then where have you been disappearing to lately?" an Anchorweight asked.

Cass shot a frantic look at her crew. As if they were all of the same mind, they threw their torches at the other gangers and sprinted into the jungle. Valentine swore viciously, watching them go. He shot a glance at the mob as if judging how quickly they could cover the distance between them. He launched himself after the Crocutas.

The skiff lurched as it scraped against the rocks. Neva gripped the side so hard that she dented the wood. Rinaldo grabbed ahold of a rock to steady them, but the Dragonslayers waited before disembarking.

"If your king still wants us gone tomorrow, we'll go without a fight," Ballard told Spyke. "But I think you'll find he'd prefer we stay."

"We'll see, won't we?" Spyke spat a thick brown wad out of the side of his mouth. "Seadog, take a few gangers and drag Cass and her crew back to Town. Boss is gonna want to talk with her. I'll check the Dragonslayers over myself. The rest of you, go see about this boat."

Neva climbed out of the dinghy last after Rinaldo and hugged a wet boulder. Spyke inspected the Dragonslayers in short order. Finding nothing, he sped off to catch up with the contingent that was looking for the Fairline.

Tavo snorted once Spyke was beyond hearing distance. "How long before Thatcher rows the Crocutas to the colony, do you reckon?"

Screams and shouts sounded from within the jungle.

"Shouldn't be long," Durant mused. "Midnight at the latest."

"Want me to report back?" Mari offered, a hungry glint in her eyes.

"Please do," Ballard said.

Mari gave a quick nod.

"Mari," Neva croaked.

The Djinn hesitated.

"Ensure the Crown finds rot on them, will you?" Neva asked.

Mari saluted with a devious smile before she morphed and flew away on the wind.

"How long before Thatcher sends his people after us?" Tavo mused.

"He won't," Ballard said firmly. "Spyke owes me, and Thatcher is a smart man. Getting rid of us would mean there was one less layer of protection between him and the wardens. No one else is willing to do what we do."

Ballard had the rest of them on their feet, hiking toward camp by the light of Neva's flame before long. Her motion sickness cleared up by the time they hit the tree line, and Crowe looked a far sight better, too. The gang planned for Tavo and Neva to take the beads to Alewiscious in the morning. Durant and Ballard would deliver a timeline to the Dancing Sandpiper. The others agreed to survey the Old Fort to confirm recent weather hadn't changed anything. For the first time in a long time, hope flared in Neva's chest.

Her gangmates collapsed, exhausted, upon their return to camp. She offered to take the first watch. She wanted to be ready if the Crown came for them in the night, and, if she was being honest with herself, she wanted a distraction. Although she would never admit it, she was nervous to use Astiand's looking glass after their last discussion had been cut off. She delayed pulling out the spelled device until she couldn't put it off any longer. Dawn would arrive soon, and she had meant what she'd said the last time they'd spoken. She honored her debts. Most of the time.

"It's about time," Astiand growled as his face came into focus.

His tone sparked emotion in her.

"Glad I wasn't worrying over you — seeing as you're perfectly fine," Neva said tightly. "What happened last night?"

"Last night?" Realization flashed across his features. "I told you Vivizhi wasn't happy. Well, that's what she's like when she isn't happy."

"I'm sure it's none of my business," Neva said. "I just wanted to tell you I should have things squared away here shortly."

"So you've done it?" Astiand asked.

Her mind flashed to using the Hand on Ebenezer. She took a deep breath that did nothing to lessen the discomfort gripping her chest. Astiand wasn't talking about her killing a man.

"I haven't breached their spire yet," she said. "But preparations are underway, and the Crocutas are no longer in play."

"That's good, isn't it?" he asked.

"It is," she said, but she wasn't sure who she was trying to convince — him, or herself.

"I'll tell Benjamand he can stop searching in the archives," Astiand concluded.

She wanted to tell him not to, but the words were stuck in her throat. If she intended to play fair and had things well in hand, it was true, she wouldn't need Benjamand to break the blood oath. But the fact was, she would need him to void the contract if she wanted to avoid decades of indentured servitude after she double-crossed the donazhi. But Neva couldn't say that to Astiand, who seemed to always put honor above all else and who was still, and forever would be, one of Trinizhi's aliados.

"If anything goes awry, I might need him to break it," Neva told Astiand. This much was true no matter her aim.

"Very well then," Astiand allowed. "Nevazhi, about our discussion last night, before we were interrupted —"

"It's late," Neva said abruptly. "Before you continue, I don't want you to say anything either of us would regret. We should say good night, Astiand."

Astiand's eyes caught hers and didn't let go. She lost the ability to breathe. *He cannot see into your soul,* she told herself, though she wasn't sure it was true. He didn't say anything for a moment.

"Good night, Nevazhi."

The light of the enchanted mirror faded, and she extinguished her power. She forced her limbs to relax. She sometimes wondered if her lies deceived him. Other times, she contemplated whether she was misleading herself, thinking of him as something more to her than he was. It was probably safer to keep herself at arm's length.

Her thoughts flashed to Emiliand and how she had encouraged him to go with the Da'Roha when they parted. Then, how she had agreed to go from one of the farthest corners of the world to one of the most isolated islands with only a remote chance at escape. On a couple of levels, she had done so to keep her friends and family safe — from her and from the Da'Voda.

But she'd never expected to find the Dragonslayers.

Her gangmates were crass, bombastic, superstitious, and brave. Wise and caring. Annoying and lovable. Each of them was willing to risk their life for the others, even Mari, who was more of an honorary member. Although Neva hadn't been looking for it, she'd found family again.

It was an unsettling realization, because that meant she had something to lose.

Atop her branch, Neva stared blankly at the moon, listening to critters of the night as they croaked and chirped. Her spine pressed against the tree trunk, making the chore of being on watch more tiresome than she had hoped. She adjusted restlessly, trying to find a position that wasn't so uncomfortable, then froze.

Had she imagined it? The outline of a dragon gliding across the face of the moon? But another distinct silhouette followed, and another. They didn't flap their wings, so they didn't make a sound. Instead, they coasted in on the wind. Neva sprang to her feet and whistled loudly — a poor man's alarm bell.

"Dragonslayers to arms," Ballard shouted, but everyone was already in motion, collecting their weapons and leaving their branches.

Neva flung her spear down. It reverberated where it stuck in the ground. She leaped off her branch and landed in a crouch. She ripped her spear free, blood heating with the thrill of an impending battle.

"What's the threat?" Ballard asked her.

She gave her report, ending with, "They were headed toward Town."

The Dragonslayers sprinted for the village, shouting loudly enough to rouse any ganger within earshot. Rinaldo was in the lead. As they neared the hub, Tavo tossed his net to her. Neva slipped her spear through and fastened it on the end. Ahead, the dragons descended. There were at least six she could see. Maybe more. One of them unhinged its jaw and sprayed flame into the jungle toward them. The Dragonslayers slid to a stop, a wall of fire blocking their path.

"We can't go through that," Durant shouted.

"Split up," Ballard ordered. "We go around."

Smoke billowed through the trees, obscuring their visibility, and the fire roared as if it, too, were a monstrous beast. Neva coughed on the acrid air, but she kept running. She risked a glance at the sky. With horror, Neva noticed a pattern in their attacks. The dragons were circling, diving at will and forming a ring of fire around Town. Once they completed it, the gangers inside would have no escape.

Neva jerked to a stop, yanking her net to pull Tavo back.

"Ballard, look," she shouted above the mayhem. "This isn't a hunt — they're going after Town."

The dragons were still spraying fire to complete the circle, but they were also targeting all the structures. When they were done, nothing would remain.

"Two hunts this close together? It's payback," Tavo said.

Neva's knuckles turned white on her spear as the truth sank in. The Dragonslayers had taken down Malakai. The wardens were seeking revenge.

"Lose the nets." Ballard cut his spear free. "We save as many as we can, and we get out."

He was looking at Neva when he spoke. Her speed, strength, and agility meant she was the best hope for the gangers. But it was more than that. He was giving her the opportunity to make a choice.

"Why do it?" yelled Crowe, hanging back. "We'll be gone before the week is done."

"Because," Ballard yanked the newcomer by the gorget. "We're the only ones who trained for this. We're the only ones who can. We have to live with what we do tonight for the rest of our lives. Now, go."

Neva took off in an all-out sprint, holding nothing back and leaping over anything in her path. She spotted a break in the ring of fire and threw herself across. About a third of the gangers who lived in Town remained inside the ring with her. Many of them cowered and covered their faces to keep the smoke at bay. Neva frantically searched through the smoke for a way to get everyone out. The heat from the dragonfire toasted her skin from a distance.

She could push aside the flames with a shield, but she didn't want the dragons to learn a Da'Valia was on the island. The last thing they needed was the dragons going on high alert ahead of the heist. Plus, Neva couldn't trust that the Hand would stay within her control again. Adding to the inferno was not her intent. So what was she to do? Her gaze landed on the largest orbo tree in Town.

"C'mon, everyone," Neva yelled. She ran toward it and started scaling the footholds. A line formed behind her. She scrambled faster, flames from nearby trees reaching for her.

When she crested the flames, Neva set her sights on a massive branch that extended to the other side of the ring of fire. Using a limb above the inferno as their escape route would be dangerous, but not as dangerous as staying in Town. This was the best chance any of them had.

"Crawl to the end of the branch," Neva shouted to the ganger behind her, an older man with leathered skin. "Jump for it when you reach the end."

The older man crawled out. The next gangers followed his example. Ganger after ganger got down on his hands and knees. The far end of the branch drooped. From near the end of the line, a panicked woman with her night shift drooping off a shoulder dragged two children after her. The boy climbed up the tree first, with the girl and mother following. They stopped next to Neva, clustered at the base of the branch. The mother shook her head, trails of tears cutting through the soot stains on her cheeks.

"I can't do this." Her voice shook with the edge of hysteria. "We can't do this."

The wardens were incinerating the last of Town's structures. They didn't have long before the dragons turned their attention to the fleeing gangers. Below, Neva saw the Dragonslayers helping the first gangers to the relative safety of the jungle.

Neva squatted down.

"You see those men down there?" Neva asked the little boy and girl.

They nodded, eyes wide and wet.

"Those men fight dragons, and we're here to help you," Neva explained. "All you have to do is climb down the branch, and they'll catch you. Can you do that?"

The children continued to cry, and their mother held them against her. More gangers climbed the tree, inching past them and onto the limb. Neva wouldn't put it past them to push the woman and her children out of the way if they didn't get moving.

"Listen to me." Neva slapped the woman a little harder than she intended. "You have one job to do right now, and that's to get these children to the end of the branch. Understand? Good. Then, move."

Neva sounded like a Da'Valian commander all of a sudden, and she was pretty sure it was because of Ballard's drills. The woman and her children inched out onto the branch, increasing the load to seven gangers. Flames licked at the underside of the limb, and the edges of its deep green leaves smoldered. Neva motioned for the last ganger in line, a middle-aged man with few remaining teeth and desperation in his eyes, to start heading out.

"Ballard," Neva shouted.

He peered up at her.

"Catch the children."

Ballard pulled Debo over, and they positioned themselves under the end of the branch. Rinaldo had his crossbow propped atop a fallen orbo tree, searching the sky for any incoming dragons, and the other Dragonslayers held their spears at the ready. The far end of the branch, where it was no wider than Neva's leg, bobbed each time a ganger dropped. When the branch calmed, the gangers started moving again — all except the girl with blonde curls, who had been following behind her mother.

"Keep going," Neva shouted, making a shooing motion.

The little girl was oblivious, her eyes squeezed shut.

"Outta me way," the last ganger yelled at the girl, threatening to climb over her frozen form.

The wind kicked up. A dragon cried out. A neighboring tree shattered and crashed into the one they were using to escape. The branch shook with the impact, a combination of ash and embers rained down around them. The last ganger lost his hold and screamed as he fell.

The percolating noise that preceded dragonfire sounded above them. Neva made a split-second decision. She still couldn't risk the lives of others by releasing the Hand, and she still didn't want reveal to the dragons that a Da'Valia was on the island. The gangers were going to have to jump for it. *Now.*

"Dragonfire incoming," Neva shouted. "Take cover!"

She ran out to the girl as gangers fell, one after the other. The end of the branch bobbed, hectic. The Dragonslayers kept ushering everyone deeper into the jungle.

"I've got you," Neva told the little girl, prying her fingers free. "Your mother is waiting for you below."

The girl still didn't look. If she had, she would have seen Debo helping the boy and their mother under the cover of the jungle. Neva lifted the girl and jumped. Jungle and flames blurred, dragonfire chasing them. Neva cradled her passenger, landing awkwardly. Pain exploded in her ribs. The branch cracked and came crashing down. A widow-maker. It smashed into Ballard and set fire to several gangers' clothing. Neva rolled the girl to a clear patch of ground. Wisps of dragonfire dissipated behind them. The dragon shot back into the night sky.

"Bloody dragons will circle back." Durant hooked his arms under Neva's. "C'mon."

Crowe collected the girl and delivered her to her mother. Debo and Tavo darted for the branch that had pinned Ballard to the ground. He was unconscious but didn't seem to have any mortal wounds. His armor had shielded him from the fire. Half a dozen gangers were rolling on the moss-covered ground to stifle flames on their clothing. Others were tossing water on them.

"Some help over here," Tavo grunted. He was puffing, his face ten shades of red as they tried to lift the branch off Ballard.

Neva limped over with Durant. Each step jarred her ribs, and her ankle was sprained. Her eyesight sharpened. She grabbed a section of the branch that wasn't aflame and lifted it so the Dragonslayers could pull their leader free. Ballard's head lolled. Shouldn't he have roused with as much as they were jostling him? But his helmet had been dislodged, and the bruise swelling over his temple was raised.

A bright yellow spot beneath the branch caught her attention, bringing tears to her eyes. Warbler, Ballard's trusty companion, had been crushed by the tree. Quickly, Neva scooped him out of the dirt. Ballard would want to say a proper goodbye. Along with the gangers who'd fled with her, Neva trailed after the Dragonslayers. They lugged Ballard into the jungle and huddled together as the dragons circled above, presumably to pick off any lagging gangers.

The inferno raged. A storm rumbled in the distance. Eventually, the dragons flew off. The sky opened up. Raindrops splashed on Ballard's forehead and stuck to his beard.

"Why isn't he waking up?" Crowe asked.

"What if he never wakes up?" Debo asked.

"Don't talk like that," Tavo grumbled. "He will."

"Mayhap he needs to sleep it off," Durant speculated. "We should get him back to camp. See how he's faring in the morning. We can fetch Alewiscious if need be."

If need be? Neva looked down at Ballard again. His chest rose and fell steadily, but his eyes remained shut. She had heard tell of head injuries that would put a person to sleep forever. It was a slow death. And if Ballard died, it would be her fault. She took a shuddering breath. She could have kept this from happening. The Hand was inexorable. Why hadn't she been brave enough to use it? Her mind went blank. She couldn't think anymore. Thinking wasn't going to make this right. *Nothing* was going to make this right.

"If Ballard..." she trailed off.

"Everyone can shut it," Tavo said. "He'll wake up. In the meantime, we carry on. That's what Ballard would want."

Chapter Twenty-Nine

Seventh Cravell, 1651

Dear Elkizhi,

Trinizhi has secured the Eye. She has it locked away, guarded at all hours, and she has persuaded Nevazhi to steal the Mouth for her from Lithlorian Island. Two prongs of the Trishula. Can you imagine? I'm not certain if it is a futile hope, but if we return the Trishula to Dhianz, perhaps he would release you from your madness. Perhaps he would restore sanity to all majilas who broke in the firérite.

Your brother,
— Astiand

As Neva carried Ballard back to their camp slung over her shoulder, the drizzle gave way to a deluge, and spots of lightning skipped sideways across the sky. Smoke from Town thickened and then thinned as the storm stamped out the fire. Neva blinked away the raindrops that landed in her eyelashes and shifted Ballard so his armor wasn't digging into her neck. Her ribs jarred with each step. Tavo and Rinaldo offered to help, but she waved them off. She owed it to Ballard to carry him to safety.

Would he have found it funny that all that training on the beach dragging trees had actually been preparing her for this? It was a dark and humorless thought.

Neva lowered Ballard next to the campfire, which she lit without a word, and propped his head up with her threadbare blanket. Rinaldo might have said something to her, but she didn't hear what it was. She was trapped in her own thoughts.

Neva rose and continued walking. The compulsion to find *something* propelled her. One of the Dragonslayers followed her for a way but wisely let her be when she reached the shore. Neva stood at the edge of the Tyvse Sea and watched the waves wash in. Each one overtaking the last. Never changing. She felt like that sometimes. Stuck in the same pattern, repeating the same mistakes. And the worst part was that she couldn't think her way out of it. No matter what she did, she messed up again and again. She was tired of hurting the people she cared about.

She found her way to the rocks where she'd lost their supper her first time on grub duty and settled against the hard stone. The storm pelted her. Slowly and with purpose, she unbuckled her belt, her fingers running over the abrasive side. She wrapped the white leather around her hand and palmed a dagger. A mark among the Da'Valia was a badge of honor, or it was supposed to be, and she hadn't yet made a mark for Ebenezer. She closed her eyes and let the sound of the waves crashing take her over, yet she made no further move to notch the leather.

"You done wallowing?" Tavo asked.

Uninvited, he took a seat next to her. Neva opened her eyes to find her gang, Mari included, gathering around her. Sunrays peeked through the clouds swarming the island.

"I'm not wallowing, Old Man," Neva said.

"Durant, you're an expert with words — what would you call it?" Tavo quizzed their gangmate.

"It's definitely wallowing," Durant agreed.

Neva let out a long sigh.

"What do you want?" she asked them.

"No offense," Debo said. "But you have the look of someone who is admitting defeat, and that's just not going to work for us."

"I appreciate you trying to make me feel better." Neva cracked a small smile. "But you don't understand. You couldn't understand even if you wanted to."

Debo shifted on his feet, taking a peculiar interest in his boots momentarily. The rain dwindled to a fine mist.

"You've seen my mark?" Debo asked, flashing his wrist. A single, large <u>M</u>. Murder.

"Aye," she answered.

"Ryder was my best friend," Debo said sadly. "They called us the Brawlin' Boys. We ruled the underground fights in the Sorrows back home."

Neva looked at him with a new appreciation. She'd heard of the Brawlin' Boys. They rarely lost and had near-legendary status in Ashford.

"An acquaintance talked us into a big fight, but this time it would be against each other. The purse would be triple or more, he claimed, and it could be ours. Ryder just had to fake a fall after a few rounds of pummeling me. It was a crooked deal, but it could've set me and the missus up for a good chunk of years. So we agreed." Debo's voice cracked and he cried openly, unabashed. "My best friend died by my own hand, and I imagine that's a feeling you know about."

Neva's thoughts flashed to Adam's scarred flesh to Ballard's still body to Warbler's to the camp on the outskirts of Glacier Pass so long ago...

"It is," she said softly.

"There were plenty of witnesses — but mind you, none of them would talk," Debo continued. "I knew that, so I turned myself in. I killed Ryder. I was guilty. I deserved my punishment."

Neva was quiet. She had lived that feeling every day for the past year.

"But Ballard took me aside when I first got here," Debo surprised her by saying. "He'd heard of me and Ryder and what happened. He told me that Ryder wouldn't have wanted me to blame myself. He said that I'd be better off honoring Ryder's memory by living for the both of us."

Neva rubbed her temples, torn. "Do you think that's true?"

Debo cursed and spit for emphasis.

"Gods, no," he replied. "Ryder was the type to hold a grudge, let me tell you. But Ballard's argument got me thinking. Mayhap if I start forgiving myself, then it won't be like the two of us died in the ring. If I can get back to my kids and raise them right, if I can be a good husband to Eileen for once, then maybe the mistakes I've made won't matter so much anymore."

"I want you to think real hard about what kind of person you want to be," Ballard's challenge to Neva when she'd first arrived on the island surfaced in her memories. Oh, how she had failed him. She had let her fear and guilt make her decisions for her, and his injury had been the result.

"What happened in Town, it was my fault," Neva said. "I could have used the Hand and made a shield big enough to protect everyone, but I was afraid."

"I hate to break it to you, but dragons have been taking down Dragonslayers as long as we've existed," Tavo said bluntly. "And although I don't like to admit it, we're all afraid, frequently —" the Dragonslayers nodded their agreement — "but it's a lot easier to fight a dragon with the whole gang backing you up."

"For all our sakes, Neva." Durant cleared his throat. "We need you in this fight for us, and for Ballard."

Neva averted her gaze. She had seen how much the prospect of returning to Cirandrel had meant to Durant when she'd revealed the reason she was on Lithlorian. She wasn't about to abandon her friends or her mission. But while they made it sound easy, her attempts at contributing to the gang thus far had largely fallen short, and she was tired of letting them down.

What would it look like if she forgave herself, she wondered. What would it look like if she used the Hand without fear of the past repeating? What would it look like if she trusted herself again? If she stopped pushing away her family and Emiliand, and if she told Astiand the truth about her feelings toward him. About what she'd done with the Eye.

She sobbed and buried her face in her hands. She could let the past go. She would let the past go. *For Ballard.*

She rose and hurled her belt into the sea. It swallowed the offering, and the last of the clouds dissipated to reveal blue sky.

"All right," she said, tying the ends of her wrap into a makeshift belt. "I'm done wallowing."

The attack on Town had devastated the ganger community, but it wasn't anything to which they were unaccustomed. They had already begun efforts to rebuild at a new location by the time the sun was up. What was more important, Tavo explained, was that the attack had opened a precious window of opportunity. There was a reason that the Docking Day truce followed every big hunt. Even when dragon hunts had been more frequent and often occurred multiple times a week, the creatures would rest following an attack. No stretching their wings. No aerial guard duty, or diving for fish in the sea.

In Tavo's self-proclaimed expert opinion, the respite was for digestion — a theory he attributed to the pellets they regularly found below the spires. Like birds of prey, the dragons would regurgitate those parts that they couldn't pass. That meant the Dragonslayers had a day, maybe two, to pull off their escape while the dragons were prone to lethargy.

Their first order of business was to get Ballard, who still hadn't roused, aboard the Dancing Sandpiper and prevent Mad Merrick from setting sail as many of the other pirates had done in the aftermath of the dragon attack. The beach was cluttered with gangers trying to trade what they had left for the supplies they would need to rebuild, and pirates readying their ships.

Neva wasn't sure they needed to worry. Contrary to good sense, Mad Merrick was lounging on the deck with his sunburnt belly on display, while the other captains fled. Durant went to him to discuss when and where the Dragonslayers would need the assistance they had been promised, while Genivra showed the rest of the gang the way to the sickbay. Neva deposited Ballard on a swaying hammock. She tucked Warbler into Ballard's hand, hoping the familiar pet would be a comfort even though Warbler's soul had passed.

"We don't have a healer anymore," Genivra said apologetically.

"Apothecary ought to fix him right up," Tavo replied.

Neva could tell Tavo was faking confidence. Despite her own miraculous recovery, she'd been conscious enough to swallow the mage's healing tonic — and she was part Da'Valia. Ballard, although his however-many-greats grandfather had been a mage, was an ordinary human.

Their errands aboard the Dancing Sandpiper taken care of, the Dragonslayers headed for the mage's hovel. Rinaldo was particularly twitchy, jumping at any noises in the underbrush during their hike. Durant whistled a tune as if he was trying to distract himself from burdensome thoughts, and Neva touched the pouch of obsidian salt in her pocket more than once, just to reassure herself it was still there.

She wasn't looking forward to seeing Alewiscious. He must have sent her to the Outpost with at least an inkling of what she would need to do to get beads of obsidian salt. But he was one of the most powerful people on the island, and they needed him. She shoved her frustration down and held her head high as the stench of a rotting carcass wafted to her.

"I wasn't sure I'd be seeing you again," Alewiscious said when he opened his door.

"Weren't you?" Neva asked skeptically.

An air of gloating surrounded Alewiscious as he stepped aside and allowed them entry. He inspected his shelves as if searching for something specific. When he turned around, glass jar in hand, he froze. Mari flashed him a devious smile and leaned across his workspace.

"Brother Alewiscious," Mari said in greeting.

"Tavo, tell me you're not bringing a Djinn into my dwelling," he said.

"She's twice the brawler I'll ever be." Tavo shrugged. "Besides, we didn't have much choice. After the attack last night, we've moved our escape up."

"To when?" Alewiscious's face scrunched.

"Tomorrow morning," Tavo said.

"That's — that's preposterous." Alewiscious threw his hands up.

"That's the shape of things," Durant interjected, a crease between his eyebrows. "Is that a problem?"

"I'm working big magic, and you're not giving me much time." Alewiscious toted a cauldron from his counter to his stone hearth. "I'll have to begin immediately."

"It'd be best if you complete it now," Durant agreed. "You know, in case anything untoward happens during our escape."

"Complete it now, he says." Alewiscious laughed. "Most mages wouldn't even be able to conduct magic this complex."

"But you're not most mages." Neva placed the pouch of obsidian salt on his counter.

"No. No, I am not, and I aim to be much more before long." A glint entered Alewiscious's eyes. He carried several more jars to the other side of the counter. "All right. I will need a cut of skin from each of you. Flesh with at least part of a tattoo."

"You trying to kill us? Why, you no-good backstabber," Tavo shouted, lunging for the mage.

Alewiscious transformed. The cabin darkened, and the candles flickered, sending inky shadows spilling across his face. His spine seemed to straighten as he stood taller, his flabby arms appearing muscular. Lightning fast, the mage was out from behind the counter, lording over Tavo.

Tavo pulled back.

"Stand down, Dragonslayer," Alewiscious commanded. He caught Tavo's fist and squeezed. The pressure in the room made Neva's ears pop.

"Alewiscious!" Neva demanded his attention.

The mage turned, his eyes locking with hers, and the strangest thing happened. Neva's power rose within her, but instead of flame erupting, a thin string of fog-like power shot from her — faster than lightning — and tapped the center of his forehead. The next moment, Neva and Alewiscious were in a different place entirely.

They stood in the landscape she'd built for the Hand. Snowflakes drifted from above. A vast, flat desert stretched out around her, with snow-capped mountain ranges in the distance. Quicksand surrounded Alewiscious, dropping away from the tips of the mage's sandals, ready to suck him in if he took so much as a step. Scorch marks like those she'd left behind when she'd released the Hand in the desert darkened the earth, swirling out from where they stood.

Warbler glided over and landed on her shoulder, chattering away. Neva's eyes grew wide. She had not conjured him intentionally. What was this place?

"You dare bring me here?" Alewiscious asked, his lip lifting into a snarl.

"Would you prefer we remain in your cabin with my Djinn friend?" Neva asked, acting as if she'd had every intention of bringing him to her private landscape. As if its creation was at all a matter of intent.

This place was familiar to her, of course. She'd imagined it while deep in meditation aboard the Order's ship, but she had never suspected that her own landscape was made of the same fabric as those the donazhis commanded.

"I need you to explain yourself, Alewiscious," Neva said evenly. "I'll accept only the truth, so choose your words wisely."

Alewiscious held up his wrist, which bore a conviction mark unlike anything she'd ever seen. A single line formed three overlapping triangles, with white scar tissue running through them.

"I need part of the marks to work my magic," Alewiscious said. "It's true that gangers who try to rid themselves of the tattoos perish shortly after, but this is different. I need but a small sliver of the ink. I've done the same thing to myself many years past and lived to tell the tale. I assure you that you and the Dragonslayers will live to tell it as well. Your deaths would not serve me."

"Ebenezer said that the Brotherhood exiled you here." Neva crossed her arms. Warbler twittered and flapped his wings.

"Who do you think created the magic for the conviction marks?" Alewiscious dropped his hands to his sides. "Think, Da'Valia. I want to leave this place as much as you, and you're the one who is going to make it happen. It would make no sense to double-cross you now."

Neva ran her tongue over her teeth. As much as she didn't want anything to do with Alewiscious, she needed him. And he needed her.

"I'll take us back to your hovel," she said finally, hoping she could do it. "And we'll wait for you to complete the spell."

"I'm sure I can hardly change your mind," Alewiscious said.

Neva pet Warbler's forehead as she'd seen Ballard do so many times and whispered goodbye. Pressing her lips together, she imagined them back in the mage's lair, willed them to return.

"Anyone who cuts off their tattoos dies, everyone knows that," Tavo grumbled to the others.

The scent of the mage's lair offended Neva's nostrils once again, and Warbler was gone. The Dragonslayers had formed a semi-circle around her, and they were watching her concernedly. She blinked back at them, her gaze settling on Tavo.

She pulled a knife, flipped the blade, and cut off the side of a conviction mark with a wince. She held out the sliver of skin on the knife tip.

"Work your magic, Alewiscious," Neva said. "And be quick about it."

Before long, Alewiscious had blue glass jars lined up in front of him, one for everyone except for Rinaldo and Mari, and Neva had sealed the Dragonslayers' cuts. Durant and Rinaldo volunteered to fetch a piece of Ballard's tattoo from the Dancing Sandpiper and hurried off. Debo and Crowe shifted awkwardly.

"You can wait outside," Alewiscious told them.

Mari leaned against the counter as the Dragonslayers walked out.

"I'll stay with you two," Mari said casually, twirling the ends of her hair through her fingers. "Help ensure there's no funny business."

"If we were in Qitarah, I could make you leave," Alewiscious said.

"Lucky for me then," Mari tilted her head to the side, "that we're not in Qitarah." Her tongue flicked out, and she smiled.

Chapter Thirty

Fifth Cravell, 1632

Brother Noridemus,
While your resistance has hindered my research, I have
discovered something that will change everything. I have
completed a sacrifice under the full moon, and I expect to have
a godly relic in my possession shortly. Once that happens, trust
I will reach out so you may have the opportunity to express your
regret for your actions thus far. My imprisonment was an
excessive miscarriage of justice, as I have never acted in
opposition to the Brotherhood, but only for its advancement. I
expect the Serculus to embrace me when I return to Qitarah
with physical preservation for all. Surely, they will grant me a
position with the utmost authority and esteem.
Brother Alewiscious
Prisoner 173, Lithlorian Island

The fog that blanketed the island was so thick that mist coated
everything from their clothing to the canopy. Neva fidgeted with the
bandage on her wrist and enjoyed the aroma of wet earth rising from the

island as she huddled in an outcropping at the base of the ashmounts. For the past hour, she'd suffered through the odor of sulfur, but the wind had finally shifted.

Debo, Crowe, and Durant were with her, debating what they would do first when they made it back to the mainland. Since the matter of their conviction marks had been taken care of properly, Rinaldo was off saying goodbye to his family, and Tavo was with him, presumably doing his best to persuade Rinaldo's sister to accompany them. Alewiscious was aboard the Dancing Sandpiper — working healing magic on Ballard, if he knew what was good for him.

Meanwhile, Mari fiddled with a charge. None of the Dragonslayers had experience with explosives, so Mari was their de facto expert, based solely on the brief time she had spent shadowing the Crocutas. If worst came to worst, Neva could ignite the explosives directly, but they were using them as a distraction. She wanted to be at the Old Fort in the morning, not under the ashmounts where they intended to draw the dragons.

"Any luck?" Neva asked.

"Nearly there," Mari said, popping up from behind the powder keg.

"Good," Neva said. "I've been meaning to ask you something... When the Crown abandoned the Crocutas on Leper Island, was Thana still there?"

"Thana who?" Mari asked.

Neva frowned.

"The blind girl who guided us to the Outpost? A limp and boyish haircut?"

"I don't remember any girl," Mari said with a shake of her head. "Gents, do you remember any girl on Leper Island?"

The Dragonslayers paused in their discussion long enough to answer. They didn't remember Thana, but they also couldn't recall how they'd found their way to the Outpost.

Neva rubbed her temples. Why was she the only one who remembered Thana? The girl had disappeared from plain sight, which was something Neva had witnessed before, but her gangmates' memories had clearly been altered. It took a lot to rattle her, but being the only one who could recollect the details of what happened on Leper Island sufficed.

"I'm going to take a walk," Neva announced, giving Mari a meaningful look. It was time she check in with Astiand.

"Do you want one of us to come with you?" Durant asked.

She waved him off, and he returned to conversing. Neva picked her way over the rocks, careful not to jostle her ribs too badly. The incoming waves misted her. She settled down beside the tide pools. Since the Dragonslayers found her on the rocks on the other side of the island, she'd wanted to tell Astiand that she'd been wrong to treat him the way that she had. That she had pushed him away to protect him. That she was sorry.

She pulled Astiand's mirror from her wrap to find a spider web of cracks running through it. She'd kept the mirror in her wrap since Mari gave it to her, but it must have been broken in the dragon fight.

"No," she murmured under her breath. "Please work."

She arranged the pieces together and thought of Astiand, hoping for a miracle. Nothing happened. She closed her eyes, remembering the shame she'd felt at mistakenly believing he would betray her and the rightness of his touch under the stairs in Picquereau. Still, nothing.

Neva swiped the shards into the nearest tide pool and dropped her head in her hands. She wanted to scream. The idea that Astiand was out there somewhere, doing his best to protect her without knowing that she respected him — that she valued him — was torture.

What had she told him the last time they talked? That he shouldn't say anything either of them would regret? How naive she had been, thinking being honest with Astiand was what she would regret more than not saying anything at all.

Her stomach churned. Given what she would face when she returned to Cirandrel, she wasn't certain she and Astiand would be able to steal a moment away from Trinizhi. What had she done?

An early morning rain petered out as Neva hunkered down among the tall grass outside the Old Fort with the Dragonslayers and Mad Merrick's pirates. Their clothing was soaked through, and mud stuck to their boots.

Her legs had fallen asleep long ago, and tension knotted her shoulders, but she didn't dare move until Mari put things in motion.

Beside Neva, Rinaldo murmured a mantra for courage, and Tavo covered a yawn. Neva raised her eyebrows at him. For varying reasons, she hadn't been able to sleep the night before, yet she found it impossible to be anything but *awake* with what they were about to attempt. She imagined infiltrating the Old Fort and coming face to face with a dragon. How long would it take him to eat her if she was trapped in enthrall? She shivered.

"What if the fuse didn't light?" Rinaldo asked, gnawing on ingo stalk.

"Just wait," Durant said.

Twin explosions rocked the island. Black smoke billowed from the base of the ashmounts, which rumbled ominously. A half-dozen dragons launched from the lantern of the spire and headed for the far side of the island. Smoke streamed from the fiery ashmounts, obscuring the morning sun.

Abandoning the concealment of the reeds, Neva ran with the Dragonslayers and their pirate comrades for the entrance of the Old Fort. Neva made it to the towering double doors first. She channeled her power into the wrought iron hinges. It took a little longer than she'd hoped, but they soon glowed orange, indicating they were weakened, malleable.

Neva pulled on the handle and helped the team of pirates quietly catch the door as it fell outwards. They lowered it to the ground. They had agreed on limited talking for this mission, but Tavo's raised eyebrows said he was impressed.

Neva grinned at him. She removed the gloves from her wrap and pulled them on. She stepped inside the Old Fort.

The dragon hoard stopped her in her tracks. She barely caught an involuntary laugh before it was too late. The Dragonslayers exchanged looks of glee, and the pirates raised their arms in a silent celebration. The Old Fort itself was magnificent, with checkered floors and marble columns. Rose gold paint gilded arched windows and matched the filigree along the bannister. Spiral stairs that led up the spire, where a giant aquaclock made of glass and metal hung suspended from the ceiling. But all of that paled in comparison to the treasure.

The amount of gold and jewels before them was positively grotesque. The Dragonslayers had promised Mad Merrick exceptional riches, but without seeing the contents of the Old Fort, it'd been part bluff.

Neva gaped at the peaks and valleys of treasures piled before them, which included everything from chandeliers to trunks to instruments, and more. They had only stepped through the front doors. What filled the remaining levels of the spire would be too much to sort through, and they wouldn't be able to take all of it.

But that wasn't for her to worry about. The Dragonslayers and the pirates were in charge of loading the ship. She had a job to do.

The Old Fort was a big place, and dragons coveted rare and priceless items. The Trishula was both. She would find the Mouth where the dragons were. The heart of the Old Fort, the spire.

Neva sought out Durant and pointed toward the stairs. He would not come after her if they were found out, but she wanted him to know she was off to enact her part of the plan. He nodded to her.

Neva quickly maneuvered through the mess of treasure, heading for the stairs. She pulled her arms in close and avoided stepping near anything that might fall over. Ceramic pots, antique paintings, and silver urns of varying sizes were stacked along the banister and down the halls. Neva glanced over the goods and did a cursory inspection of each room on the second floor.

Where are you?

Rodents scurried away from piles of priceless rugs as she approached. There was so much stuff in the tower that even gold and jewels didn't seem like treasure after a while. It was a good thing the dragons could fly off the roof, because they couldn't possibly make it down their own stairs.

Neva stilled. If she continued like this, she would never make it to the ship in time. She pulled at the collar of her wrap. If she had any hope of finding the Sword of Elon in this palace of forgotten riches, she would need an advantage.

She shook her hands out at her sides, giving herself over to her senses. When she had stolen the Eye from the House of Trescony, she'd been drawn to it. Perhaps that hadn't been a coincidence.

She listened for something — anything. The Hand beckoned her. She ignored it. She ignored the delicious chill of the stone walls separating her from the sun and the thrill of thieving humming through her veins. Finally, faintly, she sensed another presence.

She tilted her head back. The Mouth was above her.

That narrowed it down to eighteen more floors or so.

Neva raced back to the stairs. She took them two at a time, stopping to feel for the Mouth on each floor. She was panting and already to the fifteenth floor when Mari materialized beside her in a cascading hourglass of shimmering yellow sand.

"Mari," Neva hissed. She slid to a stop, narrowly avoiding a pile of uncut gems. "You shouldn't be here."

"The gang has everything well in hand," Mari whispered. "I just wanted to give my report. Everything is going according to plan. The next charge should go off in about..."

Mari ticked one, two, and three off on her fingers. An explosion sounded in the distance. She grinned as the floor shook under them. A human skeleton toppled off the bannister on the floor above, dropped past them, and smashed into smithereens on the checkered tiles of the entrance way.

Neva and Mari locked eyes.

"Don't move," Neva mouthed. She had heard a few noises during her search. Most had come from the crew downstairs, but a few had come from the spire's lantern. Their distraction had drawn away some of the dragons, but not all.

After a few more moments of silence, Neva relaxed.

"How many?" Mari asked.

"One? Two? More?" Neva asked. If the treasure in the Old Fort was hers, she certainly wouldn't leave it unguarded. They'd seen half a dozen dragons fly away when the first explosions struck, but she hadn't seen the eldest, Enoch, whom Tavo had said was the deadliest. "Go help the gang. I'm getting close, and I'll be at the rendezvous as soon as I have the sword."

"You don't need me here?" Mari asked in hushed tones, pouting.

"I need the boat loaded and a smooth getaway," Neva said.

"Aye-aye," Mari saluted. "One smooth getaway ahead."

The Djinn morphed into dust before Neva could admonish her for jinxing them. Neva shook her head as she continued on. Each floor seemed to house better wares than the one below it. She was so close to the top of the spire that regurgitated bones littered the trove. Neva grimaced as she stepped over a large pellet, which she was sure Tavo would find terribly interesting.

She stopped at a landing and peered into to the stairwell that led to the lantern. She activated her invisibility glamour and scratched at the insatiable itch on her neck as the magic awoke. She crept up the stairs. She took a deep breath, rounded the corner, and froze.

A dragon the color of a juicy plum was curled up just inside the wide entrance, wisps of smoke escaping with every laborious exhale. His horns, many times larger than her own, curled forward like a bull's. His tail twitched. The telson on the end clinked against the tile floor. He must have been dreaming because his eyes were closed. Drool pooled beneath the razor tips of his teeth. Neva's bladder constricted, and her throat went dry. She was so close, she could reach out and touch him if she wanted to.

She absolutely did not want to.

Neva silently ran through a prayer to Dhianz. When the dragon failed to stir, she exhaled slowly and straightened. What were the shades Tavo had related to each dragon? The eldest were the darkest, and this one was nearly black. Enoch.

Enoch's tail twitched a second time, and Neva lowered herself into a crouch, fighting the instinct to flee. She reached out again for the Mouth with her senses.

There you are.

She called on her Da'Valian vision. A faint glow came from the farthest corner of the room. She squinted. In tales of lore, the sultan who'd forged the Sword of Elon polished the basket hilt until it gleamed, but the ornamentation hadn't been polished in a very long time. She sidled past the dragon, keeping her attention locked on his horns just in case. A calm wind poured through the arching windows, coercing the smoke away from her.

Neva froze at the sound of scaly wings flapping. A burst of wind preceded the graceless landing of a white dragon. It angled through two pillars of the lantern in a fluid motion. Then, it was tumbling across the marble floor in a mess of scales and talons.

Neva took advantage of the ruckus to dive across the opening. She halted in front of the sword. It was wedged between a large ceramic vase, an antique hand-carved screen, and a pile of other weapons that looked to be worthy of a bard's song. A quiver of golden arrows. An engraved battle axe. A suit of armor large enough to fit an ogre. Move one and the rest would come tumbling down.

The sound of another dragon reached her. She relaxed her fingers. A dragon the color of desert sand dropped gracefully into the room, spitting an Anchorweight out onto the floor.

Neva yanked the sword free. She lowered it swiftly and cringed as the collection of weapons toppled.

Enoch's head snapped around.

"Young Chaard, what is the meaning of disturbing my slumber?" Enoch hissed, his voice carrying a thick brogue.

Neva held her breath.

"A meal, grandfather," the pale dragon said, nudging the ganger closer to Enoch. The Anchorweight groaned. "I found him near the explosions."

"Do you smell that?" Enoch stared directly at Neva, searching for something. Searching for her.

Every muscle in Neva's body tensed. Three dragons were between her and the door. They suspected her presence. She couldn't wait them out, so what could she do? She was trying to come up with a plan when she spied Mari's golden dust swirling outside the doorway.

Stupid Djinn, she thought. *Thank the gods for you.* At least Neva wasn't alone.

"I smell another ganger." Enoch unfurled with a snarl. "Stop playing with your dinner, Lennox. Chaard, guard the door."

The white dragon — Lennox — raised his head from the flailing Anchorweight. "Another ganger?"

Enoch stalked closer to Neva. "Show yourself," he demanded.

Neva's heartbeat pounded in her ears.

"I said to show yourself," Enoch roared. His tail whipped out, striking a mountain of glistening gems. Neva flinched. Deep red rubies, amber citrine, and dazzling emeralds slid across the floor to further complicate her escape.

Mari's dust form drifted in along the floor and commingled with the smoke pouring from Chaard's nostrils. On an inhale, Mari slid inside the dragon. Chaard's eyes flashed yellow.

Neva rose from her crouch and dropped her invisibility glamour.

"What mischievousness is this?" Enoch hissed. Smoke billowed around him. "Who are you?"

"You can call me the Lynx," Neva kicked the sword up, caught it, and stepped toward the door. "I was just on my way out."

"Put down my sword." Enoch's chest rumbled, signaling a rising flame. "I will eat you alive, Da'Valia."

"I think not," Neva said. "You're going to let me walk out of here — isn't that right, Mari?"

"That's right," Mari said, stretching out on her back, belly up. "If you value your offspring that is."

Sparks shot from Enoch's nostrils.

"Chaard?" Enoch asked.

"Mari. My friend is a Djinn." Neva strode toward the door, stopping next to Mari. "And she is very powerful, as you can see, so I suggest you step aside."

"Prepare to die, Da'Valia." Lennox hissed.

Swiftly, Neva freed the Sword of Elon from its scabbard and pointed it at Chaard's chest. Thick, black blood seeped out. "Your word that you will let me walk out of here alive. *Now.*"

Enoch whipped his tail around and slammed it into the marble tiles, cracking them.

"Leave our den, foul creatures," he growled.

"Your word," Neva demanded. "Both of you."

"You have it," Enoch said. "Be gone with you."

Lennox lowered his head flush against the floor.

Neva backed out the entrance. "Mari, let's go."

Neva lowered the sword and slung the scabbard over a shoulder. She couldn't believe they'd done it. Her chest swelled with the thought that she would have made both her parents proud.

A cloud passed overhead, casting a gloomy shadow over the lantern. A beat passed. Neva's gaze darted to Mari and back to Enoch's horns. Mari had never possessed a dragon before. Had something gone amiss? After another beat, just enough time for fear to impede Neva's air supply, golden dust streamed from Chaard's mouth. Mari returned to her corporeal form and flashed Neva a smile.

"What was it that you said about a smooth getaway?" the Djinn gloated, blowing dust off her knuckles with a haughty look over at Chaard.

"I —" Mari stopped walking. Her fingertips faded to dust for just a moment before returning to their solid state. Her eyes were frozen in place, pinned on Chaard.

Neva's blood turned to ice.

"We had a deal," Neva said through gritted teeth.

"We did, indeed." Enoch turned on her. "And according to that agreement, you may live. Your Djinn, however, is ours."

No! Neva screamed frantically inside her mind. She jerked, ever-so-faintly hearing Emiliand call her name in response, but he was gone the next moment.

Chaard curled his tail around Mari.

"Look at my new treasure, grandfather," Chaard said.

"She wasn't part of our agreement," Neva said.

"You're right. She wasn't." Enoch stalked across the grand room. "The question is, are you prepared to join her?"

He unhinged his lower jaw to reveal the flame that dwelled in the back of his throat.

Neva forced herself to take a step backward. Then another. Self-preservation kicked in. She spun and fled the lantern. She flung herself down the stairwell and braced her forehead against the stone wall. She sucked in short, rapid breaths, her hands tingling. She felt sick to her stomach.

The dragons had Mari. What was she going to do?

"Hello, dove," a voice sounded behind her.

Chapter Thirty-One

Eighth Cravell, 1651

Brother Noridemus,

It is with pleasure that I report to you I have a relic within reach — Dhianz's Hand, in fact. Obviously, my spell to call it here took longer than anticipated, but perhaps that's what one might expect when one is tethered to an island as remote as Lithlorian. Regardless, I conducted a test to confirm. Don't bother sending a boat. I will return to Qitar with haste once I secure the relic, and the Serculus can initiate me in front of the entire Brotherhood.

Brother Alewiscious
Prisoner 173, Lithlorian Island

Neva spun around, coming face to face with Thatcher. What was he doing here? She didn't have a chance to find out before he threw an illuminator up, and the cast ball of magic burst into a brilliant flash of light. Neva shielded her eyes. The next spell he tossed at her hit her like a slap across her cheek. The conflicting tastes of copper and blackstrap molasses coated her mouth.

Time slowed.

...Wait. That wasn't right. Water still flooded the center of the aquaclock. Thatcher still moved toward her at full speed. It was she who had decelerated.

Neva reached for the Hand, trying to track his movements. The Hand would obliterate the hold that Thatcher's spell had on her. She looked down.

Too late.

He ripped the sword from her grasp with gloved hands.

"So sorry, dove," Thatcher said, assuming a classic fencer's stance. He thrust the blade at her heart.

The ancient blade glanced off the soul scourge crystal, slicing a shallow, bloody streak down her sternum. In the brief moment that it touched her, Neva's lips parted and her lungs swelled, the Mouth claiming her.

Thatcher yanked the sword away. A massive shockwave exploded, sending a searing white light through Neva's mind and tossing them apart.

Neva regained consciousness with her face in a shallow puddle of blood. Her nose was bleeding, and she had suffered a gash on her eyebrow, but she'd only been out for a split-second, according to the aquaclock. She shoved herself up, seeing double. She grabbed the banister and struggled to stand.

Her eyesight sharpened. Thatcher had been tossed opposite her, back up the stairwell. She unleashed her power, but he had already ripped the cork free from the vial he held to his lips. He disappeared with a strange sucking sound. The Sword of Elon went with him.

Neva dropped to her knees, her mind blanking. She watched her attack burn out against the ceiling as if she was seeing it from outside her own body. Debris fell, sending fine cracks through the glass of the aquaclock. Hope shriveled in her chest.

Vanquist spells were known for accidentally disappearing body parts more than they were known for transporting people great distances, so Thatcher must not have gone far. But wherever he'd ended up, he was untraceable. Meaning that if Trinizhi had sent Thatcher, Neva had failed.

She allowed herself a moment — just one moment — to wallow in self-pity. If she ran now, she might reach the Dancing Sandpiper before it set sail, and her gang might be able to make an educated guess about which pirate ship Thatcher was most likely to use as his getaway. But doing so meant that Mari would be left at the mercy of the dragons.

Neva whispered a curse. She was trying to relinquish the guilt that had been crushing her for the past year. The only way she could remain unburdened was to live with no regrets, and leaving Mari behind would be a regret. Neva couldn't do that to someone she considered family. But could she instead allow Trinizhi to seize the Hand and the Eye? To force Da'Valia everywhere under her ruthless rule?

Neva tugged her gloves off with her teeth and yanked a short sword from the pile of treasure to her left. Her mouth went bone-dry, and her ears roared. She clutched the sword as if it were a lifeline and she was trying not to drown in the Tyvse Sea.

Mere threads held together her wrap, but, luckily, the cut that ran down her middle was superficial. She would tend the wound later. If there was a later.

Three dragons, a Da'Valia, and a Djinn walk into a pub, but who walks out? She was insane — absolutely insane — doing what she was about to.

She braided a shield of power in front of her and bounded up the stairs. She bolted into the lantern to find Chaard wrapped around Mari, leisurely squeezing. Lennox clamped his massive jaw down on the Anchorweight with fervor, shaking the ganger like a ragdoll. And Enoch — Enoch was waiting for Neva. He unleashed dragonfire.

Neva dropped and slid, using a blast of power to propel herself across the room to Chaard. Dragonfire flowed over her shield like a river over rocks. Chaard snarled and bucked his hind claws at Neva. She flung her shield at him and let go of the power as Enoch whipped his tail out, the telson on the end narrowly missing her head. She flipped to her feet and sent a barrage of strikes at Lennox and Enoch. She brought her sword down on the narrow place where Chaard's telson emerged from his tail.

The dragon's caterwaul pierced the air. Neva fought the need to cover her ears. Her sword was wedged under a scale. She abandoned it as Chaard ripped his tail away, telson dangling. Neva skipped back beyond his reach. Mari convulsed and fell to her knees as she was released from enthrall.

"Take Enoch," Neva shouted.

Mari shot toward Enoch. But it wouldn't matter if Mari possessed one warden, because they were all about to unleash dragonfire. Neva darted between two columns. She twisted to catch her balance on the ledge of the lantern and manifested a new shield.

Dragonfire slammed into the shield almost as soon as she erected it behind her. The impact sent her flying.

Neva plummeted. With a cry, she summoned an enormous stream of power to slow her fall. She landed hard on a tile roof and rolled, out of control. She slipped off the edge and into one of the fort's vast courtyards. Her ribs hit the stone edging, stealing her breath. Struggling to her feet, she took in the field of sizeable black eggs that stretched out before her. The top of each egg was shattered. Dragon spawns, hundreds of them, had been born here.

Dread knotted her stomach, but there was no movement. She was alone down here. She peered up to see Mari unhinge her jaw and chomp down on Chaard's neck. Lennox leaped atop Mari with another ear-gouging cry and sank his fangs into her rear.

Run, Neva ordered herself.

She was a blur as she escaped the Old Fort. Her heels struck the hard earth, the solid lava moat, the wet moss, the rotting logs. She moved so fast that the jungle was nothing more than a stream of color flying past. Her skin stung as she failed to avoid leaves and branches. She blasted a strangling vine in her path. She crested a bluff to find the Dancing Sandpiper raising its anchor in a small bay.

"I'm here," Neva screamed, barreling down the beach. She stumbled to a stop at the water's edge, sinking into the wet shore.

Mari crash-landed next to her, her hindquarters painted with black blood. Sand showered down around them.

"Can you climb on?" Mari asked.

"Aye." Neva was already moving toward her friend.

Mari offered a claw. Neva climbed up. Her ribs screamed at her. The Hand was pounding against its cage. Next to it, another less-discernible power stretched and swirled. The Eye was no longer bound. It was free for her to use — something notable but which she would contemplate at a later time. Neva pushed them back, channeled her pain to strengthen her concentration, and hoisted herself atop Enoch's back.

She looked out over the bay and gestured for Durant and Crowe to return to the Dancing Sandpiper. They had finished unloading the last skiff full of treasure and were already sailing her way, but Mari would be faster. Durant waved in response, and they executed a fast jibe, nearly capsizing. Neva let out a breath when they managed to stay upright.

"I won't be able to control Enoch much longer," Mari said.

"Just get me to the ship." Neva leaned flush against Enoch's neck.

Mari pushed off, violently pitching Neva. She clutched Enoch's dark purple scales. The slash down her middle pulled, her ribs burned, and her arm throbbed. She swallowed down bile as they gained altitude. They weren't halfway to the ship when the wardens broke out of the enormous cloud of smoke from the ashmounts, heading straight for them.

Mari flew faster. Ahead, Durant and Crowe reached the Dancing Sandpiper, and the pirates raised the sails. Mad Merrick and Genivra shouted orders from opposite ends of the ship, the crew orchestrating their getaway with an array of ropes, levers, and pulleys. Rinaldo and a small contingent of pirates had arrows trained on Enoch. Just out of range, Mari hovered until Rinaldo made everyone lower their weapons.

"Ready?" Mari asked Neva.

"As I'll ever be," Neva said, identifying a clear spot on deck.

Mari dove, and Neva's stomach fell out from under her. She let go. She used one of Mad Merrick's men to break her fall.

"Take aim," Rinaldo ordered.

The archers raised their bows. Mari burst free from Enoch in a brilliant cloud of golden dust.

"Fire!"

Most of the arrows hit Enoch's impenetrable scales and fell away, but one struck true. Enoch thrashed, an arrow sticking out of one eye. Some foolish pirate had dared to look at the dragon's eyes.

"Incoming," Mad Merrick shouted across the deck.

"Get up." Tavo ran over and yanked Neva to her feet.

Neva blasted Enoch. Her power hit him in the chest, but not before the wounded warden sprayed dragonfire. A sudden gust of wind made the sails go taut, ropes straining and wood creaking, propelling the Dancing Sandpiper beyond the flames. Neva sought out Mari, but her gaze landed on Genivra, whose eyes were glowing. Wind whipped around the woman, drawing her dreadlocks away from her face. The stories about the Dancing Sandpiper's exceptional getaways suddenly made much more sense.

Neva spotted Mari and didn't like what she saw. Mari was wan, fading in and out of her dust form as she made her way to the cluster of archers.

Alewiscious flung a spell at Enoch from the quarterdeck. A magical rope with an electric aura looped around Enoch's neck. Neva's eyes widened — it was an enchanted strangling vine.

Enoch roared. He sprayed another blast of dragonfire at the ship's sails, but he was laboring and losing altitude. Neva flung up a shield large enough to protect the mast. In her peripheral, she spied the incoming wardens. Ghostly bluish-white dragons jumped ahead of where the beasts were. Neva blinked hard. The hallucination disappeared.

"Fire in the hole," Mad Merrick shouted.

Thunderous explosions boomed and ricocheted off the water as the crew discharged the cannons below deck. The blasts rocked the ship. Neva dug her fingers into the damp wood of the taffrail. Then, she was running, and sliding, for the stern. The dragons scattered to avoid the cannonballs, giving her a brief opening to take her position for their getaway. Mad Merrick's crew brought the ship about, resuming their trajectory away from Lithlorian.

"You've seen our tricks. Show us yours, Da'Valia," Genivra shouted.

Neva cracked her neck and rubbed her hands together. She couldn't believe she was about to do this, but she had to or else everyone aboard the ship would become dragon fodder.

She willed away an avalanche of fears: of the ship catching fire, of it sinking, of the crew or the Dragonslayers being hurt — or worse. Raising shaking arms to channel the Hand into being, Neva turned the spindle wheel on the vault in her mind. The Hand surged to meet her.

Neva jerked at the outpouring of power and wedged a foot against the base of the mizzen behind her. Her heart went wild, and she momentarily forgot to breathe. She bit the inside of her cheek. Hard.

Heed me, she ordered. She sucked in a deep breath to steel herself. Fiery tendrils streamed into the sky, and she latched onto them, drawing them where she wanted them to go. She wove the power together with speed and efficacy. This wasn't an accidental release or a release for the sake of release. The Hand followed her every command. It wanted to be used, and for the first time, she was using it in battle as Dhianz had intended.

A smile flitted across Neva's face as her net took shape. For once, she was grateful that Ballard had made her practice weaving nets beside the campfire. Exhilaration stamped out her fears as she raised the net of fire from the sea to well beyond the clouds, forcing the advancing wardens to veer. The crew of the Dancing Sandpiper stopped. Across the deck, they gaped.

Mad Merrick was the first to recover.

"To your stations. Mind your tasks, you halfwit twits." The captain's bellows startled his crew from their dazes.

"I stand corrected," Genivra muttered. "That's no mere trick."

Laughter bubbled up inside Neva at the first mate's words. She wove the net higher. She loved her sword, her spear, and her knives. But employing the Hand was a gift from Dhianz. She was fearless and formidable. She was a force to be reckoned with. Who could say what would be... She only knew that she would never doubt herself for using everything at her disposal to protect those aboard the Dancing Sandpiper. Tavo. Mari. Ballard.

Tears stung her eyes, but she didn't mind. They were tears of relief. This, all of this, felt right. She was meant to embrace the Hand and use it as it was meant to be used. She would never imprison this part of herself again.

Cheering gangers littered the main beach on Lithlorian, widening her smile. Neva rolled her shoulders and stood up straighter. Sure, she had failed to keep the Sword of Elon, but she was doing something no one had ever done before. She was escaping from Lithlorian Island.

Splash … splash … splash!

The wardens dove into the Tyvse Sea. Neva pivoted, sending the Hand below the surface to meet them. The ocean boiled where the Hand disappeared from view. Beads of sweat dripped down the sides of her face as she doubled her efforts to maintain the net under the water. It would only take one dragon getting through and ramming the hull to put an abrupt end to their grand escape.

A warden smashed into the Hand below the surface, a blow to the gut. Neva doubled over. The dragon was tangled in the burning net, flailing, and each yank and tug on the Hand was an assault on her person.

The flailing stopped.

The remaining wardens broke the surface with a cacophony of caterwauls. Mad Merrick's ship continued to make away, and Neva continued to feed the net, expanding it so that the dragons could not go around. A faint, telltale sound reached her on the wind, and she set her mouth in a hard line. The wardens were preparing to unleash dragonfire. Together, would they be able to puncture the net she'd constructed? She wasn't going to give them the chance to find out.

With a guttural yell, she gathered the net and brought it down on the dragons. They dove back into the ocean. She cinched the burning net underwater and pulled it in to prevent the wardens from escaping. They thrashed about, spraying dragonfire. Neva fell to her knees. Her insides were being torn apart. She channeled the pain into keeping the net alive.

Finally, the dragons ceased. Neva collapsed onto the deck, her back against the mizzen.

The Hand pooled, burning brightly and calmly, in the back of her mind.

"Thank you, trishulita," it whispered, content again.

Chapter Thirty-Two

Ninth Cravell, 1651

Dear Elkizhi,

I've done all that I can, yet it does not seem to be enough. Nevazhi pushes me away at every turn, and I've not heard from her in days. I fear her dislike. I fear her demise. I fear our failure for all Da'Valia.

More recently, I find myself questioning Trinizhi's motives for trying to ensnare Nevazhi with a blood contract. What if it's not just because she wants the Mouth from Lithlorian Island? The things I've seen Nevazhi do... There's never been a majila like her. I approached a Da'Xana scholar on her behalf the other day, and he said something under his breath. I heard the word 'Trishula.' What if Vivi has been right all this time? That Neva was chosen by Dhianz. What if, somehow, the power from the second prong lies within her? May Dhianz have mercy on us all.

Your brother,

— Astiand

Mad Merrick insisted that Neva rest in his quarters after she had helped solidify his place as one of the greatest pirates in history, and she was only too willing to accept. Neva leaned back atop the captain's bed, and her moan of pleasure abruptly turned into a groan of disgust. Mad Merrick's pillow smelled like fish. She threw it to the foot of the bed with a sigh. She felt less burdened than she had in a long time, but after a heist, a battle, and an escape, she couldn't help fidgeting. Her Da'Valian side was primed to fight. She needed a distraction.

Neva had just begun to reach for the Eye when the Dragonslayers and Alewiscious arrived. A rotund pirate pushed into the cramped cabin behind them and gave Neva a black-toothed grin, his eyes flashing yellow. Mari stepped aside, and Ballard trailed in.

"It seems I slept through all the excitement," he said, hooking his thumbs on his belt.

"Ballard." Neva leaped up and threw herself at their leader.

"Thank you for Warbler," he whispered, returning her embrace. Louder, he said, "Alewiscious forced some of that healing tonic down my throat. Works wonders. I hope to never experience it again."

Neva grinned. His apparent dislike matched her own feelings about the concoction.

"Speaking of..." Alewiscious rummaged around in his pockets as if he couldn't remember where he'd put something. He pulled out a vial. "Heat it, and drink it."

Neva made a face and took the tonic. As much as she loathed the stuff, doing anything with fractured ribs was uncomfortable. Throwing up would be worse — and they were embarking on a long boat ride.

"My thanks, Apothecary," Neva said, raising the vial in salute.

Alewiscious watched her as she heated the vial and raised it to her lips. She frowned at him, not liking the attention, and was struck by a vivid image.

Alewiscious, standing over her prone body, his arms raised as he chanted an incantation in a language Neva had never heard before. Snakelike tendrils of his electric-edged power wrapped around her wrists and ankles.

"Neva?" Tavo snapped his fingers in front of her face. Her vision cleared.

"Tavo?" she asked, dizziness making her sway on her feet. "What happened?"

"Your eyes went white and you just sort of... froze up?" Mari said it like a question.

"I — I saw *you* conducting magic against me." Neva pinned Alewiscious with a glare. "What's in this tincture, Apothecary?"

Neva threw the vial at him. He fumbled after it. The glass cylinder bounced back, striking her leg and shattering against the floor. The contents of the vial seeped across the floorboards, and a foul-smelling smoke rose from the mess. Neva had no doubt that it would have been equally as caustic on her insides.

"Why you no-good —" Tavo pulled back his fist.

Neva raised her palm, white fire licking over it, ready to teach the mage a lesson. Alewiscious went for another pocket, and Tavo swung. He screamed when his fist came back and broke his own nose. Blood spurted and poured down his face. That shouldn't have happened. *Magic.* Neva yanked her power back at the last second and grabbed Durant's arm before the swindler tried to sink his blade into Alewiscious's gut.

Rinaldo and Mari grabbed Alewiscious by the arms.

"He must've spelled himself," Debo guessed. "What do we do with him?"

"That's enough of your tricks, Al." Rinaldo ripped away Alewiscious's cane and tossed it out the door.

"This is Mad Merrick's ship," Ballard said as Rinaldo and Mari tied the mage's hands. "He'll decide what to do with him."

"You can't put my fate in the hands of a mad man." Spittle accompanied Alewiscious's objection.

"I'd consider myself lucky if I were you," Neva told him. The image of her at his mercy was burned into her memory.

The Dragonslayers dragged Alewiscious to the deck and called down Mad Merrick. The captain and Genivra approached from the quarterdeck with curious expressions.

"What is it?" Genivra asked, hands on her hips.

"Alewiscious tried to poison me," Neva said, clenching her teeth.

"A serious allegation," Mad Merrick mused. "Have you any proof?"

"They all saw it." Neva gestured to her gang. They chimed in with their agreement.

"Even you, Roberto?" Mad Merrick asked Mari's host.

"Aye, Captain," Mari said gruffly.

Mad Merrick and Genivra exchanged a look.

"Lay out the plank," Mad Merrick yelled. "Apothecary is taking a walk."

The crew stopped what it was doing, and two men went about fulfilling their captain's order, sliding a plank out over the fast-moving water.

"Don't do this, Merrick. Take pity on an old man." Alewiscious struggled against Rinaldo and Mari. "It is a mere misunderstanding. I'm innocent, I swear it."

Before them, Alewiscious shriveled and withered into a skeleton that vaguely resembled a man. His beard thinned and became straggly. His skin stretched to hang from his bones. A hump strained against the clothes on his back. His bound hands locked themselves in claw-like positions — reaching toward the cane that Rinaldo had thrown out of the cabin.

The cane rolled across the deck, straight for Alewiscious. Neva pounced on it and tossed it overboard. If he wanted the cane, that was reason enough for her to be rid of the thing.

"No!" Alewiscious lunged after the cane, his expression turning dark and angry. Mari and Rinaldo yanked him back. Alewiscious's feebleness faded away. The hump shrunk, and he grew taller, muscular even.

"May the gods curse you." Alewiscious snarled.

"They already have." Neva crossed her arms.

"Enough," Mad Merrick yelled. "I'll not have anyone attempting murder aboard my ship — unless it's me. I hereby sentence Alewiscious to death in the depths of the Tyvse Sea. Walk, Apothecary!" Mad Merrick waved his sword.

"Mind your blade," Ballard cautioned quickly. "He protected himself with a spell."

"Is that so?" Genivra pulled a small metal ball from a pocket and juggled it in one hand. "Let's rectify that."

She threw the illuminator into the air. It burst into light and hovered over the deck, shining brightly and deactivating all spells within its reach. The tang of nickel coated Neva's tongue.

"Let me at him," demanded Tavo, holding a kerchief to his nose with one hand and his curved sword in the other.

"You're making a mistake," Alewiscious said as Tavo and the pirates advanced. "Don't do this, I beg of you."

Neva held out her palm and called her power to the surface. An image of Ebenezer flashed through her mind. She didn't know what would happen to a mage whose soul was tethered to this world when the Tyvse Sea ate him up, but it must be a fair trade for what he'd been about to do to her. Alewiscious backed away from her. He inched onto the plank, murmuring something too quietly for her to make out the words. Probably praying to whatever gods were left that he hadn't offended.

Probably not many of those, Neva thought. She raised her hand.

Alewiscious stepped off the plank. A splash sounded below. Neva and the others rushed to the railing. Foam churned below as the Dancing Sandpiper cut through the water.

Alewiscious did not emerge from the frothy depths.

The Eye swirled, an incandescent star gently pulsating deep within Neva's mind. Sitting cross-legged atop Mad Merrick's bed, she filled her lungs to center herself and then wished she hadn't breathed so deeply. The ship rocked to and fro, and she had been steadily pinching herself to keep her nausea at bay.

All things considered, she was grateful to still be alive after having taken on the Lithlorian wardens, but her future was looking dim. It was only a matter of time before she would have to relinquish her power and become indentured to Trinizhi. Her stomach roiled at the thought.

Neva reached for the Eye, prodding around the edges of the power. Her heart was pounding so hard that she could hear it. But she needed an edge.

Flash — Battlefields burned. Flash — An army stormed a city. Flash — Emiliand and Xandrazhi stood against a trio of Vodou witches. Electric magic flickered around them, a false wind yanking at their clothes and hair.

Emiliand and Xandrazhi struck out at the witches, but their shots hit an invisible wall. The wind died, and the air died with it. Xandrazhi and Emiliand struggled for breath, drowning on dry land.

Flash — Thatcher threw a set of dice into a box on the deck of a pirate ship. The Sword of Elon was shrouded in a blanket at his side, and a bloody bandage covered his ear. The ship's sails were sun-bleached with a sea urchin insignia and crossbones. The Ezmerelda. For a moment, Thatcher glanced up and seemed to see her watching him. He lifted the bottle of rum and tipped the top, taunting her.

Flash — Blood flooded a river. Flash — A group of Upyri conversed with a group of mages in a temple. Flash — Soaking wet, Alewiscious dragged himself and his cane onto the shore of a small, deserted island. Sand speckled his face and his clothes. Flash — A shadow transformed a kilstroke circle from white to black.

Warm blood trickled from Neva's nose, tickling her upper lip. She directed the Eye to the back of her mind, putting an end to the visions. She opened her eyes to find Mari in her petite Djinn form, leaning against the door, watching her.

"Welcome back to the realm of the living," Mari said, passing her a bandana from a collection Mad Merrick had hanging on the wall. "Where did you go?"

"The Eye…" Neva started. She held the bandana to her nose. "It showed me the future."

"Sounds ominous," Mari observed. "What's your new escape plan?"

Neva looked at her friend sharply.

"I'm done running," Neva said. "You can tell Mad Merrick I have our new coordinates."

To be continued.

GLOSSARY

Adam Tate — A former thief and up-and-coming weapons trader out of Ashford. Living on the run from the Da'Voda, he fell in love with Neva. Half his body was burned when she lost her hold on the Hand

Ailish (A-lish) — The goddess of courage and protection.

Alewiscious — A mage sentenced by the Serculus of the Obsidian Brotherhood to an undetermined amount of time on Lithlorian Island for the theft and accidental destruction of one of their prized texts.

Aliado — A hilan member of a majila's alliad.

Alliad — A group of Da'Valia that agree to work together and share their power following a private bonding ceremony, usually performed by an otima.

Amania — The country to the east of Cirandrel, across the Tyvse Sea.

Amanians — The people who live in Amania.

Anchorweights, the — The second strongest gang on Lithlorian Island mostly consisting of former pirates. They seem to have an endless supply of rum and are expert fishermen.

Andreo — One of the dragon wardens of Lithlorian Island.

Apothecary, the — How Alewiscious is often referred to on Lithlorian Island.

Archibald — One of Neva's uncles and a member of her old thieving ring in Glacier Pass.

Army of Onidas — A legendary army that led a successful crusade under King Onidas across the Serpentine Sea, fighting off all manner of giant sea creatures.

Arroyand Da'Voda-Esava — One of Trinizhi's aliados, a sexual sadist and a ruthless fighter.

Ashford — The premier trading hub of Cirandrel, a city of prosperity and waterways that connect to other parts of the kingdom.

Ashmount crew, the — A gang on Lithlorian Island that has a monopoly on all the fresh water resources.

Ashmounts — Twin volcanic mountains on the back of Lithlorian Island.

Astiand Da'Voda-Cuchilla — One of Trinizhi's aliados and Neva's sworn guardian.

Baker, the — A polyamorous ganger who raises chickens and bakes pies on Lithlorian Island.

Ballard Tavish — The leader of the Dragonslayers gang, convicted for privateering. He was born at sea, grew up as part of the Tavish family, and served under King Onidas.

Baroness Fisk — A widow whose double-cross helped lead to Tavo's conviction.

Beastie — A slang term for unaligned hilans.

Benjamand Da'Xana-Escriva — Head librarian and warlock among the Da'Xana, and an old friend of Monazhi's.

Bertie — A former Anchorweight who contracted leprosy.

Brakane Desert (bray-cane) — The desert region where the Da'Foha reside.

Brawlin' Boys, the — An underground street-fighting duo from Ashford.

Brother Cyrus — A high-ranking mage of the Obsidian Brotherhood, who Alewiscious hoped was his friend.

Brother Noridemus — A mage of the Obsidian Brotherhood and member of the Serculus.

Brother Osirus — A mage of the Obsidian Brotherhood who is a secretary for the Serculus.

Bryand Da'Voda Solatta (bry-and) — A former toppel aliado of Trinizhi, the Da'Voda's donazhi, and longtime friend of Astiand Da'Voda-Cuchilla.

Calabray's pub — The public house where Neva's family is hiding in Ashford.

Cass — A violent, paranoid thief and a member of the Crocutas crew.

Ceasekin — A squad of toppel majilas who are raised as assassins.

Ceris (C-ris) — The goddess of bounty and the hunt.

Chaard — One of Lithlorian's great-grandchildren and a warden of Lithlorian Island.

Chameleon, the — An alias of Thatcher Sullivan.

Charube (chair-ub) — A green, clawed crustacean.

Cirandrel (ser-an-drel) — The country in which Neva grew up. It is governed by King Stephan and his Order of Cirandrel, twelve dukes who run Houses across the realm.

Colavalia (col-ah-vall-E-ah) — A race of supernatural guardians Dhianz created as a gift to Riska to protect the gates to the Underworld.

Conviction marks — Tattoos developed by the Obsidian Brotherhood and used by the Order of Cirandrel to keep track of who has been convicted of a major crime. For convicts who have been sent to Lithlorian, the ink is spelled to keep them from escaping. Anyone who cuts them off dies from blood poisoning within days

Corazhi — A Da'Foha majila Bryand fell in love with during the Great War.

Corkay trees — Gray trees with deep roots and powdery bark that grow around oases in Ramanaji Desert.

Cravell (craw-vell) — The season after Vestive and before Auton. When the weather is warm.

Craven's Roosy — A well-fortified citadel carved out of the mountains in central Cirandrel. With sufficient food stores, those that dwell there can hold off invaders for exceptional lengths of time.

Crocuta Crew, the — An up-and-coming thieving ring led by a woman named Cass with a penchant for using explosives.

Crowe Corbyn — One of the newest members of the Dragonslayers, convicted by the Order for multiple thefts.

Crown, the — The strongest gang on Lithlorian Island, led by their "king," Thatcher Sullivan.

Crystal of Souls — A stone gifted by the goddess of death, marking those she's touched in the realm of the living.

Cul Corner — The poorest district in Glacier Pass, full of prostitution and drug use.

Da'Bruna (da-broo-na) — The most brutal Da'Valia clan remaining. The cannibalistic Da'Bruna reside in the Grasslands on the northernmost edge of the desert.

Da'Foha (da-foe-ha) — Another Da'Valia clan that keeps with the old ways and eats its dead, the Da'Foha reside in the Brakane Desert.

Damiand — A Da'Voda hilan who was a commander under Trinizhi during the Great War.

Dancing Sandpiper, the — One of the fastest pirate ships around, it's captained by Mad Merrick.

Da'Roha (da-row-ha) — A nomadic Da'Valian army led by a donazhi and consisting of hilan warriors who sign on for service with the desire to find majilas to align with from other clans.

Da'Valia (da-vall-E-a) — Fierce creatures created by Dhianz, the god of war, for battle. They're strong, fast, cunning, and they have exceptional senses. They value skilled fighters, power, and honor. They were forced out of Ramanaji hundreds of years ago by the Obsidian Brotherhood and Djinn. Only five clans remain, and each is ruled by a donazhi. The hilans, the males of the race, were brought into being at midnight. The majilas, the females of the race, were brought into being at dawn, which is reflected in their coloring and power. They were subsequently cursed by Dhianz with an imbalance of power that is more punishing to all the majilas.

Da'Voda (da-vo-da) — The most remote Da'Valian clan remaining. They're extremely wealthy and reclusive, and reside in the northern mountains of Cirandrel.

Da'Xana (da-zan-a) — The most prestigious Da'Valian clan. They have many scholars and warlocks and reside in the coastal fortress known as Picquereau in Cirandrel.

Debo Smythe — One of the newest Dragonslayers and a former member of the Brawlin' Boys, convicted by the Order for murder. He hails from Ashford, where his wife Eileen lives with his children.

Dhianz (diane-z) — The god of war.

Djinn (gin) — Creatures demonic in essence who specialize in possession, created by Goj.

Docking Day — The first day that the pirates return to Lithlorian Island to trade with gangers and make repairs, usually timed for the days following a dragon attack in an attempt to avoid unnecessary loss of life.

Donazhi (doe-na-zee) — A toppel majila, who is favored by Dhianz and who rules a Da'Valian clan. This is not an inherited position, and a majila must win her place as ruler. Her reign ends when she dies.

Dragonfire — An incredibly hot fire produced by a dragon.

Dragonslayers, the — A small gang on Lithlorian whose aim is to defeat the dragons.

Durant Tanyon — A member of the Dragonslayers gang, he was convicted by the Order for being a swindler. He hails from Sills.

Ebenezer Tavish — The original patriarch of the Tavish family and a member of the Obsidian Brotherhood.

Eileen — Debo's wife.

Elkizhi — Astiand's younger sister.

Ellazhi Da'Voda-Ostra (ella-zee) — A young Da'Voda majila who went through her rite of passage at the same time as Neva.

Emiliand Da'Voda-Riga (E-me-lee-and) — A handsome and humble half-breed hilan soldier who is an extraordinary fighter. Orphaned at birth, he never met his mother, a former Da'Bruna, nor his father, a Colavalia. He's a toppel who can secretly read minds.

Enoch (E-nock) — Lithlorian's son and the leader of the wardens on Lithlorian Island.

Enthrall — The inherent power of dragons to lock eyes with their prey and capture them in an immobile death lock.

Erlach (er-lack) — One of the dragon wardens of Lithlorian Island.

Evokamor (evoke-a-more) — A sensual magical practice. The company of evokamor practitioners is highly coveted, for they are very selective in choosing their clients.

Eye, the — A powerful tool of prognostication and the first prong of the Trishula.

Ezmerelda — One of the fastest pirate ships in existence, captained by Zeerust.

Fairline, the — A small, agile ship that crash-landed on Lithlorian Island.

Farakai — One of the youngest of the dragon wardens on Lithlorian Island.

Farer's Strait — The primary trade route between Amania and Cirandrel.

Finneas (fin-E-us) — An eccentric and unscrupulous mage who mentored Alewiscious.

Firechild — A character from a fable wherein a poor boy prays to the god of fire and is blessed with the ability to start fires.

Firérite (fee-ray-rite) — An incredibly painful, sometimes debilitating and sometimes deadly, rite of passage among the Da'Valia. Hilans are quite young when they go through the process, and majilas do so when they reach adolescence. After the rite of passage, a Da'Valia has immediate controlled access to their power.

Fireside — The coldest season of the year, Fireside follows Auton and comes before Vestive.

Ganger — A member of any gang on Lithlorian Island, often a convict from Cirandrel but sometimes a native-born child.

Garen Warehouse — The warehouse where the Garin family sells firewood to those who deliver it about Glacier Pass.

Gem Quarter — A section of R'shara, where all manner of stone is processed, polished, and cut.

Genivra — Mad Merrick's first mate.

Glacier Pass — The northernmost city in Cirandrel, originally established by those who sought riches by mining, now a thriving metropolis and the top exporter of both base and precious metals. Home to the House of Trescony.

Glamour — A usually cheap spell attached to a charm of some sort that imbues the wearer physical attributes they think are advantageous or attractive. Typically created and sold by hedge witches.

Goj (gah-j) — The vengeful god of trickery, Dhianz's half-brother.

Grand Magi — A position that belongs to the wisest mage in the Obsidian Brotherhood's Serculus.

Grasslands — The harsh bog-ridden plains that are the de facto boundary separating Cirandrel and the deserts. This is where the Da'Bruna reside.

Great War — A civil war resulting from the Order of Cirandrel's eventually successful attempt at a coup, which lasted from 1633 to 1644 as King Stephan stole the throne from his cousin, King Charles.

Gregand — A Da'Roha solider from Emiliand's squadron.

Hanazhi Da'Voda-Gnerre (hana-zee) — A Da'Voda soldier and single mother who Neva killed when she lost control of the Hand.

Hagave (ha-ga-vay) — A spicy alcoholic beverage, which unlike many other spirits does have an effect on the Da'Valia.

Hand, the — The second prong of Dhianz's greatest weapon, the Trishula. It can be wielded to level a fiery force of destruction against one's foes.

Harpies, the — A gang of women on Lithlorian who will not suffer a rapist to live.

Helband — A Da'Voda commander who answered to Trinizhi during the Great War.

Hedge witch — A human blessed with a sprinkle of power from no god in particular, a hedge witch usually lives off making glamour charms, tinctures, and telling the future.

Hilan (hee-lan) — A male Da'Valia.

House of Balmoral — One of the twelve houses of the Order of Cirandrel, located in Escalona.

House of Halcyon — One of the twelve houses of the Order of Cirandrel, located in Leon.

House of Trescony — One of the twelve houses of the Order of Cirandrel, located in Glacier Pass.

House of Madrona — One of the twelve houses of the Order of Cirandrel, located in Port Telgard.

Ian — Cass's brother and a member of the Crocutas crew.

Ictand — A soldier in Emiliand's squadron among the Da'Roha.

Illuminator — A globe that is spelled so when it is activated, it reveals all — casting light in the dark and disarming spells.

Illyia — A city in Cirandrel that specializes in brightly colored dyes.

Ingo stalk — Part of a naturally occurring plant on Lithlorian Island that's used by the gangers to keep their teeth clean and healthy.

James Kittle — Neva's eldest cousin on her father's side, a twin to Kendall and son of Aunt Margret.

Jeaux — Ebenezer Tavish's wife.

Jingali warrior — A unique brand of fighter from Ramanaji Desert, they appear half-human and half-lion, and they have prehensile tails. They rely on silker root to fight for days on end.

Junipero (hoo-nee-peer-O) — A tasty, minty alcoholic beverage that, unlike many spirits, has an effect on the Da'Valia.

Kendall Kittle — Neva's youngest cousin on her father's side, a twin to James and son of Aunt Margret.

Kilstroke — A fight to the death among the Da'Valia. It must be sanctioned by a donazhi and the rites conducted by a prima otima. The kilstroke is considered the catalyst for Dhianz's judgment.

King Charles — The previous ruler of Cirandrel who was usurped by King Stephan and the Order of Cirandrel in a decade-long war for the realm.

King Onidas — The ruler of the Nacien Islands, and leader of the Army of Onidas.

King Stephan — The ruler of Cirandrel, who colluded with the Order of Cirandrel to steal his position from his cousin, King Charles.

Knight and Knave — A knife-throwing game where the winner claims bragging rights as the Knight and the loser becomes the Knave.

Landscape — A term for the plane of existence between the realm of the living and the Underworld, where those favored by Dhianz may pull another's spirit with them for a private conversation.

Leper Island — The name for Lithlorian Island's sister isle, where those afflicted by leprosy are exiled. Home to the old Outpost.

Levasta root — A natural pain remedy.

Lithlorian — A deceased dragon patriarch with a legendary treasure trove who struck a deal with the Order of Cirandrel to become warden of Lithlorian Island in exchange for a steady supply of convicts to eat. He also struck a deal with Trinizhi to intercept the Mouth, which he added to his collection.

Lithlorian Island — A prison island where Cirandrel sends its convicts. Located in the Tyvse Sea between Amania and Cirandrel, it is guarded by dragon wardens, who are the descendants of Lithlorian.

Livorna — A city along the north-western coast of Cirandrel.

Lowel (low-el) — The lowest level of power among the Da'Valia.

Lynx, the — Neva's thieving moniker.

Mad Merrick — A pirate and captain of the Dancing Sandpiper with unrivaled aim and a reputation for risk-taking.

Maeve — The goddess of strength, resilience, and childbearing.

Mage — A formally trained male magic worker who was bestowed with power by Yokam, the god of soil and stone. They can be identified by their black eyes when they are infants.

Magic — God-given power that has been molded via a spell.

Maither (may-ther) — Mari's brother, a top-level Upyr.

Majila (ma-hee-la) — A female Da'Valia.

Malakai — One of the youngest dragon wardens of Lithlorian Island.

Mandana — Leader of the Revenants and Rinaldo's mother.

Margret Kittle — Neva's aunt and Shaun's sister, Margret is also James and Kendall's mother.

Mari — A disgraced Upyr, she's a Djinn who works as a desert guide against the winds.

Master at arms — The highest military position among a Da'Valian clan. The person holding this position reports to the donazhi directly. The master at arms oversees all military training, strategies, and assignments, and their direct subordinates are commanders.

Maven — The god of wine and merriment.

Melanzhi Da'Foha (mel-an-zee) — The donazhi of the Da'Foha.

Mikel — Neva's best friend and coworker from Glacier Pass.

Misty Tavish — A pirate in the Tavish family and Ballard's grandmother.

Monazhi Roberts (mo-na-zee) — Formerly Monazhi Da'Voda-Lira, she was a former frontrunner for the position of the Da'Voda's donazhi and a talented warlock. She is the mother of Nevazhi Roberts.

Morafeno — The northernmost metropolis in Ramanaji Desert.

Mouth, the — The third prong of the Trishula. Its power has not been witnessed in centuries.

Nacien Islands — An independent nation of islands off the coast of Cirandrel.

Naiads — Vicious water nymphs who enjoy playing tricks on seafarers.

Nevazhi Roberts (ne-va-zee) — A half-human, half-Da'Valian thief who grew up in Glacier Pass. She's the daughter of Shaun Roberts and Monazhi Roberts.

Nikolazhi (nico-la-zee) — A Da'Voda warlock.

Obsidian Brotherhood — The order of mages who rule Ramanaji Desert with Djinn.

Odonus (O-don-us) — The god of prosperity and mercantile.

Old Fort, the — A former palace commandeered by a Cirandrellian king for a sea-based military station on Lithlorian Island. It was later gifted to the dragons as part of their agreement to serve as Lithlorian Island's wardens.

Old King's Highway — A network of roads maintained by the Order that connect all the Houses in Cirandrel.

Olivia — A sister of Rinaldo's.

Orbo tree — A gigantic red-trunk tree that is native to Lithlorian Island with oversized leaves and branches.

Order of Cirandrel — A group of twelve dukes who conspired against the former king of Cirandrel to put King Stephan on the throne, the ruling government. Each duke rules a House.

Orphague — A home for orphaned Da'Valia. Each clan has one, except for the Da'Roha, and they're run by the otimas.

Otima (O-tee-ma) — A holy servant of Dhianz who is androgynous and adept at magic.

Outpost, the — A former militaristic settlement on Leper Island.

Perzhi Da'Xana (per-zee) — The donazhi of the Da'Xana clan.

Picquereau (pick-er-oh) — A storied fortress on the cliffs of coastal Cirandrel, where the Da'Xana reside.

Pirates — Descendants of convicts on Lithlorian Island who raid and loot for a living. They return regularly to Lithlorian Island to visit their families, tend their ships, and trade supplies.

Port Telgard — A trade hub for commerce with Amania, home to the Order's prison ships and the House of Madrona.

Porsha — A thief who lured Neva into a trap in R'shara.

Power — Power is god-gifted to people, places, and things in Cirandrel. It can be molded and directed by those who know how to use it, either in its raw form or in spells.

Prima otima (pree-ma O-tee-ma) — The lead otima of a clan, they are an expert in rituals and casting magic in honor of Dhianz. Their specialities include healing, kilstrokes, alliad ceremonies, geldings, death rites, and similar events.

Pussole — A puss-filled orifice.

Qitar (kit-R) — The city in Ramanaji Desert with the most diamonds, home to the Obsidian Brotherhood's university.

Ramanaji Desert (ra-man-a-G) — The harsh desert country where the Obsidian Brotherhood and Djinn drove out the Da'Valia.

Revenants — A gang on Lithlorian Island.

Rinaldo — A native of Lithlorian Island, he grew up among the Revenants and later became a member of the Dragonslayers.

Riska (risk-a) — The goddess of death and ruler of the Underworld.

Roberto — A pirate and crew member aboard the Dancing Sandpiper.

Roses, the — A district in Ashford that is notable for the red roses growing in front of all the homes, a reminder of a bloody skirmish in the Great War.

R'shara — The southernmost city in Ramanaji Desert.

Ruffo — A pirate and crew member aboard the Dancing Sandpiper.

Ryder — One of the Brawlin' Boys, Debo's former best friend.

Salaman — A notorious crime lord in R'shara who specializes in the theft of precious jewels.

S'donzhi — A powerful majila who fell in love with Dhianz and later betrayed him by stealing the Trishula.

Seadog — A ganger who's a member of the Crown.

Serculus — The group of mages that rules the Obsidian Brotherhood.

Shacklay — A magical bracelet used by the Da'Valia to subdue a majilas' uncontrolled power before her firérite and to constrain the power of those in custody.

Shaun Roberts — Neva's father, a former thief of notoriety.

Shaundrazhi Da'Bruna (shaun-dra-zee) — The donazhi of the Da'Bruna clan.

Shizit — A curse or insult implying a person or thing is a combination of a shit and a zit.

Silker — A root that is a stimulant from Ramanaji Desert.

Sorrows, the — The slums of Ashford.

Soul scourge — A mortal wound inflicted by the Winds.

Spyke — Thatcher's second-in-command among the Crown.

Strangling vine — A naturally occurring plant on Lithlorian Island. It strangles its victims and feeds off them for months.

Summit — A non-obligatory meeting of the Da'Valian clans that occurs once per year at Picquereau.

Sword of Elon — A weapon that once belonged to the first sultan of Morafeno. S'donzhi imbued the sword with the Mouth, and Trinizhi later made a deal with the dragon Lithlorian to keep Neva's parents from securing it centuries later.

Tavish Fleet — The predominant pirate fleet in the four seas.

Tavo Ott — A member of the Dragonslayers gang, convicted by the Order for murder. He hails from Escalona.

Teonets (tee-oh-nets) — The god of fire.

Tethering — A method of magic, where a spell is anchored for permanence.

Textile Quarter — A section of R'shara, where all manner of furs and plants are processed, dyed, and woven.

Thatcher Sullivan — A notorious thief who rules the strongest gang on Lithlorian Island. Alias: the Chameleon.

Thurland — A Da'Bruna sentry who dallies with Arroyand.

Toppel (top-el) — The highest level of power among the Da'Valia.

Town — The principal place of trade on Lithlorian Island, largely consisting of temporary dwellings since dragon attacks force gangers to frequently rebuild.

Trades, the — A commerce-driven social event hosted by the House of Trescony.

Trinizhi Da'Voda (trin-E-zee) — The donazhi of the Da'Voda. She is aligned with Arroyand and Astiand, and previously Bryand.

Trishula (tri-shoo-la) — The greatest weapon ever created by Dhianz. The tridents' three prongs held three great powers: the Eye, the Hand, and the Mouth. S'donzhi stole the weapon from him, broke it apart, and hid the powers.

Tyvse Sea, the (tie-vees) — The ocean separating Cirandrel from Amania.

Tyvse Slit, the — A massive fracture scarring Cirandrel.

Underworld, the — Where Riska collects souls after they leave the realm of the living.

Upyri (oop-eerie) — The highest caste of Djinn, or a plurality of members of the caste. They are in cahoots with the Obisidian Brotherhood and have helped rule Ramanaji Desert through fear for centuries.

Upyr (oop-eer) — A member of the highest Djinn caste.

Valentine Cross — A member of the Dragonslayers gang, convicted by the Order for multiple murders. He hails from Traveath.

Valis — The mythical city at the entrance to the Underworld in the Dark Wood.

Vanquist — A spell that transports the user to a different location. The main side effect is the loss of body parts.

Venantulas — Poisonous creatures that look similar to spiders.

Vestive (vest-ive) — A rainy and sunny season following Fireside and preceding Cravell.

Vivizhi Da'Voda-Mourda (viv-E-zee) — A toppel majila, the master at arms for the Da'Voda is a mentor to Emiliand and was romantically involved with Astiand in her youth. She was raised in an Orphague.

Vodou witch (voo-dow) — A powerful witch from the Vodou line, known to be deadly and dangerous to Da'Valia.

Wahlberries — Berries that grow on Lithlorian Island and which are poisonous if dried.

Warbler — A yellow songbird who belongs to Ballard.

Warlock — A Da'Valia trained in magic with an emphasis on battle magic.

War of the Canals — A war between humans and Naiads when they fought over ownership and control of the waterways in Ashford.

Watch, the — A government force that protects the citizens of cities across Cirandrel.

Water nymph — See Naiads.

Winds, the — Supernatural windstorms that are charged by souls displaced by Djinn, the Winds were created by Goj when he scattered the ashes of Dhianz's son on the wind.

Witchaven — A municipality along the Old King's Highway and the Dark Wood.

Xandrazhi Da'Roha — The donazhi of the Da'Roha, the youngest donazhi in a generation.

Yokam — The god of soil, stone, and permanence.

Yolandrazhi — The top warlock among the Da'Bruna, and Shaundrazhi's lover and confidant.

Yorand — A Da'Roha solider in Emiliand's squadron.

Zeerust — Pirate and captain of the Ezmerelda.

Zephyr — One of the dragon wardens of Lithlorian Island.

About the Author

CHRISTINA DAVIS was born and raised in Santa Cruz, California, where she was home-schooled in the mountains and read every book she could get her hands on at the local library. She graduated *summa cum laude* with a Bachelor's degree from San Jose State University and enjoyed a career in sports and digital journalism before moving into financial services marketing. She is now a stay-at-home mom who writes every chance she gets. She loves reading, writing, baking, tea, coffee, chocolate, board games, hiking, cosplay, and watching hockey. She lives in beautiful Monterey County with her husband and daughter.

Join her newsletter for updates, secret scenes, giveaways, and more.
Visit www.ChristinaDavisWrites.com to sign up now!

www.ingramcontent.com/pod-product-compliance
Lightning Source LLC
Chambersburg PA
CBHW061556190726
48288CB00007B/2049